The Cellist

By
Kevin Marsh

Author of:
The Belgae Torc

Dedication

For Bernie

Mentor, Colleague, Friend

Published by Paragon Publishing
© 2017 Kevin Marsh

ISBN 978-1-78222-529-4

Book design, layout and production management by Into Print
www.intoprint.net
+44 (0)1604 832149

Printed and bound in UK and USA by Lightning Source

DECEMBER 1995

"Come on you two, we have to go now. Look, the weather is closing in."

Their mother was standing at the bottom of the hill hopping from foot to foot in an effort to keep warm. She was too far away to be heard clearly, but from her body language, her message was obvious.

Mia looked up to where she was pointing. The sky overhead was as thick as an old grey blanket that stretched all the way to the horizon. It reminded her of a time when she and her father had watched from the cliff top as a storm raged out in the channel. The sky had been as dark as night with clouds so heavy they seemed to boil right up from the raging sea. It was a spectacular sight and full of drama especially once the lightning loosened its tongue.

"Come on," her brother Ethan shouted, his cheeks rosy from exertion; he had just dragged their sledge up the hill and was now eager to ride it down again.

"We're going to make this thing fly." He said, his voice full of excitement.

Squatting down on the wooden slats that spanned the runners, Ethan dug his heels into the snow and held the sledge steady as Mia climbed on. She tucked her knees up under her brother's elbows and held onto him tightly then, peering nervously over his shoulder, she could see their mother at the bottom of the hill. She looked so small and doll-like dressed in her long red coat with matching woollen hat and mittens. It was then that Mia realised just how big the hill was and she squealed as her brother lifted his feet and they began their descent.

A blast of cold air stole her breath away and her eyes filled with tears, but she dared not loosen her grip so burying her face into her brother's back, she squealed again, louder this time as the sledge picked up speed. All at once, it was over, the runners ploughed into the drifts at the bottom of the hill and they came to an abrupt stop.

"Wow," Ethan cried, "that was awesome."

"Come on you two." Mia could hear her mother's voice clearly now even above the sound of her pounding heart.

"I'm freezing. Get into the car quickly before it starts to snow again."

Ethan complained as their sledge was heaved up onto the roof rack.

"Come on, in you go."

Pulling open the door, he scampered in leaving a dusting of snow across the seat. Mia brushed it away before following him and when settled, she reached for the seatbelt. She hated having to wear it but her parents insisted that they buckle up tightly so pulling it across her body, she tucked it under her arm. It was not designed for children and if she did not hold it in place, it would ride up and rub against her chin.

Their mother climbed in and tapping her boots against the bottom of the door, loosened the worst of the snow before swinging her legs in.

"Goodness, I'm frozen." She said and removing her mittens rubbed her hands together before blowing on her fingers.

Mia adored her mother's hands; they were soft, warm and always scented, her nails often painted red to match the colour of her lips. She studied her own fingers and frowned, her nails were chipped and uneven, but she was determined to have hands just like her mother's one day.

After a few moments, the engine started and the heater was turned up to maximum. At first, the blast that filled the car was icy cold but soon it would become warm. Mia glanced at her brother, he didn't seem to notice, he amused himself by peering longingly out of the window at the snow covered hill. There were not so many people around now the worsening weather had driven them all away. Snow was beginning to fall, huge flakes that would soon cover their tracks, but for now, the road ahead was clear.

The sound of the wipers swishing against the glass was hypnotic and now the air inside the car had warmed, Mia began to feel sleepy. She smiled, this was the perfect start to the holidays, no school until next term and tomorrow their father would finish work early then the fun would really begin. Only three more sleeps until Christmas day, this was going to be the best ever.

A red light up ahead filled the car with its glow and gently their mother brought the car to a stop, moments later the light turned green and they were off again.

Suddenly a sickening force shook the car and Mia was thrown sideways. Air bags deployed but this did nothing to stop her brother from crashing into her and as the car rolled, she was pinned against the door, her face just millimetres from the road. Sparks flashed alarmingly from the door as it scraped along the tarmac, but fortunately, the window remained intact.

Their mother screamed but as the car came to a rest, her cries stopped and it was a few agonising seconds before Mia dared to look up. The front seat was leaning at a funny angle with her mother's head pressed up against it. Mia could see the look of shock on her face, her red lips parted slightly and blood was beginning to stain her white teeth. Mia groaned and tried to move but it was impossible, her brother was on top of her and it was too much effort to push him away. She called out his name, but there was no response, her mother continued to stare then Mia began to cry.

There was hardly any pain as she lay there crushed inside the wreckage. Drifting in and out of consciousness, she became detached from the horror that surrounded her, it was as if it was happening to someone else, it was all just a dream. Emergency crews worked tirelessly to free her and occasionally she heard the sound of their voices. Noise from their equipment became distant and as she closed her eyes, she could feel her strength beginning to drain away. Her arms and legs were growing cold and as realisation took hold, she became frightened. Something terrible had happened to her mother and her brother, that much was clear, but it all seemed so unreal. Forcing these unwelcome thoughts away, she drew on her inner strength; she had to remain strong. She refused to allow death to claim her.

Chapter

ONE

The romance of the swan as it glides majestically across the stage is guaranteed to win the hearts of every audience.

'The Swan', is in every cellist's repertoire. Written by Camille Saint-Saëns in 1887 it remains an instantly recognisable piece from his Carnival of the Animals suite.

Mia held her cello in a lover's embrace, in her arms it became a living thing and together they made the sweetest music. Closing her eyes, she immersed herself completely in the moment. Her passion was infectious and as she charmed her audience she could do no wrong, then with a final draw of her bow, the piece ended gracefully and silence filled the auditorium. Mia looked up and smiled.

The audience, enthralled by her faultless performance, were held in rapture and unable to respond. Several seconds passed before they rose to their feet, then the air was filled with sounds of their appreciation.

Mia was stunned and peering out from behind the stage lights, individual faces began to appear. Their cheers leaving her in no doubt, her performance was a success. Carefully setting her cello to one side, she rose from her chair and approached the edge of the stage. The applause became thunderous and bowing politely, Mia gave thanks to their praise then as she left the stage, the excitement gradually subsided as the audience began to disperse.

Terry smiled, the swan remained swimming inside his head, and as he looked down onto an empty stage, his emotions began to stir. He had never seen his daughter perform to such a large audience before and suddenly all those years of dedication, hard work and financial commitment seemed worthwhile. Her childhood had been disciplined with endless nights of practice as she learned to play pieces that were ever more complicated. She regularly took part in junior competitions that were fiercely competitive and Terry worried that the strain would be too much for Mia, but she had taken it in her stride. Music school followed and all the while, she continued to blossom into a sophisticated and beautiful young woman. She was a rising star in the world of classical music and her performance tonight left him in no doubt. Her mother would have been very proud and it pained him to think that she was not there beside him, but now was not the time to dwell upon that. He watched as people moved around the auditorium and realised that Mia was living her dream, she seemed content sharing her talents with her audience and it pleased him. In an attempt to distract his maudlin thoughts, he studied the crumpled programme that he was holding. The promotional photograph of his daughter with her cello impressed him enormously, she looked incredible and his smile widened; he was a very proud father indeed.

"Mia darling. What a fantastic performance." He spotted her the moment he joined the backstage celebrations. She was still wearing the long black dress that she had performed in, it was formal but chic, a uniform preferred by musicians and it suited her perfectly.

"Daddy," she smiled and brushed her lips against his cheek. "I didn't know if you would be able to come."

"Wild horses wouldn't have prevented me from being here tonight."

Most of those around them were members of the orchestra, but there were a few VIP guests from the city and of course family members. The party was in full swing and as a waiter swept past, Terry reached for two glasses of champagne, and passing one to Mia, he studied her as she took a sip. She was the image of her mother, her long dark hair was drawn back from her face and colour had been applied to her lips, it was her mother's favourite shade.

"There were so many people here tonight, I had no idea," he said, finding his voice.

"Yes, I'm told it was a full house."

"And all for you, you must be delighted."

"Mia must get used to the fact that she is now one of the most popular female cellists of the moment."

Terry turned to face a tall young man. He was smartly dressed and appeared confident in an arrogant kind of way.

"Daddy, may I introduce you to my friend Belenos."

"Belenos Falzone at your service sir." His smile was genuine enough and as he held out his hand, his loftiness seemed to fade away.

Terry was surprised at the firmness of his grip. He could tell a lot from a handshake and suddenly he was impressed.

"Mia has spoken about you before," Terry declared.

"What has she been saying? Not giving away all of my secrets I hope."

"Does my daughter know many of your secrets?"

"Stop fishing Daddy." Spots of colour were beginning to form on her cheeks.

"So, Belenos," Terry was tempted to ask about his unusual name but decided that would keep for another time. "Are you also in the music business?"

"Oh heavens no," he replied quickly. "I posses no musical talent at all I'm afraid. I'm a journalist for my sins."

Raising his eyebrows in surprise, Terry replied. "Broadsheet I assume, I can't imagine you working for a tabloid."

Belenos laughed and raising his glass took a sip before going on.

"I'm an independent, plying my trade to any reputable newspaper that will have me. I also submit to glossy magazines with articles of interest, celebrity gossip, that kind of thing. Not your kind of reading I would imagine."

"Indeed not," Terry agreed.

"So what kind of business are you in sir if you don't mind my asking." Belenos was keen to move the focus away from himself.

"Security," Terry replied vaguely.

"Oh Daddy," Mia smiled and turning to Belenos she continued. "My father is a Detective Inspector here in London."

"Scotland Yard?" Belenos asked with no hint of surprise in his voice.

"Afraid so, The Met."

"Why so coy?"

"Daddy is afraid that by telling my friends what he does for a living it will frighten them away."

"Well I'm not sure about that, I can certainly see the benefits of having a detective in the family." Belenos said diplomatically.

Before Mia could reply, a flamboyantly dressed woman swept her away.

"That's Alicia Wicks," Belenos whispered and taking Terry by the arm guided him away from the noise of their excited chatter.

"Mia's agent?" he glanced enquiringly at Belenos.

"The very same and I have no wish to be drawn into their conversation."

"Do I detect a reluctance on your part to socialise with that woman?"

"I'm afraid you do," he made a face. "I must admit that I can't stand her. The feeling is mutual so we agree to remain distant. She may be very good at her job but I believe that as a human being she fails miserably."

"Is that your opinion or do others think the same?"

"I would say that most people would agree with me, Mia included if she were to be honest, but the truth is Alicia Wicks is a very influential woman."

"I see," Terry whispered as he studied her from a safe distance.

Chapter
TWO

Mia woke up to a room full of winter sunlight. Climbing out of bed, she stretched luxuriously before enjoying the view from the panoramic window. The City of London was laid out beneath her, the River Thames glistening in the cold morning light as it made its way through the heart of the city. She watched the small boats and vessels plying their trade as they had done for countless generations and she smiled at the bustle of the crowded pavements. Red buses and black taxis crawled along at walking pace caught up in the hum of traffic and she was relieved to be high up above the constant noise.

Turning away, she crossed the room and headed towards the en-suite bathroom where she showered and washed her hair. Twenty minutes later, she moved back into the bedroom and stared thoughtfully at herself in the huge gilded mirror. Memories from the previous evening stirred inside her head and she smiled, the concert had been a success she was sure of it, but she was yet to read the reviews. It was one thing to satisfy an audience, but quite another to win the hearts of the media.

Mia was pleased that her father had been there, she had seen so little of him recently. His work often claimed him, in fact, he seemed to do nothing else, he had no hobbies to her knowledge, and his circle of friends was very limited. He was totally committed to his work, but he appeared to be happy enough. This did little to stop her from worrying about him.

When at last her hair was done, she threw on a pair of denims and her favourite woollen jumper and went in search of breakfast. She had made herself a promise long ago that once she became a successful musician she would make the most of luxurious hotels, even if her flat was just a taxi ride away. She was determined to enjoy life, but unfortunately, there seemed little time for anything else these days apart from rehearsing and performing.

"Ah, Miss Ashton," The hotel manager said the moment she appeared. "I trust you slept well and everything is to your satisfaction."

"Good morning to you," Mia smiled and wondered if the man had been waiting to pounce. "I have no complaints at all, in fact your hotel is second to none and I congratulate you." She knew how to humour men like him but wondered if she would have the same opinion once breakfast was over.

He escorted her to a reserved table in a beautifully furnished room overlooking a little courtyard garden.

"Enjoy your breakfast Miss Ashton."

"Thank you," she said as she sat down. "Oh how thoughtful, the daily newspapers."

When reserving the room her agent Alicia Wicks had given strict instructions that all the daily papers were made available and he was more than happy to oblige.

Serving staff moved in the moment he had gone and nothing was too much trouble. A pot of fresh coffee appeared and Mia made her choices from the menu before turning her attention to the newspapers.

The ravishing cellist Miss Mia Ashton treated us to a faultless performance. If ever there is a name to watch out for then this is the one.

Mia sipped her coffee and quietly read her reviews. They were all much the same, words positively written to suit the tastes of every reader. Belenos had been kind again with a succinct paragraph of praise and sincerity that fitted neatly into the celebrity pages. She wondered what he expected in return. He was a brilliantly honest journalist, a rare thing indeed, but his reports could also be quite scathing. In the past, she had bore the brunt of his less flattering reviews, but his criticisms never came between them. If he considered her performance less than perfect, he was not afraid to report it.

"Mia," a cheery voice sounded from across the room.

"Belenos," she exclaimed with delight. "I was just thinking about you."

Hurrying towards her table, he took her hands in his and kissed her cheeks continental style.

"Do you mind if I join you?" Without waiting for a reply, he sat down and began to re-arrange the table making room for another plate.

"How could I possibly refuse after such a kind review," she tapped the magazine with her fingertip and as she waited for him to reply, she admired his boyish good looks. They had never been romantically involved but she could understand why some women found him irresistible.

"Well, it's true," he said ignoring the way she was looking at him. "You were fantastic last night; your audience simply adored you."

She knew that what he said was true. Once she had conquered her nerves, she began to enjoy herself.

"You're not expecting that nauseous woman Alicia Wicks to turn up anytime soon are you?" He peered theatrically over his shoulder and Mia laughed.

"Oh come on, she's not so bad."

Alicia was terribly suspicious of Belenos and she terrified him with her feministic views and low opinion of men.

"She is a domineering and shameless woman and what's more you know it," he grinned. "In fact, I'm sure she's a lesbian."

"You are awful," Mia looked up and feigned shock. "So what if she is, it's none of your business." She paused, waiting for him to comment but he remained silent so she went on. "I deliberately left my mobile phone in my room, I refuse to have her interrupt my breakfast."

"She'll be angry with you."

Mia rolled her eyes.

They chatted endlessly about a multitude of subjects and after her second cup of coffee, Mia was ready to face the day.

"So why are you here?" she asked and sitting back in her chair crossed her legs under the table.

"Well, it was something that your father said last night concerning a topic I'm working on. It wasn't appropriate to discuss it with him then. Look, the thing is, I didn't get the chance to take his card, but I would like to talk to him about it."

"So you want me to give you his details."

"Well, you could do better than that," peering at her he grinned crookedly before going on. "You could organise an informal get together, a quiet drink, or something, besides as you said before you owe me one." He glanced at the newspaper and she laughed.

"Okay, I'll see what I can do."

Chapter

THREE

Benjamin Sykes walked into his sister's shop. The calming atmosphere of this cleverly designed space never ceased to amaze him. Soft music drifting on the delicately perfumed air helped to put even the most fraught nerves at ease. His sister had done a fantastic job setting up her business and he smiled. Situated just off the main routes running through the West End there was never a shortage of shoppers and visitors to this part of the city.

"Hi Ben, how are you?" Emilia moved elegantly towards her brother and wrapping her arms around his neck, hugged him briefly.

When she stood back, he studied her closely. Today her hair was a deep chestnut brown. Emilia liked to change the colour of her hair regularly and he never knew what to expect.

"You look great," he said nodding his approval. "Business seems to suit you, you've done a great job here."

Taking him by the hand, she led him to a small office at the back of the shop.

"Coffee?" she asked and without hesitation dumped the dregs from the pot into the sink. "I suppose you still take yours full of cholesterol."

"You can talk," he laughed. "What happened to rosehip tea or whatever ghastly concoction it was you used to drink?"

"I was a student then, now I have grown up, besides, there's no substitute for caffeine and a working girl needs something to get her going in the morning."

"All morning it seems," he said eyeing the discarded dregs in the sink.

She frowned and stuck out her tongue.

"So," she said becoming serious. "How was the concert, you did go to the theatre last night?"

He nodded enthusiastically his eyes bright with the memory and when he had finished telling her about it, she eyed him mischievously.

"I take it you enjoyed yourself then. Impressed by Mia Ashton it seems."

She handed him a steaming mug of coffee and waited for his confession.

"The music was simply marvellous. I've not considered the cello before but it was one of those magical moments when…" Words seemed to fail him and he struggled. "It was like falling in love for the first time!"

"Goodness," Emilia exclaimed. "She did have a profound effect on you and every other man in the audience I shouldn't wonder." She could see right through him, it was hardly the music that had stolen his heart.

He looked hurt.

"Don't worry dear brother," she said patting his arm softly. "I'm sure you'll get over it."

Ben simply nodded and sipped at his coffee. He loved bantering with his sister they were easy in each other's company and often knew what the other was thinking.

"So, how's business Em?" he asked after a short silence.

"Steady," she replied, "I guess it will pick up soon. My busiest time will probably be in the spring. Easter weddings are still very popular."

Emilia specialised in arranging weddings. She could provide everything a bride would need to make her day special.

"No celebrities in lately then?"

"No, not recently although I do have a big society wedding booked in for next year." She told him the name of the bride and he was suitably impressed, but she swore him to secrecy.

"So, White Lace and Promises is well and truly on the map."

She nodded enthusiastically as she dabbed coffee from her lips.

"Tell me, how did you dream up such a name for a bridal shop?"

"Don't you know?" she frowned. "You obviously didn't listen to the Carpenters closely enough when we were growing up."

Suddenly the bell over the door sounded and Emilia jumped to her feet. In a swirl of fragrance that he would never be able to identify, she swept past him and into her shop.

He was truly happy for her, she was obviously satisfied with her lot, surrounding herself with such beautiful things. He assumed that everyone who came in would be full of happiness and excitement. Emilia was always upbeat, nothing ever seemed to get her down.

Turning his thoughts back to Mia Ashton, he sighed. He had re-lived the concert a hundred times, it had even dominated his dreams, but he realised that was all it was. He could not go on like a love struck teenager, besides, he had never even met Miss Ashton, and the chances of him doing so were very remote indeed. Draining his mug, he put it down on the table and made his way into the shop. Emilia was talking quietly to a young woman about colour schemes and designs and as he listened, he heard something about shades of white. After a while, he managed to attract her attention and leaving her customer to browse, Emilia came to where he was standing.

"Listen Ben," she stared up at him. "If she means that much to you then go after her. What have you got to lose?"

"Oh dear," he replied pulling a face. "Is it really that obvious?"

Slipping her arms around him, she brushed his cheek with her lips and whispered. "I can read you like a book dear brother."

Ben opened the door to his maisonette to the sound of his telephone ringing.

"Hello Ben," his sister's voice greeted him.

"Em, what's up?"

"Listen, I take it that you would jump at the opportunity to meet Mia Ashton."

"Yes of course," he replied suspiciously. "Why do you ask, what have you got up your sleeve?"

"Nothing, you know me, just minding my own business, but a little bit of gossip has just come my way."

He carried the telephone into the living room and sitting down he felt that he would probably need to.

"You remember the woman who came into my shop earlier?" she went on before he could reply. "That was Jenna O'Brien, she is getting married next year."

"Yes," he said trying to sound interested.

"Well, she told me that Mia will be at the new French Restaurant that opened a few months ago. You know the one?" she paused before going on. "Raymond Duval's."

"Oh yes, I know. He's hosting some kind of social evening, everyone is talking about it."

"He's keen to encourage the community to come together," she told

15

him, "he's a clever man. I'm sure it's a marketing ploy, anyway, he has invited a few celebrities and some good journalists."

"Is there such a thing?" he asked humorously.

"Of course there are, you know what I mean."

"So, where do I fit in?"

"Can't you see? You have to be there; it would be the perfect opportunity for you to meet her."

"Oh come on Em, how could I possibly do that? I don't have an invitation for one thing and as you've just said, this is an event aimed at people who network and promote their businesses."

"That's where I come in," she paused for effect. "I happen to know Raymond. We met recently at a commercial traders meeting and it turns out we have a lot in common. Anyway, he told me what he was planning and I'm certain that I can get us both an invitation."

"Are you sure?" he asked tightening his grip on the receiver.

"Leave it to me."

They ended their call and he sat still for a moment going over what his sister had just said. His heart quickened at the prospect, but he had to come up with a plan. They hardly socialised in the same circles, but now all that was about to change and he could hardly believe his luck. The prospect of meeting Mia Ashton had suddenly become a reality and he smiled. This was typical of his sister, she always managed to engineer the perfect situation, it was what she did best.

Chapter
FOUR

Mia had just completed another two hour rehearsal at home in her music room and she was feeling mentally exhausted, this was her second session of the day. Rising from the stool, she carefully returned her instrument to its stand. It was a beautiful Viennese Guadagnini dating from 1777 and it was her prized possession. She knew most of its provenance, but there were a few gaps in its history. Often she wondered about its past, how many musicians had cherished it over the years as much as she did. She hardly considered herself its owner, just another custodian, one of many privileged to have the opportunity to work with it. Picking up a soft cloth, she wiped finger marks from its wooden surfaces before cleaning the strings. Her cello was her best friend, they had been through so much together and now their relationship was about to become even more intense. Her upcoming concerts were increasingly more important and her future career depended on them being a success. She went over the music in her head until she was satisfied that each piece was committed to memory only then would her performance be perfect.

Moving away from her music room, she went into the galley-like kitchen and filled the kettle with water, her mind still occupied with work as she spooned coffee into the pot. Her next concert was in York where she was going to perform with a pianist. Alicia had agreed to the concert without consulting her and now she hardly had sufficient time to learn the scores. She had never played the Brahms Cello Sonatas No.s 1 & 2 completely before and only once had she practiced part of Schubert's Arpeggione Sonata. She would be expected to play these pieces in York and piling on this extra pressure whilst performing a concert in London hardly seemed to concern her agent, but it strained Mia to breaking point. She would however not complain, she would do whatever it took to realise her goal.

Whilst waiting for the kettle to boil, she made herself a sandwich and the moment she took a bite the telephone began to ring.

"Alicia," she mumbled before swallowing painfully. "How nice of you to call."

"How are you finding the York programme?" she asked without preamble.

"Everything is fine, I've been through it twice today."

"Well, that is a relief," Alicia sighed dramatically. "I simply couldn't change a thing not at this late stage, everything has been arranged."

"Don't you think that in future it might be a good idea to consult with me before making such huge decisions?"

Alicia was in the habit of agreeing complete performance schedules and booking other musicians without discussing it with her.

"Details darling, details. You don't have to bother yourself with such trivia anyway, as you have just said, everything is fine."

Mia groaned inwardly and resisting the urge to argue, clamped the telephone under her chin as she poured hot water into her coffee pot. Biting into her sandwich, she was confident that she would not have to respond, Alicia would make sure of that. Words tumbled from her mouth at an alarming rate and Mia had almost finished eating before she was required to speak.

"You have next week's schedule?" Alicia asked.

"Yes, I was just about to go through it."

"Well, you'll see that everything has been organised. The timetable is a little tight, but I'm sure you will manage."

Mia was about to ask a question but Alicia beat her to it.

"Your train leaves from Kings Cross at 11:30, your driver has all the details."

"The journey time is a couple of hours?" Mia asked.

"Yes, you should arrive in York at about 1:30. A car will be waiting for you at the other end, it will take you to the Lyons Concert Hall at the University where you will be performing. The stage should be set up and you will have an opportunity to practice with the pianist who is a local woman by the name of Grace Hooper."

"So we spend a couple of hours rehearsing, then I'm taken to my hotel?"

"Yes, the driver will give you a telephone number so when you are ready just give him a call and he will come and pick you up."

"The schedule is really tight," Mia said as she scanned the programme, "I would have liked more time with the pianist."

"You have Monday afternoon and most of Tuesday. The concert is on Wednesday evening and of course you could squeeze in a couple of hours on Wednesday morning."

Mia knew that the day of the concert would be busy, she had an appointment at the beauty salon during the morning then a lunchtime radio interview, and she had to try to find some time for herself, it was crucial to relax before an important concert. She listened as Alicia droned on and yawned whilst rubbing away the stiffness from her neck with her fingertips.

Finally, Alicia stopped talking and with a huge sigh of relief, Mia allowed the telephone to fall from her hand. She was tempted to turn it off, terrified that her agent might call again. Going into the living room, she threw herself down into an armchair and closed her eyes. Silence surrounded her and curling her legs up beneath her, she reached for the file containing the paperwork for her trip. She had already glanced at the programme but now she took a closer look. Everything was itemised and scanning quickly down the list she could see her life mapped out neatly in black and white. After a while, she closed her eyes again and let the papers fall onto her knees. She hoped that the weather would be kind in York, it was still very mild in London, but it could turn nasty in the north especially at this time of year. She didn't mind the cold weather but she hated snow. December was a difficult month for her, but all she needed to do was to keep busy.

She could feel herself drifting off and allowing the sensation to take hold, she relaxed her muscles and the stiffness across her shoulders began to ease. It was going to be a late night at Raymond Duval's so she felt justified in resting now, besides she had been up since dawn rehearsing. She just hoped that the telephone was not going to ring again.

Chapter
FIVE

Ben saw her the moment she arrived and his heart began to lurch uncomfortably. She looked marvellous, her long dark hair caught the light as it fell loosely over her shoulders and the cut of her dress drew his eye to her perfect figure. A pink pashmina completed her outfit, and Ben couldn't help thinking how classy she looked, he then began to doubt his ability to attract her attention.

He was surprised that she had arrived on her own, he had expected her to be accompanied by an entourage. He watched as she searched the room then someone called out her name and her face lit up with a radiant smile.

"Mia."

"Belenos, hi."

A well groomed man appeared in front of her and casually slipped his hand into hers before hugging her affectionately. He whispered something in her ear and she laughed softly then glancing his way, she noticed Ben looking at her, she returned his stare briefly before turning back to her friend.

"Mia, you look simply amazing." The man was saying as he led her across the room.

"Do you know who he is?" Emilia asked as she stepped up beside her brother.

"No."

"He's Belenos Falzone, a well known journalist, so be careful what you say to him. He's also a very good friend of Mia's."

"How do you know these things?" Ben asked, astonished at her wealth of social knowledge.

"You obviously read the wrong magazines," she replied dryly.

The room was beginning to fill up as more guests arrived. Waiting staff were kept busy with glasses of champagne and trays of canapés. Laughter rose up above the general din, and occasionally Emilia would spot someone she recognised. She waved and smiled pleasantly whilst pointing out those of note to her brother who continued to be amazed.

"I know absolutely no one here," he complained.

"You should get out more often," she smiled and catching the attention of a woman across the room, turned to him and said. "Now there is someone that you should meet."

Grabbing him by the arm she held onto him tightly, frightened that she might lose him as she steered around groups of people.

"Jenna," she called as soon as she was in earshot.

"Emilia, how wonderful it is to see you." They hugged and air kissed before Jenna purred. "Now tell me, who is this?"

"This is my brother Ben."

"How lucky you are," she said before holding out her hand. "He must be your best kept secret." Moving in closer she lowered her voice. "You never told me that you had such a delicious brother."

"The subject of my family has never come up," Emilia reminded her. "We usually discuss your wedding plans."

The smile faded from Jenna's face.

"Ben, this is Jenna O'Brien."

He nodded and was about to say how pleased he was to meet her but he didn't get the chance. The girls seemed to have a lot to say to each other, but Jenna flirted shamelessly with him before being caught up in a passing crowd.

"I had no idea that she was such a tease," Emilia whispered by way of an apology.

"She is obviously determined to have a good time, besides, she's not married yet." Ben laughed. His sister could be so prudish sometimes.

He glanced over to where Mia was standing. She was deep in conversation with another woman and he was amused at the way she used her hands, waving them in the air to emphasise some point or other. Belenos Falzone was standing to one side with his back to her, he was talking to a group who seemed very interested in what he was saying. It was obvious to Ben that he and Mia were not together, there was nothing in their body language to suggest they were a couple. Emilia had told him earlier that they were just good friends and from what she understood, Mia was not currently in a relationship.

Mia laughed and absentmindedly tucked a stray lock of hair behind her ear then suddenly she looked up and caught him staring again. He was unable to look away and as she held his gaze, her red lips curved into a smile and something passed between them. Her friend made a comment and the moment was lost.

People were now beginning to move into the dining area where a buffet table had been set up. Tables and chairs were arranged where people could sit together and enjoy their food, it was all very informal. Ben marvelled at the range of delicacies on offer and wondered if Raymond had prepared it all himself or had he simply employed caterers for the occasion. He realised that the evening was primarily about promoting his business, so Raymond and his staff must have been very busy indeed.

Helping himself to a few items, he loaded them carefully onto a plate before moving along the table. With his head down, he agonised over his choices, everything was expertly presented and it seemed a shame to spoil the display. Reaching for a tempting looking pastry, he was surprised when a flawlessly manicured hand got there before him.

"Oh, I do beg your pardon," he said glancing at the woman who appeared at his side.

"Hi," she said with a smile. "I'm Mia."

"Yes, I know," he replied awkwardly and caught completely off guard he rallied frantically in an effort to avoid saying something stupid.

"So, who are you?" she stared at him through soft brown eyes and again her neat red lips curved into a smile.

"I'm Ben, Benjamin Sykes."

"Hello Benjamin Sykes, I'm very pleased to meet you." She whispered before slipping her hand formally into his.

He could hardly believe his luck, Mia Ashton was standing right there beside him and he was holding onto her hand.

"So, Ben," she said, "are you going to have that pastry or am I?"

"You," he said quickly. "I'll get you a plate."

"I have one." She laughed and held it out towards him.

"Of course you have." He grimaced and reaching for a pair of cake tongs, he expertly transferred the pastry to her plate.

"What's your connection with Raymond Duval?" she asked casually. "Do you know him?"

"No, I'm an imposter I'm afraid," he glanced at her and recovered some of his composure. "I'm here with my sister, she's the connection, not me."

"Benjamin the imposter," she laughed. "I like that. So the woman you are with is your sister?"

It was his turn to smile. "Yes she is. Are you with anyone in particular?"

"No, not really. I know quite a lot of people here though, but I came alone this evening"

Moving away from the buffet table, they were jostled by those coming up behind and by some unspoken mutuality, found themselves at a table tucked inside a charming little alcove.

"I was at your concert the other evening," he confessed the moment they had settled.

"Oh yes, and what did you think?" Laying down her fork, she studied him intently.

"That you were marvellous, your performance was fantastic."

"Have you been reading my reviews?" she laughed.

"No, honestly I..."

"Don't worry Ben, I believe you." Reaching across the table, she touched his arm with her fingertips before laughing again then she nibbled on her pastry before asking. "What do you do? You know what I do for a living, but what about you?"

Cleverly, she steered the conversation away from herself and focussed on him. It was a safe bet, she knew that men liked to talk about themselves and she listened attentively as he admitted that he was currently between jobs. He had recently returned from what he called his 'Grand Tour', having spent some months travelling around Europe.

"A welcome change from years of study," he told her.

"How marvellous, what have you spent years studying?"

"Ergonomics," he said before going on to explain. "It's the study of people in relation to their working environment, the adaption of machines and general conditions to fit individuals so that they may work at maximum efficiency." It sounded as if he was reading from a manual.

"Goodness," she looked up at him, "how interesting. So what now, how can you make use of your knowledge?"

"I have been looking at various industrial management systems, but to be honest what interests me most is working on projects that will benefit disabled people."

"A very noble cause," she nodded. "You are lucky to be in a position to contemplate such a vocation."

He changed the subject by telling her about his sister and her shop. He thought that she might be more interested in that.

"How long has she been in business?"

"Just a few months, long enough to establish herself. Now all she needs to do is drum up some customers."

"She sounds like a very determined woman, but I imagine that it must be no easy task," she paused to take a sip of champagne. "Why did she choose to go into retail? Bridal wear is a very specialised business. Does she arrange the whole package, you know, organise everything, plan the perfect day?"

"That is what she wants to do eventually, but it's early days. There is just herself and one part time assistant at the moment. I imagine it to be quite a stressful task organising someone's wedding."

"Yes," Mia nodded. "It is the most special day in a woman's life. I wouldn't want the responsibility of arranging that, I would be terrified of getting it wrong."

He agreed and studied her for a moment before going on.

"She is looking for someone to help organise and develop that side of her business. Emilia's specialism is fashion design. She is brilliant at coordinating colours and stuff like that, it's what she studied at university."

They talked endlessly whilst enjoying their food and whenever a waiter passed, their champagne flutes were topped up.

Ben thought Mia charming, she far exceeded his expectations. She was easy to be with and not in the least pretentious and when he finally managed to get her to talk about herself she was very modest.

Mia was pleased with him too, she loved the way he spoke freely about all aspects of his life. He obviously loved his sister very much and he respected her enormously, Mia liked this about him. He was quite unlike other men she knew and it was not long before she realised that she would like to get to know him better.

Emilia studied them from a distance. She knew very little about Mia Ashton, but was amazed at how relaxed her brother appeared in her company. She had to admit that they looked good together and she would never have believed that they had just met. Ben looked up and their eyes met, he could sense her scrutinising him.

"Em," he said as she approached their table. "Come and meet Mia."

"Hi Emilia," Mia smiled welcomingly. "Ben has told me all about you."

"Oh has he indeed?" Emilia laughed.

"Your shop, White Lace and Promises sounds amazing. I can't wait to pay you a visit."

"Are you planning a wedding?

"Oh goodness me no," Mia shrieked. "Haven't met Mr Right yet."

Ben got to his feet and offered his sister his chair and the women continued their conversation. He was completely forgotten but he did not mind, he was content that they had taken to each other so readily.

Ben glanced around at the other guests and spotted Belenos Falzone. He was at the centre of a large group with Jenna O'Brien holding onto his arm, she seemed to be monopolising him. Everyone was enjoying themselves, the conversation was interesting and the atmosphere relaxed. Raymond Duval must be overjoyed, Ben thought, the evening was a great success.

Mia was happy with her new friends and was glad that Emilia had turned out to be Ben's sister. At first, she thought they might have been a couple, she had noticed them the moment she arrived. Ben had been watching her and she was afraid that maybe they had met before. In her line of work, she met so many people that it was impossible to keep track.

She got home just after midnight, her mood mellow from the effects of champagne and good company and sinking down onto the sofa she sighed and kicked off her shoes. She was pleased that she had gone to Raymond Duval's restaurant and was looking forward to returning there again soon. She had briefly met him during the early part of the evening, he was the perfect host, taking time to welcome all his guests.

Closing her eyes, she laid her head back and breathed deeply. Emilia Sykes was an interesting and knowledgeable person and she was certain they could become friends. Ben was sweet and seemed genuine enough. She smiled, she had enjoyed his company immensely.

Chapter
SIX

The following day Mia woke early from a fitful sleep, opening her eyes to the grey half-light of another winter morning she groaned. Elements of her nightmare were still there inside her head so she rolled over and buried her face in her pillow. After a few moments, she pushed away her fears and concentrated on pleasant memories from the previous evening.

Thoughts of her York trip were never far away, she still had lots to do before she would be ready to travel and peering at the bedside clock, she groaned again. Why had she woken so early after such a late night? Clearly, her nightmare was the reason for that.

Chastising herself for allowing such negative thoughts to fill her head she rolled out of bed. She was naked, so reaching for her dressing gown she shrugged it on and frowned. She usually wore a nightdress in bed, so why was it still on the end of the bed? Shrugging her shoulders, she pushed her hair out of her face and went into the living room.

Light struggled to penetrate the room and pulling back the curtains made little difference so reaching for the lamp she switched it on. Her left hand felt stiff and sore, scrutinising it under the light she discovered a fading bruise. Flexing her fingers gingerly she tried them out, it was hardly a good time to pick up an injury. How could this have happened she frowned and touching the side of her head, she felt out of sorts. It could hardly be the result of a hangover, she had not overdone the champagne the night before, so she put it down to her disturbed night.

Turning away from the light she looked around the room, it was peaceful. Her dress was there on the sofa looking as if it had been cast lazily aside. She would never leave her clothes like this so picking it up she smoothed her hand over the soft, cool material. It still bore the scent of her perfume and she smiled, it was then that she noticed the zip had been damaged, the fabric around it torn. How could this have happened? She was always so careful with her clothes and searching her memory she realised that she could not remember getting ready for bed. She could however recall her conversation with Ben and his sister and even returning home, but then nothing, her memory became blank.

Her shoes were on the floor, not together neatly as she would have left them but cast aside as if in anger. Gathering them up she checked for damage but luckily, there was not so much as a scuff. It was then she spotted her underwear. Her panties and bra were on the carpet beside the armchair torn to shreds.

"What the hell is going on?" she asked herself before going to the bathroom. Standing in front of the mirror, she removed her dressing gown and scrutinised her body searching for scratches or bruises but there was nothing, no evidence that an attack had taken place, her only injury was a bruised hand and stiff fingers.

She was certain that she had returned home from Raymond Duval's restaurant alone. Her flat was definitely empty when she let herself in, she was sure of that. She checked the windows and doors, before peering out at the lawn and flower borders. There was no evidence of footprints or that anyone had been there waiting for her to return home.

Going into the kitchen, she made herself a mug of strong coffee. Caffeine would help to wake her, give her the strength to think clearly. Sitting down, she took her time and breathing deeply used a relaxation technique to help calm her nerves. She was saddened to think that unpleasant experiences from her teenage years might have returned, but now was not the time to start worrying about that.

After a while, she felt easier and going into her bedroom, got dressed before working on her fingers. Simple exercises would help to reduce the stiffness, loosen the joints before playing her cello.

The house was quiet and filled with the calm of a Sunday morning but it would not last for long. She had to spend time practicing so pushing away any remaining negative thoughts she concentrated on making herself ready.

Her music room was quite unlike the rest of her home. Although the atmosphere was relaxed this was a place of work. A large window set into one wall usually allowed plenty of natural light into the room, but not today. It was gloomy outside so she turned on the wall lights. The floor was of polished oak and the walls decorated with a soft buttermilk covering, Mia was pleased with the effect. Music stands flanked her cello, which had pride of place in the centre of the room. The only furniture in the room was a cabinet containing sheet music. A small CD player that she used to play backing music stood on top of the cabinet.

Mia took her time, taking deep breaths she settled on the stool before embracing her instrument then she began to play.

Ben and Emilia met for breakfast at a small cafe on the edge of the park.

"It was a very pleasant evening," Ben said as they settled at their table.

"You did well, you dark horse." Emilia's eyes flashed with admiration as she looked up at her brother. "I had no idea that you were such a smooth operator."

"Don't be daft," he told her as he reached for the breakfast menu. "She is just so easy to get along with."

"Yes," Emilia nodded in agreement. "You are right there. So tell me."

"Tell you what?" he teased, knowing exactly what she was asking.

Emilia pouted and feigned disappointment.

"Don't worry, I have her number written on the back of my hand."

Her eyes strayed to his hand.

"Not really," he said. "She wrote it down on a serviette and I'm to telephone her later in the week once she has returned from York."

He explained that she was giving a concert there and would not be back until Thursday.

"So, as you see, maybe we'll meet up again next weekend."

"Okay," she nodded satisfied that she had got to the bottom of it.

Changing the subject, they talked for a while before she got down to what was really on her mind.

Mia worked her fingers along the strings trying out her bruised hand, but she need not have worried. Drawing the bow back and forth, she tuned her instrument until the tone was perfect then she continued to play. Closing her eyes, she shut out every distraction and concentrated entirely on her music playing a couple of her favourite tunes before turning to the pieces for the concert. Using a recording of the piano accompaniment, she launched into the first piece.

Immediately her troubles were forgotten and as she connected with her instrument, several hours passed without her even noticing. Her fingers danced with memory reflexes, her performance perfect and when it was over, she was breathless, her heart skipping as if in time with the beat. It was at times like this that she felt truly alive, if music was a drug, she would be dependent on it and without it, her life would be pointless.

Leaning backwards, she stretched her arms above her head and from somewhere in the house she could hear the sound of a telephone ringing. It stopped, but when she went into the living room a few minutes later it began to ring again.

Hello," she said picking up the receiver and waiting for an answer, she stood upright and placed a hand on her hip. "Hello, who is there?"

"I hate you."

"Sorry, what did you say? You are very faint, I can hardly hear you."

"I hate you." The voice was louder this time. "I hate you." It repeated before the line went dead.

Mia was stunned, still gripping the receiver all she could hear was the dialling tone. Slumping down into a chair she sighed, saddened at the fact that someone could be so callous. How did this person have her telephone number? She was ex directory and only ever gave it out to friends, besides she relied on her mobile phone more often these days. Groaning with frustration, she slammed the receiver down.

Chapter

SEVEN

Belenos Falzone frowned and tapped the end of his pen against his teeth. This was a habit he had perfected as a student and moments like this reminded him of his study days. He was working on a proposal for a leading magazine, his brief, a series of articles about serial killers. Interest in this subject had soared since the abduction of local artist Josie MacDonald and the appalling deaths of a number of her friends.

On the desk in front of him, lay a number of newspaper articles from the time of the atrocity, but what intrigued him most was the lack of information regarding the details of the murders. He would have expected to find in depth reports about the people involved especially the murderer himself, but this was not the case. It was as if there had been some kind of news blackout, there was just a rudimentary report about events leading up to and after the killings.

Sitting back in his chair, he sighed before running his hand through his hair. The more he thought about it, the further from his brief he strayed. He was supposed to be putting together a series of articles comparing the methods preferred by a number of serial killers. He was to delve into their psychological state and come up with a logical and informed presentation, but his investigative journalistic instincts were telling him to look deeper into the Josie MacDonald case. He would of course have to do the legwork, come up with a plan and carry out some primary research. It would be necessary to get close to those who were there at the time if he were to discover the facts. He scribbled down a few notes and without realising it, an hour slipped away. Glancing over his shoulder, he guiltily pushed his notes out of sight, hiding the evidence before reading the piece he had downloaded about serial killers from the internet.

A serial killer is a person who murders three or more people, in two or more separate events over a period of time, for primarily psychological reasons. There are gaps between the killings, which may range from a few hours to many years...

Suddenly his telephone rang.

"Mia," he said recognising her voice immediately and they exchanged greetings.

"Did you have fun last evening?" she asked.

"Jenna O'Brien was entertaining," Belenos laughed. "You know what she is like."

"Yes, she can be a little loud sometimes," Mia agreed, "but I admire her. She is a free spirit, an independent woman who knows her own mind."

"Don't get me wrong, I like her too." Belenos said. "She's adorable in an enviable kind of way, but it would take a very strong character to cope with her on a daily basis."

"I hear that she is to be married next year."

"Really?" Belenos snorted, "I had no idea. From the way she was acting last night I guess that she doesn't take her engagement very seriously."

"I met a lovely man," Mia confessed in a change of subject.

"So I noticed," he replied. "Who is the lucky fellow, but more to the point, who was the lovely creature accompanying him?"

"Well that was me of course," she laughed before becoming serious. "His name is Ben and the woman he was with is his sister Emilia."

She told him about her new friends and he listened with interest.

"I'm sorry that I didn't get to say goodbye," he said when she was finished. "I saw you leaving but couldn't get away from Jenna and the gang."

"Listen," she interrupted. "How did I seem to you when I left?"

"What do you mean?" he asked.

"Did I look sober for example?"

"What a curious question," he began and stalling for time considered his answer carefully. "You looked very happy and alarmingly sober to me. Why do you ask?"

"It's just that I don't remember very much after arriving home."

"You left with your friends Emilia and Ben."

"Yes, I remember that. We shared a taxi and because I had the furthest to go they insisted on dropping me off first."

"You did go home?" he asked amused by her tone.

"Of course I did, I went home alone."

"So what's the problem?"

"There is no problem," she lied, refusing to tell him what she had discovered when she woke up.

"Well, you seemed to be having a great time. I guess the full effects of the champagne did not kick in until you were on your way home."

"True," she said realising that what he said made sense. She could not bear to tell him about the mysterious telephone call so she said. "I spoke to my father earlier."

"Okay," Belenos replied wondering where the sudden change of subject was leading.

"You asked me to set up a meeting between the two of you."

"Oh yes, of course."

"He can see you at lunchtime tomorrow at the Richmond Hotel."

Belenos knew the hotel, it was a popular place for police officers to meet and unwind at the bar. He had interviewed a number of detectives there in the past when he was working as a local reporter.

"That is good for me," he said glancing at his diary on the computer screen. "What time is lunchtime?"

"One pm, is that okay?"

"Yes one o'clock it is. Thank you for doing that for me," he said. "You are leaving for York tomorrow?"

"Yes," she replied. "Kings Cross on the eleven thirty."

"Have a great time and make them adore you." The sound of her laughter cheered him. "Let me know the moment you are back and I'll take you out for supper."

"You're on," she said.

The following day Mia was up early and moving cautiously around her flat she found nothing out of place. She had checked the windows and doors twice over before going to bed the previous evening and now as she went from room to room she was greeted by nothing more than a warm and comforting atmosphere.

Was she being paranoid, she asked herself with a sigh of relief. Her father was always telling her that she could never be too careful. He rarely spoke about the unpleasant aspects of his work, but she had read too many crime novels so was under no illusion as to the horrors he faced on a daily basis.

Going into her music room, she embraced her cello and allowed herself a few moments to explore the instrument. It was warm and comforting, the wood darkened with age, it smelt of polish and was always a pleasure to touch. The strings were new, she had replaced them after the last concert and now after a few hours of practice, they were perfect for the musical arrangements in York.

Lifting the instrument carefully from its stand, she placed it in its case and left it by the door. Next, she gathered up her sheet music and put it into her briefcase along with a couple of sets of spare strings. Doing these simple things helped to steady her nerves. As the concert drew closer, she began to feel the pressure of performing to a live audience. However much she prepared she still felt nervous, but she knew this would soon pass, once she was there and the concert began, her nerves would settle.

Leaving the music room, she went into the kitchen and made herself a mug of coffee, the car that would take her to the station would be arriving soon and she did not have long to wait. Before she had time to finish her coffee, the doorbell rang.

"Good morning Miss Ashton," the man said cheerfully as he presented her with his identification card. "All set are you miss?"

"Good morning," Mia replied as she inspected him carefully, her father's advice ringing in her ears. She had not met this man before but he was from the private hire company that she favoured.

"Shall I take your bags?"

"Yes please," Mia nodded as she reached for her coat and scarf. "I'll follow on with this." Picking up her cello case, she eased it along the hallway before pulling the door shut behind her.

At the train station, the driver took care of her luggage, transferring it to the first class baggage storage area. This amused Mia, she had never experienced this before and it amazed her that the driver should be so attentive. Alicia had reserved two seats in first class, one for Mia, and one for her cello. Her beloved instrument never left her side.

The train pulled out of the station at eleven thirty sharp leaving behind the madness of Kings Cross and just under an hour later luncheon was served, sandwiches, cake and a reasonable pot of tea.

The weather deteriorated steadily as the train sped north and by the time she arrived in York, the sky was heavy and slate grey. A dusting of snow covered the countryside on the outskirts but in the city itself, the pavements were wet and cold.

Mia looked out of her window as the train slowed and came to a stop. People were going about their business dressed in thick coats with scarves wrapped warmly around their necks. The scene was similar to the one she had left behind in London, but here in York there seemed less urgency. The scale of things was pleasantly less, the crowds smaller, the atmosphere not as stressed.

Stepping onto the platform Mia looked around. She was not sure where to go to collect her bags so spotting a guard further along the platform, she hurried in his direction.

"Excuse me," she called, approaching the man before he had time to disappear. "Where do I go to get my luggage?"

The man eyed her for a moment before replying. "All taken care of miss."

"Miss Ashton?" A voice sounded from behind and as Mia turned, she could see a smartly dressed woman hurrying towards her.

"Miss Ashton?" she asked again.

"Yes," Mia replied. "How do you know my name?"

"Well," her smile was friendly. "I don't see anyone else carrying a cello case."

It was Mia's turn to smile and searching for something sensible to say she was beaten to it.

"Welcome to York. My name is Cassie and I will be your driver whilst you are here."

"Oh I see." Cassie came as a total shock. A female chauffeur was not what she had expected especially one so pretty and so young.

"I have taken care of your luggage," Cassie told her. "If you would like to follow me, the car is this way." She did not offer to carry Mia's cello case, clearly working on the orders of Alicia.

A large dark coloured car was parked close to the entrance, its gleaming bodywork inviting, its warm leather interior a luxury that Mia could hardly refuse. There was plenty of room in the boot for her cello, only then did Mia reluctantly part with her cherished instrument.

"The traffic in town is not too bad. If we go that way I can show you some of the sights." Cassie said holding the door open as Mia slipped into the rear seat.

"Have you been to York before?" Cassie asked once she had settled in the driving seat.

"No I'm afraid not, this is my first visit."

"The Christmas market began last week and is now in full swing. You might like to take a look later, but I would leave it until after dark because the festive lights are very pretty."

Mia nodded but made no comment.

"I'll take you to your hotel where you can drop your luggage and freshen up then we'll go to the university where you will be performing."

"That sounds perfect," Mia said. "Is the university far from town?"

"No, it's just a couple of miles out."

Five minutes later, they pulled up in front of a grand looking building.

"You'll find it quiet here even though the hotel is situated in the centre of town."

It was not long before Mia was back in the car and on her way to the university where Professor David Star was waiting to meet her.

"Miss Ashton," he said smiling enthusiastically as Cassie opened the door then stepping forward, he introduced himself. "David Star, Head of the Music Department."

"Professor Star," Mia took his hand. "I'm so pleased to be here at last."

"The honour is all ours Miss Ashton," he said shaking her hand firmly. "We are so looking forward to your concert."

Cassie had the boot open and was about to reach for the cello.

"Allow me," Professor Star said and moving quickly he recovered the instrument from the car.

"Please collect me at six." Mia spoke to Cassie who nodded politely.

"If you'll come this way," Professor Star led her away from the car. "I'll take you through to the concert hall where you will meet Grace."

They made their way along a brightly lit corridor, which led away from the reception area. There were not many students in this part of the building so falling in beside him Mia studied him from the corner of her eye. The Professor was a tall, lean man who she guessed to be in his early fifties. He was dressed immaculately in a tweed suit and wore a pair of tan brogues on his feet. His hair was dark, but slightly too long for the shape of his face. Although his hair appeared natural, she was certain that it was coloured, his eyebrows were two shades lighter and beginning to grey.

"Here we are," he said and holding the door open, allowed her to enter before him. "The Lyons Concert Hall."

Her first impressions were how compact it was, much smaller than she had imagined. Hexagonal in shape it could seat three hundred and fifty people. This much she knew from the information Alicia had given her. She also knew this to be the home of the York Symphony Orchestra.

"The Lyons Concert Hall," Professor Star was explaining, "is named after Sir Jack Lyons, our benefactor from times past. The hall is the heart of the music department."

She could tell from his enthusiasm that he was monumentally proud of his domain and when he was finished, he peered down at her and smiled.

They stopped at the edge of the stage where a grand piano stood in magnificent solitude. The atmosphere inside the concert hall was relaxed, the light subdued and Mia began to feel more confident. Seeing a place for the first time always filled her with concern. If the vibrations of the building were not to her liking then she would have to work much harder on her performance, but here the ambience was perfect and it pleased her.

"Ah, here's Grace."

A side door opened and a tall, black woman made her way confidently across the stage.

"Miss Ashton, may I introduce Grace Hooper."

"Mia, please call me Mia," she said as they shook hands.

"I'm so pleased to meet you," Grace smiled. "I've heard so much about you."

"Only good things I hope."

They laughed together and Mia knew instinctively that she would enjoy working with this woman.

"Did you have a good trip?" Grace asked displaying a genuine interest.

"Yes thank you. I see you've had snow already, nothing like that in London yet."

"Oh yes, we had a dusting this morning. A little more is forecast over the next few days but I wouldn't worry, I'm sure it won't come to much not here in the city anyway."

Professor Star stood silently watching the women as they became acquainted and when he saw his chance, he said. "Grace is a member of our orchestra, she plays the piano of course but also a range of musical instruments."

"Oh," Mia smiled. "What instrument do you favour?"

"I enjoy them all. Piano is my first passion but I also adore Gypsy Jazz. I play acoustic guitar and sing."

"Wow," Mia exclaimed. "How fascinating, I am impressed. Classical piano and Gypsy Jazz, the disciplines are so different."

"I play a lot of jazz on the piano, but I like to let my hair down sometimes and jam with the guitar." Her eyes glowed with enthusiasm.

Grace was much younger than she expected, Mia had conjured up an image of an ageing aunt, an austere piano teacher, not an attractive and talented woman who enjoyed all kinds of music.

"I'm so pleased to be accompanying you, I'm so lucky." Grace was saying.

"I hope I won't be a disappointment to you." Mia laughed. "I suppose we had better get down to it, we don't have much time."

They sorted out their sheet music and Grace stared at Mia's cello as she adjusted the strings.

"What a beautiful instrument and such a fabulous sound." She sighed with appreciation.

Professor Star took a seat a few rows back from the stage, he too was eager to hear her play.

Grace nodded then they began. Mia, taking the lead, launched into the first movement and stopping occasionally, they discussed slight changes but together they were perfect and later when the rehearsal was over both musicians were satisfied.

Chapter
EIGHT

Belenos made his way to the Richmond Hotel. The lunchtime rush had just begun and the well-appointed dining room was noisy with diners. It never ceased to amaze him that whatever the economic state of the country places like the Richmond still seemed to thrive. There appeared to be no end of people willing to part with obscene amounts of cash in order to enjoy good food and wine.

Going into the bar where it was less noisy, he glanced around and recognised one or two of the faces from the small groups enjoying a liquid lunch. DI Ashton was alone at one end of the bar nursing a tumbler of single malt. At his elbow sat a small jug of spring water and he seemed to be having trouble making his mind up, should he add it to his scotch or enjoy it neat.

"Inspector Ashton," Belenos said, disturbing his thoughts.

"Falzone," Ashton replied and looking up they shook hands. "Care for a snifter?"

"Don't mind if I do." Belenos smiled. He was unaccustomed to lunchtime drinking but today was prepared to make an exception.

When his drink arrived, they left the bar and moved into a little side room that reminded Belenos of a formal gentleman's club. Wingback chairs and leather sofas stood in groups around tiny polished tables and the walls were adorned with hunting scenes, there was even a stag's head mounted on an end wall. A masculine air hung about the place and Belenos was certain that he could detect stale cigar smoke.

They sat down and eyed each other as they sipped at their drinks.

"So," Belenos said breaking the silence. "Mia is on her way to conquer the frozen north."

Terry was amused by his remark, it conjured up pictures of his daughter dressed as a Celtic warrior queen riding north to do battle with the Romans.

"Indeed she is," he nodded. "What is it that you want to discuss?" Terry eyed him suspiciously. "I assume you are not here to ask for my daughter's hand in marriage."

"Oh goodness me sir." Belenos choked, "whatever gave you that idea?"

"Drop this sir business will you, you can call me Terry."

Belenos shuffled in his seat, not comfortable with the prospect of addressing Mia's father by his Christian name.

"I'm working on a series of articles for a well known publication," he explained. "I've been researching serial killers such as May Wilson, Harold Shipman and Dennis Nilsen to name but a few and have an understanding of the term serial killer." He paused before reaching for his drink.

"How can I help you? You seem to be doing very well with your research. There are many books about this subject and of course much more on the internet."

"Yes, that may be true, but it's not the same as actually talking to people who have to deal with these cases. I'm looking for a personal perspective, I would like to know what you think about these murderers."

"I've not met any of the people you have mentioned, these are all high profile cases, killers who have caught the imagination of the public."

"They must all share a common characteristic. What is it that turns them into monsters?"

"These people are not all as you put it monsters. You have to remember that some of them appear pleasant and trustworthy. Take Harold Shipman and John Bodkin Adams for example. These men were middle class doctors, well respected in their communities who would hardly be expected to harm anyone let alone commit murder."

"True, but in the case of Adams, he was never found guilty of murder or even professional negligence for that matter." Belenos said quoting from the wealth of information that he had picked up during his research. "Years after his death," he continued, "conflicting views remain about whether he was guilty of murder or euthanasia. To some he's regarded as a forerunner to Harold Shipman, whilst others believe that he simply carried out mercy killings at a time when pain killers were the only way to alleviate terminal suffering."

"Indeed," Terry nodded. "It depends on your point of view. Some of those whose loved ones became his victims may think differently."

"Of course," Belenos agreed, "but some murders display brutality beyond imagination." He chose his words carefully, hardly needing to spell out the horrors that some of the victims had endured.

Terry studied him carefully but remained silent so Belenos continued.

"It's the psychological aspect that intrigues me most. In many cases, a traumatic childhood is held accountable for many behavioural problems that manifest themselves in later years."

"True," Terry inclined his head. "There may be a number of psychological reasons why people do the things they do. We are all driven by circumstances, it's what makes us who we are, but there can be no excuse for cold blooded murder."

"Is that a policeman's point of view?"

"No, I don't think so, I believe it's the view shared by most civilised people. Surely it's a fundamental basis for our entire culture."

"Indeed it is," Belenos liked what he heard and mentally filed the quote away for future use.

Terry, reaching for his drink twirled the heavy tumbler between his fingers and wondered where this conversation was going. He had a gut feeling that they had not yet arrived at the primary objective of this meeting.

"What about William Randolph?" Belenos asked suddenly.

"Ah yes, the recent case involving local artist Josie MacDonald." He smiled to himself knowing that finally he was getting to the point.

Belenos sat up in his seat and his eyes flashed eagerly.

"What can you tell me about him?"

"Very little I'm afraid. He was killed before he could be brought to trial." Terry thought for a moment, recalling the facts. "He was shot dead by a man called Rufus Stone during a daring rescue attempt."

Belenos knew this to be true. "A successful rescue mission by all accounts that revealed the extent of the crimes committed by Randolph."

"Indeed it was. If it wasn't for this man Stone, there would undoubtedly have been more killings."

"Wasn't Rufus Stone a victim himself?"

"Yes he was," Terry shuddered. "His daughter disappeared many years earlier and her remains were discovered on the Montague estate along with others of Randolph's victims.

"William Randolph interests me," Belenos admitted and looking directly at Terry, he pressed on. "Can you put me onto the investigating officers in Scotland who dealt with this case?"

"What makes you think they would be willing to talk to you?"

"The truth it seems has never been told. Not much is known about Randolph and his killing spree. Maybe it's time the story was published."

"The tabloids in Scotland reported the facts at the time." Terry reminded him.

"Yes I'm aware of that, but there seems to have been some kind of news blackout."

"Isn't it obvious then that someone doesn't want the story to be told?" Terry said. "The Randolphs were a powerful family with ties to Scotland going back many generations. Someone must be protecting the family name."

"That is a crime in itself. Randolph was a serial killer who tortured his victims mercilessly before taking their lives."

"That does not give the tabloids the right to bring down his entire family, destroy the reputations of those who are innocent."

"There is no family," Belenos reminded him. William Randolph was the last of his line."

Terry stared at him, there was something terrifying about this young man. If he was capable of destroying a person or a family with the stroke of his pen, then was he much different from the criminals they were discussing? He had seen it before, trial by tabloid they called it at the Yard, and just or not, it was a reality. People generally believed what they read and once a rumour had started, it was impossible to stop it from spreading. Belenos Falzone could cause untold damage.

The atmosphere in the room changed, it was no longer as congenial as it had been earlier.

"Randolph is merely an interest of mine," Belenos said, making eye contact with Terry. "He's not really part of my investigation so I don't intend to include him in my article."

"In that case my advice is that you stick to your brief and forget about Randolph."

With one swift movement, Terry finished his drink and got to his feet.

"I can't stop you from carrying out your enquiries, but I would be very careful if I were you. There may be more than simply a story at stake here." He nodded curtly before walking away. Their meeting was clearly over.

Chapter
NINE

Snow lay on the ground, a mantle that covered the Vale of York, a wild winter landscape as silent as the unspoken word. For now, the city had escaped the worst of it, but the pewter coloured sky threatened more.

Mia emerged from her hotel and sniffed at the air. It was cold and crisp outside, the scent of snow making her nostrils flare as images of her childhood filled her head. Suddenly her mother's voice sounded and glancing over her shoulder, she shuddered. Mia could still feel the excitement as their sledge hurtled down the snow covered hill and holding onto her brother, she never wanted to let him go.

"Good morning Miss Ashton."

Cassie appeared and startled, Mia blinked back a tear.

"Good morning," she replied, her voice high with emotion. "The cold air is making my eyes water."

Cassie smiled as she held the rear door open. The warmth of the car was inviting and as Mia settled on the smooth leather seat, she pushed away the memories of her childhood.

"Traffic is slow this morning," Cassie said as she took her place behind the wheel. "Some of the trains have been disrupted on account of the bad weather, but it's not too bad."

The car eased away from the kerb and as they joined the others in a crawl around the city Mia began to think about the day ahead.

"I will be rehearsing all day," she said but then realised that her driver would be familiar with her schedule and she felt foolish.

"Inside in the warm is probably the best place to spend the day."

Cassie told her. "The weather forecast promises an improvement, there shouldn't be more snow today, it's not expected until later this week."

From the look of the angry sky overhead, Mia doubted this prediction and catching sight of Cassie's eyes in the rear view mirror she smiled then looked away.

There was no more snow but the temperature dropped alarmingly and as the day went on the wind increased in strength bringing with it arctic weather conditions. By late afternoon when they were tired of rehearsing both Mia and Grace went into town.

The Christmas market was busy despite the biting wind and moving with the crowds they sheltered by the little sheds that housed the market traders. The stalls were full of Christmas delights and Mia began to look around for gifts for her father. The lights were as pretty as Cassie had said and the sweet, spicy aroma of mulled wine added to the seasonal spirit. A choir stood in a little square just off the Shambles, their voices pure with ancient song and further along the street a group of buskers delivered sounds just as old. Mia stopped to listen and to study their unusual stringed instruments.

"They are very good," she said dropping coins into the case that lay open on the pavement.

"I can't remember their name but they are part of the folk scene. They always play tunes from our Viking past, giving them a modern twist but remaining faithful to the original melody."

Mia smiled, this was truly a magical place, and the pressures of the day began to melt away. Everything was set, the rehearsals were complete, and she could do no more. She was pleased at how well things had gone; now all she had to do was perform faultlessly at the concert.

Mia bought gifts from the market stalls and decorations for her flat. She had found a stall selling scented pinecones and now her bags were filled with the scent of winter spices.

"I'm exhausted," Grace said as they ducked into a brightly lit cafe.

Dumping their shopping beneath a table, they shrugged off their coats and made themselves comfortable.

"I'm going to have mulled wine and mince pies," Mia said, her eyes flashing mischievously.

Christmas carols were playing softly in the background and the hum of people enjoying hot drinks and cakes only added to the atmosphere.

"What do you make of Alison?" Grace said the moment they sat down.

Alison Morley was the young violinist performing solo at the concert. She was due to go on stage before Mia and Grace.

"She is a brilliant musician," Mia began, wondering just how honest she should be, "although I think a little arrogant."

"Yes," Grace nodded, "I agree, she's certainly not very friendly."

Mia made a face.

"Don't worry, it's not you." Reaching across the table Grace touched Mia's arm. "Alison is not very popular with the other members of the orchestra. David would get rid of her if he could but she is such a damned good musician."

"Well, as long as she does her job tomorrow it hardly matters if she likes me or not."

"I guess you are right," Grace smiled. "I can honestly say that I dislike no one. I seem to get along with everyone I meet."

"Me too," Mia nodded. "Life is too short to make enemies."

Their mulled wine and mince pies arrived delighting them with mouth-watering aromas.

"Tell me more about yourself," Grace began. "Do you have any brothers or sisters?"

Mia held her glass close to her face and breathing in the spices peered at Grace over the rim before replying.

"No," she said softly, "no siblings."

"I have a sister," Grace smiled and her eyes lit up. "She lives in Leeds with her husband and two delightful children."

Mia listened without comment.

"What about a boyfriend or partner?" Grace could see that Mia wore no rings and there had been no mention of a husband.

"No one serious," she confessed before breaking open her mince pie with her fingers, she frowned as if making up her mind before continuing. "I have however just met someone, but its early days yet."

"Oh wow," Grace looked up enquiringly. "How exciting, do tell."

Mia told her about Ben, describing him and recalling how they had met. She also mentioned Belenos admitting that he was just a good friend.

"He sounds very interesting and what an unusual name."

Mia told Grace that he was one of twins and his brother was called Gwydion. Their Welsh mother named them both after Celtic gods.

"How fascinating," she said her eyes wide with delight. "You are so lucky to have such good friends."

"Belenos is a journalist so you have to be careful what you say sometimes."

"Really? Surely he wouldn't publish anything without your permission."

"Don't you believe it," Mia laughed. She went on to tell her about some of her less flattering reviews. "I must admit though," she paused before taking another sip of her mulled wine, "he's not so bad these days. He still writes my reviews, but has graduated to much larger stories. He's no longer into sensationalism and now produces interesting and balanced articles for colour magazines." She mentioned some of the publications and Grace was impressed.

"I often buy those magazines so must have read some of his work."

They were silent for a while, content to watch as shoppers passed by the window. The evening was drawing in and now the festive lights were at their best.

"How about your parents?" Grace asked, once she had finished eating her mince pie.

"My father is a policeman," Mia said looking up at her. "A Detective Inspector at Scotland Yard."

"Really?" Once again, Grace was impressed. "You really are full of surprises, you know such fascinating people. My life is quite dull by comparison."

"Oh I doubt that," Mia laughed.

They chatted about their fathers for a while comparing stories from their childhood, then Grace asked about her mother.

"My mother died when I was eight years old," Mia said softly.

"Oh I am sorry," Grace said uncomfortably. "I shouldn't be so nosy."

"Don't be silly," Mia reassured her. "It was such a long time ago, besides I'm completely over it now."

She studied Mia and knew that was not true.

"This mulled wine is delicious," Grace said, "especially now it's cool enough to drink without scalding your tongue."

Mia nodded and lifted her glass to her lips. "We are going to be so good tomorrow," she said. "Professor Star will be delighted."

Grace nodded. "I can see him now taking all the credit for our success."

They giggled like teenagers and thoughts of Mia's mother were forgotten.

"He's an extraordinary man," Grace said, becoming serious. "He looks after us very well, the orchestra wants for nothing. He is the heart and soul of the music department and I'm certain that without him the orchestra would not be such a success."

They ordered more mulled wine and talked about the university and life in York and as they got to know each other, Mia realised that she had made another good friend.

"It's been a lovely day," she said glancing at her watch, "I'll call for my car. Can I drop you off somewhere?"

"No need for that," Grace reminded her. "Your hotel is just around the corner and I live only a short bus ride away."

Chapter
TEN

Mia and Grace stunned their audience, there were never any doubts, their preparation was perfect and their performance faultless. Alison Morley played her part delivering a complicated piece with practiced ease and displaying skills of the highest degree. Alison was the perfect choice to open the concert and from the moment her performance began it was clear that the bar had been set very high indeed.

"Come on you two," Alison called as she appeared at the changing room doors. "We have a party to attend and David is waiting."

"I suppose we had better go and show our faces," Grace laughed as she set her empty glass down beside the ice bucket.

"It's a shame we can't take this with us," Mia said as she got to her feet.

"Turning up with a half empty bottle of plonk is hardly appropriate." They laughed again, the flame of excitement burning fiercely in their eyes.

Smoothing her hands carefully over her dress, Mia studied herself in the mirror. Her long dark hair was groomed to perfection and her freshly applied lipstick was bright. She had coloured her nails and now the varnish was almost dry. She would never perform with bright red nails, but now with the concert over they matched her lips, her mother would have approved.

Outside the snow began to fall, huge white flakes floating serenely down from an over burdened sky, but inside it was comfortably warm and people were waiting to meet them. Mia was of course the main attraction, but Grace had been drawn into her light and standing together, they were ready to support each other once again. Grace was determined to enjoy her newfound fame.

David was waiting to introduce them to a line of dignitaries made up of the Mayor and his wife, leading churchmen from the Minster along with directors and governors of the university.

"Ladies and Gentlemen," he called for silence. "I give you Mia Ashton and Grace Hooper."

The applause grew louder and lasted longer than Mia would have liked. She searched the crowd for Alison, but the young woman was nowhere to be seen.

"I would just like to say a few words," David continued, holding his arms up in a gesture for silence.

"I think that you will agree that we have been privileged to witness a superb performance this evening."

Murmurs of appreciation rose up from the delighted audience so he went on, telling them about his work in the music department and their connection with the York Symphony Orchestra. His speech was rousing and enlightening, it would go a long way in maintaining support for his department at the university. More applause sounded and when he was finished the Mayor stepped forward.

To Mia he appeared as a typical politician dressed in a fancy suit. He was trying too hard to impress and the moment he opened his mouth her suspicions were confirmed.

"I have rarely heard Brahms played with such vigour," he began and she doubted that he had heard a Brahms Cello Sonata before. Chastising herself for such uncharacteristic thoughts, she arranged a smile on her face and listened politely.

His speech was longer than David's and when he was finished, an almost inaudible sigh of relief went around the room. Clearly, the Mayor needed to work on his speeches and his presentation.

With the formal part of the evening over Mia and Grace were free to enjoy the attention lavished upon them. Mia was happy to tell everyone about her future concerts, the next one just two weeks away on Christmas Eve.

The weather was deteriorating fast, the snow falling heavier now, soon it would be difficult to travel. Cars were standing in order of importance at the entrance, dignitaries and senior churchmen first with the others vying for position. Cassie was towards the back of the procession, having already collected the cello she realised that Mia would be one of the last to leave.

Grace was waiting at the entrance watching with increasing apprehension. She smiled warmly at those who were leaving then she spotted Mia's car. Moving cautiously through the snow, she desperately needed to sit down. Her shoes pinched her feet mercilessly and were most inappropriate for such weather conditions. The pavement was treacherous and she almost slipped.

"Mrs Hooper," Cassie called out as she pushed open her door.

"Don't get out," Grace said as she reached the back of the car.

Climbing in, she sighed with relief then kicking off her heels, sank back into the warm leather seat.

"Oh my, what an evening, I really do admire Mia," she sighed thinking about all the concerts that Mia had done and those she was yet to perform. "It's very kind of you to offer to take me home."

"Not at all," Cassie said turning to face Grace. "No point in having someone come out on a night like this."

"My husband is relieved I can tell you." Grace smiled. "He was supposed to be accompanying me to the concert but on account of the bad weather we decided to cancel the baby sitter."

"A very wise decision, although it's a pity he missed your performance."

Snow settled on the windscreen and as Cassie glanced forward, the window wipers swept it away.

"Mia won't be long," Grace said, "she has just popped back into the changing room to collect her things."

Alison Morley pushed her way through the crowd gathered at the door and pulling her hood up over her head, slipped her hands into her pockets. It was only a short distance to her room so without a second thought she hunched her shoulders against the weather and set off across the campus. Snow covered the pavement until it disappeared completely and the only way to follow it was to walk beneath the trees that lined the way. A hedgerow, now a lattice of winter twigs separated the pavement from the road and when the cars inched passed their headlights illuminated the wintery landscape ahead. Turning away from the road, Alison cut across the drifts that had built up on the grass and headed towards a collection of distant buildings. There were no street lamps here.

Chapter

ELEVEN

Belenos stood with his face pressed up against a shop window, but he saw nothing of the display. His mind was elsewhere, he was thinking of William Randolph. He could not understand why so little had been published about the man and the terrible events in Scotland earlier that year. There should be at the very least reports on the internet, but there was nothing. Perhaps Mia's father was right and someone was deliberately covering up his actions by blocking the information, but his journalistic instincts reminded him that the public had a right to know. This made him even more determined to discover the truth. He felt sure that Josie MacDonald and her friend Sarah Hamilton were the key. Both women had survived their appalling ordeal and to his knowledge, neither of them had told their story. He had e-mailed both the Scottish newspaper in Elgin and the police investigation team who had handled the case, but they were yet to respond. He would wait a few more days before following up with a telephone call, there was no point in appearing too eager. In the meantime, he decided to speak to Jenna O'Brien, she was a profound gossip who was sure to have something to say on the subject. Jenna had agreed to meet him for lunch at a little restaurant on the embankment, so pulling up his collar he headed off towards the river.

His thoughts turned to Mia and her concert in York the previous evening. He had sent her a text message earlier and was waiting for a reply. He had no idea of her travel arrangements, he assumed that she would be back in London sometime that day.

Twenty minutes later, he found the restaurant and was surprised to find Jenna there already.

"Belenos," calling out loudly she rushed towards him and squealed as she jumped back. "Oh, you are all wet,"

"It's just started to rain outside."

"Never mind that, lose your coat then come over to our table."

Doing as he was told, he followed her. Thankfully, there were not many diners in this part of the restaurant. Jenna had a habit of being loud, she seemed insensitive to others around her.

"So tell me, what's this all about?" Sitting down she arranged her skirt around her knees before going on. "You must be up to something because if you were trying to seduce me, surely you would have invited me to a far more romantic restaurant."

Belenos glanced around hoping that no one had heard.

"Your perception does you credit," he smiled nervously, "you are correct of course. Now why would I try to seduce you when clearly you are promised to someone else?"

Her smile became frosty and she fiddled with the huge diamond on her finger.

"Sorry," he said, "poor joke."

She scowled at him.

"Of course I would love to seduce you," he whispered," but not today." He winked at her and she laughed loudly.

"Right," he said sharply, "down to business. I understand that you know Josie MacDonald."

She regarded him suspiciously and he noticed a shadow pass fleetingly across her face.

"I don't know her exactly," she told him after a pause, "but I do know of her. There is a difference you know."

"Okay," he nodded. "What I'm interested in is what you can tell me about her. These terrible abductions and murders intrigue me."

He told her about the articles he was working on, impressing on her that the business with Josie MacDonald was an unrelated interest and nothing that she could tell him would find its way into print.

"What do you know so far?" she asked, perusing the wine menu.

"I know the name of the woman killed at Spey Bay when Josie was there painting."

"I'll have a large glass of Pinot," Jenna said as the waiter stopped at their table. She also made her choices from the food menu, but made no comment on what Belenos had said.

"Her name was Jennifer Bosworth," he continued, "a business woman who was delivering a talk about health and safety products and staff training services to the oil industry in Aberdeen."

"What was she doing in Spey Bay? The last time I was in Scotland Spey Bay was in Morayshire and that's miles away from Aberdeen."

"Exactly, therein lies the mystery." He paused before going on. "Perhaps Randolph abducted her and took her there or maybe she just decided to take a break, go further north to enjoy the scenery. I understand that part of Morayshire to be an area of outstanding natural beauty." He was certain that Jenna would not care one bit about that, he could hardly imagine her wearing hiking boots and dressed in a Barbour jacket. Outdoor pursuits were definitely not her thing.

"We know that Josie was witness to this woman's death."

Belenos was about to tell her that Josie had been painting a water-colour of the old iron bridge that spanned the River Spey. He knew something of its history and the industry that once thrived in the area, but again she was unlikely to have been impressed.

"Local newspaper reports from the time would have us believe that this woman was Randolph's first victim, but that was not the case. There was also no mention of the suffering she was subjected to before being killed."

"Yes," Jenna held her hands up in front of her to stop him from saying more. "Unfortunately I can imagine well enough what those poor women went through thank you very much."

Their drinks arrived and Jenna took a large gulp before going on. "You do realise that Josie MacDonald is pregnant don't you?"

"So," Belenos stared at her as he put his glass down on the table then licking foam from his lips he replied. "Doesn't she have a long term boyfriend?"

"Don't you see?" Jenna said leaning towards him. "At the time of her abduction she hadn't been with Timothy Granger for long, a few weeks at the most, certainly not long enough to have been planning a happy family."

Belenos stared at her from across the table, his mind processing what she had just said, but he was struggling to follow her meaning.

"Do I have to spell it out for you?" she rolled her eyes. "Josie is an aspiring artist on the verge of national acclaim. Now tell me why she would suddenly want to have a child." She paused, waiting for him to respond, but when he remained silent, she continued. "You are aware of what happened to the women when they were tied up in that squalid little dungeon aren't you."

"Of course," he replied looking a little uncomfortable.

"Randolph was one sick bastard," Jenna whispered then with a shudder she sat back and folded her arms tightly across her chest.

"So, what you are suggesting is that Josie MacDonald is carrying the killer's child." The blood drained from his face as realisation set in making his five o'clock shadow appear darker.

Jenna experienced mixed emotions, she wanted to reach out across the table and comfort him until his gorgeous smile returned, but at the same time was content to watch as he considered the cold reality.

"You really think that the killer made her pregnant?"

"It adds up don't you think?" she replied with a shrug of her shoulders. She lowered her voice before going on. "I would imagine that she was taking an oral contraceptive at the time of her abduction."

Belenos frowned but allowed her to explain.

"With oral contraceptives you only have to miss one and you are vulnerable to becoming pregnant. Even if a woman is ill and vomits whilst on the pill it's advisable to use an alternative method of contraception."

Belenos nodded his understanding. "So why didn't she simply have an abortion if she knew that she was pregnant?"

Jenna stared at him in shock; she could hardly believe that he would make such a comment and taking a deep breath, she reined in her anger.

"Well," she began, choosing her words carefully. "That might seem the perfect solution to you, but for some women the thought of having a termination would never cross their minds."

He frowned again. "But surely in her situation..." he did not get to finish what he was saying.

"Terminating a pregnancy is not something to be taken lightly," she snapped, "not every woman is willing to take the risk. It can be a very dangerous procedure with devastating consequences, besides there are huge emotional and ethical aspects to be considered."

"That may be so, but given the circumstances I would have thought it a no brainer."

She stared at him aghast at his insensitivity. Was he naturally this callous or was it merely the characteristics of his sex?

"We have no idea what was going through that poor woman's mind," she said softly.

"I suppose you are right," he agreed. "You can forget logic."

Jenna could see that still he did not understand and her expression hardened. She thought that maybe this handsome man would be different from the others, but she was wrong. All men were basically the same and it saddened her.

When they had finished eating a waitress arrived to clear their table and Jenna could see the effect Belenos was having on the girl, so reaching out, she took his hand and squeezed it affectionately before glaring at the woman.

Belenos glanced at Jenna and smiled completely unaware of the confrontation playing out in front of him.

"Would you like a pot of tea?" he asked and Jenna smiled sweetly.

Chapter

TWELVE

Mia was relieved to be back in London. She had enjoyed her stay in York especially the Christmas market searching for gifts with Grace. It had been a perfect remedy for what could have been a very stressful few days.

The deteriorating weather disrupted the train services in the north of the country and this had a knock on effect, consequently her train rolled into the station almost an hour late. She did not mind the delay, but for some that lost hour was a catastrophe and the railway network was to blame.

London was as manic as usual, but at least there was no snow. It was cold and wet and darkness seemed to have arrived early casting shadows across the city.

'Back to the real world,' Mia thought as she eased her cello from its seat in first class, then following the others through the carriage she stepped onto the platform. Her driver was somewhere at the main entrance, but in the mass of bodies it was an almost impossible task to locate him.

"Miss Ashton," a man's voice sounded from behind her and as she turned, she was astonished to see her driver. How was he able to find her so easily?

"Did you have a good trip Miss?" he asked casually as he slipped her cello into the car. Her luggage was already there and she wondered how he had managed to collect it so quickly, the train had been standing in the station for less than ten minutes.

"Thank you," Mia smiled as she climbed into the car. "It was a successful trip. York is such a beautiful city but the weather up there is freezing."

"I'm sure it is," he replied.

She studied him as he slipped into the driver's seat. He was so different from Cassie. Always willing to chat, Cassie possessed a natural charm that was pleasing. There were no airs and graces with her, but she was professional at all times. This man however reminded her of a rather stuffy but efficient chauffeur from the set of a period drama.

Alicia had already been on the phone demanding that she report to her office the moment she arrived back in London, but Mia had other ideas. She had no intention of carrying out these demands, so going home first, she dropped her bags off and carried her cello into her music room returning it safely to its stand. The driver waited with the car as Mia freshened up and when she ready they returned to the city.

"Come in, come in," Alicia screeched as Mia appeared at the door.

Alicia was sitting at her desk almost hidden from view by a huge computer screen. Mia thought the office resembled a goldfish bowl, its glass walls overlooking an open plan workspace where as she liked to say her minions worked. Huge windows gave way to an uninspiring part of the city, Mia considered the view grim, but Alicia seemed to like it.

Strong colours were her theme today. Alicia was dressed in bright pink dungarees and a thick woollen jumper, which matched her red turban. Her make-up was perfect and as usual, she looked marvellous. Mia felt rather dowdy by comparison.

"Sit, sit," Alicia gestured wildly with her hand not taking her eyes from the computer screen for a moment. With a grunt of satisfaction, she double clicked the mouse before looking up.

"I've already heard from David," she began, swivelling her executive chair so that she faced Mia. "He telephoned this morning and is overjoyed. He told me that your concert was a roaring success."

"Roaring," Mia said raising her eyebrows. Surely not a word the professor would have used, she thought.

"He is full of praise," Alicia continued. "He can't thank us enough."

"Well that's good then," Mia replied managing to get a few words in.

"Your next concert is all arranged, Christmas eve at St John's Smith Square in Westminster."

"Won't we be in direct competition with the carols at the Abbey?"

"You don't have to worry, there are plenty of people to go around I can assure you of that, besides, most of the seats have been sold already, so you can expect a full house."

She slipped a file across her desk.

"As you can see, it's naturally a festive theme, a mix of popular and traditional carols arranged for the cello and piano."

Mia opened the file and studied the notes. Three pianists were listed, Paul and Jessica Andrews along with Victoria Stevens.

"Why are there three pianists?" Mia asked.

"There will be two pianos on the stage, the Andrews like to play duo and have arranged some of the carols to incorporate two pianos and cello."

"Okay," Mia said, expecting more.

"Victoria Stevens is an aspiring musician who recently won a young musicians award," shaking her head in an effort to recall the information Alicia frowned before going on. "We thought it a nice touch to encourage this young performer, so she will be accompanying you for some of the evening."

"That's fine."

"You'll find all the details in the file. It shouldn't be too taxing," Alicia smiled. "You must know all the carols listed."

"That's true," Mia laughed, "but it's not as easy as that, it all depends on the arrangement. I'll have to rehearse with the pianists, can you arrange that?"

Alicia made a note on her pad.

"Don't leave it too late, I don't want to have to put this together at the last moment."

"You go away and do what you need to do and I'll take care of all the details." Alicia sounded reassuring, but Mia was not convinced.

"Just don't underestimate this. It may be a collection of simple Christmas carols to you, but it's a little more complicated than that."

"I'll have to take your word for it."

Later that evening the body of Alison Morley was discovered buried under the snow not far from the Lyons Concert Hall at the University of York.

Chapter
THIRTEEN

The victim had been removed from the scene of crime during the early hours and she now lay on an examination table in the mortuary at the York Teaching Hospital.

Dr Ralf Hughes, the duty pathologist, shrugged his middle-aged frame into a gown and prepared himself to meet the deceased. On his way into work that morning, he heard the news on the radio. The body of a young woman had been discovered on the university campus. Details were sketchy but he realised this was likely to be his first job of the day.

"Good morning gentlemen," he said as he breezed into the examination room.

Inspector Mallinson and Detective Sergeant Keable were standing in the viewing gallery behind a glass screen. Dr Hughes liked it this way, the glass panel was scant protection from the grizzly scenes that the detectives were likely to witness, but at least they would not fall under his feet at the sight of parting flesh.

Dr Hughes picked up a small digital recorder and began speaking in hushed tones. His assistant had already taken preliminary photographs and had undressed the body, which now lay covered by a sheet. Dr Hughes stepped up to the table and revealed a once pretty young woman whose face, neck and breasts had been mutilated by a sharp object. He continued talking in a language that the detectives were struggling to follow. He would translate later, but for now, all he was interested in was recording his initial findings.

"Let's roll her onto her side," he said to his assistant.

Moving in for a closer look, he bent his knees so that his face was level with the back of the victim's head.

"I would say that we have discovered the cause of death," he directed his words towards the detectives and probing gently at the fractured skull with his fingertips he nodded with grim satisfaction.

"It was not a particularly vicious blow," he told them as he worked. "Not much force seems to have been used, but the result as you can see was sufficient to end this poor girl's life."

The detectives could not see the back of the victim's head, she was facing them so they had a perfect view of her mutilated flesh.

"She wasn't stabbed to death then?" Keable asked, his mouth going dry as he stared at the injuries.

"I would say not, those lacerations look superficial to me, however I will have a little poke around, see if we can't find a life extinguishing wound."

The horrific cuts appeared more than superficial to the detectives but they chose to keep their observations to themselves.

"The victim was wearing her coat with the hood covering her head at the time of the attack, fibres from inside the hood have massed around the site of the head wound." Dr Hughes said before moving towards the table where the coat and the rest of her clothing were laid out.

"There are traces of hair inside the hood, I would of course expect to find that, there is also a small amount of skin impregnated into the fabric." Moving towards a powerful light, he took a closer look. "This is consistent with a sudden blow to the back of the head."

"The victim was not wearing her coat when she was discovered so it must have been removed by the killer." Mallinson told him. "Why just her coat and not other items of her clothing?"

"Mine is not to reason why detective," Hughes replied as he continued to probe. "I can only give you the facts."

"Whoever did this must have hated her, it was a frenzied attack."

"There are deep lacerations to her face," Hughes said talking into his recorder. "Her cardigan and blouse have been shredded and pulled to one side exposing her breasts."

Keable swallowed noisily as he followed the pathologist's dialogue.

"There are deep cuts to soft tissue but as I suspected, no penetrating stab wounds. This looks like an attempt to destroy the looks of this woman."

"What do you mean Dr Hughes?" Mallinson asked.

"Sorry detective, I'm afraid I was thinking aloud, I don't want to put ideas into your head, lead you along the wrong path as it were."

"I wonder if she knew her attacker."

"They usually do," Dr Hughes nodded. "We bar our doors against strangers as darkness falls, but it's those we care about most who pose the biggest threat."

"That's rather a cynical view doctor." Keable said.

"I've seen all kinds of tragedies come through that door detective, you would not believe the stories these poor unfortunate souls have to tell." He glanced up. "Oh yes my friends, the dead have the ability to speak."

Sometime later Dr Hughes began his summing up.

"I can confirm that there is no evidence of sexual assault, this woman was not raped. I can't say if this was a random attack or if she was hunted down by her killer, it will be your job to discover the facts. What I can tell you however is that the killer struck from behind with a decisive blow that would have killed her instantly or if not she would have died very soon after. There are no defensive wounds to her hands or arms so it is unlikely that she got a look at her killer. The rest is as you see, is the work of a short bladed knife wielded in a frenzied attack. The person you are looking for is right handed, of medium height but slightly built. Some of the marks on the body suggest that a light touch was used, there is not much bruising you see, which leads me to think that the killer was not particularly strong."

"Could this have been carried out by a woman?" Mallinson asked.

"I think it unlikely detective. Why would a woman inflict such injuries to one of her own sex?"

Mallinson nodded, but he knew of cases like this especially where jealousy was involved.

"I'll see what I can do with her face; a reconstruction job is required before a formal identification can take place."

"We received a missing persons report earlier this morning," Keable began as he dug out his notebook, "a young woman by the name of Alison Morley. She was one of the musicians performing at the university last night and did not return home after the performance. Her flat mate thought that she might have stayed over at a friend's house because of the bad weather."

Dr Hughes returned to the body and inspected the left hand more closely.

"There are calluses here that would indicate this young woman was indeed a musician, a violinist or other stringed instrument perhaps."

Keable nodded as he scanned his notes. "There are no details of what she was wearing and there were no personal items found at the scene but the description matches, hair colour, height etc."

"Then I think we may have found Alison Morley."

Chapter

FOURTEEN

Sitting comfortably on her stool, Mia took a deep breath and sat up straight before letting it out slowly and at the same time, she emptied her mind. Thoughts of Ben had distracted her ever since she had returned to London. He had messaged her twice during her trip to York, once the moment she arrived then again soon after her concert. She realised now that she should have made more of an effort, telephoned him perhaps, but in her defence she had been rather busy working to a very tight schedule. She did not want him to think that she was not interested, so making up her mind, she decided to telephone him as soon as her practice session was over.

Reaching for her cello, she wriggled and settled it between her knees before drawing the freshly rosined bow lightly over the strings then, after a few adjustments she went through her warm up routine. At first, her fingers were stiff and refused to work, but as they moved over the fingerboard, they seemed to take on a life of their own and it was not long before the session began. She loved playing her cello, it never failed to bring a smile to her face.

The rhythm of the simple carols lightened her mood. There was just a week to go before Christmas and at last, she was beginning to appreciate the building excitement. This was never a happy time for her or her father, but this year she was determined to make the best of the festive season, beginning with the carol concert on Christmas Eve.

Losing herself in her music, her body swayed rhythmically and her heart rate quickened to the beat. It was at times like this that she felt truly alive, music was her life and without it, she would have nothing.

Almost two hours passed as she went through all the carols for the Christmas concert including a few of her favourite pieces. She was feeling more confident now although there was bound to be changes. Alterations to timing and other technical aspects were inevitable especially when performing with others. These would be discussed when they met up to rehearse together.

Leaning backwards, she pushed her arms up above her head and groaned as she stretched out the muscles in her back. From somewhere in the house she could hear the sound of a telephone ringing.

"Mia, are you okay?"

"Hello Daddy, of course," she could hear the tension in his voice but carried on. "I got back earlier this afternoon. The train was delayed because of bad weather, but the concert was great. It went off very well."

"Haven't you heard the news?"

"News, what news?" Her father sounded stressed and she was becoming concerned.

"Alison Morley has been found dead."

"What do you mean, how can she be dead?"

"The poor girl has been murdered," he told her, the tone of his voice softening as if to lessen the blow.

Mia gasped and staggered backwards until her legs touched the edge of the sofa then she sat down heavily.

"Murdered, when?"

"It must have been last night after the concert. She was attacked as she left the theatre and was found early this morning."

"No, it can't be true."

"Listen Mia, the police in York will contact you. They will have questions."

"Questions?" she murmured, her thoughts tumbling through her head in a mass of confusion.

"Look, there's no need to worry, it's simply routine stuff. They have to build up a picture, piece together her movements."

"I see," Mia whispered, her grip tightening on the receiver.

"Did she say anything to you about meeting up with anyone after the concert, friends, or a boyfriend perhaps?"

"I hardly knew her, we had only just met. Grace," she paused, "Grace Hooper, the pianist, she would probably be able to tell you more."

"It's not me she needs to tell, the detectives working on the case will be interviewing everyone who was there last night."

He was sounding efficient now, the policeman taking the place of her father. She realised this was his way of coping, it was a voice that she knew so well.

"Just be careful," he told her, "be vigilant."

She wanted to tell him about the telephone call she had received a few days ago, but she didn't want to worry him. If he knew, he would be impossible to live with. No, she could not tell her father, not just yet.

"Let me know when the police have spoken with you. Keep a note of what you say."

Mia agreed to do as he asked but said no more. The shock of the news had upset her and now her nerves were on edge. She wondered how Grace had taken it, but decided it would be unwise to contact her, not until after she had spoken to the police. It was no use continuing with her rehearsal, it would be some time before she would be able to focus clearly on anything and thoughts of speaking to Ben were lost in the confusion of her mind.

Ben was working in the little office at the back of his sister's shop, White Lace and Promises. He had agreed to go through some of the files and was studying a pile of stock sheets. Whilst staring intently at the pages, his fingers darted over the keys of his laptop transposing figures into a line graph. The graph was designed to show the turnover of stock, highlighting items that were profitable against those that were not so popular. His sister seemed to have a good grasp of her customer's requirements but areas for improvement were beginning to emerge. It was still of course early days, her shop had only been open for a few months, and a little more market research would be necessary before accurate figures could be projected. The bell over the door chimed but he paid no notice, Emilia was in the shop and it soon became obvious that whoever had arrived was more than just a customer.

"It's Jenna O'Brien," she whispered, popping her head around the door. "She has some very interesting news."

He looked up from what he was doing and shrugged his shoulders. He was immersed in his work and had no time for idle gossip. Emilia, reading his expression pouted.

"I really think you should hear what she has to say."

With a sigh, he got to his feet and closed down the screen before following her out into the shop.

Jenna was standing with her back to them scrutinising a display of brightly coloured silk ribbon. They did not see the look of joy that spread across her face as she ran her fingertips gently over the soft material.

"Jenna," Ben said, moving towards her. "How nice it is to see you again." He had only met her once and hoped that his enthusiasm was not too overwhelming.

"Ben," she smiled as if greeting an old friend. Taking his outstretched hand, she squeezed it softly before brushing her lips against his cheek.

He did not need to worry, Jenna was an exceptionally friendly woman, and as she leaned into him, the waft of her expensive perfume beguiled him as readily as her charm. He was unable to avoid the look his sister gave him.

"Em tells me that you have some news to share." He almost stuttered.

"Yes I'm afraid I have." Her smile faded as she let him have his hand back.

"Have you been listening to the news on the radio this morning or seen it on the internet?"

"No, we have been too busy." Ben told her glancing towards Emilia who simply nodded her head in agreement.

"Well, it concerns Mia Ashton and her concert in York."

"We heard that it was a great success." Emilia smiled enthusiastically.

"That may be true, but one of the musicians who appeared with her has been brutally murdered." Speaking in muted tones, she was eager to impart this information but realised that restraint was the best approach. "The dead woman," she went on, "is thought to be Alison Morley, a student at the university who was playing the violin at Mia's concert."

"Murdered?" Ben whispered hardly able to believe what she was saying. He stared at her, searching her face for confirmation.

"That's what the news people are saying. Of course details are sketchy at the moment, there has been no information about how the poor girl died." Jenna shuddered and looked visibly upset. Gone was her initial excitement, but as they were acquainted with Mia she regarded it her duty to relay this news to all their friends.

"Do you think Mia knows?" Ben turned towards Emilia.

"She must do by now, it's been all over the news channels."

"I thought that maybe you had already seen her." Jenna looked at him hopefully, having recovered some of her composure.

"No," Ben shook his head. "I've not spoken to her since before her concert."

"Oh," Jenna groaned as hopes of expanding her knowledge of the situation evaporated. She had obviously underestimated Ben and his relationship with Mia. Clearly, they were not as close as she had imagined.

Chapter
FIFTEEN

The moment he heard the news Belenos was on the phone to Mia.

"I've spoken to the police in York," she told him. "They are sending someone round from Scotland Yard once they have prepared my statement."

"They recorded your telephone conversation?"

"Yes," Mia replied, "I suppose so." She could hear the concern in his voice. "I guess that once it's been printed off they will require a signature."

"Be sure to read it through carefully before committing yourself to it."

"You are beginning to sound just like my father," she said in an effort to lighten his mood.

Belenos wanted to say so much more. He felt compelled to tell her to look out for herself, that she could never be too careful, but he guessed that from her comment her father had already been there. They talked for a while longer about her trip to York then she told him about her Christmas concert.

"It's going to be held at St John's, Smith Square." She knew nothing about the place other than it was in Westminster.

"Wow," Belenos enthused. "That is a fantastic venue. It's a beautiful baroque building renowned for its splendid architecture and atmosphere."

"Well that's good then," was all she could think of saying.

"It's easy to get to," he continued," just a short walk from St James's Park tube station."

He went on to describe the interior, conjuring up images of huge white columns supporting ornate vaulted ceilings.

"There is plenty of room for seating but as it was not designed as a theatre the seats are not stepped, those sitting at the back will have to stretch their necks in order to get a look at you."

"Oh," she replied. "Well hopefully the audience will be there to listen to the carols rather than for the view. There won't be much to see just me and two pianos."

"Two?" he exclaimed, wondering if he had heard her correctly.

"Actually there will be three pianists. A couple who like to perform together and a young musician called Victoria Stevens. Alicia thought it a good opportunity for her to accompany me with some of the carols."

Belenos could tell that she was not entirely happy with the arrangements.

"Is that a problem?" he asked.

"No, not really," she sighed, searching for a good enough reason to convince herself. "It's just that Alicia insists on leaving rehearsals to the last minute. I need to get together with these people to sort out the musical arrangements well in advance of the concert."

He wanted to tell her that Christmas carols had been around for years. They were simple pieces of music that probably required very little arranging, but he chose to keep his views to himself. This was an argument that he could not see himself winning.

"Listen," he began. "If you need a helping hand you know that you can always rely on me. I might not be of much use but I have very broad shoulders and I'm good at listening."

"Oh, thank you," she sobbed, swallowing down her emotions then she reminded him. "I seem to remember your promise of supper once I returned from York."

"Yes," he laughed and they organised a date in their busy schedules.

As soon as their conversation was over, Mia reached for her ipad. What Belenos had told her about St John's, Smith Square interested her and she wondered why she had not thought about looking it up on the internet before? It did not take long for her to find what she was looking for and as she studied the photographs, she could see why he had been so enthusiastic. It was described as a beautiful building, surrounded by modern structures, an architect's dream sharply juxtaposed with the bricks and glass of another man's vision.

She began to read the text that accompanied the photographs and soon discovered that it had once been a church. Ruined by firebombs during the blitz, it was restored soon after the war and turned into a concert hall.

Her eyes were drawn to a little map in the corner of the screen, so enlarging it she studied the area. Information appeared beside the street map and following Dean Bradley Street, she found a little garden overshadowed by large buildings.

This garden was acquired by the church of St John the Evangelist, Smith Square, for the use as a cemetery and was consecrated by Dr Wilcox, Dean of Westminster on 29th July 1731.

Looking closer at the map Mia could see that the garden had been designed around a central fountain. There was good disabled access with wide paths flanked by London Plane trees, tall shrubs, and pretty flower borders.

She felt that there was something significant about the place, but was convinced that she had never been there before or to the Millbank Medical Centre that overlooked the garden. Perhaps it was just another of those inexplicable Déjà vu moments.

Sometime later, the doorbell rang. Startled, her heart was beating furiously and there was a sharp pain in her head. Her ipad lay at her feet and she frowned, what was it doing there? The doorbell chimed again so climbing unsteadily to her feet, she bent down to recover it before going to answer the door. Glancing at the clock, she was shocked at the time.

"Ben," she exclaimed, surprised to see him standing there.

"Mia, sorry to drop in on you unannounced, I should have telephoned first."

"Don't be silly," she croaked as if still half asleep. "I'm pleased to see you."

"I've heard the news."

"Oh," her smile faded. "You had better come in." Stepping to one side, she opened the door wider.

Ben had not been to her flat before and he felt like an intruder as she closed the door behind him. It was spacious and tastefully decorated and the air was as sweet as her perfume.

"I'm sorry that I have not telephoned," he began, "but Em, my sister, has been keeping me busy." He sounded so stiff and formal, not what he intended at all.

"Don't be silly," she said again, running her fingers through her hair as if to claw away the pounding inside her skull. "We are both very busy people."

They sat down together on the sofa and turning towards him, she smiled. It was a sad almost forced smile, but Ben appreciated what she must be going through.

"I heard what happened in York and I just had to see you." Reaching out he touched her arm lightly.

Mia began to tell him about her time away focussing on the good times and how much she had enjoyed herself, especially shopping with Grace. Nothing could take away those happy memories despite the tragic circumstances surrounding the death of Alison Morley.

Chapter
SIXTEEN

The next few days were even busier than before, a never-ending round of music and rehearsals occasionally interspersed with social events usually provided by Ben or Belenos. The added pressure of preparing for Christmas was beginning to take its toll. Mia was waking up suddenly during the night confused, often wondering where she was or haunted by some nightmare or other. Most mornings it felt as if she had not slept at all. At the weekend, it would be Christmas, the rehearsals, the concert and the anticipation of the season would be over then she could relax.

Mia met Jessica and Paul Anderson and quickly ironed out any technical issues that had been bothering her. They spent time rehearsing together at the couple's home in St John's Wood. Victoria Stevens was unable to attend on that occasion so arrangements had been made for Mia to meet her the following day.

Victoria lived with her parents on the outskirts of London in a huge Georgian house. An avenue of shrubs and small trees led her along a short driveway towards an impressive carriage sweep and stepping from the taxi, Mia stared up at the house. It was magnificent and she couldn't help thinking that Victoria Stevens must have enjoyed a privileged childhood.

"Good afternoon Mia." A well-presented middle-aged woman met her at the door. "It's so kind of you to come all this way."

"Mrs Stevens?" Mia asked. Although they had never met before, Mia was certain that this was Victoria's mother.

"Indeed," she nodded, her thin lips curving into a smile. "Come in, we are so pleased to meet you."

Mia stepped into an impressive hallway that was so spacious it could quite easily have accommodated her entire flat. Her shoes echoed noisily against the floor tiles as she followed the woman towards a splendid staircase and feeling self-conscious, Mia walked on tiptoes.

"Victoria is in the music room."

Mia made no comment she expected nothing less.

Mrs Stevens pushed open the door and Mia stifled a gasp as she entered the room. A Baby Grand took centre stage in the perfectly proportioned room and along one wall stood a number of electronic keyboards. Beside a huge floor to ceiling window was a display cabinet filled with recorders and tin whistles that reinforced Victoria's musical talent.

"I used to play the recorder." A well spoken voice informed her from somewhere behind the piano.

Mia spun round; she had failed to notice Victoria when entering the room, her attention drawn to the assortment of instruments and of course, the impressive space that was in total contrast to her own humble music room.

"Victoria?" Mia asked as she placed her cello case carefully on the floor. She knew that Victoria Stevens was seventeen years old but was not prepared for what she saw as she moved around the piano. A stunningly beautiful young woman stared back at her. Her large blue eyes, blonde hair, and fair complexion were in total contrast to her own. Victoria was sitting upright at her piano, her elegantly long fingers resting on the keys, but instead of perching on a stool, she was sitting in a wheelchair. The look of shock on Mia's face must have been obvious because Victoria began to laugh.

"Sorry," she spluttered ungainly. "Obviously no-one told you."

"I apologise," Mia replied, conscious of her reaction. "It's so rude of me, but you are right, I had no idea."

"Don't worry about it, I'm used to the way people look at me especially when we first meet. I'm paraplegic," she explained. "The result of an operation that went wrong." She couldn't help laughing again.

"I'm sorry to hear that." Mia replied, not quite knowing how to respond.

"Don't be sorry, no-one is to blame." With complete self-confidence, Victoria went on to tell Mia about herself.

When she was finished, Mia lifted her cello from its case and cradled it in her arms, it became a shield to protect her against the reality of the situation.

"I hope you don't mind me telling you all this," the girl said cocking her head to one side and squinting thoughtfully at Mia.

"I applaud your ability to speak so openly about your disability. I can't imagine that I would have the courage to do the same."

"I feel it clears the air, prevents people from asking awkward questions. It also avoids embarrassing silences and misunderstandings don't you think? Most people have no idea how to react when they come across a person in a wheelchair. We are no different from anyone else."

"Quite," Mia said, impressed by her plain speaking.

"Right, now we have got that out of the way, shall we make a start?"

"Yes Victoria I think we should."

"Please call me Vicky."

The moment they began to play Mia realised that she was dealing with a very talented musician. Victoria Stevens may be young and incredibly bright, but she also played the piano with an unbridled confidence. Her determination was evident in every way and it was not long before Mia realised that she liked working with her. It was a pity that Victoria did not have a greater part to play in the concert, it had been difficult working with the Andersons.

"Wow," Vicky exclaimed, flushed with excitement. "You make those dusty old carols sound amazing. I just adore your cello."

"Thanks to you and your playing, those dusty old carols, as you put it just seem to come alive."

"I'm sure the audience will be knocked out by them. Christmas is going to be such amazing fun this year."

Mia could remember having the same thoughts, but that was a long time ago.

"Well, I think that we are done." Vicky wheeled herself away from the piano and turned to face Mia.

"We are going to meet up on Christmas Eve morning and introduce ourselves to the stage crew. We'll have time to set up and do sound checks." Mia told her as she packed away her cello.

"Yes," Vicky nodded. "I have that in my diary. I guess we'll have an opportunity to rehearse again once we have set up."

"Of course," Mia smiled. "The Andersons will be there too so you'll be able to meet them before we go through the whole performance."

"Great," Vicky's eyes gleamed with pleasure. "Some of my friends will be there for the evening; we are planning to go for a celebratory drink afterwards. You are most welcome to join us, I'm sure they will be thrilled to meet you."

Mia smiled at the prospect of going to a pub with a bunch of teenagers but it was unlikely to become a reality. She was beginning to feel her age in the company of just one.

"That's very kind of you, but I have my own arrangements."

"Okay," Vicky replied brightly.

Chapter
SEVENTEEN

It was early on Christmas Eve and Belenos was in his study working at his desk. The first draft of his investigation into the psychological profiles of serial killers was open in front of him and he was scrutinising every word. This article was designed to explore the childhood of selected killers and search for similarities in their early lives. He knew that most of them had experienced traumatic episodes during their formative years, but he was looking for a pattern. He also knew that defence lawyers would deliberate on this area of a killer's childhood, using it as an argument for leniency when it came to sentencing. Belenos was hoping that this article would encourage his readers to consider the workings of the justice system and to think objectively about what had driven these people to carry out their heinous crimes. The question that he wanted them to ask themselves was should they be nurtured in secure psychological units where they could receive help and rehabilitation or should they simply be written off as cold-blooded murderers.

He was happy with this first instalment, he would type it up and e-mail it to the magazine editor for approval right away, it might even be in time for inclusion in the New Year edition. He felt certain that the editor would agree with the slant he had taken and further episodes could expand on the issues that had been raised.

He looked up and stared out of the window. The street beyond was quiet, nothing stirred in the twilight of morning. Peace had settled upon the neighbourhood, it was as if Christmas had already begun. Sitting back in his chair, he allowed his mind to wander. He thought about what

Jenna O'Brien had told him when they had met up for lunch a few days ago. She seemed to know a lot more about Josie MacDonald than he expected and had obviously been digging deeper into the subject, in fact she had come up with another revelation. She had telephoned him the previous evening to tease him about it, but had made it quite clear that if he wanted to know more it would cost him. Her demand this time was a 'romantic dinner', she would settle for nothing less than candlelight and champagne. He just hoped that what she had to tell him was worth it. He had to admit that although she was a little loud she was extremely easy on the eye; heads would turn when she entered a room and often it was not only the men who stared. It pleased him to think that she sought his company, but it would probably not last for long. Women like Jenna were fickle creatures who lived for the moment. Being betrothed to another seemed to mean very little to Jenna, her impending marriage was seldom mentioned. The journalist in him wondered why this was, what kind of a marriage was she getting herself into, no one seemed to know not even her closest friends. He would have to tread very carefully if he were to investigate, upsetting a woman like Jenna O'Brien would be a very bad idea, she could do irreparable harm to his reputation.

By mid morning, Mia was in her music room collecting up her papers and sliding them into a briefcase. She was feeling relaxed and rested having slept unusually well the night before and was looking forward to this evening's concert. In the living room presents had been carefully arranged under the tree, there were gifts for her father and Belenos and this year Ben and his sister Emilia had been included.

She was expecting her father for Christmas dinner, but he was working the morning shift so would not appear until around three in the afternoon. This suited her, she could enjoy a leisurely start to the day before preparing a Christmas feast. Suddenly the telephone began to ring so leaving her thoughts with her cello she went into the living room.

"Hello," she said holding the receiver to her ear, but there was nothing, only silence. "Hello," she said again louder this time.

The sound of laughter greeted her, it was faint at first becoming louder until finally he spoke.

"Mia, hello, is that Mia?"

"Who is this?" she said not recognising the voice. Suddenly she shuddered, it was as if an icy blast had swept through the house.

"Did you enjoy the snow?"

Mia frowned and pressed the receiver tighter to her ear.

"The timing of the snow in York was perfect don't you think?" he said laughing as he spoke.

She tried to place his voice but it was no good, it sounded like no one she knew. It was almost childlike and she shuddered again.

"Alison Morley, now wasn't she fun?"

"What," Mia exclaimed loudly. "Who is this?"

"You didn't like Alison did you. Aren't you pleased that she's gone?"

"What are you talking about?" She wanted to slam the receiver down, end the call but she needed to know who was saying such hurtful things. "Who is this?"

"You know who I am."

"I think that you are mistaken, I have no idea who you are or what you are talking about. What do you want?"

"What do I want? I want for nothing, it's all about you Mia, it's what you want."

"Stop playing games with me and tell me who you are."

"My name, you want to know my name? Well I will tell you, my name is..."

The line went dead leaving her shaken. Her heart rate had soared and now a sharp pain had formed in her head as colours flashed in front of her eyes. She needed to sit down, so dropping the receiver she staggered backwards until she found the sofa. Burying her face in her hands, she took a deep breath and held onto it for a count of ten before letting it out slowly. Feeling slightly better, she began to analyse the call. It sounded like the person who had called previously, the call she had pushed to the back of her mind, an unpleasant memory best forgotten, but now it had returned. How had he got hold of her number, she thought. This would have to be reported to her father, but there was something holding her back. A thought stirred deep in her memory but before she could grasp its meaning, it was gone.

Suddenly the telephone rang again and leaping to her feet her hand trembled as if reluctant to pick it up.

"Hello," she spat angrily.

"Good morning to you too," Alicia said, "get out of bed the wrong side this morning did you?"

Her sarcasm did nothing to ease Mia's distress, Alicia Wicks was the last person she wanted to speak to right now.

"I just hope your mood improves before this evening."

"Of course," Mia replied doing her best to sound normal, "you don't have to worry about a thing."

"Good, I'm glad to hear that." Alicia wondered why Mia sounded so fraught, but she did not bother to ask, instead she got straight down to business. "The car will be with you in about half an hour. You will be ready won't you?"

"Of course," Mia said again. "I was just collecting up my things."

"Good. The driver will drop you off at Smith Square then when you are ready you are to telephone him, he will collect you and run you to the beauty salon for your hair and make-up appointment."

Mia already knew the arrangements, the whole operation had been organised weeks ago, but as usual, Alicia had to have the last word.

"There will be a short reception after the concert," Alicia reminded her. "You will be there won't you?"

"Of course I will," Mia replied. "I have invited a number of friends to the concert and to the reception afterwards."

"Good, I won't be there myself but it's important that you are seen by the media. Get that friend of yours, Belenos Falzone to write up a favourable review." She almost sneered as she said his name.

Mia rolled her eyes and studied the fingers of her left hand. They had stopped shaking now and she was feeling a little calmer although the sound of Alicia's voice was not helping much. She spoke constantly for another fifteen minutes and when finally she was finished there was barely ten minutes left before the car was due to arrive. She would have to get a move on, the driver would be punctual, of that she could be certain.

The Andersons were already there when her car pulled up outside the concert hall. Mia hardly had time to admire the magnificent building or enjoy the splendour of its interior before she was intercepted.

"We've already instructed the technicians." Jessica said her tone full of arrogant importance.

Mia simply nodded a greeting then sweeping past, made her way towards the stage where two magnificent pianos stood gleaming under the brilliant lights. A man, working on one of the instruments, glanced up at Paul Anderson who was sitting at the keys waiting to play random notes as instructed.

"That one is out of tune," Jessica snapped. "Paul won't play until it's perfect."

"I hope the change in temperature when everyone arrives later doesn't play havoc with it," Mia replied tartly, hoping to annoy her further. "Changes in temperature are a nightmare with my cello strings."

77

"I'm sure everything will be fine," Jessica retorted before turning away. "I've no idea when that young girl is planning to join us."

Clearly, Jessica was stressed and it surprised Mia to think that an informal concert like this could be the source of her discomfort. It was not as if any important dignitaries would be present.

"Miss Ashton," Jim Peters, one of the sound engineers came over to where they were standing. "I will be looking after you today. As soon as you are ready, I'll set up your mike, all you have to do is play a few tunes and I'll do the rest. I'll do everything I can to make you sound even better than perfect." He winked cheekily at her before turning away.

Mia had worked with Jim before, he could be relied on to do a good job.

Victoria Stevens arrived with her parents and entering through the main doors, made her way along the central aisle to where Mia was standing before realising that there was no disabled access to the stage.

"There is access from the side door." One of the technicians explained helpfully, but jumping down from the stage, he called. "Dave, Chris, give me a hand will you."

Gathering round Victoria's chair, they prepared to lift her up onto the stage and she giggled with girlish delight. Her mother made a fuss, fretting about health and safety, but no one took any notice. Mia glanced at Jessica who rolled her eyes, from the expression on her face, it was clear that she was not amused.

"Right," Victoria said as she wheeled herself across the stage. "Which one is mine?"

This made Jessica even worse, the thought of someone else touching the piano assigned to her was almost too much for her to bear.

The next couple of hours passed without major incident and by the end of the session, everyone seemed pleased. Jessica Anderson had calmed down and the second piano had performed faultlessly. Mia led them through every carol with the confidence and ease of a professional musician and when they were finished, she telephoned her driver. Whilst she waited for him to arrive, she chatted pleasantly with Victoria and her parents.

Chapter
EIGHTEEN

Ben arrived at his sister's flat at around seven o'clock. She lived in a collection of rooms at the top of an old house that had once been a desirable residence for a wealthy family. These days however the building was looking rather shabby and it was his opinion that it should have been destroyed in the firebombing during the blitz of the 1940s. Emilia seemed to like it, she muttered something about having a sense of history, but he could not see the attraction. It was true that her neighbours were likeable, the collection of flats housed inside the building were set up like a little community were everyone knew each other. Emilia had used her design skills to turn her dingy servant's quarters into a cosy little nook and she could see herself living nowhere else.

"Ben," she smiled with genuine delight as he appeared out of breath at the top of the stairs, then pulling him through the open door she said. "You really must exercise more often."

"I swear those stairs get steeper each time I climb them," he puffed pressing his hand against his side.

"It's merely you putting on weight and getting older." She planted a kiss on his cheek then squeezed past him. "Is it freezing outside, do I need to wear my scarf and gloves?"

"I would," he nodded. "It's not too bad at the moment but I guess it will turn cold later."

Stepping into the living room, he ducked his head under the doorframe and studied her Christmas tree. He did not care for festive decorations, he thought her tree only cluttered what was already a tiny space, but he had to admit, it looked amazing. Emilia could see the look on his face and she knew exactly what he was thinking so winding a scarf around her neck, she said.

"Come on Mr Scrooge, if you have recovered sufficiently from your climb then I suppose we had better be off."

The tube was crammed with revellers determined to celebrate the season, but it didn't take them long to reach their destination. Leaving St James's Park station it was just a short walk to St John's, Smith Square.

The concert hall was filling up quickly with people of all ages. There were a number of families with children and Ben noticed a group of nurses from the nearby medical centre.

"Can you pick up a programme whilst I nip to the loo?" Emilia said as she disappeared into the crowd.

When she returned she was carrying two cardboard cups filled with mulled wine and as she settled beside him festive spices rose up around them and mingled with the scent of her perfume.

"I thought you might like one of these," she said handing over a steaming cup then glancing up at the stage, she frowned. Mia's cello was on its stand between two pianos, Ben noticed the look on her face, and passing her the programme, it all became clear.

"That's unusual," she whispered. "A piano duo."

"Yes," her brother nodded. "It's a husband and wife team, but there's also another pianist, someone called Victoria Stevens."

Emilia studied the photograph of a beautiful young pianist then reading the paragraph that accompanied it, shook her head. She had never heard of Victoria Stevens before or the Andersons for that matter.

"Apparently she is the BBC Young Musician of the Year." Ben said before pointing out that she was only seventeen.

Emilia looked at the photograph again before sipping at her mulled wine.

It was not long before the concert got under way and Mia appeared wearing a long black gown adorned with festive accessories, she looked magnificent. Using a microphone, her voice filled the room as she began to explain the proceedings.

"First I have the pleasure of introducing our young pianist Victoria Stevens. Victoria is an exceptional musician who has won many classical music awards and we are lucky to have her here to perform with us this evening. We will open the concert with three favourite carols. Feel free to sing along if you wish."

Applause rippled around the audience as Victoria made her way out onto the stage. Ben was surprised; there was no mention in the programme about her being disabled.

She positioned herself at the piano before glancing over her shoulder at Mia, then, with a nod of her head, she found the right key and played it twice. Mia, settling her cello between her knees played the same key, their instruments were perfectly in tune.

The concert got underway and music filled the hall. It was rich and jolly and it soon became clear that both musicians were enjoying the moment immensely. Mia and Victoria seemed perfect together, they harmonised beautifully, the piano and cello in perfect accompaniment. Some of the people in the audience sang the words, but the majority remained silent and simply enjoyed the music.

It was not long before Victoria had played her part and the audience showed their appreciation, her friends cheering loudly as she left the stage. There was a brief interlude before the Andersons appeared, then the concert resumed.

When it was all over, Emilia and Ben joined the small gathering in the room at the back of the stage. Mia was talking to Belenos Falzone, a photographer was at work taking her picture, and Ben looked on from across the room. He was eager to get up close to Mia. He wanted to talk to her, congratulate her on another wonderful performance.

Mia brushed her red lips against his cheek as Belenos prepared to leave. It was clear that he had finished his interview, the photographer had already moved away. Having got his pictures of Mia and the Andersons, he was now homing in on Victoria Stevens and her group of excited friends.

Mia looked across the room, her expression neutral, but the moment she saw Ben her face lit up with a smile that set his heart racing.

"Ben," she called out as she moved quickly towards him. "I didn't see you in the audience." Wrapping her arms around his neck she held onto him long enough to enforce their developing relationship.

"We were there." Emilia assured her, "buried in the crowd."

"Em, how lovely it is to see you again."

They embraced before Mia stood back then both women began talking about their festive arrangements and it was not long before they had come up with a plan.

"We should meet up on Boxing Day, walk off some of the excesses of our yuletide banquet."

"Good idea," Emilia nodded and glancing at her brother she continued, "I'm guessing that we'll consume a week's worth of calories tomorrow."

A time was agreed and Ben was content to go along with their arrangements.

Mia turned her head towards Victoria Stevens who was now finished with the photographer. Her group of friends had thinned out, they were going to meet up again at a nearby pub, but Mia wanted to have a word with Victoria before she left.

"Mia," the sound of Ben's voice cut through her thoughts. "Emilia and I are off now, so we'll see you on Boxing Day. Have a great day tomorrow."

She nodded and hugged him again. "Merry Christmas," she whispered into his ear.

The room was less crowded now as people began to leave and Mia searched for Victoria, but she had left it too late, Victoria had already gone.

"Mum it's okay, there's no need to fuss," Victoria said as she met up with her parents beside their car, "the pub is not far. You two have a lovely meal and I'll see you back here in a couple of hours."

Her father helped her into her motorised wheelchair before stowing her manual chair in the back of the car.

"Take care love," he dropped a kiss on top of her head then she sped away.

Eager to catch up with her friends she raced along Dean Bradley Street before arriving at the junction with Horseferry Road. Here the traffic was heavy so transferring to the footpath she went to the pelican crossing and waited impatiently for the green light to flash. Once across the road it was just a short distance to St John's Gardens, where her friends had agreed to meet her. The pub was just around the corner but by cutting through the gardens, it would save a couple of minutes.

Turning into the shadows, she went along the footpath towards the fountain. Lights from the windows of the medical centre spilled out over the grass, this was where her friends should be waiting, but the place was deserted. Slowing her pace, the whine from the motor quietened and it was then that she heard footsteps. Turning her head, she swerved slightly to the right for a better view then she sighed with relief.

"Oh, it's you," she said.

Chapter

NINETEEN

Six o'clock on Christmas morning and DI Terry Ashton arrived at work. It was surprisingly quiet but he could feel the anticipation of the action to come. The atmosphere inside the station seemed charged and foreboding not quite what he had anticipated for Christmas Day morning.

"Morning boss," DC Dennis James greeted him. "Have you heard the news?"

"Don't tell me," Terry grinned. "A fat man wearing a red suit has been apprehended, accused of breaking and entering."

"No boss," Dennis said shaking his head. "It's worse than that."

Terry looked at him and could tell from his tone that something serious had occurred.

"You had better tell me then."

"The body of a young woman was found earlier this morning in St John's Gardens," he paused to look at his notes. "Victoria Stevens."

Terry shook his head, he did not recognise the name.

"She was a musician by all accounts. She performed last night at the concert hall in Smith Square."

"St John's, Smith Square?" Terry looked at him, his eyes flashing with alarm. "My daughter was performing there last night."

The blood drained from his face as he made his way around the desk. Standing beside Dennis, he logged onto the computer and typed in the name of the venue. Once the information appeared on the screen, he scrolled down until he came to the details of the Christmas Eve concert.

"Wow," Dennis said. "Is that really your daughter?"

Terry glanced at him unsure if his interest lay purely in her good looks or the fact that she was a professional musician.

"Here," he said scrolling down further.

There was a short piece about Victoria with a photograph.

"I'll get that printed off," Dennis said becoming businesslike.

Terry reached into his pocket and pulled out his mobile phone, he went through his list of contacts until he found what he was looking for then he stabbed the call button with his thumb. The dialling tone almost went to voicemail before she picked up.

"Hello," she croaked her voice thick with sleep.

"Mia, are you okay?"

"Daddy," she recognised his voice instantly then turning her head towards her bedside table she frowned as she peered at the alarm clock. "Yes of course I'm okay, why what's this all about?"

Reaching for the lamp, she switched it on and blinked before pulling the duvet up around her shoulders. The central heating had not yet come on and the air in her bedroom was chilled.

Terry breathed a sigh of relief then hesitated. He regretted giving her the news over the phone, but he owed her an explanation.

"There's no easy way to tell you this," he began speaking quietly. "Victoria Stevens has been found dead."

"What?" Mia replied thinking that he had made a mistake. It was Alison Morley who was dead.

"She was discovered earlier this morning in St John's Gardens. I'm not sure of the details yet but it's being treated as a suspicious death."

"Oh my God! Are you saying that she has been murdered? Surely, it must be a case of mistaken identity."

Terry studied the report that Dennis had given him.

"There is no mistake I'm afraid. We have a description, besides her wheelchair was found at the scene. SOCO are still there."

"I can't believe it," Mia sobbed. "I was only talking to her and her parents last night. She was so young and full of life, she had a promising musical career ahead of her."

"Listen, I'm sorry to be the bearer of such bad news, but are you sure you are alright? All your windows and doors are secure?"

"Honestly Dad I'm fine. It's just such a shock, I can't believe it." She paused before going on. "Will I still see you later?"

"Yes of course," he nodded hoping that would be the case. If he was going to have to lead the investigation then it might prove difficult for him to get away.

Mia pulled the duvet cover tighter around her shoulders and shivered miserably. Chewing at her bottom lip, she was horrified by the terrible news and slowly thoughts began to swirl around inside her head. Her nightdress was still on the end of her bed and under the duvet, she was naked. Slipping her legs over the side of the bed she drew in a sharp intake of breath as a stabbing pain shot through her hip. Standing up slowly she turned towards the lamp and leaning forward inspected her right hip. An ugly bruise had spread across her skin and where her hipbone stuck out there was a small abrasion that had scabbed over. She frowned and reaching for her gown, shrugged it on before going into the living room. Turning on the lights, she discovered her underwear on the floor beside the sofa and her dress slung over the cushion. Her frown deepened, why was it not hanging up? Reaching for it, she ran her hand over the soft fabric smoothing out the creases then she found that it was damaged. Looking closer she could see a tear in the fabric, a small amount of blood had dried into the material and there was mud smeared along the hem. Sitting down heavily she searched her memory, how could this have happened? She must have bumped into something hard and sharp, she thought.

Pushing herself up she went into the hallway where her shoes were beside the front door. Bending down carefully she inspected them, there were traces of mud along the sole and around the heel, the same as on her gown. Her coat was on the peg so checking it for damage she found nothing, no rips and no mud stains.

Going into the kitchen, she filled the kettle with water then put it on to boil before stepping into the bathroom. Here the light was brighter so opening her gown she inspected her hip in the mirror probing the wound gently with her fingers. The cut was superficial but the bruise had spread, the joint was stiff and tender, but luckily, there was only a mild discomfort when she moved. Arnica would take care of the bruise she thought as she reached up into the bathroom cabinet.

Her cello was safely in her music room, which was a huge relief and now curled up on the sofa with a mug of coffee she was ready to probe her memory further. She could remember leaving the concert hall with her driver, he had insisted on carrying her cello case. Something must have happened in the car on the journey home, she felt sure of it or perhaps someone had been waiting outside when she returned home. She had let herself into her flat, but after that, it all became a little vague. Shaking her head, she could still hardly believe that Victoria Stevens was dead. She spared a thought for the girl's parents. It was a terrible thing to lose a loved one especially at this time of the year. She knew exactly how that felt, Christmas would never be the same for them again. Her heart went out to Victoria's parents.

Chapter
TWENTY

It was not until the twenty ninth of December that the post mortem on Victoria Stevens was carried out. DI Ashton had already received the SOCO report and was sitting in his office discussing it with DC James. They wanted to be clear of the facts before going to their appointment at the mortuary.

"The report says that Victoria Stevens was found in her wheelchair, it suggests that the attack was carried out whilst she remained sitting there."

"Well, she could hardly get up and make a run for it." James observed as he studied a photograph of the victim. "If she had just received a blow to the head then I guess she was stunned to say the least."

"So why leave her in her chair. The attacker could have dragged her to the ground before carrying out his attack."

"If rape was not an issue then I guess he didn't need to have her lying down, besides I imagine that he wouldn't have had much time. There must have been plenty of people about at that time on Christmas Eve."

Ashton looked at his colleague and rubbed his finger across his chin thoughtfully.

"Whoever wrote this report has used an element of artistic license," he said reading from the script.

"Well, Miss bloody Marple should have stuck to the facts," James growled. "Our job is hard enough without having to read through a crime novel."

"There were traces of blood and fabric fibres found on the arm of the chair." Ashton continued ignoring James' remark. He pointed out the relevant page where close up photographs had been included. "She must have run into someone during the evening or as she made her way along the path, either that or this was done during the struggle."

"It could be her own blood," James said as he studied the graphic photographs.

"Or it could belong to our murderer."

"Let's not jump to conclusions," James said looking up. "The pathologists will no doubt be able to tell us more."

"I just hope he didn't cut her whilst she was conscious." Ashton shuddered as he gathered up the scene of crime photographs.

James nodded grimly.

The Westminster Public Mortuary was situated just a short distance from their office and when DI Ashton and DC James arrived, they went straight to the Iain West Forensic Unit where the Metropolitan Police team had taken Victoria's body.

Dr Patricia Fleming was addressing a group of medical students.

"There would have been a coroner in this area dealing with murders for around 800 years," she told them, "so it's completely appropriate for Westminster to be at the forefront of forensic pathology."

"How extensive are the facilities here?" one of the students asked.

Ashton and James joined the back of the group hoping to blend in but they failed dismally. The tour seemed to be winding up so they were content to bide their time and try to look interested in what Dr Fleming was saying.

"We can store up to 102 bodies here, so we can cope with mass fatalities should the need arise, however in the unfortunate event of something like that happening we would have to recruit reinforcements from across the city."

"What about dealing with bio-hazards?"

"That is not a problem," she smiled. "There are strict procedures in place to deal with such incidents, we have a bio-hazard post mortem room."

Several more questions were asked over the next few minutes and Dr Fleming dealt with them all satisfactorily, the students seemed happy with her answers. Ashton was impressed, he liked the way she worked, she had the ability to hold everyone's attention when she spoke, he would never grow tired of listening to her voice.

"What we have here is a reflection of the more sophisticated scientific techniques employed in homicide investigations these days."

This was her finishing statement and a short applause followed before the students began to thin out. One of two remained to ask their final questions but the detectives did not have to wait long.

"Terry," she said moving quickly towards them bearing a smile.

"Good morning Pat," he said grasping her outstretched hand.

"This is DC Dennis James," he introduced his colleague before going on. "Dennis and I are here for the Victoria Stevens post mortem."

"Busy morning?" James asked as he took her hand. He was impressed, hers was a firm grip, but her hands were soft and warm.

"Well, you know how it is," she laughed.

"You give guided tours as well?" he asked keeping their conversation going.

"Sure, we all do our bit. I enjoy working with Med students. When I was their age nothing like this existed, the path lab had not moved on much since Victorian times." She laughed again as memories filled her head. "I will never forget my first visit to a post mortem room. The body of the victim was laid out on the examination table and I'm sure the resident medical examiner resented our being there. He was no better than a butcher. Several of my colleagues fainted or rushed to the sink where they hastily deposited their breakfast."

"That would never happen today surely?" he said with raised eyebrows.

"Don't you believe it," she looked up at him. "Students still have the ability to pass out or decorate the floor."

They laughed.

Dr Patricia Fleming was a magnificent woman and no one would agree more than DC Dennis James. He would have been amazed to learn that she was fast approaching her fiftieth birthday. Her short dark hair was stylish and the only evidence of creases on her face was laughter lines around her eyes. She obviously took great care of her appearance.

"Right gentlemen," she said becoming serious. "You know the drill. Whilst I go and slip into my working clothes, you make yourselves comfortable in the VIP lounge."

The VIP lounge was what they called the viewing area, a high tech space with a live CCTV link to the post mortem room where investigating officers could watch the pathologists at work. With issues of DNA and fabric transfer, the fewer people present in the 'cutting room' the less chance there was of contamination so the stronger the evidence.

Fifteen minutes later and sitting in front of a huge screen the detectives watched as Pat and her assistant appeared. Victoria Stevens was already laid out on the examination table her body covered by a green sheet.

"Are you comfortable gentlemen?" she asked looking into the camera.

"Some lemonade and popcorn might have been welcome," James replied although he doubted his ability to hold down popcorn once the post mortem began.

"I'll bear that in mind for next time." Pat said before reaching for a recording device. "The victim is a seventeen year old female who we know to be Victoria Stevens."

The girl's parents had confirmed formal identification, although there had never been any doubt.

"Her coat seems to have been removed carefully," Pat said speaking clearly into the microphone. She was standing to one side where Victoria's clothes were displayed. "Her blouse shows evidence of damage," she examined the item closely before going on. "Several buttons are missing and there is a small tear around the seam of the right arm. The clip on her bra is damaged this is consistent with it being pulled roughly from her body. I can see no blood on these items of clothing."

Turning towards the examination table, she nodded to her assistant who pulled back the sheet exposing the naked body of Victoria Stevens. DC James sucked in his breath, shocked at the sight of her injuries, but DI Ashton moved closer to the screen.

"There is a blunt force trauma to the side of her head," Pat bent forward for a closer look and carefully removed matted hair from around the wound.

Working her way methodically around the body she searched for evidence of torture but the story she was seeing was quite different.

"There are a number of cuts to her face and neck, these extend down onto the upper torso. Her breasts have been slashed in what can only be described as a frenzied attack." She paused as her assistant took photographs of the wounds.

"These injuries have been caused by a small narrow blade." She measured several of the wounds noting length and depth. "There are no penetrating stab wounds so at the moment I would say that the probable cause of death was from the blow to the head." She looked up at the camera. "To answer the question that I guess you are burning to ask, the injuries to her face and torso were almost certainly inflicted after death."

"It looks like the same MO as the murder in York a couple of weeks ago." DI Ashton said. He was thinking about the links between his daughter's concerts and the deaths. Both victims were young female musicians who had just performed with her, but pushing these thoughts aside, he asked.

"Can you tell us anything about the person who did this Pat?"

"Well, the killer is right handed," she began as she moved to the head of the table, "and must have been standing in front of her when the blow was delivered." She looked up at the camera again and frowned. "Our victim was looking up when she was struck and from the angle of the blow." She paused and stood back, cocking her head to one side as if imagining the scene. "I would say that the person who did this is not more than medium height."

Crouching down she probed the wound again.

"The weapon used was wielded with just enough force."

Ashton waited for her to continue but she remained silent as she worked and after a while, he said. "What do you mean Pat?"

"I'm suggesting that our killer is either not particularly powerful or incredibly restrained."

"Why do you say that?"

"Well the blow was sufficient to fracture her skull," she paused again before standing upright, then turning towards the camera she went on. "There is a depressed fracture which undoubtedly was the cause of death. I will confirm an intracranial haemorrhage in a short while. With an uncontrolled attack, I would have expected the wound to be more severe. A hefty blow would have shattered her skull and knocked her out of her chair, but I can find nothing to substantiate that. There are no scuffmarks of damage to her coat and no bruises to her hands, arm or shoulder from a sudden impact with the ground."

"Can you tell us what kind of weapon was used?"

"Oh yes," she said, "a stone of some kind. There are fragments of soil in the wound. I would say that it's likely to have come from the edging of a flower border, something like that."

"She was found in St James's Gardens." Ashton murmured. "What about the trace evidence that SOCO found on her chair?" he asked, speaking more clearly this time.

"Yes," Pat nodded and moving away from the examination table, she reached for her notes and began to scan the pages.

"Blood was found on the arm of the chair along with fragments of fabric." She paused to read from the report. "The fabric looks as though it comes from a quality item of clothing, something like a dress or blouse, it's too fine to be from something that a man would wear."

"What colour dress or blouse?"

"The sample was dark in colour, black or dark blue maybe."

"So the blood could be from a woman?" Ashton asked joining up the dots. "If the fabric belongs to a dress or blouse..."

"Oh yes, without a doubt." Pat nodded before he had time to finish his line of thought.

"Has that been confirmed?" He asked looking directly at her but not knowing if she could see him on a monitor in the post mortem room.

"A blood smear can be a clear indicator of gender," she told him before holding up the file. "XX chromosomes, blood group A RhD Positive."

"Is that a rare blood type?" James asked.

Pat shook her head. "Around 40% of the population share that blood group."

"So our killer could be female?" he said.

"It most certainly belongs to a woman, but it's not from our victim. Her blood group is O. I cannot confirm that it belongs to the killer."

"Why do you say that?"

"Well for one thing, it's not my job to tell you that the killer is female, I can see no clear evidence of that, besides who's to say that Victoria didn't run into someone by accident."

"We'll have to speak to everyone that she was in contact with at the concert, by all accounts there was quite a crowd so an accident may well have occurred."

It was a line of enquiry they would have to pursue, but DI Ashton realised that to draw blood and damage clothing, any collision must have been pretty spectacular.

"So, the mutilation was carried out post mortem?" Ashton asked.

"Yes, the wounds are not deep, although some do extend to the bone, but no main arteries have been severed."

"Not much in the way of bleeding then?"

"No, not a considerable amount, not what you would expect."

"Our killer would not necessarily be covered in blood?"

"Unlikely, you see it's not like a conventional stabbing where there would be arterial spray. In this case there would be blood seepage, but from post mortem wounds like this there would not be a significant amount, besides as I just said, no main arteries have been damaged."

"One other thing Pat," Ashton said. "Our victim was disabled, so just how much mobility did she have?"

"Victoria's notes tell us that she had impairment in the function of her lower limbs, in other words she did not have the use of her legs. She had normal movement in her hips, arms and upper body."

"So she could have fought off her attacker?"

"Of course, there was nothing wrong with her arms."

"There are no injuries consistent with defence wounds?"

"Correct; no bruises to her hands or arms and no skin particles beneath her nails. In fact her nails are in very good condition."

"Do you think she knew her killer?"

"Either that or she didn't have time to defend herself."

"So why was she cut like that?" James asked shaking his head.

"Well, I would guess that it was to obliterate her good looks." Pat replied grimly as she studied the photograph of a smiling Victoria Stevens.

"Thank you Pat," Ashton said. He had heard enough. "We owe you one as usual."

Later that day the post mortem confirmed that Victoria had indeed died from an intracranial bleed caused by a blow to her head.

Chapter
TWENTY ONE

It was a bitterly cold day in London and although barely mid morning, the weather was miserable and darkness threatened. The wind chill was several degrees colder than the ambient temperature, the New Year had brought with it a cold spell. Snow was forecast for the days ahead and Mia shuddered at the thought. She stared miserably out of the window watching as hoards of shoppers spilled from the pavements in search of those post Christmas bargains, the sales had just begun in earnest. It never ceased to amaze her that whatever the season tourists packed the streets jostling the locals in a bid to seek out the gold that paved the city. American, Japanese and now a never increasing number of Chinese visitors arrived daily in an effort to help boost the economy of the country.

The taxi stopped at the side of the road and leaning forward between the seats Mia paid her fare. She had yet to fasten her coat and as she pushed open the door, an icy blast sent a shiver through her body. Swinging her legs out onto the pavement, she pulled herself upright just as the door closed suddenly. It caught her hip throwing her off balance and as she fell back against the car, Mia cried out as pain shot through her pelvis. Biting down on her bottom lip, she held her breath.

"Are you alright luv?" the driver called, his head appearing above the back of his seat.

Mia was stunned and tears threatened her mascara. She would have collapsed onto the pavement had it not been for the door pinning her against the side of the vehicle. Cautiously she put some weight onto her leg and as another stab of pain shot through her hip a memory stirred.

"Are you okay?" The driver appeared in front of her and taking her arm, held her upright.

Mia stared at him in confusion; she expected to see her driver from the private hire company who had driven her to the concert on Christmas Eve.

"Yes, I think so," she managed to say as reality took hold.

She was certain that this had happened before, the door of the private hire car must have been the cause the injury to her hip and the damage to her dress. How could she have forgotten such a thing? These lapses in her memory were beginning to bother her, whole periods of her life were a complete blank, and still there was the matter of the telephone calls. Clearing her mind of these unwelcome thoughts Mia made her way towards Alicia Wicks office.

DI Ashton strode purposefully into the murder room at the Metropolitan Police Headquarters. Earlier that day he had stopped outside the building to look at the iconic revolving sign, it told the world that this was the home of New Scotland Yard. To think that he was part of the most recognisable law enforcement organisation on the planet never failed to thrill him, but now he was feeling deflated, so taking a moment he looked around and sighed. A desk had been set up for him in the murder room, this was where he felt obliged to be. As the officer in charge of the investigation, it was his job to ensure that the wheels of justice turned smoothly. He still had access to his office, but here at the centre of the investigation, he could keep an eye on the proceedings, he could also observe and listen to the bickering that went on amongst his colleagues. Rivalry was rife and he did not want anyone holding back important bits of information or going off on some ego-filled tangent that may or may not impress the top brass. It was his reputation on the line here.

The investigation into the death of Victoria Stevens had only just begun. The poor girl had been dead for over two weeks already, but progress had been painfully slow. To be fair a large part of the time had been taken up by the festive and New Year celebrations, but this was no consolation to her parents. He was certain that they were not feeling very festive. He had been at work all over the Christmas period but it was hellish trying to get things moving. It was an impossible task working with a reduced back-up system, but now with things back to normal he was hopeful that progress would be made. His small team were busy setting up their work stations, some more interested in the position of their desks, telephone and computer points than with what mattered most.

Detectives Mallinson and Keable from the North Yorkshire Police were due to arrive sometime that morning. They were bringing with them details of the Alison Morley case, there were startling similarities between the two murders that could not be ignored so it made sense to pool their resources and work together.

DC Dennis James appeared carrying a file under his arm.

"Morning boss," he said cheerfully, "post mortem report." He waved the file in the air before continuing. "I asked Pat for a summery in plain English. These documents are hardly bedtime reading, you need a degree in medical jargon just to understand them."

"You are looking remarkably dapper this morning Dennis." Terry said eyeing him suspiciously. The fact that he had used Dr Fleming's Christian name so amiably had not passed him by. "Tell me that you didn't go running to Dr Fleming's office personally to collect that."

"Well, someone had to do it, might as well be me."

"So, no other reason to go popping off to the medical examiner's office then?"

"Of course not," Dennis grinned. "You know me boss, lead from the front. No need to send a junior to do the footwork when I can take care of it myself."

Terry grunted. He knew Dennis well but he knew Pat better. Dennis had no idea how far back they went, but he got the impression that his colleague was about to discover just how unusual their friendly pathologist could be.

"DI Mallinson and DS Keable are at reception sir." A young police officer delivered her message before hurrying away and Dennis stared after her as she went.

"She's young enough to be your daughter," Terry mumbled under his breath. Dennis was about to reply but thought better of it.

Mallinson was a tall, well turned out figure with a shock of thick dark hair that gave nothing away. His age would have suggested greying at the temples at least, but there was no incriminating evidence. Keable on the other hand was at the opposite end of the fashion spectrum. His was a stocky figure with legs too short for his trousers that did not match his jacket. He also wore a thick woollen jumper pulled tight over his spreading paunch.

Introductions were made before the detectives could be admitted into the inner sanctum of New Scotland Yard.

"Welcome to the great metropolis," Dennis chuckled. This was his standard joke and Terry groaned inwardly, but Mallinson and Keable laughed dutifully.

It turned out that Mallinson's Christian name was Edward although he preferred to be called Ed, whilst Keable was Jason, he decided not to mention the fact that he liked to be called JJ at home.

"This is the nerve centre," Dennis pointed out when they reached the murder room.

"It doesn't look much at the moment," Terry added quickly, "but I can assure you it will become a hive of activity once the investigation picks up momentum."

"Coffee gents?" Dennis asked before recruiting a junior to do his bidding.

"Lead from the front Dennis?" Terry whispered as he ushered the guests into his office.

As soon as they were comfortable, Terry began. He was eager to get down to business. It was important to establish a pecking order, although Mallinson was equal to him in rank, he remained the officer in charge.

"We have the autopsy report on our victim," he said, pushing the file across his desk. "Her name is Victoria Stevens," he continued giving Ed and Jason some background details. "She was seventeen years old and lived with her parents in the suburbs. She was an accomplished musician having just become the BBC Young Musician of the Year."

Ed raised his eyebrows as he opened the file.

"A fine looking young lass," he said staring at the photograph.

"She was found on Christmas Eve with a fatal head wound. She had spent the evening performing at a Christmas concert, she was a pianist." Terry continued with his summary.

"Pretty much the same as our girl," Ed confirmed. "Alison Morley was just short of her twenty first birthday. She was a student at the University of York and also a musician." He told Terry nothing more than he knew already.

"The MO is the same. Your girl died of a head wound?"

"Yes," Ed nodded as he removed a file from his briefcase. "I have a copy of the autopsy report but unfortunately it's the full version." He grinned apologetically. "Didn't think to ask for the condensed edition."

"Anything we don't understand, I'm sure Pat will be pleased to translate." Dennis chipped in.

"Dr Patricia Fleming is the pathologist who carried out the post mortem on Victoria Stevens." Terry explained.

"Our victim was killed by a blow to the head, probably delivered by a heavy glass bottle. What was used to kill Victoria?" Jason asked.

"A stone from the gardens where she was found." Terry replied.

"An opportunistic killing then."

"You say probably a glass bottle." Terry looked up at Ed.

"Yes," he nodded. "The medical examiner thinks it a likely weapon as he found marks consistent with a rim or edge, the sort found on the bottom of a wine bottle or something similar."

"There were no fragments at the scene?"

"No, it seems the weapon remained intact."

For the next thirty minutes, they compared notes discussing the similarities between the two cases.

"We thought at first that Alison Morley might have been the victim of a random attack which unfortunately led to her death, but when we consider the mutilation and the fact that we have another identical killing then obviously there must be more to it." Terry stared across his desk at Ed, waiting for him to continue. "Our investigation is hardly underway and we've only just put this information on the system so how is it that you know so much about our victim?"

"Well, apart from watching the news, we know of someone who was acquainted with Alison Morley." Terry was not about to tell him that it was his daughter who had performed at the concert in York. DI Mallinson had not yet worked out that the musician topping the bill shared his surname.

"Mia Ashton, the renowned cellist is Terry's daughter," Dennis confessed suddenly, pleased to be able to share this bit of information.

Terry stared at him thunderously leaving him in no doubt that he had made a grave error.

"Is she indeed?" Ed said, his eyebrows rising again. "When were you going to mention this small fact Inspector?"

"It's not relevant at this stage of our investigation," Terry replied defensively.

"Not relevant," Ed pressed. "I would say that it was completely relevant. We have two suspicious deaths, and both young women had connections with your daughter."

"It's true that they both performed with my daughter, but she didn't know them."

"So a coincidence then?" Ed snapped. "Looking at the evidence and given that both murders took place directly after a concert which included your daughter, one in York and now again in London, I would hardly call that a coincidence, would you?"

Terry remained silent.

"I would be rather concerned if it were my daughter," Jason told him, the pair slipping naturally into the Good Cop, Bad Cop routine.

"We have discussed the situation and I have no reason to believe that she has anything to add to our investigation."

"We are not suggesting that she is involved in any way," Jason leaned forward, "but she may know the killer even if she is unaware of the fact."

"I understand all that," Terry replied.

There was now an edge to his voice, which made Dennis feel uncomfortable. He should have kept his big mouth shut but it was too late, the damage had been done. This was not a conversation that Terry had intended having so soon after meeting Mallinson and Keable and if it wasn't for Dennis they would be none the wiser.

"Anyone for more coffee?" Dennis asked rising to his feet.

"Look," Terry said ignoring his colleague. "Our investigation as you can see is still in its infancy. We have been busy over the holiday period with other aspects of the case. Talking to my daughter is going to be a little awkward."

"I agree," Ed nodded. "That's why you can't be involved in a formal interview. Dennis is also probably too close, so I suggest that DS Keable and I take care of that."

Terry stiffened at the prospect of Mia being questioned by these detectives.

"Okay," he snapped. "Leave it with me, I'll make the arrangements."

"We've already spoken with her regarding Alison Morley," Jason added. "I telephoned her myself. It was all routine stuff and she was unable to add anything to our investigation."

"Get a transcript of that conversation Jason. I want it in front of us when we conduct the interview."

Dennis arrived with a tray of coffees. This time he had got them himself, glad to be out of the office for a while, distance himself from the awkward situation that he had unwittingly created.

When their meeting was over, he volunteered to take Ed and Jason on a guided tour of the building. It would be a good idea to leave Terry alone, allow him time to calm down.

Chapter

TWENTY TWO

Mia left her agent's office feeling unusually troubled. Alicia could have this effect on her but today she had been particularly unsettling. She had agreed that the recent concerts had been a success but they were of course overshadowed by the terrible murders. Alicia had also pointed out that the ongoing police enquiry and the developing rumours surrounding the case could have a negative effect on her reputation.

'Who knows what might happen when the media get their grubby little claws into you.' Alicia's words echoed hatefully through her head. 'You had better get that friend of yours to write something in your defence.'

Why should Alicia think that she needed to defend herself, she had done nothing wrong. Her thoughts continued to spin inside her head as more of what Alicia said came back to her. She had threatened to cancel some of her concerts and Mia was shocked and saddened by her lack of support. It was as if Alicia believed that she was guilty of something. She stopped on the pavement and narrowly avoided being knocked to the ground by a group of excited tourists. What she needed, she realised was an antidote to Alicia's poisonous attitude, a friend who would help raise her spirits. Emilia Wicks came to mind, she would pay her shop a visit. She had been meaning to call in, see what her new friend did for a living but she had not yet had the opportunity, now however she was determined to make the most of this dismal day.

Rising up from beneath the pavement, Mia left the tube station and began the short walk to the shop. Glancing up at the sky, she shuddered and pulled her scarf tighter around her neck. It was becoming increasingly darker overhead and barely afternoon it was as if evening had already arrived and now rain was beginning to fall.

White Lace and Promises was far more impressive than she had expected. From the pavement, Mia studied the immaculate double fronted Georgian building. In the gloom of the winter's day, it looked cosy and inviting. Light coming through the small square windowpanes spilled warmly onto the pavement and the original front door with its polished brass handle invited her in. It reminded Mia of a scene from a Dickens novel. A bell tinkled merrily as she pushed open the door and a pleasant rush of warm perfumed air greeted her.

"Mia," Emilia cried as she looked up from behind a small work counter. Her smile was genuine as she rushed to embrace her. "How lovely it is to see you again."

"This is fantastic," Mia replied and standing back, she took in her surroundings. "I had no idea that your shop would be so grand." The smile froze on her face. "Oh, please forgive me; that came out wrong. It was rude of me to say that."

Emilia laughed and nodded her forgiveness. "My little shop has that effect on all my friends."

"It appears much bigger from the inside and you have so many beautiful things."

"I'm so lucky," Emilia agreed. "It's such a joy to work here."

Mia's eyes were everywhere as she tried to take everything in at once.

"You must be frozen, it's such a dreary day. Would you like a cup of tea or coffee?"

"Tea would be lovely."

"I warn you, it's nothing fancy, just a teabag in a mug."

"A teabag in a mug will be fine."

She followed Emilia into the small office at the back of the shop.

"Ben has been working here," Emilia explained as she filled the kettle at the small sink in the corner of the cramped space. "He's been marvellous, working out marketing strategies that I plan to put into action immediately."

"So, what he told me was true then."

Emilia looked up from what she was doing and Mia went on quickly.

"He said that he was busy, that was why we haven't seen much of each other lately. To be honest I thought it sounded like an excuse to distance himself from me. Given the terrible things that have been happening recently I wouldn't blame him."

The kettle clicked off loudly and clouds of steam rose into the air, Emilia poured boiling water into their mugs before speaking.

"You have got it all wrong. He has spent a lot of time working here with me, he even stays late into the evening saying that he finds it easier to concentrate when it's quiet."

Reaching for one of the files on the desk, she opened it and showed Mia a colourful chart.

"It all looks rather nice," Emilia admitted, "but don't ask me what it means. Ben tells me that charts like this will help to make the business more profitable. I would never have thought about producing stuff like this, but he assures me that my accountant will be thrilled."

They both laughed before Emilia asked.

"When are you going to see him again?"

"I really have no idea," Mia replied quietly, sipping at her tea.

Emilia studied her closely thinking how tired and pale she looked. The pressure of recent events was obviously taking its toll.

"We haven't made any arrangements," Mia continued. "We've hardly spoken to each other since Boxing Day. It's probably my fault, I should have telephoned him, but to be honest I'm not sure that he would have wanted me to. When we met up last, I got the impression that he was uncomfortable in my company."

"Look Mia, I know that's not true Ben idolises you, he really does. Believe me he is not losing interest, quite the opposite in fact, but you know what men are like. He would be the last person to tell you that." She paused wondering just how far she dared go playing lover's advocate. "He probably thinks that you are busy preparing for your next concert, besides as you can see I have been rather monopolising him recently."

"My agent is threatening to cancel some of my concerts, given the current situation."

"Can she do that?" Emilia asked, shocked at her sudden statement. "Surely that's not the answer."

"I suppose she can and as you might appreciate I'm rather upset about it."

"I can imagine," Emilia replied. "Can't your father do something, have a police presence at the next concert?"

"I don't know." Mia shook her head.

"It could be the perfect opportunity to catch this murderer especially if they think he might strike again."

"My father is leading the investigation but I have no idea what is going on. He never discusses his work with me."

Emilia moved some of the files from the top of the desk.

"Sit down," she said indicating to the chair before perching on the edge of the desk.

"I've had some awful telephone calls." Mia told her quietly.

"What do you mean, threatening phone calls?"

"No," she shook her head, "not exactly." She described the calls as taunting and disturbing.

"Have you reported this to the police?"

"No," she shook her head again avoiding eye contact. "Not yet."

"Well don't you think you should?"

"Of course," Mia replied, "but I don't want to worry my father."

Emilia raised her eyebrows, shocked at her friend's response. There must be more to it than that, she thought.

"Do you know who it is making these calls?"

"No, I don't think so."

"You really should tell your father about this." Emilia said softly.

"I know," Mia whispered. She wanted to say much more, tell Emilia about her lapses in memory, the mysterious injury that she had received, but she didn't know how to begin. How could she possibly discuss something that she hardly understood herself.

They talked for a while longer and Emilia soon realised that Mia needed reassuring. Whatever was going on would not affect their friendship and it was important that she understood that. She could rely on her.

"I'll work on Ben," Emilia promised. "I'll get him to telephone you."

"You won't tell him about any of this will you?"

"Of course not, whatever we say to one another remains confidential. I will never betray your confidence."

Mia nodded then smiled. This was not how she imagined her afternoon would go. Confiding in Emilia had not been part of her plan, she would never have thought to burden her with her own problems, and now she was beginning to feel guilty.

"Right," she said placing her empty mug down on the desk. "Won't you give me a guided tour of your shop?"

Chapter
TWENTY THREE

Ben did not telephone Mia, he went one step further by turning up on her doorstep clutching a bunch of winter blooms and an expensive bottle of wine. Mia was overjoyed to see him and throwing her arms around his neck, almost dragged him into the hallway. Casting her inhibitions aside, she urgently sought his mouth and kissed him with a passion that she had seldom felt before. It was then that she knew, he would be staying the night.

"Hi," she breathed heavily and pulling away from him, she could feel the heat rising towards her cheeks. "You have no idea how pleased I am to see you."

"Me too," was all Ben could manage. Her enthusiastic greeting had taken him completely by surprise, but Mia could see that he was overjoyed by her affection.

Releasing him, she reached for her flowers and stepped back. She wanted to kiss him again but resisting the urge, she watched him closely as he shrugged off his coat and unwound the scarf from his neck. He stooped to recover the bottle of wine that had fallen to the floor then she took him by the hand and led him into the kitchen.

"I'll pop these in a vase," she said stretching up towards a cupboard. "They are beautiful, thank you so much."

She set about arranging her flowers leaving him to remove the cork from the bottle.

"I've been so busy lately," he said as he reached for a couple of glasses then pouring the wine he passed one to her.

"I know," she nodded as she studied her handiwork. "Emilia showed me. I'm impressed with what you have done, but do you really think it will make a difference to her business?"

"Sure," he replied positively. "If she follows my recommendations and guidelines..." He stopped talking and smiled. "I didn't come here to talk about my sister's business."

Taking his hand again, she pulled him closer and placed a kiss on his cheek before leading him into the living room where she gently pushed him down onto the sofa then snuggled up beside him.

He was not very good at small talk, didn't want to spoil the moment by telling her how worried he had been about her so he simply held onto her hand, and sipped at his wine.

"It's such a relief to be into the New Year don't you think?" Turning to face him, she continued. "I don't do Christmas very well I'm afraid."

He knew something about her past by reading articles on the internet. She was only a child when her mother and brother were killed in a road accident, which left her with serious injuries. Although her physical injuries had healed, no amount of counselling could ease the psychological damage that had been done. How can a child be expected to come to terms with such a terrible situation, he wondered. Her father had brought her up single-handed and she had thrown herself into her music in order to escape her nightmares.

"When is your next concert?" he asked steering himself away from such depressing thoughts.

"February," she replied. "It's a Valentine concert, it's called 'Romantic Solos.'"

"That sounds nice."

"It will be providing my agent doesn't cancel the whole thing." Her voice took on a hardened edge.

"Why would she do that?"

Mia told him about her meeting with Alicia and his reaction was the same as his sister's.

"Can she really cancel a concert just like that?"

"Well," Mia took a sip of wine before going on. "She could take steps to prevent it from going ahead but it would be an almost impossible task without the backing of the authorities."

"That's madness, surely by working with the police this may be an opportunity to flush the killer out."

"Yes," she agreed. "But would they be willing to take the risk?"

"Surely those who have already purchased tickets won't be very pleased, especially as it's just a few weeks before the event."

"I'm sure you are right."

"Where is the concert going to be held?"

"The Barbican."

"Wow," Ben exclaimed. "Not just a small concert then." He was impressed, he had been there once before to listen to the London Symphony Orchestra, and was amazed at the scale of the complex. He discovered that the Barbican Centre was the largest of its kind in Europe, hosting not only a range of classical concerts and contemporary music, but also theatre performances, film screenings and art exhibitions. He guessed that the Valentine's concert was being run in conjunction with a romantic meal offer from one of the centre's three restaurants.

Mia got up and went into the kitchen before returning with her vase of flowers and the rest of the wine. The vase she placed on the table where she could admire them then she topped up their glasses before settling back down beside him.

"Emilia's shop is simply amazing," she told him. "I had no idea that it would be so..." she paused searching for the right word, "well presented."

"She has done a marvellous job," Ben nodded proudly. "She has a busy time ahead with Easter weddings. One of those is a very grand affair, I just hope that she can cope with it all."

"Are you going to help her?"

"Yes," he nodded. "I'm afraid I have been recruited to help organise some of the weddings. Em wants me to make contact with suitable venues and come up with proposals for complete wedding packages."

"That sounds fascinating," she looked at him and laughed. "Planning a wedding is every woman's dream but I imagine it can be as stressful as moving house."

"I guess so," Ben shrugged. He had never given it much thought, but he had to agree, it did sound like a daunting task.

"If you are going to do this, might I suggest that you do it well because woe betide the organiser who gets it wrong."

"Em is far too organised for that, she never courts failure, everything she does is well thought out and meticulously planned. She leaves nothing to chance."

"Well in that case she can organise my wedding when the time comes." Mia smiled and shot him a sideways glance.

"What do you have in mind?" he asked, interested in what she had to say.

Mia chewed at her bottom lip and narrowed her eyes as she pictured her perfect wedding.

"I would like a medieval theme," she began as her ideas took shape. "Set in a romantic ruin it will be a perfect day with a huge marquee and tables beautifully laid for the wedding breakfast. Of course, there will be lots of music and everyone will be dressed in medieval costume. Can you imagine those fine dresses, the wonderful colours, and the merry making?"

"Wow," Ben replied picturing the scene.

"Oh yes," she continued quickly. "My new and gallant husband would carry me away on a pure white stallion to a waiting vintage car then we would drive off into the sunset and live happily ever after."

"Sounds idyllic," Ben said and after a short pause he said. "I'll see what I can arrange."

"Is that some kind of proposal?" she giggled, nudged his shoulder with her elbow before draining her glass.

Their evening passed pleasantly enough, they managed to avoid talking about the prospect of cancelled concerts, and murdered musicians. When their bottle of wine was empty, Mia got up and went to make coffee.

Their coffee remained untouched, going cold in the cups as their lovemaking began right there on the sofa. Eventually they moved into her bedroom where they started all over again before finally falling asleep in the small hours of the morning.

Belenos Falzone was at his breakfast table reading the daily newspaper. The front pages were devoted to Brexit and the Government's pledge to move quickly with talks in Europe, but on page two he found a report on the murder of Victoria Stevens. The police investigation was ongoing but there had been a recent development. It was believed that the killing of a music student Alison Morley in York was not a random act and now police were investigating a possible link between the two cases.

There were no further details but it seemed that a serial killer could be responsible. The article went on to say that the police would soon be making a statement.

There was no mention of Mia Ashton but Belenos knew that as soon as journalists got the heads up then things would change. There would be a frenzied scramble to see who could come up with the most sensational story.

His own work regarding serial killers was progressing satisfactorily, he had already submitted two more articles and was now waiting for feedback from his editor. He had taken Jenna O'Brien out a few days earlier for a meal that he would be paying for out of his next two pay cheques and narrowly escaped her advances. She had made it quite clear what she had in mind, but he drew the line at sleeping with her. The deal as far as he was concerned was information about Josie MacDonald's friends in exchange for a slap up meal, which unexpectedly included copious amounts of expensive wine. To be fair she had come up with the goods, but he was not sure yet how he could use it without upsetting all those involved.

Reaching for his teacup he took a mouthful of cold tea and shuddered, it had been standing far too long. Ideas flashed through his head so picking up his pencil he scribbled furiously in his notebook then he tapped the end of the pencil against his teeth thoughtfully.

Ben awoke to the half-light of morning. He was confused, the bed he was in felt wrong, it was clearly not his own. He lay there listening to the noises of the house in an attempt to get his bearings, the surroundings might be unfamiliar, but the scent that greeted him as he rolled over he knew well. Climbing out of bed, he smiled as memories of their lovemaking filled his head. There was no sign of his clothes, they must still be in the living room he thought, so reaching for the door he paused and wondered where Mia had gone. She had not disturbed him when she got up and he had no idea how long he had been laying there without her. Opening the door a crack, he peered out. The kitchen door was open, but he could hear no movement so opening the bedroom door wider he slipped into the hallway. He found his clothes in the living room strewn over the floor beside the sofa and he smiled again unable to believe that they had actually made love.

Soft music was coming from another room, so dressing quickly he went to investigate. Easing open the door he slipped silently into the room beyond. In the middle of the polished wooden floor, Mia was sitting on a stool with her back to him playing her cello. He recognised the tune immediately but it sounded different, the arrangement was enigmatic and eerily haunting. He stopped still hardly daring to move, the last thing he wanted to do was disturb her so easing himself silently to the floor, he sat with his back to the door and allowed her music to wash over him.

"Wow," he murmured when she was finished.

Turning her head towards him Mia blinked. Her unfocussed eyes were moist with tears that rolled unchecked over her cheeks.

"Mia, that was beautiful."

She blinked again as if seeing him for the first time then sniffing back her tears she returned from the place where she had been.

"Hi," she whispered.

Ben stared at her afraid to speak and break the spell. Her music was still resonating in his ears and the room seemed charged with a sensation that he had never experienced before. Mia looked so sad and vulnerable sitting there all alone.

"I get so emotional when I play," she explained. "I have to shed my tears when rehearsing. Can you imagine what I would look like on stage bawling like a baby?"

Getting to his feet, he went to her and wrapping her up in his arms, she rested her face against his chest and breathed in his scent. The animal passion that she had experienced the previous evening was gone leaving her feeling satisfied and whole. Her affection for him had deepened and she realised that she never wanted him to let her go.

Chapter

TWENTY FOUR

Inspector Mallinson was planning to interview Mia formally at the station, but Terry would not allow it.

"You have no reason to put my daughter through that. Don't you think that she is upset enough?"

"I don't know Inspector, why don't you tell us."

"So now I am the one being interrogated," he snapped.

"Of course not Terry," Keable reassured him, the good cop again.

"Well, for the record I will confirm that my daughter has been badly affected by these terrible events."

"In what way?" Mallinson stared at him.

If there was ever a moment when Terry wanted to throw a punch then this was it.

"How do you think?" he snapped, "she is devastated." He eyed Mallinson hatefully before going on. "Two of her colleagues have been brutally murdered shortly after performing with her."

"Okay Terry, calm down." He could see the flames burning brightly in his colleague's eyes.

"I won't have you accusing my daughter of having something to do with this."

Mallinson and Keable shared a glance. They were both of the opinion that Terry was too close to be involved in the case. He had a conflict of interest and should not be the one leading this investigation. The Chief should be informed immediately.

"We are simply following a line of inquiry."

Terry set up a meeting for later that afternoon. Mallinson and Keable would speak with Mia informally at her home. Terry wanted a female colleague to be present but something told him that Mallinson would never agree to that.

Once the formal introductions were over Mia invited them in. Mallinson followed her along the hallway with Keable trailing behind, first impressions were important and neither detective missed a thing. The flat was tidy almost to obsession, just like a show house. The decor was bright and neutral and there was no indication that she shared her home with anyone else.

"Sit down gentlemen," Mia indicated to the sofa but Mallinson chose to sit in one of the armchairs.

"Would you like a cup of tea or coffee?"

"No thank you Miss Ashton," he replied answering for them both, his strong Yorkshire accent strange to her southern ear. "How long have you lived here?"

Mia lowered herself into the other armchair, the coffee table between them.

"Just over three years," she told him.

"Nice flowers," he nodded towards the vase. "An admirer?"

Mia frowned before answering. "Why do you ask? Maybe I bought them myself."

"Just being friendly," he smiled, sensing her hostility. "We are here to ask you questions about Alison Morley and Victoria Stevens but it does no harm to lay down foundations, discover a little about you first."

"What do you want to know?" she asked, raising her eyebrows. Crossing her legs, she folded her arms protectively across her chest.

The detectives could read the signs. She was willing to tell them something about herself, but there was a limit to how far she would go.

"Well, it's obvious that you live here alone Miss Ashton, but do you have someone special, a close relationship, a boyfriend perhaps?"

She almost told him that there was no crime in living alone but she kept her thoughts to herself.

"I have several good male friends, but none of them are particularly close." She felt uneasy saying that, it was as if she was betraying her feelings for Ben, but she did not want to say anything that might draw their attention to him.

"What about girlfriends?" Keable asked.

111

"I have a healthy amount of female friends, but I'm not gay if that is what you are suggesting."

"Indeed not," he smiled awkwardly. "Your sexual preference is no concern of ours."

She knew exactly what they were doing. They were trying to goad her into saying something that she might later regret. It was an old trick, once they had established a rapport her guard would be down and she could fall into their trap, but she had nothing to worry about, she was innocent.

Moving away from making personal observations they began talking about Alison Morley and Mia told them everything that she could remember about her trip to York. Keable cross referenced what she said against her original telephone statement.

"Can you think of any reason why someone would want to harm her?" Mallinson asked.

"Like I said before Inspector, I had only just met Alison and know nothing about her."

"You didn't socialise with her during your stay?"

"No, the only person I went out with was Grace."

"That is Mrs Grace Hooper?" Keable asked, glancing at his notes.

"Yes. Grace was the pianist who performed with me at the concert. She would know more about Alison than me."

"Why do you say that?" he asked and leaning forward he almost dropped his pen.

"They were both associated with the York Symphony Orchestra based at the university so they must have known each other."

"I see," he said scribbling in his notebook.

"What about Victoria Stevens, did you have any contact with her before your concert?"

"Like Alison I had never met Victoria before, but I did go to her parents' house to become acquainted and to rehearse before the concert."

"Why was that, would you not have rehearsed together before the concert at the venue?"

"Yes of course, but I like to meet the people I'm performing with beforehand, well in advance of the concert in fact."

"I see," Mallinson took up the questioning. "Did you meet the Andersons before the concert?"

"Yes of course, I arranged to meet both Jessica and her husband Paul at their home in St John's Wood."

"Was Victoria invited to attend that meeting?"

"She was, but she couldn't make it, that is why I met up with her a few days later."

"Do you know why she was unable to keep her appointment with the Andersons?"

"No, I didn't ask. Victoria was disabled, she used a wheelchair so perhaps going to a stranger's house was difficult for her." Mia offered, trying to be helpful.

"On the evening of your concert in St John's, Smith Square, you attended the reception afterwards?"

"Yes," Mia nodded. "We were all there, Victoria and the Andersons." She told them about the interviews and the photographs.

"Victoria was keen to get away because she had arranged to meet up with friends at a pub."

"How do you know this?" Mallinson asked.

"She told me, in fact I was invited to join them."

"And did you?"

"No, I declined the offer."

"Why was that?"

"Well, as I said before, I hardly knew Victoria and the thought of spending Christmas Eve in a noisy pub with a bunch of drunken teenagers is not my idea of a having a good time."

Keable snorted. He could understand her reasons.

"If you had accompanied Miss Stevens that evening then things might have turned out very differently."

"Don't you think I haven't thought about that Inspector?" she glared at Mallinson. "I wanted to speak to Victoria before she left, wish her a Merry Christmas and all the best with her promising musical career, but I didn't get the chance. She left before I had the opportunity to say anything."

Mia was saddened at this and they both noted her pained expression.

"Where did you go after the reception?" Keable asked.

"I came straight home."

"Can anyone verify that?" Mallinson barked.

"Well, as you see, I live alone, there is no one waiting here for me when I get home."

"What about neighbours, did any of them see you arrive home?"

"No, I don't remember seeing anyone, it was late on Christmas Eve, it was a silent night."

Keable was writing furiously in his notebook and Mallinson stared thoughtfully at her.

"My driver can vouch for me." Mia continued. "He could tell you exactly what time I arrived home."

Mallinson was tempted to ask if she had gone out again after the driver had dropped her off, but that was not necessary. Victoria Stevens was already dead by then.

"Thank you Miss Ashton." He smiled amiably, his attitude towards her changing suddenly. "You have been most helpful."

The interview was over and both detectives got to their feet.

"When is your next concert?" Mallinson asked.

"February," she told him. "A Valentine concert at the Barbican."

"That sounds interesting," Keable turned to face her. "I might bring my wife down to London for that. Any chance of a couple of complimentary tickets?" he smiled, pushing his luck.

"I'll have a word with my agent," she replied dryly.

When they were gone, she sat quietly going over what they had said. She might have found the interview much more upsetting, but with Ben's flowers arranged so beautifully in the vase on the table and thoughts of their lovemaking, nothing could spoil her mood for long. Suddenly the telephone began to ring.

"Hello."

"What are the police doing paying you a visit?"

She recognised his voice immediately and her stomach tightened.

"How do you know it was the police and how do you know they were here?"

"Oh, I know everything," he laughed, an evil sound that made her shudder.

"I know that your boyfriend stayed the night," he continued. "Was it nice Mia, having him on your sofa?"

She was speechless and had heard enough. Slamming the phone down she pulled out the plug before it could ring again. How did he know about Ben, she asked herself? He must have been watching, he must be close by now. She shuddered again and wrapping her arms tightly around herself, she got to her feet and turned towards the window. Could anyone see in from the garden, she wondered. Surely, with the curtains closed, even if his face was up against the window it would be impossible to see in. It was the same with her bedroom window, so how could he possibly have known?

Chapter
TWENTY FIVE

Belenos studied the names on his list. These were the victims of the serial killer William Randolph Jnr. Randolph went by the name of Greg MacLaren, then eventually became known as Mr Mac. He had changed his name soon after his release from a secure psychiatric centre in an unsuccessful bid to put his past behind him. He had spent years in a prison hospital then finally was transferred to a psychiatric unit where he had received treatment before undergoing a rehabilitation programme. Once he was placed back into the community, a string of social workers supervised him closely, but after a few months, it was considered that he no longer posed a threat to society so these visits came to an end and the local police were made aware of his situation.

Randolph had enjoyed a privileged upbringing living on a large country estate not far from the village of Fochabers. He was born into a wealthy family and was the sole beneficiary of a large house, the estate included a number of outbuildings surrounded by extensive parkland and forest. It was here that he came to live after his release, it was a solitary existence where he hardly dared to venture out. The locals could still remember the events leading up to his arrest and he was blamed for the sad and untimely deaths of his respected parents. He could hardly expect a warm welcome home.

For a long while, there had been no trouble, but then one day a woman by the name of Jennifer Bosworth went missing. At first, this had nothing to do Randolph it was an Aberdeen investigation. Belenos knew that Jennifer was an executive up from London to promote her business to the oilmen in the offices that surrounded Aberdeen. Belenos thought it likely that this was the woman murdered at Spey Bay in Morayshire when Josie MacDonald was there painting. He re-read the notes and checked again the local newspaper reports on-line. Randolph had returned to his old ways, torturing then killing his victims before finally being stopped for good.

Jenna O'Brien had supplied him with some very interesting gossip concerning one of Randolph's victims. Her name was Elizabeth Baines, known as Lizzie by her friends. Jenna had told him that she was a transgender woman. Lizzie had been living and working as a woman and the truth was not out until her body was recovered. She had evidently been going through transition but was awaiting surgery. This in itself would not have interested Belenos, but his next assignment was to investigate transgender issues in society. His editor was keen to have him do this because it was a subject gaining in popularity. His brief was to look into discrimination issues and write a number of articles based on housing, employment, education and healthcare. There were also concerns regarding violence against transgender people.

Lizzie Baines, he realised might be a good starting point, but he was hesitant, he would have to handle this with some sensitivity. There was no end of information on the internet but it would be useful to have a primary resource. His instinct was to visit Lizzie Baines' parents but given the circumstances, he felt that this approach might be too painful and inappropriate at this time. There were others that he knew who would not hesitate to make such an insensitive move, but he did not want to cause these people further anguish. Lizzie had been their only child and to publish their daughter's private life was a step that he was not prepared to take.

He had two more articles to write about serial killers, the final piece he decided would focus on William Randolph, AKA Mr Mac. It would be an opportunity to compare him with other serial killers who liked to subject their victims to torture before murdering them. It was hardly a pleasant theme to dwell upon, but his editor had assured him that their readers were fascinated by these kinds of stories and this helped to keep sales figures healthy.

Assistant Commissioner Brian Calvary was a busy man but he found the time to summons DI Ashton to his office.

"Ashton," Calvary said the moment he appeared at his door. "Take a seat."

The chair known as 'the naughty boy's seat' had been ceremoniously placed in front of Calvary's desk for the occasion. Ashton was convinced that the legs were cut short, allowing the Chief to tower above his victim and glare down like a ferocious headmaster.

"Ashton, I'm sure you must be aware of why you have been asked to come and see me." Calvary began with no preamble and glancing at his watch it was clear that he was pushed for time. "You should have owned up to the fact that Mia Ashton is your daughter."

"I didn't think it necessary at this stage of the investigation."

"Not necessary," Calvary bellowed. "Surely an officer of your rank is aware of protocol."

"Of course sir, but I could see no reason to bring this up. My daughter is not under suspicion here."

Calvary eyed him sternly, his face giving nothing away.

"That may be so, but this is a murder investigation and I will not have a leading investigating officer harbouring a conflict of interest. Just think about what the media would make of it if word got out."

"I assure you..." he did not get the chance to finish.

"To that end Inspector I am taking you off the case. Mallinson and Keable are to remain with us for a while longer so Mallinson will head up the investigation. They will be working closely with DS Woods and other members of your team."

Ashton was expecting to be taken off the case but he did not think that his colleagues from Yorkshire would be staying around. For them to be given his case was unthinkable, they were not even from the Met. He realised that DS Woods was going to have a rough time of it, he was certain that Mallinson had something against female detectives.

"I want you to look into a series of assaults," Calvary said, bringing Ashton's thoughts back into focus. "You will have to delve into the archives because some of the assaults took place a while ago. I want this one cleared up quickly Terry, we are under pressure to clean up the streets. The Government's New Year Initiative to make the city a safer place has of course been handed to us so it's important that we are seen to be doing something about it."

"Yes sir," Ashton replied. There was no point in arguing, besides, the Chief had used his first name so perhaps he had already been forgiven his previous charge.

"Will DC James be available or will he remain working on the murder case?"

"He will stay where he is for the moment, but if you need another experienced officer to assist you then I will re-assign his duties. Until then do what you can, I'm relying on you to get the job done"

In other words, Terry thought, I'm on my own.

Ashton left Calvary's office furious that Mallinson and Keable had usurped him. It rankled him even more to think that they were outsiders. His father had been a proud Lancastrian, so there was no love lost between himself and men from Yorkshire. If only DC James had kept his big mouth shut, he may have been able to lessen the fallout once the Chief discovered about his daughter.

He had to pass the murder room in order to get to his office and it annoyed him further to find Mallinson already occupying the desk that had been set up for him. When he arrived at his office, the first thing Ashton did was to call DS Woods.

DS Isobel Woods was a tall and substantial woman who was known as 'The Matron' by those in uniform who worked beneath her. Her reputation for getting results stood her in good stead with her superiors, but Ashton was convinced that she was heading for a rough time and he did not want her character tarnished.

"Izzy," he smiled as she appeared at his door. "Thanks for coming to see me." He indicated to a chair and she made herself comfortable.

"You are no doubt aware by now that I am no longer in charge of the murder case."

"Yes guv," she replied, unable to maintain eye contact.

"It has nothing to do with you," he told her and she visibly relaxed.

He went on to voice his concerns regarding the men she would be working with and he urged her to cover her back.

"I want you to know that you can come to me with any problems that you might encounter. Don't allow yourself to be victimised by these men."

She nodded, knowing exactly what he meant, but she was also aware that she had not been called into his office to discuss his misgivings about her working relationship with Mallinson and Keable.

"I want you to keep me updated with regular reports," he stared at her before going on. "I want to be kept in the loop regarding this case."

She nodded but remained silent. She knew that Ashton was a reliable officer and one of the better seniors to work with. He had no reason to single her out so his concerns must be genuine.

"Okay guv," she smiled as soon as she realised that he was waiting for confirmation.

When she was gone, Ashton turned his attention to the file that had appeared on his desk, it had been delivered when he was in his meeting with the Chief. It was not a very thick file, it contained just two sheets of paper. On one, he found a list of names, addresses, and mobile telephone numbers. Statements had been condensed to a few lines and were next to useless. The other page contained details of at least thirty victims of assault, all were over twelve months old, the oldest going back almost three years. Beside each name were reference numbers for files that were held somewhere in the archives, these he would have to search out for himself.

Turning back to the first page, he picked up his telephone and began to dial the number at the top of the list.

Chapter
TWENTY SIX

Ben had been planning a Valentine treat for Mia. Raymond Duval was hosting a romantic evening at his restaurant where diners could enjoy a specially prepared meal and sample wines from his extensive cellar, but Mia was performing that evening. Not to be outdone he considered reserving a table at one of the restaurants at the Barbican. He knew that something special was on offer, a Valentine meal in conjunction with her 'Romantic Solo' concert, but again he was disappointed.

"It would be impossible for me to get away," she told him. "It's a wonderful idea but I couldn't possibly perform on a full stomach especially if wine is involved."

The only thing he could do to make up for missing the Valentine offers was to arrange an alternative romantic evening of their own.

Mia's first impression of Suzie Chahal was how energetic she was. At barely five feet tall, Suzie was a mini powerhouse. Her long dark hair appeared almost blue under the lights and her huge almond shaped eyes sparkled with mirth as she smiled. As stunning as a model, Suzie exuded charm and dressed casually in faded jeans and a knitted jumper, she made Mia feel dowdy.

"Mia," she squealed with excitement as she rushed to meet her. "Do you mind if I call you Mia?" Her brilliant smile left Mia in no doubt of her sincerity, her warm Bolton accent mixed with deep-rooted Asian vowels worked perfectly.

"Yes of course. You must be Suzie."

They shook hands before Suzie said.

"Let me introduce you to Simon," she giggled dizzily. "I've only just met him but he's my best friend already."

Mia could believe that. Nothing that she had read about Suzie Chahal could prepare her for the genuine warmth of her character. She had read up on Simon too and presumed they had done the same.

"Sorry about this place," Simon said as he stepped forward to meet her. "It's the best I could do I'm afraid."

Mia looked around at the hall they had hired, it was looking a little tired. Simon was responsible for finding a place for them to rehearse but Mia realised that she should have been the one to undertake this job. It was hardly fair to leave it to him he had no local knowledge.

"The piano is not brilliant," he said, "but at least it's in tune."

It was an upright model and looked as ancient as the hall itself.

"I remember we had one just like that at school." Mia laughed, but Simon was not amused.

"I'm sure it will be okay," Suzie shot him a glance before treating him to one of her smiles.

"I'm so pleased to be performing with you." She enthused as Mia carefully removed her cello from its case.

"It's so exciting to be playing at the Barbican," she continued. "I've never worked anywhere as grand as that before."

"It's a fantastic opportunity," Mia agreed, "a good one to have on your CV."

She unscrewed the top from her water bottle and took a mouthful before settling down with her cello. Simon was already running his fingers over the piano keys softly playing a tune of his own. He was writing a series of classical pieces for a youth orchestra with which he was closely involved.

Mia tuned her cello as Suzie checked her viola then they began.

Jenna O'Brien was talking to Emilia about her wedding plans and from the little office Ben could hear every word. He thought it strange that Jenna never expressed excitement about her wedding day, all the other women who came into the shop were overflowing with anticipation and excitement.

"So, this is your chosen colour scheme," his sister said and he could imagine her showing Jenna a range of styles from a colour diagram.

"What about your bridesmaids?"

"Oh, I won't be having any bridesmaids, or at least I don't think I will."

Emilia frowned and looked at Jenna who appeared to be increasingly more uncomfortable. She realised that something was wrong.

"What will the groom and best man be wearing?" she asked in an attempt to lighten the mood. At first, Jenna did not reply, so Emilia continued. "Is it a formal wedding, top hat, and tails?"

"Oh," Jenna blinked. "I suppose it will be a traditional wedding, but I don't think formal, not in that sense."

"Will it be a big affair?"

"Oh yes, you can be sure of that."

Jenna stared at Emilia and her confidence wavered, her cool exterior slipped, revealing a frightened and vulnerable young woman. She hesitated before making up her mind and when she began to speak, Emilia was not prepared for what she had to say.

"My father has it all arranged, I'm simply required to turn up looking every bit the blushing bride."

"I don't understand." Emilia replied, her eyebrows disappearing under the fringe of her strawberry blond hair.

"Well, quite simply it's an arranged marriage." Jenna said as the blood drained from her face leaving her pale. "I have been promised to one of his business associates."

"Wow," Emilia groaned. She was shocked at this sudden revelation and rallying her emotions, she asked. "Are you happy with this arrangement?"

"What do you think?" Suddenly the hard exterior that Emilia associated with Jenna returned.

"Oh dear," was all Emilia could think of saying.

It was obvious that Jenna needed someone to talk to and Emilia realised that she was going to have to provide that role.

"Why did you agree to marry this man?"

"I didn't, but I have no choice in the matter."

Emilia was amazed that a woman like Jenna could be caught up in a situation like this.

"Surely your father has no right to expect you to go through with an arranged marriage."

"You don't know my father," Jenna sneered. "It's not as if I don't know this man, our families have been friends for years. I'm pretty certain that an agreement was made years ago and now it's time to cash in on the deal, so to speak."

"Where does this man come from, is he British?"

"He has lived in this country for most of his life, but his family are from Saudi Arabia. I'm expected to go with him to his country after we are married, learn how to be a dutiful wife."

Emilia was shocked and sickened. She could hardly imagine Jenna living the life of a married woman in Saudi Arabia. The cultural differences were vast, she would never survive living under Saudi rules.

"This will of course mean a considerable financial boost to my father's business." Jenna continued. "Once our families are united in marriage it will open up opportunities for him in the Middle East."

"You cannot be serious." Emilia exclaimed. "This is no basis for a happy marriage. What if you were to refuse?"

Jenna studied her in silence. She looked totally defeated and struggled to maintain a dignified appearance.

"If I do not go through with it my father will cut me off completely. He will disinherit me. The shame that it will bring down on my family will be devastating."

"Don't you realise that this is emotional blackmail, it's against the law."

"That may be so, but my father is a powerful man. Believe me, he would carry out his threats, and I would be ruined."

"Is it worth it? Surely your happiness is more important than wealth."

"It's not just about the money. My fiancé's family would be slighted, so it's not only my father's business that would suffer."

"What do you mean?" Emilia asked reaching for Jenna's hand.

"If I don't go through with this then I'm fearful for my life. I would almost certainly be made to regret my decision."

Ben could hear everything and was as shocked as his sister, he could not understand how such a thing could be allowed to happen.

When Jenna left, Emilia appeared at the office door looking strained.

"I guess you heard all that."

Ben nodded but made no comment. He watched as his sister fought with her emotions. She was saddened for Jenna but also angered and confused at the absurdity of the situation.

"We have to do something to help Jenna." She said at last.

"What can we do? If she doesn't want to go through with this then it's up to her to do something about it."

"You heard what she said. She is terrified that they will kill her. It's bad enough being disinherited by your family, but living under the threat of death..."

"Then surely this is a matter for the authorities." Ben replied.

"We should look into the legality of an arrangement like this, see if there is some way of helping her."

"If she is as scared as she makes out, then surely it would be dangerous to support her. These people sound murderous, we don't want them targeting us, we really shouldn't get involved"

Emilia thought for a moment before shuddering. "We can't sit back and do nothing, I'm certain she came to me for help."

Chapter
TWENTY SEVEN

DI Ashton made a discovery that he did not expect. The information stored in the archive linked six names on his list with an organisation called TG International. At first, he believed this to be a transport company but on closer inspection, he found that TG stood for Transgender. A quick look on the internet told him that TG International was a clinic based in the dockland area of east London.

Stepping out of his car Ashton looked up at a converted Victorian warehouse and checked his notebook, confirming this to be the address he made his way towards the entrance. There were no signs advertising the clinic, but on the wall, beside the door, he found a collection of brass plaques displaying names of the businesses that shared the building. TG International was on the first floor so ringing the bell he stood back and waited. A metallic voice sounded before the lock on the door clicked given him access.

"Detective Inspector Ashton I presume?" An educated voice greeted him from the top of the stairs. "I'm Robert Nixon."

"Thank you for agreeing to see me Mr Nixon," Ashton said grasping the man by his hand. "Terry Ashton."

"Do you mind showing me some form of identification please Inspector?"

"Of course," Ashton replied and reaching into his pocket, drew out his wallet.

Once Nixon was satisfied, he led him into his office.

"Sorry about that Inspector, one can never be too careful these days,"

Nixon apologised, his face flushed pink.

"Don't be, I should have had my Warrant Card ready for you to examine. My fault entirely."

"Can I offer you a drink, tea, coffee? It's from a machine I'm afraid."

"No thank you," Ashton shook his head. "Not long had my lunch."

Unclipping a pen from his notebook, he turned to a clean page before asking his first question.

"What is it that you do here Mr Nixon?"

"We offer social and emotional support to transgender men and women, anyone in fact who identifies as trans and of course their families." He pushed a glossy leaflet across his desk.

Ashton produced a folded piece of paper and passing it to Nixon asked.

"Do you know any of the women on this list?"

Nixon scrutinised the names carefully before replying.

"Yes Inspector, these are women who are or have been associated with TG International."

"They are all transgender women?"

"Yes Inspector," Nixon nodded, "all transgender women."

"Are you aware that these women have been the victim of an assault within the last twelve months?"

"Sadly I am Inspector," he looked at Ashton before going on. "Some of these women have received counselling as a result."

Ashton nodded. "I have contact details for everyone on that list, but I want to be clear about what I'm dealing with before I speak to them."

Nixon stared at him for several seconds before deciding how to proceed.

"These are normal people Inspector; treat them as you would any other woman."

"Don't get me wrong Mr Nixon, I harbour no prejudices, but I've never come across a transgender person before."

"How can you be sure Inspector?"

Ashton considered his remark and was about to make a comment but thought better of it.

"The people who visit this centre are not drag queens, men simply wearing a dress or women trying to be butch. Mostly you wouldn't be aware of their situation. Part of what we do here is to provide education, necessary learning so our clients can function and get on with their lives. From a young age, one learns all the habits and tricks that one needs in preparation for the real world. Imagine spending your childhood with the knowledge that you are living in the wrong body. It's easy to hide from the truth when you are young, but as puberty sets in, nature cruelly reminds you of what you are about to become. Each time you look at yourself in the mirror, you see the wrong image staring back at you, it's not how you feel inside and you know that it's all wrong, but there is very little you can do about it. In some cases, social demands prohibit your true self from emerging. It can be a terrible thing Inspector that is why we are here, it's what we do, we help people to cope with changes, we encourage and support them with their decisions."

"I see," Ashton said wondering if Nixon was speaking from personal experience. He studied him closely looking for the signs.

"It's a very complex process Inspector, but we offer a network of support to everyone who comes to us."

"You keep records of your client's treatment?"

"We do," Nixon replied carefully. "You are aware of course that our records are confidential, in fact we are covered by the Data Protection Act."

"Yes, I understand that, it's not personal information that I'm after at this stage of my investigation." He looked up and smiled at Nixon before going on. "I simply need to know more about the assault victims and their everyday lives."

"A generic report?"

"Yes," Ashton agreed.

"You are aware Inspector that there is a lot of information on the internet about transgender people."

"I understand there is, but you are missing the point. I want to know why the names on that list led me here."

Nixon sighed noisily and looked sad.

"Inspector, assaults on transgender people are unfortunately a fact of life driven by ignorance or misunderstanding. I would imagine that these attacks occurred in this area simply because this is where we are situated."

"Could they have been carried out by someone from this centre?"

Nixon was visibly shocked by this question.

"I find that very hard to believe Inspector. I suppose in theory it could be possible."

"Do you have transgender men here as well as transgender women?"

"Of course."

"Does everyone get on?"

"As well as in any other community. We have a cross section of society who are mostly supportive of each other. As I said before there is nothing unusual about us."

Again, Ashton was tempted to say something but stopped himself just in time.

"Are your members in equal numbers, men to women ratio I mean?"

"I would say that we are roughly 60% female."

"Okay," Ashton nodded as he scribbled in his notebook.

"How many do you total in number?"

Nixon paused as he made a mental calculation, then counting on his fingers he said. "About seventy including staff."

"What about age range?"

"Our clients are all adults, we have no one under the age of eighteen. The age range varies from late teens to the over sixty."

Ashton was surprised and couldn't help saying. "As old as that?"

"Age is simply a number Inspector."

"Indeed it is. Now, you said earlier that you employ counsellors."

"Yes, we have three qualified counsellors. All of our staff are carefully vetted, their credentials checked thoroughly before being offered the opportunity to work here."

"Have any members of staff left within the last twelve months?"

"No Inspector and in answer to your next question we have not taken on any additional staff in that time period or had visiting experts."

"Thank you Mr Nixon," Ashton said scribbling as fast as he could.

"What other staff do you employ apart from counsellors?"

"Three therapists, a life coach and an occupational therapist. We use art as a form of expressive therapy, the creative process is said to improve a person's mental and emotional being."

"So eight staff in total?" Ashton asked, showing no interest in the psychological benefits of art.

"Nine if you include me."

"Full time?"

"No they are all part time except for me."

"Could I have a list of their names? I would also like a complete list of your clients, everyone who visits this centre regularly including those who have stopped coming within the last twelve months."

"Okay Inspector," he nodded. "If you would be kind enough to leave your e-mail address, I will send you a file. It may take me a while to gather that information together but you must understand, I cannot include details of our client's personal notes."

"Of course not Mr Nixon. Your help is much appreciated, it's important that we catch those who are guilty of carrying out these attacks. They have to be stopped."

"Amen to that." Nixon replied.

Chapter
TWENTY EIGHT

It was the morning of St Valentine's Day and her doorbell had rung twice already. The first time was the postman with a card that was impossibly too large to go through the letterbox flap in her door, then a short while later a florist delivered a stunningly beautiful bouquet of flowers. Both gifts had been sent anonymously but she knew they were from Ben. This time when the bell rang Mia opened the door to her driver.

"Miss Ashton, good morning to you," he said and like a proud father appraising his daughter he beamed. "Please, allow me to carry your bags."

Mia had packed a small bag containing a change of clothes. The dress she was going to wear that evening was on a hanger in a full-length protective suit cover. She handed both items to him before turning to pick up her cello case. Lifting it carefully over the step, she closed the door firmly behind her and checked that it was locked before walking to the car. It was a little brighter today and turning her face towards the sky, she smiled. It was as if St Valentine himself had charmed the snow clouds away. Breaking with her rule, Mia had decided not to stay at a luxury hotel after the concert, she was sure that Ben would have something arranged.

"Allow me," the driver appeared at her side and held the door open.

"Don't want the door closing on me again," Mia looked at him before going on. "My hip has only just recovered from before."

He stared at her and frowned and she could see that he was confused.

"The door," she explained, "it closed on me as I got out of the car last time."

"You are mistaken Miss," he replied shaking his head. "It wasn't the door that caused your injury."

"Oh." It was Mia's turn to look confused.

"No Miss, don't you remember?" Closing the door carefully he walked around the car and climbed into the driving seat. "You slipped on the footpath and lost your footing before careering into the central heating outlet on the wall over there."

She looked to where he was pointing and frowned. On the wall beside the flower border was a small metal outlet, she had not noticed it before.

"I fell against that?"

"I'm afraid so Miss."

From his amused expression, it was obvious that he believed she had had too much to drink. It was Christmas Eve after all.

"Nasty accident, I'm surprised you don't remember."

Mia sat back in the seat and puzzled over what he had just said. That would explain the mud stains on her shoes and hem of her dress. The vicious looking metal could easily have ripped her dress and cut her hip, but she had no memory of that happening.

Suzie Chahal and Simon Coleman were already at the Barbican when Mia arrived. Driven by the excitement of performing at such an amazing venue they were there early watching as the engineers prepared the stage and soaking up as much of the atmosphere as possible. The moment the concert piano was wheeled into position Simon checked it over. It was an impressive instrument, its deep black woodwork gleaming under the harsh stage lights. He stood and marvelled, wondering who had been lucky enough to have played it before him.

"This is fabulous," Suzie beamed. "The stage is enormous."

Cables and tools littered the floor and clearly, it would be some time before they could rehearse.

Mia appeared and as she made her way across the stage, a path amongst the cables and tools opened up magically before her.

"Miss Ashton."

She stopped at the sound of her name and was surprised to see Jim Peters coming towards her.

"Jim, fancy seeing you here."

"My friend got me in for your concert," he explained. "I'm working with the sound crew so I'll be sorting you out later," he smiled as he glanced around at the chaos.

"I'm sure they know what they are doing." She laughed.

"General repairs to the lighting or so I understand," he told her. "They want to make sure you look your best tonight."

"Have you met the others?" she asked turning towards them. "Suzie and Simon are performing with me tonight."

"Hello," Suzie chimed as she danced her way towards them. "Are you doing my sound checks too?"

"No," Jim shook his head as he scrutinised her. "One of the other guys will be looking after you, but I'll be setting everything up."

"I can't wait to get started," she squealed with excitement.

Simon stood back and watched as Mia and Suzie talked to Jim. He had not met the sound engineer before, but there was something strange about him. Jim Peters was slight of build and barely as tall as Mia. His fresh faced features and small hands made him appear effeminate. He seemed friendly enough but Simon could not bring himself to join in with their conversation.

It was well past midday before they could get on stage and begin their technical set-up. Jim and another sound engineer fussed around them as they took their places. Positions had been marked out on the stage floor and it was here that microphones and stands were being placed. Simon settled at the piano and ran his fingers lightly over the keys and in the control room at the back of the auditorium a sound engineer made adjustments to the equipment.

Mia and Suzie tuned their instruments whilst playing a series of short bursts. Volume indicators flashed and sound levels were calculated, this allowed speakers around the stage to be harmonised and balanced.

Mia was happy with the musical arrangements. They had gone through all of the pieces earlier, but they had not yet practiced with the orchestra who were providing the background music. There was no opportunity to get to know the musicians and barely time to rehearse together so it would be the responsibility of the conductor to ensure that everything ran smoothly.

When they were happy with their preparations, they stopped for refreshments. It was now late in the afternoon and time for Mia to have her hair and make-up done.

The audience began to arrive, the auditorium buzzing with the excitement and anticipation of a romantic evening. Ben took his seat, he was alone, his sister was elsewhere, out with an admirer. She had been coy with the details earlier, choosing to remain secretive about her arrangements. He considered the fact that he might know the fellow and that was why she wanted him to remain anonymous. A tap on his shoulder brought him out of his reverie and with an apologetic nod, he got to his feet and allowed a couple to squeeze past and find their seat. Once they were settled he sat down again, his arm just inches from the woman beside him. She was peering at her programme, reading about Mia and he was tempted to say that the star of the show was his girlfriend, but he kept his thoughts to himself. It was strange to think of Mia that way but it filled him with warmth. He could hardly believe his luck, it was not so long ago that they were strangers and if it had not been for his sister, he would probably never have met her. Emilia always spun in the right circles, she knew people who could make things happen, it had always been that way. She had the ability to draw people into her circle. Ben looked up at the stage as movement caught his eye. Someone was dodging amongst the ranks of chairs arranged for the orchestra and he watched as one of the seats was replaced, the offending item of furniture relegated to the shadows. He had been to the Barbican once before, but it was not quite how he remembered it. The stage seemed much wider this time, but it must be an optical illusion. Mia's cello was on its stand beside the piano with the orchestra arranged around them and a small platform had been set up for the conductor. It resembled a tiny dais complete with chrome tubular handrails enclosing three sides. Ben smiled as he took in these small details. This was his way of entertaining himself, he loved to observe people and sometimes he even listened in on conversations. It was surprising what could be learnt by eavesdropping, but this evening there were so many people talking that most of their words remained indecipherable. It struck him then that this was probably Mia's largest concert so far. She had told him that on rare occasions, she had been a guest cellist, invited to play with a large orchestra, but tonight it was all for her. She was a rising star in the world of classical music and it was her popularity alone that had drawn these people here tonight. Of course, it was true that a carefully coordinated marketing plan had helped, the occasion and the venue making for a successful outcome. He glanced around him, almost every seat was occupied, row upon row of people in rising tiers all eagerly awaiting 'Romantic Solos' the aptly named Valentine concert to begin.

The orchestra arrived sending a sigh of expectation around the auditorium. Applause rippled politely, rising in volume, as Mia appeared leading Suzie and Simon onto the stage. Mia looked stunning and Ben felt his heart quicken. She had no idea where he was sitting but he was certain that she had spotted him. She looked in his direction and smiled but he realised that the stage lights were a barrier between her and the sea of eager faces.

It did not take them long to settle and then the music began. The first tune, a haunting rendition of a popular song set the scene, its magic weaving a spell over the entire audience. Ben was thrilled as he watched Mia play, she seemed to drift away to another world, a place of her own making where nothing else mattered but the music. Her facial expressions and body language captured the sentiment of each melody and there was hardly a dry eye in the house.

When the concert ended the applause was rapturous, an explosion of sound that filled the entire space. The couple beside him were on their feet, eagerly displaying their appreciation along with the rest of the audience and Ben was so happy for Mia and her colleagues. He wondered if Belenos Falzone was present. His review would no doubt be triumphant, it could be nothing less going on the mood of the audience.

Mallinson and Keable were doing their best to blend in. Pressed up against the wall as a tide of people made their way slowly along the corridor they observed everyone who passed. They were dressed smartly for the occasion. Keable was sporting a bow tie, a little out of character Mallinson thought, but then he had never seen his colleague dressed for anything else but work.

A gathering of musicians was taking place in a private function room at the end of the corridor, several trays of canapés and expensive sparkling wine had gone in that direction earlier. The crowd thinned allowing the detectives to make their way towards the closed door where they could hear the muffled sounds of a speech in progress. Admission was by invitation only, but several police officers had been smuggled in disguised as serving staff, the rest of the party was made up mostly of the performing musicians.

Mallinson had his people covering all the exits, he was leaving nothing to chance. If a crime pattern was to be established then he was under no illusions, Suzie Chahal was the target. Women police officers were stationed in the female toilets and changing areas, their orders not to let the musician out of their sight.

"I'm still on a high," Suzie squealed with delight. "That was so fantastic."

"We did exceedingly well." Mia replied their heads together as they shared the moment.

"I'm more than happy with that." Simon appeared and handed them both a glass of wine.

The conductor, a tall lean fellow, came over to congratulate them then a stream of musicians followed in his wake. The party was a jolly affair, full of warmth and laughter but it was not long before it began to break up. Mia guessed that spouses and partners would be waiting, it was Valentine's Day after all.

She thought of Ben and wondered where he was. Unfortunately, he had not been invited back stage but he would not be far away. She was looking forward to meeting up with him soon.

"Are you going on somewhere?" Mia asked Suzie but it was Simon who answered.

"No," he shook his head. "We have an early start in the morning so must get back to our hotel."

Mia realised from Suzie's expression that she would have liked to go on to a nightclub. They were not a couple, she was sure of that, but Simon was protective of Suzie. He seemed reluctant to let her out of his sight even for a moment.

The room began to empty as people said their goodbyes. Wine glasses were abandoned on tables by the exit and as Mia watched, she was certain that she recognised a woman standing by the door. She reminded her of one of her father's colleagues and Mia frowned. She began to see other faces that she knew and suddenly the penny dropped. The police must be of the same opinion as Emilia and Ben, she thought. They were obviously taking no chances and she wondered why her father had said nothing.

"You take care going back to your hotel," Mia told Suzie. "Do you have a taxi arranged?"

"Yes," Suzie nodded. "Your agent Ms Wicks kindly organised a car for us."

"Did she indeed?" Mia raised her eyebrows. Alicia was either mellowing or there was some financial incentive that influenced her benevolence.

"Don't worry," Simon whispered. "I'll see her safely to her room. No harm will come of her tonight."

Mia made eye contact with him and an unspoken understanding passed between them.

"Right," she said breaking the spell. "Time to go I think."

They hugged and promised to remain in touch hoping to perform together again in the future.

Mallinson watched as Mia left the room. His earpiece chirped as one of his colleagues announced that the other musicians were on the move. He followed Mia along the corridor as far as the main entrance where a young man that he knew to be Benjamin Sykes was waiting.

A shadow stirred just outside the main doors and he stiffened, a figure was watching from the cover of darkness. Mallinson was about to alert Keable, but then he realised that the covert observer was DI Ashton. He wondered if Ashton was here in an official capacity or that of a concerned parent. He thought perhaps both, he made no attempt to find out.

"Miss Ashton has left the building." He whispered into his radio.

An unmarked car would follow her private hire car, the same arrangement had been made for the taxi conveying Suzie Chahal and Simon Coleman back to their hotel. He sighed with relief, all the young musicians were safely away. It seemed that the pattern of murder had been broken.

Chapter
TWENTY NINE

The following day DI Ashton was sitting at his desk in his office. Along the corridor, the murder room was silent and calm. Turning his attention to his computer, he was surprised to find a message waiting for him. It was an e-mail from TG International and opening it, he discovered an attached file. Nixon had sent him the information that he had requested, names sorted into two columns, one for staff and the other for clients. The list of staff names included job descriptions and details of the services they provided. A colour coding had been used to separate the names of the clients; female names in pink and blue for the men. Ashton studied the list and could not help wondering what drove people to believe they had been born the wrong gender. What trials had they faced during their lives? He had never interviewed a transgender person before. Whatever his views he would have to be tactful.

The pink names were in the majority and glancing down the list he found the six from his original case notes, this confirmed that these women were associated with TG International. Nixon had told him as much but now he had proof. He hit the print button and as the printer began to work, he leaned back in his chair and pulled the daily paper from his desktop. It was already open at the review page and reading it again, he grinned. Mia's concert had been very well received and all the reviews were in agreement. Her performance had been perfect and there was a short paragraph praising Suzie Chahal for her violin solo. Simon Coleman was also mentioned, he was a rising star in his own right, a brilliant pianist, but it was praise for his daughter that pleased him most.

Not many of his colleagues knew that Mia was his daughter, but now that was about to change. With the police presence at the concert word would soon be out. The printer stopped churning out paper and there was a few seconds of silence before a sudden commotion came from the murder room.

Dr Patricia Fleming was already at the King Edward Hotel when Mallinson and Keable arrived. They found her in a first floor corridor pulling on a pair of white disposable overalls, she was about to enter a taped off area. They had not yet met so after a brief introduction she handed them both a sealed polythene pack before ducking under the tape and disappearing into a room. Once they were suited up and had pulled on paper overshoes the detectives followed.

The room was impressively huge, even the queen-sized bed seemed lost in its stylish surroundings. A door leading off to one side opened into an en-suite bathroom where there was an elegant Victorian bath and a double sized shower cubicle.

The victim was lying on the bed, her arms and legs splayed out stiffly. She was naked, her face and breasts had been slashed.

"Suzie Chahal." Keable whispered in disbelief. "How could this have happened?"

One of Dr Fleming's team was taking photographs and as he moved around the room, the flash from his camera revealed the full horror of the scene. Mallinson silently took it all in imagining the final moments of Suzie's life. A towelling robe lay crumpled on the floor beside the bed.

"She had just stepped out of the bathroom," Dr Fleming said as she appeared at his side. "She had used the shower. Look at her hair, she didn't have the opportunity to brush it out and dry it before the killer struck."

"So, she must have been wearing the dressing gown when she answered the door."

"It seems so," she looked up at him. "Her clothes are either hanging up or folded neatly away in the drawers."

"She must have known whoever it was at the door," Keable reasoned. "Surely she wouldn't have opened it to a stranger dressed only in a robe."

"It could have been room service," Dr Fleming nodded towards a trolley parked by the door. It contained an ice bucket complete with champagne and a vase of blood red roses.

"The bottle hasn't been opened and the bucket is full of water." Keable told them as he went to investigate. "Looks like it's been here all night."

"Is there a card with the flowers?" Mallinson asked.

"No," Keable shook his head. "There's no wrapping either." He checked the waste paper bin beside the dressing table.

"We need to know who delivered that trolley to this room. Find out who was on duty last night." Mallinson paused and touched the side of his head with his fingertips.

"Find out where those flowers came from, also the champagne. I want to know if it's from the hotel cellar or was it delivered with the flowers."

Dr Fleming moved away from him. The photographer had finished taking his pictures and now it was time for her to make her initial assessment. Calmly she circled the bed observing the scene from every angle before touching the body.

"Death took place around six to eight hours ago," she began as if talking to herself then pausing she moved in closer. "There is a wound to the side of her head and looking at the extent of the mutilation and the lack of blood on the duvet, I would say that the knife attack took place post mortem."

"The same as Alison Morley and Victoria Stevens," Mallinson remarked. "We must be looking at the same killer."

"I'll be able to tell you more once I've carried out the post mortem."

"What's your gut feeling, are we looking at the work of our killer, or is this a copy cat?"

Dr Fleming straightened up and frowned as she studied him from across the room. With an almost imperceptible nod of her head, she made up her mind and began to tell him what she could see.

"The killer is right handed," she began then after a short pause she went on. "The cuts are not deep, no main arteries have been severed, they appear to have been delivered using minimal force."

Turning Suzie onto her side she checked her back for injuries before concentrating on the head wound.

"Not a huge force was used here either, just sufficient to deliver a killer blow."

"So, the same MO, the same killer."

There was another pause before Dr Fleming nodded her head in agreement.

"I would say so, yes."

"What do you think caused the head wound, what was used as a weapon?"

"From the severity of the injury something heavy and blunt," she examined the wound more closely. "There is a ridge with a line of

139

indentations around the skull fracture." Standing up she glanced towards the bottle resting in the ice bucket. Mallinson could see where she was looking.

"We'll get SOCO to check that out," he mumbled. He avoided touching it himself, not wanting to contaminate anything that might be waiting for them to discover.

Scene of Crime Officers were standing by to gather forensic evidence from the room and once the body had been removed they would begin their painstaking job. It might be days before Mallinson got their report, but in the meantime, he was responsible for getting this murder investigation underway. He would also have to explain to the Chief why they had failed to protect this young woman. The police presence at the concert the previous evening looked to have been a complete waste of time and he realised that he would also be criticised for running up an expensive overtime bill.

Mia woke to the sound of deep rhythmic breathing. Ben was lying beside her and as she turned her head towards him, she smiled. Creaking from the central heating pipes behind the bed was the only other sound in the room.

She felt marvellous, memories of their lovemaking had made for sweet dreams, the pleasure lasting all night long. Stretching her arms above her head, she arched her back and groaned silently before looking around the room. It was the first time that she had been to his maisonette and had not yet had an opportunity to explore. The previous evening the driver had dropped them at her flat where she returned her cello to her music room then they had set off for Ben's place. Ben had prepared a surprise picnic, a romantic gesture laid out on a tartan blanket across the living room floor. The furniture was pushed back against the walls and candles were placed on every surface, when lit, the room had filled with a spicy scent that she did not recognise. He had presented her with a variety of snacks from around the world, Indian, Thai, Italian and French dishes. There was even a wicker basket full of miniature bottles of wine, a different taste for each dish. A dozen red roses accompanied a verse, which he had written himself, lyrics confirming his love for her. It was an evening that she would never forget.

All these thoughts ran through her head as she lay there beside the man she loved. She did not want the moment to end but from somewhere in the next room she could hear the sound of her mobile phone ringing.

Chapter
THIRTY

Belenos Falzone was putting the finishing touches to his final article about serial killers when his telephone began to ring.

"Hello," he answered vaguely, gripping the receiver between his shoulder and chin.

"Belenos old chum, how goes it in the world of freelance?"

"Freddie," he replied recognising a voice from his past. "How long has it been?"

"Too long."

"So what are you up to mate?"

"I've finally gone up in the world. I now work from the dizzy height of an office above the newsroom floor."

"Well good for you, it's what you have always wanted." Belenos couldn't remember the name of the organisation that Freddie worked for but he knew it was a huge multi-media concern.

"Listen Belenos, I have stumbled across something that you might be interested in, it's red hot."

"Okay, let me grab a pen."

"It's not yet been made public but will soon be all over the TV news channels. As you are currently working on the subject of serial killers I thought I would give you a heads up."

Belenos pulled a clean piece of paper towards him and waited for his friend to begin.

"There has been another murder in what the police in Yorkshire are calling the 'Classical Killings'. Have you heard of a violinist called Suzie Chahal?"

"Yes of course," Belenos replied. "She performed last night here at the Barbican with Mia Ashton. The concert was brilliant."

"Were you there?"

"No, not personally but I managed to catch some of it on a local classical radio station."

"Well, I'm afraid to have to tell you that Suzie was found dead in her hotel room this morning."

Belenos was stunned and unable to respond to the sudden news. His first thoughts were of Mia.

"Belenos, are you still there?"

"Yes, sorry Freddie, it's a bit of a shock. Are you sure of your facts, how do you know about this?"

"We have our methods."

"Reliable methods?"

"I assure you there can be no doubt. I'm afraid Suzie Chahal has suffered the same fate as Alison Morley and Victoria Stevens."

"So there is a serial killer on the loose."

"Yes I'm afraid there is. How well do you know Mia Ashton?"

"Well enough, we spin in similar circles and have become good friends."

"Might I suggest that you keep a very close eye on her?"

"Is that you talking as a friend or do you know something that the authorities don't?"

"I've not heard anything to suggest that her life is in immediate danger, but she does seem to be in the thick of things. If I were a young and beautiful musician, the last person I would want to be associated with at present is Mia Ashton."

Belenos grunted but remained silent. He knew that what Freddie was saying was true and he wondered what Mia's agent Alicia Wicks would have to say about it.

"You are working on articles about serial killers, now is your chance to perhaps get up close to a real one."

They chatted for a little while longer before Belenos ended the call then he sat staring at his notes.

Mia was huddled on the sofa covered in the tartan blanket they had used for their picnic, her legs folded beneath her, she was sobbing silently. Her mobile phone was on the floor where it had fallen and she stared at it miserably wishing that it would never ring again.

The call had been from him again, the cold and taunting voice describing in minute detail what he had done to Suzie Chahal. His hate for her and his victims was clear and she gasped violently as another wave of grief washed over her.

"Mia," Ben said as he appeared at the door. "Whatever is the matter?"

Sitting down beside her, he pulled her gently towards him and could feel her body shudder as she cried. He was desperate to know why she was so upset, but all he could do was wait patiently. Wiping away her tears with his fingertips, he whispered words of comfort in her ear and after a while, she began to relax. Her eyes were red and her face pale as she peered up at him then holding nothing back she told him about the telephone calls describing as best she could the anonymous voice that hated her so much. She went on to tell him about her forgetfulness, embarrassed at mentioning the times she had found herself in bed naked, her clothes scattered around her living room and having no memory of how it happened.

"It's completely out of character," she told him as more tears stung her eyes. "It's just not what I do."

She showed him the fading scar on her hip and repeated the story her driver had told her, then she spoke of the time she had woken with stiff fingers, the back of her hand painful and bruised.

"I thought that somehow I might have something to do with these terrible murders."

"That's a crazy idea," he whispered softly.

She smiled weakly at him before resting her head against his shoulder.

He had not yet taken in what she said about Suzie Chahal. She must be mistaken, he thought.

"It was horrible talking to those policemen," she shuddered. "They almost accused me of killing Alison Morley."

"I'm sure they were just doing their job. Have you spoken to your father about any of this?"

"No," she replied, sounding like a frightened child. "I didn't want to worry him."

"I think it's time for you to come clean. You must bring this to his attention, the police need to know about what is happening. Either these telephone calls are from a crank or they really could be linked with the murders."

Suddenly her mobile phone began to ring again. She was terrified at the prospect of answering it and staring wide eyed at Ben she watched as he leaned down to pick it up.

"It's Belenos Falzone," he told her as he checked the screen.

"Will you answer it," she pleaded.

Ben hesitated as the phone rang and vibrated in his hand then he pushed the button and held it up to his ear.

DI Ashton was stunned at the news, everything possible had been done to keep Suzie Chahal safe. His colleagues were at the Barbican the previous evening and cars had been arranged to escort both Suzie and Mia home. He could imagine what Mallinson and Keable would be thinking now. The Chief won't be pleased either especially after all the effort put in by everyone.

He wondered how Mia was this morning and reaching for his phone, he began to dial her number but then he stopped himself. She would be safe at home, probably enjoying a leisurely breakfast and reading her reviews in the morning papers. She would not yet be aware of the terrible news so there was little point in disturbing her.

Chapter
THIRTY ONE

Mallinson was speaking with the hotel manager whose office was situated just behind the reception area.

"I'm afraid that I have no idea who delivered the trolley to Miss Chahal's room." While affable and willing, he was unable to add much more. "There is no record of her ordering room service." He shook his head gravely and studied the computer printout as if it might hold the answer.

"Could she have telephoned down with her order?"

"Yes, reception would have taken the call. Alternatively she could have spoken to someone when she returned to the hotel before retiring to her room, but there is no record of her doing either of those things."

He passed Mallinson the printout containing details of every room service request made in the last twelve hours.

"Would it be on here if Miss Chahal had used her mobile phone instead of the telephone in her room?"

"Indeed it would. Everything is outlined there on that list."

Mallinson nodded. Suzie's mobile phone would be checked for calls and texts.

"Could it have been ordered earlier during the day, when she checked in perhaps?"

The manager nodded and turning to his computer opened another file labelled Room 211.

"As you can see, room service was never ordered by Miss Chahal. If she had, it would be registered here."

Mallinson sighed and ran his fingertips along the edge of the document that he was holding then he decided on another question.

"What about CCTV?"

"We have cameras in the lifts and at each end of the corridors. We also have several covering reception, the bar and dining areas including all the main function rooms."

"None in any of the rooms?" Mallinson knew the answer but he had to ask the question.

"Goodness me no, that would contravene every privacy law in the land."

Mallinson nodded again.

"I need to see all the CCTV footage from last night. Could that be arranged?"

"Of course, it's a digital system so can be viewed through our computers."

"So we can make a copy?"

"Yes of course or I can e-mail you the files."

"Excellent. Could my colleagues and I have access to the system immediately?"

"Yes, I will have a conference room put at your disposal. Once we have set up the equipment I can show you how to access the system."

Half an hour later Mallinson, Keable and DC James were in a room used for corporate meetings. They were sitting at a table set up for a group of twelve, writing pads and pens at each position along with a tumbler and a small bottle of spring water.

A computer was hooked up to an overhead projector and once the programme was initiated, a picture appeared on a Smart Board fixed to a wall. The picture split into a number of individual screens, one for each camera. The detectives would have a multiple view where they could see every camera at once. At first, the picture quality was poor, but improved with further adjustments.

Mallinson insisted that they begin by watching footage from earlier in the evening. This was tedious work but essential to see everyone coming and going. They watched as staff appeared regularly and took note of their faces so they could be identified later. They observed those who seemed suspicious or looked as if they had no business being there. Most of the action took place in the reception and bar areas. The hotel ran an open restaurant so there were people coming and going all of the time, many of the guests not staying the night. The restaurant and bar was busy all evening, with no end of people eating or drinking. The lifts were in constant use and it never ceased to amaze DC James what some people got up to when they thought no one was looking.

A clock in the top right hand corner of the screen kept time, each recording running in chronological sequence and at 00:15 Suzie Chahal and Simon Coleman appeared. Mallinson froze the recordings and scrutinised each screen looking carefully for anything out of the ordinary. He was disappointed, there were no ghostly faces peering through the windows or suspicious looking characters hiding behind a newspaper. He ran the films on again tracking their progress from the lift and along the corridor. Simon was good to his word, he saw Suzie to her door, but did not enter her room.

"We know the room was empty when she went in," DC James commented.

The camera further along the corridor showed that no one had entered her room. It tracked Simon as he walked away to the other end of the corridor. There were six rooms separating them.

Mallinson turned his attention to the other views, one section of the screen showed the reception area, the two lifts were covered and there was a camera at each end of the corridor where Suzie Chahal's room was situated. All they had to do was wait. He ran the film at fast forward slowing only when something interesting caught his eye.

At 00:47 someone appeared pushing a trolley into one of the lifts. At first, the picture was not clear but the camera picked up movement and then an image came into view.

"We have what appears to be a female with a trolley that we believe to be the one found in room 211." DC James said confirming what they could all see.

The camera in the corridor picked up the woman as she exited the lift and tracked her progress along the corridor. This time they managed to get a good physical description and all three detectives scribbled furiously in their notebooks. The woman disappeared as she passed through a fire door then the camera at the other end of the corridor picked her up. It was a long distance view but as she moved towards it, they got a look at her face. Her features were blurred but by freezing the frame, they were able to see that she was fair skinned, 25-35 years old with shoulder length dark hair.

She stopped outside room number 211 and knocked on the door. Standing back, she smoothed her skirt with her hands before tucking her hair behind her ears, then seconds later the door opened. They were unable to see Suzie Chahal, she remained hidden from view, but after a

147

brief conversation, the woman pushed the trolley into the room.

Twenty minutes later, she emerged and closing the door behind her, walked quickly along the corridor. They monitored her as far as the stairwell opposite the lifts but then lost sight of her as she pushed through the doors.

"Where did she go?" Keable asked.

"The stairs lead to a fire exit," DC James told them. "I checked it out earlier. The fire door opens out onto an alleyway. It has a push bar affair with no seal and there is no alarm."

"Where does the alleyway go?" Mallinson asked.

"It leads to a small staff car park at the rear of the hotel. There is another alleyway leading to the main road."

"Cameras?" he asked.

"Not that I could see."

"So we are looking for a woman?" Keable said. He did not sound convinced even though he had seen it for himself. He was certain that the killer was a man.

Mallinson ran the recording forward several hours checking to see if anyone else entered the room, but there was nothing. No further movement was recorded until 06:30 when people began to emerge.

"Get the manager in here," he said. "Let's see if he can identify this woman."

Chapter
THIRTY TWO

Belenos realised there was very little he could do with the information that Freddie had given him. He could hardly present it to a newspaper because by doing so questions would be asked. His actions would undoubtedly prompt a police investigation; they would want to know how he came by such knowledge, especially as nothing had yet been officially released to the press. He may even become a murder suspect. He imagined that journalists would already be gathering, alerted by the police activity at the hotel they would be waiting for a statement. Belenos knew how it worked, journalists on a favoured list would be the first to receive the news.

Turning to a clean page in his notebook, he began to write. Starting with the names of the victims, he dashed off a short paragraph about each one and once his knowledge was exhausted, he turned to the newspapers. After that, he searched the internet looking for anything that might be helpful. There was quite a lot of information about Victoria Stevens. She had kept a blog and a website including a diary of events leading up to her disability. A few years earlier, she had undergone surgery to help ease her condition but unfortunately, it had gone wrong leaving her without the use of her legs. There was no hint of bitterness, no campaign to apportion blame, Victoria had been an optimist, her glass always half full.

Social media was a great help and Belenos discovered all sorts of things about the young musicians. It never ceased to amaze him at the wealth of personal information freely available on the internet and it did not take him long to get to know the victims.

Perhaps this is how the killer worked, he thought. Would he have researched his victims, select them by studying their profiles. He doubted it, but there was a definite pattern emerging and it pointed squarely at Mia. Freddie was right when he made the point; *'how many young female musicians would currently be willing to perform with Mia Ashton?'*

He was certain that Mia had already voiced her concerns, she must have discussed it with her agent Alicia Wicks. He thought about the telephone call he had made to Mia earlier. Ben Sykes had answered her phone telling him that Mia was unable to take his call, but from the sound of his voice, it was obvious that some kind of drama was taking place. Ben was not a convincing liar, besides he had heard Mia sobbing in the background. Perhaps her father had delivered the devastating news and she was aware of the latest killing.

The manager of the hotel was asked to join the detectives in the conference room and accompanying him was a short rounded woman called Ursula Janowski. Ursula was the assistant facilities manager and one of her main duties was to organise the service staff work rotas. She looked nervous as she sat in the chair offered her, the thought of being questioned by the police unnerved her. DC Keable could see that she was less than comfortable so perching on the end of the table, he folded his arms and smiled before asking.

"Janowski, that's Polish isn't it?"

"Yes," Ursula nodded hesitantly. "Most people think I'm from Romania or another eastern European country."

Keable laughed. "Easily done, the English are not very good at placing accents. Most people think I'm a Lancastrian."

Ursula frowned, she knew nothing of the Yorkshire, Lancashire divide.

"I would like you to look at this image and tell us if you recognise this woman." Mallinson nodded and DC James set the recording in progress.

Although blurred, the picture taken from inside the lift was the best they had. The other facial image was a long shot, taken in the corridor as the woman delivered the trolley to room number 211. Neither Ursula nor the manager spoke until the film ended.

"Can we see it again?" Ursula asked.

They watched intently for a second time and when it was finished, they told Mallinson what he was expecting to hear.

"This woman does not work at the hotel."

Mallinson stared at Ursula but made no comment, it was a few moments before he asked his next question.

"Can you tell us anything about the contents of the trolley?" He slid a photograph across the table.

Ursula positioned it on the table between herself and the manager and they both scrutinised the image carefully before delivering their verdict.

"The bucket, the vase and trolley all belong to this hotel, but the champagne is a label that we do not stock." The manager spoke this time.

"So, the bottle and flowers must have been brought in by the killer."

The manager nodded but made no further comment.

"Where do you keep the trolleys when they are not in use?"

"There are storerooms close to the kitchens at the back of the building. We keep everything there."

"Does everyone have access to this area?"

"Yes." Ursula took the opportunity to answer. "The store is never locked."

"Is it usual to have people wondering about the storerooms at night?"

"We are a hotel, people come and go all of the time."

"What time did the kitchen staff finish?

"The last meal was served at 22:30," Ursula told him. "By midnight they would have gone."

"So that area of the hotel would have been quiet from about midnight onwards?"

"Yes, there would of course have been night staff milling around, but after midnight they usually remain in the staffroom."

"Do they often get called out during the night?"

"Sometimes it can be busy, especially at weekends with people returning from nightclubs. Some of them require room service but mostly it's lost key cards or they need help getting into their rooms."

Mallinson thought about what she said before raising his eyebrows and turning away from where they were sitting.

"I'm sorry we are not able to offer you more Inspector." The manager shuffled uncomfortably in his seat.

Mallinson turned back to face them then he asked. "Would a member of staff delivering room service also be required to serve at tables in the restaurant?"

"Yes," Ursula nodded. "Evening waiting staff or those working at the bar usually make up their hours by remaining here for the night shift. They would attend to whatever is required, including room service."

"I see," Mallinson looked thoughtful. "We will need to talk to everyone on duty last night including the kitchen staff."

"I will check the rota," the manager said, "and personally make sure that everyone comes in to see you."

"Thank you. That will be a great help."

Chapter
THIRTY THREE

Belenos was staring at his computer screen. His final article about serial killers was complete and he would soon be required to present ideas for his next project to the editor of the magazine he was working for. He should begin his research immediately if he was going to keep to the deadline, but first he wanted to know more about William Randolph or Mr Mac, the serial killer in what Belenos called 'The Josie MacDonald abduction case'. He couldn't shake off the feeling that this was somehow linked to the recent spate of murders, but he knew that was impossible. The only similarity here was the fact that all the victims were young women. Like all predators, the killer had stalked his prey before striking, but this time abduction was not part of the crime. These latest killings were different, here the victims were bludgeoned to death before being mutilated in what police described as a frenzied attack.

In each instance the killer must have been at Mia's concert or at least close by because both Alison Morley and Victoria Stevens were killed soon after performing, their bodies discovered not far from the venue. The killer could hardly have planned it this way, he must have simply been close enough to strike when the moment was right. With Suzie Chahal it was different. Because of the heavy police presence, it was impossible to get her alone after the Valentine concert so the killer had been forced to implement a daring plan. This display of thinking proved that the murders must have been pre-meditated and not just random acts. It couldn't have been an easy task getting into the hotel, finding the right room then carrying out the crime in a building with rooms full of people. Mr Mac must have been like this Belenos thought, he was a man capable of planning a murder. He had driven from one end of the country to the other in order to seek out specific individuals. This must have taken an incredible amount of organisation. Mr Mac had also reacted to situations as they arose so his plans were fluid; he was obviously a man who could think on his feet.

Belenos scribbled down a few notes then he continued to read from his computer screen. He had discovered an article on the internet about Mr Mac's father and it made for interesting reading. Father and son shared the same name, but that is where the similarity ended. William Randolph senior had been a respected man, a Justice of the Peace, who served his local community for many years. He provided employment on his estate for local people and supported many noble causes. He maintained a very healthy investment portfolio, which meant regular visits to his accountant in London. Belenos wondered why Randolph chose to travel from his home in Scotland to London when there must have been dozens of accountancy firms in Edinburgh.

Further investigations revealed that the portfolio was still active. Solicitors were sorting through the estate, which by all accounts amounted to a tidy sum. This included a large house in Morayshire set in extensive grounds with woodland attached.

Randolph's son was his sole heir and had inherited his father's wealth but apparently had used very little of it. Much of his life had been spent in an institution and it was only when he was released into the community that the murders began. Now he was dead and leaving no successor or will, there was no one left to inherit so an administrator had been appointed. It was his job to search for distant relatives living abroad or creditors who might have a claim on the estate but it seemed that the Randolph family line had come to an end. This search was a legal formality, which had to be observed and Belenos thought about what Jenna had told him. If Josie MacDonald was carrying Mr Mac's child then she might have a legitimate claim. Paternity would of course have to be proven, but if no one stepped forward then the estate would eventually go to the Crown.

Digging deeper, Belenos discovered that the accountancy firm Randolph senior had used no longer existed, they had merged with a larger company some years previously, but luckily, many of the old files had been archived. These he was able to access online and they revealed some very interesting information. Vanessa Weston was the name of the accountant who had dealt with Randolph's investment portfolio and the last time he had visited London was just before his death in 1981.

Belenos typed the name Vanessa Weston and did a general search. He was hoping to find out more about the woman responsible for the continued growth of her client's portfolio, but the search proved fruitless. Next, he went to the Records Office site to check the Births, Marriages and Deaths section and after completing an on-line application form, a list of names appeared on his screen. He realised that he would have to refine his search as too many random names had popped up, so studying the list he made his selection then, clicking on a likely candidate waited for the computer to do its work. He had made a lucky choice, a few moments later the information he was looking for appeared. Vanessa had died in 1995 but the records told him something else. She had given birth to a child in 1982, a girl called Phillipa. He clicked on the relevant section and typed in these latest details. There were several girls by the name of Phillipa Weston born in 1982 so scrolling down the list, he scrutinised them all carefully before finding what he was looking for. Phillipa was born in Camden on June 4th 1982, the information revealed that her father was unknown.

Sitting back in his chair Belenos thought about what he had found. Could Phillipa be the result of an infidelity between William Randolph and his accountant Vanessa Weston? The dates added up and Randolph would have spent a lot of time with his accountant, it was an interesting idea. The girl would be in her mid thirties now. He ran another check but found nothing more, so making notes, he copied down reference numbers from the screen so he could locate the files again. If what he suspected was true then this could be another genuine claim on the Randolph estate.

He studied his notes and marvelled at this unexpected find. He had no idea when starting his research that he would turn up something like this.

Mia was feeling better. She had showered and dressed but still the shocking news of Suzie Chahal had reduced her to a state of depression. Ben did his best to console her and tried to persuade her to eat some breakfast but all she would take was a mug of strong coffee. He was worried, Mia's face was bloodless, her eyes red rimmed and swollen from crying. Not so long ago, she would never have faced him without wearing make-up, but today nothing seemed to matter.

"I don't have to go out," Ben told her as they sat together on the sofa.

"Emilia can wait, it's not important."

"No," Mia shook her head. "If you have arranged to meet your sister then you must go."

Studying her, he sighed. "Would you like to come with me? I just have to call into her shop, it won't take long."

"No," she shook her head again. "I must speak to my father. Could you see me as far as his house?"

"Of course."

Fresh tears appeared at the corner of her eyes so reaching out, Ben pulled her gently into his arms. Resting his chin lightly on top of her head, the scent of shampoo filled his nostrils and closing his eyes, he felt her body tremble as another wave of grief swept over her.

"We'll get through this," he whispered softly. "Nothing is going to happen to you."

Mia's life was in tatters, the carefully organised schedule designed to propel her to dizzying heights was in peril. Nothing could have prepared her for the deaths of her colleagues, she would never forget those poor girls. Eventually, the tears stopped leaving her low spirited and lethargic.

Perhaps Alicia was right, until the killer had been caught, her concerts should be put on hold. It was unfair to risk the lives of others so she decided to speak to her agent later that day.

Ben was having similar thoughts. What was the killer playing at? Was this some kind of psychological game designed to unhinge Mia, destroy her career before it had begun or was he simply a psychopath who took pleasure in mutilating young women? Perhaps Mia was his next target, maybe she had suffered enough and the time had come to end it. The taunting telephone calls were obviously unsettling her and with the shock of the murders, he wondered just how much more she could take. He could already see the changes in her personality; no longer was she the carefree spirit that he had met just a few weeks ago. He would not allow this to change the way he felt about her, in fact, her vulnerability only strengthened his feelings. Mia was a very special woman. He did not believe in love at first sight, but something about her had stirred him, she had stolen his heart. He would fight for her, die for her if necessary, this thought filled him with strength and he kissed the top of her head.

"We had better get ourselves organised," she whispered, her voice stronger this time.

Ben blinked and the spell was broken so loosening his grip he allowed her to pull away from him then locking eyes with her he said.

"I love you so much that it hurts."

"Careful," she replied, "you are in danger of sounding like a cliché."

Staring at her he laughed, he was amazed that in the midst of her grief she could still come up with something as amusing as that. It might not have been the response he was hoping for but it pleased him immeasurably.

"Ben," she whispered softly. "I love you too, don't think for a moment that I don't. This..." she paused searching for the right words. "This thing, this terrible situation may have serious consequences but it will change nothing. I will always love you."

"Wow," he replied then kissing her forehead, he said. "You have no idea how good that makes me feel."

"Oh yes I do."

Chapter
THIRTY FOUR

DS Isobel Woods had done a lot of footwork interviewing staff at the hotel and now with her report finished, she walked quickly along the corridor to see DI Mallinson. He was not in his office so she left the manila envelope on his desk. Glancing at her watch was a needless task, her stomach told her that she had worked well past the end of her shift, but she had just one more person to see before heading home.

"Izzy," Terry was genuinely pleased to see her standing on his doorstep. "Come in."

Closing the door behind her, he followed her into the living room.

"You look done in," he said as she sank exhaustedly into one of the enormous armchairs.

"I worked half the night chasing up hotel staff then spent most of the morning writing up my notes." Leaning forward she reached for the bag dumped at her feet and produced a file.

"Good work," Terry said as she handed it to him. "Would you like something to drink, tea of coffee or something stronger?"

"Tea would be lovely," she replied and resting her head back against the cushion, closed her eyes.

Noises from the kitchen were somehow reassuring, Izzy lived alone and her flat always seemed cold and heartless, there was no one waiting there to greet her at the end of a long shift. She thought that it was probably the same for him, although unlike hers his home felt cosy and lived in. Perhaps it was the way the room was arranged, she had heard about Feng Shui, but harmonising with her surrounding environment never featured high on her list of priorities.

Many of her colleagues seemed to live alone these days proving that policing and personal relationships were never a good mix. They were either separated or divorced, or simply never had time to develop a relationship. Izzy fell into the third category. She had been warned at training school that the job would demand every hour of her life, it was almost impossible to clock off and some aspects of the job would remain with her forever. She wondered how DI Ashton had managed to bring up his daughter singlehandedly. She knew that his wife and son had died many years ago, it could not have been an easy task.

Terry appeared carrying a tray loaded with a fancy teapot, cups and saucers and a jug of milk.

"Blimey Guv, I never had you down as a tea aficionado. This all looks very sophisticated, but you seem to have forgotten the stand of fancy cakes."

"Don't push your luck."

Izzy laughed and watched him go through the ritual of filling their cups.

"Well done," she applauded. "I usually make such a mess when pouring tea from a pot."

"I could rustle up a few biscuits but no cake I'm afraid."

She was tempted but declined his offer even though she had still not eaten. Tea would do for now, besides her stomach had stopped complaining.

Terry enjoyed working with Izzy, they complemented and mocked each other in equal measure but instinctively knew when they had gone far enough.

"That is a copy of the report I left for DI Mallinson," she told him.

The file was resting on the table beside the tea tray.

"It's mainly routine stuff, statements from people who saw nothing, but I have included the SOCO report."

Terry nodded and pulling out the contents, began to read the first page. No fingerprints had been found on the bottle of champagne used as a weapon to kill Suzie Chahal.

"It must have been wiped clean," Izzy told him. "There should have been prints all over that bottle.

"SOCO found fibres and hair on the bed beside the body." Terry frowned as he read the next paragraph.

"Yes," Izzy nodded, "the hair looks like it came from a wig. Don't ask me how they can tell."

"Probably synthetic."

She hadn't thought of that.

"Did you speak to the people who serviced the room?"

"Yes, it's all there in my report." Her eyes strayed to the papers he was holding. "I interviewed all the housekeeping staff including the cleaners who worked the rooms on that floor of the hotel. None of them admit to wearing a wig."

Terry remained silent, she had pre-empted his next question so he turned to the images from the CCTV.

"So our killer appears to be female." It was no surprise to him because he had already heard the rumours at the station.

"Bit of an eye opener I must admit," Izzy replied. She found it hard to believe that a woman could be capable of carrying out such brutal murders.

"I wonder why she was wearing a wig."

"All part of the disguise I guess."

They studied the pictures closely. They were grainy, the detail hard to make out. The perspective was distorted by the long-range view from the corridor shots, but it was enough to confirm the profile that both pathologists had given. Pat Fleming and Dr Hughes from York had both said that the killer was no more than medium height and used minimum force to kill their victims.

"Why mutilate them?" Izzy shuddered.

"I have no idea," the sound of her voice interrupting his thoughts. He was unable to offer a solution.

"Why would a woman do that to another?" Izzy chewed at her bottom lip as they studied the photograph of Suzie Chahal lying bloodied on the bed.

"Perhaps it was an act of jealousy," Terry whispered. "All our victims were talented and very attractive."

"True," Izzy agreed but she was not entirely convinced.

"I wouldn't say that our suspect is particularly unattractive."

Izzy peered at the photograph and thought that the woman looked fairly average.

"I'm sure the Tech Heads at HQ can clean these images." She said looking sideways at him.

"Yes," he agreed, "we'll probably see the results in tomorrow's papers."

Picking up her cup and saucer Izzy sat back in her chair and sipped at her tea.

"My grandfather used to drink tea from a cup and saucer just like this."

She told him smiling at the memory. "He would pour tea into his saucer and slurp it up, making the most awful sounds."

"Don't you dare try that," Terry warned her sternly. "I don't want tea stains on my carpet."

They laughed together and the mood in the room lightened. The photographs of Suzie Chahal had disturbed them both and Terry couldn't help thinking that it could quite easily be his own daughter lying there mutilated on the bed. Izzy was having similar thoughts but chose to keep them to herself. She always made sure that she had a personal self defence spray in her bag. The one that she was advised to carry sprayed out a slimy substance that stained the target leaving an ultra violet tracer.

"I have also included in my report a list of everyone who performed at the concert including names of staff on duty at the Barbican on the night of the murder."

"Thanks Izzy, I really appreciate this." He knew that she had been thorough, she had a reputation for getting things done, her administration skills were enviable.

When she was gone, he studied the lists carefully looking for a pattern of some kind. The names of the entire orchestra were there including the stagehands and theatre crew. Many of those were foreign, eastern European mostly and he would struggle to distinguish between the male and female names. He was fully aware that this could contain the name of the killer and he hoped that Mallinson would cross reference the lists from each of Mia's concerts. It was essential to look for names that cropped up repeatedly. The suspect could however have been a member of the audience. On the evening of the Valentine concert, the audience figures numbered over nine hundred. Names could be traced through the booking office, but it would be a thankless task and he doubted that Mallinson would insist on taking that route, besides they would have nothing to compare against, he was certain there would be no data like this available from the previous concerts.

Chapter
THIRTY FIVE

The sound of the bell was fading as Terry made his way along the hallway and when he opened the door, his daughter was standing there her face pale and her eyes red from tears.

"Mia whatever is the matter?"

"Daddy, I need to talk to you."

Standing aside, he ushered her in. She would never just turn up unannounced so he knew it must be serious. Once in the living room, he sat her down in the chair that DS Woods had occupied half an hour earlier and giving her a few moments to compose herself, he busied himself by clearing away the used cups.

"Would you like some coffee?" he asked before disappearing into the kitchen.

Mia was staring at the ornate teapot its contents now stewed and cold. She wondered who her father had been entertaining, it was unusual for him to use his best china, normally he served tea in mismatched mugs. On the arm of his chair was a manila file with papers spilling out from beneath the cover. He was obviously working she thought. His guest must have been a colleague, a female colleague because a faint but sweet aroma remained in the room, the only evidence of gender, she had seen no trace of lipstick on the rim of the cup.

Glancing at the file again she was curious to know what it was he was working on. One of the protruding papers was clearly a picture or photograph, but there was not enough showing to reveal its content.

Her father appeared carrying two mugs of coffee and settling in his chair, he shuffled the papers into the file before dropping it on the carpet at his feet. Fixing his eyes on his daughter, he waited for her to say something, his expression clearly inviting an explanation. Holding nothing back, she told him about the telephone calls and as she spoke fresh tears burned at the back of her eyes.

"You should have told me this earlier," he said when she was finished and passing her a handkerchief his expression softened.

Dabbing at her eyes Mia expected him to be angry, but she knew that it was only because he cared.

"You spent the night with Ben Sykes?" he asked once she was ready to go on.

It felt strange telling him about her private life, she loved him dearly but there were things that she would rather keep to herself. Terry could sense her unease, it was not easy for him either, but once he had established her whereabouts, he moved on. It saddened him to think that Mallinson and Keable would not afford her such consideration. They were likely to want to talk to her again, this time formally at the station. She was one of the last people to see Suzie Chahal alive and she might unwittingly be holding onto a vital clue. Pushing these thoughts aside, he focussed on the anonymous telephone calls.

"Do you have any idea who might be doing this?" he asked hoping to dislodge some forgotten fact. "Was there anything about the voice that you recognised?"

"No," she shook her head miserably before looking up at him. "It's the same person each time, but he sounds so nondescript, he just sounds ordinary." She shrugged her shoulders this time before going on. "It scares me to think that he knows so much about me."

"What do you mean?" Terry asked leaning towards her.

"Well, on occasions he has said things that he could not possibly have known," she shuddered at the memory of his lewd comments.

"What kind of things?" Terry persisted.

"I'm sure that he is spying on me because he can describe things about my flat. It's as if he has been inside my home or at least looked in through the window, but I'm so careful. I close the curtains as soon as it gets dark before putting on the lights and I never walk around half naked." That was as far as she was willing to go, there was no way she was going to reveal what he had said about Ben and their lovemaking.

Terry remained silent then with a nod of his head he encouraged her to go on.

"He knows things about the murders, he told me what he had done to

Suzie Chahal." Fresh tears escaped from the corner of her eyes and rolled down over her face.

Giving her a few moments to compose herself, Terry thought about the contents of the file that DS Woods had given him. The CCTV footage clearly shows that a woman had been in the room at the time of Suzie's death. There was nothing to suggest that a man was in on it too. SOCO had found no evidence of a man being in the room.

"Did you receive these calls on your mobile or home telephone?"

"Both, but mostly on my home phone."

Terry realised that the calls could be the key so he continued with this line of inquiry.

"Have you given your mobile number out to anyone recently?" he knew that her home number was ex-directory and could not be found easily, but still he wondered how this man had got hold of it.

"I gave it to Suzie and Simon but to no one else. I rarely use it to make calls."

"Did you use it when you were in York?"

"Yes, I called Cassie my driver, but I always block my number so it doesn't appear on another device."

"Do you have any objections to me requesting information from your telephone network providers? I should be able to trace the caller from that."

He considered asking her to say nothing to Mallinson about their conversation, but she had not yet realised that he would want to question her further. He decided to say nothing for the moment, she was clearly upset enough and he didn't want to make matters worse.

There was still no news from the King Edward Hotel and Emilia was blissfully unaware that another of Mia's colleagues had been murdered. Ben chose to keep what he knew to himself, to tell his sister now would mean having to explain everything and he felt that it would be unfair to speak about Mia behind her back.

"I can't stop thinking about what Jenna O'Brien told me the other day." Emilia said as she moved restlessly around her office.

Today her hair was a bright cherry red, she must have coloured it before her Valentine date, Ben thought as he studied her. Her figure-hugging jumper was aqua marine blue, the colour working well with her hair it softened the harsh tones of her make-up.

"How can arranged marriages be relevant today, it's such an archaic idea?" Emilia stopped in front of him and fumed. "Surely her father can see how unhappy she is with the arrangement."

"It's none of our business." Ben reminded her but that was the wrong thing to say, his sister was hoping for his support.

"Well, isn't that just typical," she snapped. "I didn't have you down as a chauvinist."

"I'm not at all Em. I truly feel sorry for Jenna but surely she is grown up enough to make her own decisions."

"That's the problem." She was on the move again sending clouds of perfume around the tiny space then suddenly she swung round towards him and put her hands on her hips. "Don't you see, she doesn't have a choice? You heard what she said, her father has threatened to cut her off completely if she refuses to comply with his wishes. She even suggested that her life might be in danger."

"I'm aware of what she said. Clearly, a woman like Jenna could never do without the finer things in life. She will either have to accept the fact that she is marrying into even more wealth or slum it with the rest of us."

"Money isn't everything," Emilia snapped. "It's her future happiness that concerns me."

"I'm sure that once she has recovered from the terrible ordeal of marriage, the contents of her husband's bank account will keep her amused."

Emilia stared at him incredulously, how could he be so heartless? She wanted to scream, she thought that he would be sympathetic but clearly, she was wrong.

"Well, I'm not prepared to stand back and do nothing. Clearly Jenna was appealing to me for help so I have been doing some research of my own." She turned towards her desk and snatched up a sheet of printed paper.

"There is something called a Forced Marriage Protection Order which can be issued to prevent people from being married against their will." Holding the paper out to him, she took a deep breath.

An order can be made against any persons in the UK or outside, who is, or has been, involved in a forced marriage in any way.

"Jenna will have to appeal to the courts, a solicitor can start the application without informing her father, or any of the others involved. This is called a 'without notice' application. It means that she will have protection from the law before anyone is aware of what she has done."

"Are you sure you want to be a part of this?" Ben stared at his sister. "Jenna told you that these people could turn nasty."

"Yes but don't you see, she will have the full backing of the law."

"Don't be so naive, her father probably thinks he is above the law."

"More fool him," she said tossing her head.

He could see that she was resolute and nothing that he could say would change her mind.

"I hope you know what you are doing Em. I wouldn't like to think that you are exposing yourself to danger. Just think what these people could do to you or your business for that matter."

"I'm sure that Belenos would be very interested to hear of any threats that may be made. It would be the perfect opportunity for him to expose this treachery. It would open up a debate on arranged marriages and people's rights under European law. Besides if things do become nasty didn't you say that Mia's father is a Scotland Yard detective?"

She had made her point but still Ben was very worried.

Chapter
THIRTY SIX

Mia returned home to a house full of noise. First, she set about the alarm, entering a series of numbers that would quieten the high pitched whine before it become a full scale distress signal, but she did nothing to stop the ringing of the telephone. She had no intention of answering it and remained by the front door until it had stopped. When peace finally settled she stood with her back against the door and listened to the sounds of her home, the fridge was humming gently in the kitchen and somewhere a clock was ticking away the time. The atmosphere was now calm and welcoming, but this was the first time that she had felt apprehension at returning home alone. It was a wasted emotion because she realised that no one could be hiding inside her house, the alarm system would not allow it. Motion sensors designed to pick up movement were in place throughout her home. The insurance company had insisted on it, her cello was priceless.

Moving away from the door, she stooped to pick up the mail then peeped into the kitchen before going into the living room. Scent from Ben's flowers filled the room and she smiled then reaching for the telephone she dialled a number and listened to an animated voice. It told her that the caller had withheld their number. Unplugging the telephone from the wall, she swung her bag from her shoulder and rummaged inside it, locating her mobile phone, she silenced it too, that way if he tried to contact again she would not have to listen to the ringtone. Next, she went into her music room.

Her cello was on its stand and drawn towards it she ran her fingers lightly over its smooth surface. It was warm just like a living thing and closing her eyes she smiled. Touching it always sent a thrill through her, it was as if she could feel the vibrations of time. Over three hundred years of history was right there in the room with her, and she was proud to be part of it. She had not played since the Valentine concert and suddenly she felt compelled to pick up the bow and draw it across the strings. She knew they would need adjusting, but with an effort, she managed to resist the urge.

Turning away from her beloved instrument, she went back into the living room and shrugging off her coat, threw herself down on the sofa. The letters were on the coffee table beside the vase of flowers where she had dropped them, so leaning forward she reached for them. Sorting them into piles, she discarded the circulars, dropping them on the floor beside her feet, utility bills went onto the table then she came to a handwritten envelope. Turning it over in her hands, she slipped her thumb under the flap and pulled out a single sheet. Unfolding it, she smoothed it out then stared at it. Four names appeared in a column down the page, Alison Morley, Victoria Stevens and Suzie Chahal all in black ink, her own name was at the bottom written in red.

Mia gasped and let the paper fall to the floor, there was something familiar about the handwriting, but for the moment, she did not have the courage to take a closer look. Her mind was in turmoil as she thought about the implications of the list. After a while, her hands stopped shaking and she was able to reach down and pick up both paper and envelope. The postmark revealed that it had been posted locally two days previously. She frowned, that was before the Valentine Concert and before the death of Suzie Chahal. She peered at the writing more closely. It was an elegant feminine script a man could not have written it. Suddenly realisation took hold and her stomach lurched, it was as if she was looking at her own handwriting.

DI Ashton had arranged to interview the six women on his list. These were all victims of serious assaults that had occurred within the last twelve months and it was his job to re-open the investigation in an attempt to bring the perpetrator to justice. It had taken a little while to set up the meeting that would see all the victims together at a pre-arranged place and time. Robert Nixon of TG International had been instrumental in making the arrangements providing the women with a safe and familiar environment in which to talk about their harrowing experiences.

Terry was grateful for Nixon's help, it had saved him an enormous amount of effort. Arranging to speak to each women individually in their home or in a public place would have been time consuming, the only alternative would have been an interview room at New Scotland Yard, but this would most likely have proved intimidating for all those involved.

Terry parked his car in one of the spaces surrounding TG International. It was a huge parking area and he felt sure that it would not remain that way for long. It was undoubtedly earmarked for some future development. Getting out of his car he looked up at the building, he would have brought a colleague with him, DS Woods being his first choice but she was assigned to the murder case, working under DI Mallinson.

"Detective Inspector." Nixon was waiting at the top of the stairs and moving forward he held out his hand. "Welcome."

"Good morning Mr Nixon," Terry returned his smile. "Are all the ladies here?"

"Indeed they are, I have set them up in the conference room with tea and biscuits."

Turning on his heel, he led Terry along a brightly lit corridor where colourful posters advertising the services provided by the centre adorned the walls. One poster caught his eye; it displayed a list of popular places to visit. A contact telephone number and name was provided for those interested in going on the outings. Terry was impressed, not only did the centre offer professional services but there was also a thriving social element to the organisation.

They stopped outside the conference room and before opening the door Nixon hesitated. Glancing at Terry over his shoulder, he grinned and an unspoken word passed between them then leaning on the handle, he pushed opened the door.

The chatter inside the room stopped the moment they appeared and six pairs of inquisitive eyes stared at them. To his surprise, Terry found six very ordinary looking women sitting around the table. He was not at all sure what to expect but any preconceived ideas that he might have had disappeared in an instant.

"Ladies," Nixon said loudly as he positioned himself at the head of the table. "This is Detective Inspector Terry Ashton of the Metropolitan police."

There was a murmur of greetings as Terry looked at each of them in turn.

"Now, you are all aware of why the Inspector is here with us today, but do any of you have any objections about speaking of your terrible ordeal collectively?"

The consensus was one of satisfied unity, the interview could be conducted as a group session. Safety in numbers Terry thought and he stifled a grin.

DI Mallinson stared up at the wall of death in the murder room. Someone had added a photograph of Suzie Chahal, a small but colourful promotion picture of a young woman with an endearing smile. There were now three young faces staring back at him and he wondered how many more would appear before the killer was caught and brought to justice.

His work at the murder scene was done and now the hotel could get back to normal. He realised that might take some time because later that morning a formal statement was going to be released and the King Edward Hotel would probably become a magnet for the weird and the morbid. At least someone might benefit from this terrible situation; there were always winners and losers.

Turning away from the board, he retraced his steps to his desk where he found the post mortem report. DC James had collected it personally from Dr Fleming's office at the mortuary. The report revealed nothing new, it was simply an impersonal and objective account, a young woman's final moments reduced to a few paragraphs. There were charts and diagrams that added colour but still it remained grim reading. This was almost a carbon copy of the two he had read previously so, pushing it aside, he reached for the telephone.

"DS Woods," he said with no preamble. "I want you to bring Mia Ashton in. It's time we had another little chat."

Chapter
THIRTY SEVEN

The women introduced themselves one by one and Terry crossed them off his mental list. Angel Rix was the first to speak, she began by telling him a little about herself. At twenty two she was the youngest in the group. She lived with her mother in Bethnal Green and worked as a shop assistant. Terry studied her closely as she spoke, her voice was soft and hesitant, her body language convincingly feminine and he wondered how long she had been living as a woman. Her eyes hardened as she recalled her terrible ordeal.

"I really thought that I was going to die." She whispered tearfully.

"Did you get a clear view of your attacker?" Terry asked and as she looked up at him, she reminded him of his daughter.

"No Inspector, I was hit from behind and pushed to the ground. After that, it was all a bit hazy.

The others listened quietly and he could feel the solidarity between them thicken. They shared common emotions that went far deeper than Terry could imagine.

Debbie Sotheby and Ruth Smith were partners. He knew this from his notes, they were both in their early thirties, but now he could add more details to his file. They lived in a converted warehouse near the river and both women worked in the finance sector.

"My father set us up," Debbie said as if needing to explain how they could afford such an affluent address. She seemed almost embarrassed to admit that she came from a wealthy family.

Jodie Sanderson by contrast looked as if she came from the other end of the wealth spectrum. She appeared less like a woman than the others and he guessed that her transition was in its early stages. It was however the sound of her voice that belied her appearance. When she spoke, she reminded him of an actress whose name he could not recall, the similarity was astonishing. Jodie was currently unemployed, her background was in construction, but now it was impossible for her to find a job in that field.

"I have tried very hard to get back into the building game but there is too much discrimination. The trade is too narrow minded," she complained.

Terry could not imagine her working on a building site and he almost suggested that she apply for an administration position but he stopped himself just in time. It was hardly his place to act as career advisor, besides she might find his remarks patronising and it would not do to alienate these people.

Lexie Rothschild was the oldest in the group. Terry was aware that she was in her mid fifties but he could hardly believe it, surgical procedures had knocked years off her features. He knew this was true because whoever had interviewed her before had concentrated on her personal details rather than the task in hand. The police notes he had were next to useless.

"I was coming home from work when the attacker hit me from behind," she explained. "It is the same as the others, I didn't get a chance to defend myself, and once I had been knocked to the ground it all becomes a little confusing."

Sharon Davey was the athletic type. She was of medium build, her body made up of boyish angles. She wore a pink and black tracksuit and looked as if she had just stepped out of the gym. Her long dark hair was pulled back into a ponytail revealing her sharp boned features and when she spoke, her voice was deeper than the others.

He was amazed at what the women were prepared to tell him. He did not expect them to be so open about their private lives, but he was grateful that they were. He now had a greater understanding of what they were about and the way they lived their lives. He also learnt a lot from what they did not tell him. Over the years, he had become an expert on body language and facial expressions, it was almost impossible for people to hide what they were really thinking.

The group discussion came next. The formal introductions were over and gently he targeted the women he thought might be able to contribute a little more, and as he listened, he made notes. There was always a forgotten memory, something that at first did not seem important but could make a huge difference and Terry knew that it was usually easier for people to open up as a group and today was no different.

He was not prepared for what came next. All the women agreed on one thing; their attacker was a woman. There was nothing about this in his files, and at first, he thought that he must have missed something. None of them were able to give him a description but they told him that the attacker was right handed, fair skinned with shoulder length dark hair drawn back into a ponytail. He glanced at Sharon Davey, she fitted the description perfectly, as did so many other people roaming the streets of the city.

Terry could hardly believe that this important piece of information was missing from his files. He had no idea who had taken the original statements but he would make it his business to find out. Alarm bells were beginning to ring inside his head as he realised that these attacks could possibly be linked to the recent spate of murders.

Belenos Falzone watched from a stationary taxi as DI Terry Ashton left the building. He waited for a few moments before passing cash through the little partition window, only then did he open the door and climb out. He wondered what DI Ashton was doing at TG International. Turning away from the car park, he focussed his attention on the building. Windows set high up on the walls would have once been the only source of natural light to enter the building, but now more windows had been added. That was some years ago during a regeneration project when the old Victorian warehouse had been converted into a comfortable suite of modern offices.

Information at the entrance told him that TG International were not the sole occupier, brass plates on the wall gave details of the different businesses operating from this location. TG International was by far the largest, taking up the whole of the top floor. He had never heard of the operation before, the editor of the magazine he was writing for had suggested that he make contact with a man called Robert Nixon. Nixon ran the company and would be able to answer all of his questions.

On the other side of the city, Emilia Sykes was on her way to see Jenna O'Brien. She had suggested they meet at a little tearoom beside the river but the commuter rush had continued all morning, bringing the momentum of the city to a standstill and now she was beginning to regret her decision.

Jenna was already there when Emilia finally arrived and rising from her seat at a little table by a window, she glided effortlessly across the room to display a flourish of friendly greeting. Emilia was surprised, Jenna was not as brightly turned out as usual, her make-up was understated and even her dress was rather plain, not at all what Emilia had come to expect.

"Hi Jenna," Emilia began as she sank onto a chair. "Thanks for meeting me like this."

"It's always lovely to see you." This was one of her standard replies and Emilia wondered if it was entirely genuine.

"Have you been waiting long?"

"No, not really, I was early. The taxi simply flew across town this morning."

"All the traffic must have been in my direction then, it's been a dreadful journey."

"Poor you," Jenna pouted. "Well, you're here now so let's enjoy our tea."

They chatted easily and for a while, both women managed to avoid the subject they had come to discuss. Emilia found it refreshing to talk about absolutely nothing for a change; most of her conversations revolved around the complexities of a wedding. Ben was currently manning her shop but she was not fool enough to let him have full reign. She had arranged for her part time assistant to come in and help, so now she could relax in the knowledge that her shop was in safe hands.

"What do you think of Belenos Falzone?"

The question took Emilia by surprise.

"Belenos," she replied rallying her thoughts. "I hardly know him socially but he seems a good sort." Her eyes narrowed. "Why do you ask?"

"Can he be trusted?" she paused before going on. "What I mean is, would he make a good ally?"

"Would he be someone to turn to for help if this beastly business turns nasty?" Emilia knew what Jenna was asking.

"Yes," Jenna nodded, "that's exactly what I mean."

"I would say that you could rely on him but you must remember that he is a journalist."

"I appreciate that," She smiled. "The fact that he has a public voice may prove to be very useful."

"True," Emilia agreed.

They had been having the same thoughts. If Jenna's relationship with her father became untenable and she refused to carry out his wishes, then the threat of public exposure may just well do the trick.

"I must admit, I've flirted with him shamelessly." Jenna made a face.

"I'm sure he'll forgive you for that." Emilia couldn't think of a single man that Jenna had not flirted with, even her brother had not managed to escape her attention.

Emilia decided that it was time to get to the matter in hand. "I hope you don't mind, but I've been doing a little research and have discovered that there are steps you can take to legally avoid an arranged marriage."

"Yes I know," Jenna nodded. "I am aware of Forced Marriage Protection Orders, but what good would it do? Once my father got to hear about it the fallout would be catastrophic."

"Don't you see," Emilia said and leaning forward she lowered her voice. "You will be protected by the law."

Jenna wondered at her naivety and rolled her eyes.

"That may be so, but it wouldn't stop my father. He is adamant that this wedding will go ahead. If he so much as suspects my reluctance then I hate to think of the consequences. As I said the other day, I would be cut off completely and that's providing he could stop something more sinister from happening. Believe me, the law could offer me very little protection."

"Then what are you going to do?"

"Honestly I have no idea."

"Couldn't you at least talk to a solicitor, maybe even start the application? At least then things would be in place and no one would need to know until you are ready."

Jenna thought for a moment and reaching for her cup sipped at her tea.

"I suppose it would do no harm," she agreed at last, "providing of course that my father doesn't get to hear about it."

"He won't until you decide to take it further. Why don't you discuss this with Belenos? See what he has to say about the whole affair."

Emilia realised that she could do no more. Ben was right, it was none of her business. If these people were so lawless then it might not be such a good idea to provoke them. She shuddered at the thought then taking another sip of tea decided to say nothing more on the subject.

"Perhaps I could elope with Belenos Falzone." Jenna giggled mischievously. "We could simply disappear for a while."

Emilia nodded but thought it a bad idea. Why would Belenos want to do that? She was aware that they had been seeing each other recently and she wondered if Belenos had given Jenna the impression that he was interested in developing their relationship further.

Chapter

THIRTY EIGHT

Mia made herself a mug of strong coffee and from the first sip could feel the buzz of caffeine as it entered her bloodstream. It would hardly contribute to the calming process or even cure the feeling of nausea that dogged her but she needed to feel its effect. Her hands were still shaking from the shock of receiving the letter. The handwriting although similar to her own could not possibly be hers, it was a crazy idea. Why would she send herself a note like that? She was convinced that it must be the work of the killer, no one else could have predicted the death of Suzie Chahal.

Mia took her coffee into the living room where she sank carefully onto the sofa and cupping the mug between her hands breathed in the heavy aroma. She couldn't hold onto it for long, it was much too hot and the palms of her hands were beginning to sting, so setting it down on the coffee table, she rested her head back and closed her eyes. She thought about her father and felt guilty at having worried him; he had looked so shocked when she told him about the telephone calls. He obviously knew a lot more about the murders, but naturally kept the details to himself. Just knowing that he was there for her was a great help and with his love and support, she could endure anything.

She should tell him about the letter, but she couldn't bring herself to do it. She did not want to upset him further, besides she had to come to terms with it herself first, try to put it into some sort of perspective.

Suddenly the doorbell rang and startled out of her thoughts she climbed to her feet and glanced at the clock on the wall. She was not expecting visitors so when she got to the door, she slipped the security chain into place, then opening it a crack, peered out. A woman police officer that she knew to be Detective Sergeant Woods was standing on the doorstep.

"Isobel," Mia said and fumbling with the chain, she pulled the door open and invited her in.

DS Woods smiled a greeting and as she swept past, Mia recognised her perfume; Isobel must have been the woman at her father's house earlier that morning. She was about to say something but was beaten to it.

"Sorry to turn up unannounced like this Mia but I'm afraid I'm here on official business." She paused and searching Mia's face all she saw was curiosity.

"Detective Inspector Mallinson requests that you to attend the station." She explained. "He wants to speak to you about the latest murder."

"Why doesn't he come here like before?" She asked, leading DS Woods along the hallway.

"He wants to conduct a formal interview this time." She said before looking around the room.

"I see," Mia replied then after a short silence she asked. "Would you like something to drink? The kettle has just boiled."

"No thank you. We had better just go, get this over with as soon as possible."

DS Woods knew that she was leading Mia into an unpleasant situation but there was nothing that she could do to avoid it. Mallinson would not make it easy for Mia, Woods was sure of that. She was aware of the friction between him and Terry and Mallinson might use this opportunity to take it out on his daughter.

Retracing their steps along the hallway Mia found her coat and scarf then slipping her feet into her shoes, she set the alarm before closing the door behind her. Her mug of coffee left abandoned on the table where it was now growing cold.

Robert Nixon was very helpful and Belenos took an instant liking to him. He was clearly proud of the services provided by his organisation. He answered every question put to him and even furnished Belenos with a leaflet containing details about TG International. It was as much as he had done for DI Ashton. Belenos was tempted to ask why the detective had been there earlier, but he realised that police business or otherwise the rules of confidentiality would bar Nixon from telling him anything.

"I have arranged for you to interview two of our people," Nixon was saying. "Michael Faith and Chrissie Bird have both kindly agreed to tell you their stories." He peered at Belenos thoughtfully before going on. "Now, I'm relying on you to produce a sensitive and well structured account of our clients and what we do here. It would not do to portray us in anything other than a positive light. We have our own share of problems Mr Falzone and an article written in the style found in some tabloids would be most damaging."

Belenos looked up, shocked at what Nixon had just said.

"I assure you that it's not my intention to be prejudiced in any way. I'm an investigative journalist not a hack, I also like to think that I'm a man of honour and integrity. Whatever Chrissie and Michael have to tell me will be treated with the utmost of respect. I am quite willing to submit everything that I write for your approval before sending it to my editor."

"Mr Falzone, I'm sure that won't be necessary. If I have your assurance and you can vouch for your editor, then I respect the fact that your word is your bond."

Belenos was amused, he had seldom heard that phrase used before and it pleased him to think that he had gained the man's trust.

Mia was shown into Interview Room 1 where initially she was left on her own. The door closed loudly behind her and she shuddered as she glanced around the soulless room. The atmosphere was stale and charged with condemnation. The only furniture was a table and four chairs, the table bolted to the floor, its enamelled steel top chipped and scratched with the names or initials of those who had come before. Plastic chairs hardly designed for comfort were secured to the legs of the table by short lengths of chain. Mia studied the box-like piece of equipment bolted to the tabletop and realised that it was a recording device and high up in the corner where the walls met the ceiling she noticed a camera lens looking down on her. It reminded her of Cyclops, a member of a primordial race of giants from Greek mythology.

The station sergeant, when booking her in at reception, had reassured her, she was not under arrest and was here under her own free will, but she knew that was not entirely true. She declined the offer of a cup of tea; experience told her that hot drinks from dispensers in places like this were hardly fit for consumption.

Sitting down on one of the plastic chairs, she tried to make herself comfortable but failed. Her mood was low and in danger of sinking even further by the negativity generated by her surroundings. Suddenly, the door opened and Mallinson entered the room followed closely by Keable.

A few moments later, a uniformed female police officer positioned herself discreetly by the door.

"Good morning Miss Ashton," Mallinson said cordially. "Thank you for agreeing to take part in this meeting."

Mia snorted but remained silent, having agreed to nothing, she was hardly a willing participant.

"Do you mind if we record this interview?" Keable asked and without waiting for an answer inserted old-fashioned cassette tapes into the machine. Like before, it seemed that she had no choice in the matter. "You will receive a copy." He smiled as he glanced at her.

Speaking for the benefit of the tape, Keable recorded the date, time and the names of all those present. Mallinson who had settled in the chair opposite watched her closely then taking a pen from his pocket placed it on the table beside a dark blue folder.

"Did you meet Suzie Chahal before your Valentine concert?" he began.

Mia was surprised at the suddenness of the question and she frowned.

"Only for rehearsal, apart from that I had never met her before. Of course I was aware of her as a musician."

He asked several questions about the concert, the level of involvement they had with the stage crew, the setting up and technical arrangements.

"Who suggested that Miss Chahal and Mr Coleman stay at the King Edward Hotel?"

"I have no idea," she replied looking up at him. "These things are usually taken care of by an agent. Perhaps the recommendation came from Alicia Wicks, my agent, or it may have simply been a random internet booking."

Mallinson picked up his pen and opening his file drew out a clean sheet of paper then he scribbled down a note.

"Does your agent take care of this kind of thing for you?" Keable asked this time, continuing the line of questioning.

"Yes Alicia or one of her team."

"Where did you go after the concert?"

This change of direction took her by surprise and taking a deep breath she told him about the meal that Ben had provided at his home. She chose not tell him that it was a romantic picnic eaten on a blanket on his living room floor.

"This would be Mr Benjamin Sykes?"

Mia nodded, wondering where they had got that information.

"For the benefit of the tape could you please answer the question?"

"Yes, Ben Sykes," Mia rolled her eyes.

"How long have you known Mr Sykes?"

"A few weeks," she told him.

"Why did you not mention him when we spoke to you before?"

"I didn't think I needed to," Mia replied sharply, her anger beginning to surface. "He has nothing to do with any of this so I thought it irrelevant to tell you about him."

"Nothing is irrelevant Miss Ashton." Mallinson eyed her coldly. "What do you mean by saying that he has nothing to do with any of this?"

For a moment, she was speechless and struggled for an answer. This must be some kind of mind trap, and she realised that she would have to be very careful when replying to his questions.

"I meant nothing by it. Ben is simply a friend who is not connected with my professional life in any way."

Glancing at the police officer standing by the door Mia sought solidarity. She was uncomfortable with the aggressive tactics employed by these men.

"Would you like someone to sit in with you?" Keable asked sensing her apprehension.

"Do I need someone?"

"I'm not suggesting a solicitor. At this stage you are simply helping us with our inquiries."

She stared at him and was tempted to ask what he meant by 'at this stage', but he continued to speak.

"Perhaps we could persuade DS Woods to attend."

"How about my father?" Mia hissed.

"No," he replied shaking his head. "That would be hardly appropriate."

She was aware of police protocol.

"Do you have any idea who might be responsible for these murders?" She asked, deciding that attack was the best form of defence.

"We are following up on several leads," was the standard reply.

Mia smiled and sitting back in her chair, she folded her arms and breathed deeply. They obviously have no idea, she thought.

DS Woods went in search of DI Ashton the moment she left his daughter at the front desk. Ashton had just returned from a trip out and she found him in the staff canteen buying a cup of coffee.

"Terry," she said. "Mallinson and Keable have Mia in IR1."

Coffee spilled from his cup as he placed it down heavily on the table.

"What are they playing at now?" he growled.

"I think she is okay," Woods said doing her best to reassure him.

"Perhaps you should go and take a look."

"I think I'll do just that." Turning on his heel, he strode away leaving his cup standing on the table in a puddle of coffee.

DS Woods watched him go then turning back to the table, slumped down heavily. Reaching for his coffee she took a sip and grimaced, it was far too sweet for her liking.

Ashton arrived at the interview room and just managed to stop himself from barging in instead, he went into the little side room where a TV monitor was housed. Switching it on, a view of the interview room appeared then flinging himself down in a chair he adjusted the volume and stared at the monitor. Mallinson and Keable were sitting at the table opposite his daughter, she was alone, but he knew a female police officer would be standing by the door. The camera angle did not include this part of the room so she remained out of shot.

Mia looked strained and from her body language, he could tell that she was not happy. He wondered why she was here, the interview could easily have been conducted somewhere less formal.

Mallinson glanced up at the camera and grinned, it was as if he could sense Ashton looking down on them and he made a show of gathering up his papers. Keable was talking to the tape, recording the time that the interview had been suspended.

Ashton was at the door as it opened.

"What the hell are you playing at Mallinson?" he demanded.

"Terry," he sneered in reply. "Just doing my job that's all, female blood sample found at the murder scene, photographs of a woman at another." He waved the file in his face. "It fits your daughter's description."

"That's nonsense and you know it."

"Is it my friend? Your daughter is connected with each murder. She knew all the victims, could easily have been the last person to see them alive."

Ashton clenched his fists but kept his arms firmly at his sides.

"She fits the profile." Mallinson repeated and ignoring the tension building between them, he continued. "I just need to understand why."

"You are way off the mark and you know it."

Mallinson grinned but said nothing as he walked away. When Keable appeared, he could see that Ashton was fuming so decided to remain silent, he simply nodding his head in greeting before following his colleague along the corridor.

Mia was confused and upset, she had not been accused of anything, but the inference was there. She was shocked by Mallinson's savagery, the way he had looked at her unnerved her alarmingly.

"I'll drive you home." Terry said as he entered the room and glancing at his colleague she smiled awkwardly before leaving Mia in his charge.

It was not until they were in the car that they began to talk.

"I don't understand what that was all about," Mia admitted.

"It's just his way of wearing you down," Terry said. He could hardly tell her about the photographs or the blood found at the murder scene, these things had not yet been made public. "He obviously thinks that you are involved in some way and is using this method to try to get a confession."

"But that's ridiculous," she groaned, horrified at the accusation. "How could I possibly be involved?"

"Did you tell him about the telephone calls?"

"No," she looked at him and shook her head. "I don't feel inclined to tell him anything."

Terry sighed, withholding that kind of information could get her into even more trouble. Bringing the car to a standstill, they waited in silence for the lights to change. The sound of the traffic was a welcome release from the suffocating confines of the interview room and as Mia stared out of the window, she made up her mind.

"I received an anonymous letter in the post today."

Terry looked at her the moment the lights turned green and was rewarded by the blast of a horn from the vehicle behind.

"What kind of letter?" he asked as he slipped the car into gear.

"It was more of a note really, a list of names in fact." She explained the contents of the note then he asked.

"When was it posted?" He glanced at her quickly, aware of vehicles drawing in around them as the road narrowed ahead.

"The postmark bears the date of the concert."

Immediately he came to the same conclusion that Mia had made earlier. Whoever sent it must have known that Suzie Chahal would be dead by the time Mia received it.

"It can only have been sent by the killer." He said.

Mia remained silent, she could not help thinking that the handwriting was so much like her own.

Chapter
THIRTY NINE

Terry returned to the station and went straight to his office. Closing the door, he sat at his desk and glanced at his computer. A number of e-mails had arrived in his inbox, but none of them looked important so he decided they could wait until later. He stared out of the window that overlooked the murder room, it was deserted, Mallinson and his team were obviously busy elsewhere. The only person that he could see working was the female police officer who had been in IR1 with Mia, she was sitting at a desk going through a pile of paperwork.

Reaching for the letter that Mia had received in the post, he studied it through the plastic covering of the evidence bag. The handwriting was neat, a regulated print in blue ink from a ballpoint pen. Dropping it onto his desk he opened the top drawer and looked for a pair of latex gloves, he found only one and searching the remaining drawers he came up with nothing so snapping the glove onto his right hand, he carefully opened the bag. The envelope would be covered in prints but still he was careful not to add his own, the letter inside however was a different matter altogether. In theory, Mia and the person who wrote it should be the only ones to have touched it. Carefully, he withdrew it from the envelope and shook it open with his latex covered hand. It was as Mia had described, four names neatly presented in a column down the page. Black ink had been used for the names belonging to the dead women with the last on the list in red. This name belonged to his daughter.

The use of coloured ink was interesting, he wondered if black signified death and red, blood, taking a deep breath he frowned. Would Mia be the next victim or was this merely a statement of fact, three dead women, and one still alive. Perhaps he was reading too much into it, he should leave the analysis to the psychologists. Carefully he slipped the letter back into its envelope before returning it to the evidence bag. The postal date on the stamp was 14th February, proof that it had been sent before Mia's concert and before the death of Suzie Chahal.

He should bring this to the attention of DI Mallinson but for the moment, he decided to keep it to himself. Reaching into his pocket he produced his mobile phone and searching through the contact list he found the number he wanted then stabbing the call button with his finger he sat back in his chair. As he waited for his call to be answered, he peeled the latex glove from his hand and tossed it into the bin.

"Hello Pat."

"Terry, what can I do for you?"

No preamble, Pat Fleming was straight to the point and Terry smiled.

"I'm looking for a favour," he began and running his hand over the back of his neck, he glanced around his office.

"Go on," she replied.

"Can you get one of your team to dust a letter for me? Mia's prints are on it but I'm hoping you can find traces of the author."

"Can't someone from your SOCO team do that for you?"

"They could, but I need to circumnavigate the system."

"Should I ask why?" Pat asked after a moment of silence.

"It's complicated. If you agree to do this for me unofficially I will explain everything over a glass of wine."

"If I agree to do this for you unofficially as you so delicately put it, it will cost you a great deal more than just a glass of wine."

"You drive a hard bargain Pat. I'll drop the material into you later."

"You certainly know how to sweet talk a woman Terry," she laughed before disconnecting the call.

Reaching down he pulled his briefcase from under his desk and unlocked it, then he took out the notes from his meeting at TG International. The evidence bag containing the letter went into the case before he locked it again then glancing at his computer screen he decided to deal with his e-mails before looking at his notes. Going through them one at a time, he either responded or deleted them depending on their content. With that done, he got to work. All the women he had interviewed earlier agreed on one thing, their attacker was a woman and he wondered if this was why their complaints had not been taken seriously in the first place. Case notes from the archives were incomplete and papers lost in the filing system could be anywhere.

There was nothing to suggest that the attacker was a woman and no one had bothered to transfer the notes onto the computer system, so he had to be content and work with what he had. None of the women had suffered a serious injury but two of them had attended casualty, there would be a record of that. It seemed that no one had followed up the complaints or tried to identify the attacker, the case notes were simply filed away.

Sitting back in his chair, he first considered the facts then he began to speculate. Either the attacker had grown tired of assaulting transgender women or she had moved into another area, perhaps progressing onto something more serious. A trawl of the serious incidents file on the computer system had drawn a blank, there were no other assaults reported in the area resembling those that he was investigating.

Heaving himself up from his chair, he went to his filing cabinet and pulling a bunch of keys from his jacket pocket, he unlocked the top drawer. Sliding out the file that DS Woods had given him he removed the photographs before returning it to the cabinet where he locked it away again. Placing the photographs on his desk, he studied them closely. These were from the CCTV system at the King Edward Hotel and could possibly be images of the killer. None of the women he had interviewed was able to describe their attacker but they had all agreed, she had long dark hair pulled back into a ponytail.

Reaching for the telephone on his desk, he looked up Robert Nixon's number before dialling. He was in luck, four of the women were due to attend a Yoga session that evening so he decided to drop in after delivering the letter to Pat. He wanted to show them the photographs, see if it would jog any memories. He should do the same with Mia, if the killer was connected with the crew that she worked with then maybe she could make an identification.

"You were right you know," Emilia said as she entered the tiny office.

Ben looked up from the computer screen and wondered what she was talking about.

"Jenna O'Brien's situation is impossible and I really don't know how I can help her."

"Well, as I said before, it's hardly your problem, callous though it may sound."

She studied her brother and smiled sadly. Ben stood up and shuffling round the desk, took her in his arms and hugged her gently.

"You are far too caring Em, you can't possibly solve everyone's problems."

"I know," she sighed. "I should have listened to you in the first place. Jenna is fully aware of her options and only she can decide what to do."

"Would you like me to make you a cup of coffee?"

Emilia looked over his shoulder at the clock on the wall.

"No thank you, look at the time, you have been here far too long already. Are you seeing Mia this evening?"

"I don't know," he shrugged his shoulders and moving away from her he said. "I haven't heard from her today."

"Then don't you think you should telephone her?"

Ben thought for a moment before realising that she was right so reaching for his mobile phone he found her number.

Mia answered the moment his name appeared on the screen.

"Please bring wine," she told him. "I'm going to soak in a bath first so don't come too early."

They chatted for a few moments before Ben suggested food.

"Can you pick up a takeaway?" Mia asked, thinking about the state of her cupboards and fridge.

"Thai?" he suggested.

"Yes, Thai would be perfect."

Mia smiled as she disconnected the call, she was overjoyed at the prospect of spending the evening with Ben, but her working day was not over yet. She really should telephone Alicia. Her agent had left several messages but after listening to them all Mia had unplugged the phone, she wanted to avoid another unpleasant call. Her mobile phone also displayed several missed calls including a text message from Alicia urging her to make contact. Weighing the phone in her hand, she was tempted to make the call, but then she glanced at the clock on the wall and decided against the idea. Alicia would not be at her office at this time of the evening so she decided to pay her a visit first thing in the morning.

Going into the bathroom, she pulled down the blind and began to fill the bath, adding a dash of bath oil to the warm water before peeling off her clothes. Once the bath was full, she lowered herself into the luxuriously scented water and groaned with delight. Almost at once, she could feel her muscles relax and the tension of the last few days gradually eased. Laying her head back against the waterproof cushion, she closed her eyes and felt herself drifting away, doing nothing to fight the sensation, she simply allowed her thoughts to run their course.

From somewhere in the distance she could hear a sound. At first, she thought it was water dripping from the tap, but then something sharper followed and she opened her eyes. Peering through the steam she was sure that someone was at the bathroom window, but the blind was down and the window firmly closed. The noise came again, a sharp tap against glass followed by another sound that she did not recognise. Someone was definitely in the alleyway between her building and the house next door. Suddenly the doorbell rang and she was startled. It could only be Ben so heaving herself from the bath, she reached for the robe hanging on the back of the door. Pulling it on, she hurried along the hall towards the door and sliding the security chain across, opened it a crack before peering out. A cold breeze stung her eyes then she realised that it was not Ben standing there at all; it was her father.

"Mia, are you alright?"

The sound of his voice cheered her so slipping off the security chain she opened the door wider and allowed him to enter.

"I was taking a bath and almost fell asleep," she told him ruefully.

"That can be very dangerous you know. I've seen the result of people falling asleep in a bath full of water."

"Surely it's impossible to drown, reflexes would kick in and wake you up."

"Maybe you are right," he said not wanting to dwell on the subject.

"What time is it? Ben is supposed to be coming round."

Terry glanced at his watch. "It's eight fifteen."

"Goodness, I didn't realise that it was so late. Do you mind making yourself a cup of tea whilst I find some clothes and do something with my hair?"

Terry grinned, it was okay for him to see her in a mess, but it would not do for Ben to see her like this.

"Go and do what you need to do, I'll make myself comfortable in the living room."

Mia smiled sweetly before disappearing into her bedroom.

Twenty minutes later the doorbell rang again but it was Terry who answered it this time.

"Good evening Mr Ashton," Ben said uncertainly. He did not expect to be greeted by Mia's father.

"Ben, hello. Why don't you come in?"

He squeezed past and the aroma of a Thai takeaway rose up between them reminding Terry that he had not eaten all day. Turning to close the door, he thought he could see movement on the driveway opposite. It was dark and the streetlight did very little to illuminate the shadows. Stepping out, he walked swiftly along the garden path, and peered at the house across the road. It was in darkness, there were no lights in the windows and no car on the drive. He waited, his senses heightened. If someone were hiding in the bushes they would be able to see him, but he remained rooted to the spot then, after a few moments he gave up and retraced his steps. Returning to the flat, he closed the door behind him before dropping to his knees, then prising open the mail flap he peered out. It was a few moments before anything happened but then a figure dressed in a dark tracksuit emerged. Clearly, it was a woman and she was wearing a baseball cap pulled low to hide her features. Terry was on his feet but by the time he had the door open she was gone.

"What's going on?" Mia appeared with Ben close behind her.

"I thought I saw someone hiding in the shadows," Terry grunted. "Did you notice anyone out there just now Ben?"

"I saw a woman out running, she passed me further along the street."

"Did you see her clearly?"

"No not really," he frowned before going on. "She was wearing a cap so I didn't see her face. She was nothing out of the ordinary, medium build I suppose with her hair pulled back into a ponytail."

Terry grunted then producing the photographs from his pocket he asked. "Did she look anything like this?"

Ben turned back into the hallway where the light was better and Terry closed the door before following them into the living room. Ben studied the photographs carefully, they were grainy and not well focussed, but he could make out a woman standing in what looked like a lift. The other pictures were of the same woman pushing a trolley along a corridor. He guessed they were taken at the King Edward Hotel.

"I'm not sure," he said at last. "I didn't see her clearly, but her build is similar and she also has a ponytail."

"Who is that?" Mia asked as she appeared beside him.

"I was hoping you could tell me." Terry said regarding his daughter closely.

She scrutinised the photographs but after a few moments gave up. "I have no idea who she is, the details are not clear enough, but there is something vaguely familiar about her. Perhaps it's her body language or maybe the way she is standing."

"Could it be someone you have worked with, backstage crew perhaps?"

"We don't have many women working back stage, maybe she is from

188

make-up or wardrobe." She reeled off a number of jobs associated with women.

"Do you work with the same crew each time you perform?"

"Most venues have their own technical crew, but there are a few familiar faces that seem to crop up from time to time."

"Okay," he nodded thoughtfully. "If you have any other thoughts let me know immediately."

Mia was about to tell him about the sound she had heard at the bathroom window, but he continued talking.

"I will get a car to patrol this way but if anything at all happens then call it in, better still call me."

Mia promised that she would then hugging her father, she saw him to the door.

"Keep your eyes peeled Mia."

"I will Dad, you take care too."

Terry headed along the street away from where he had left his car but there was nothing to see. He needed to be sure that the danger had passed. If the woman had merely been out running then what was she doing lurking in the bushes opposite Mia's flat. Going to his car he opened the boot and found a torch, he was determined to check the driveway and the shadows around the bushes.

Chapter
FORTY

The following morning Mia went to see her agent Alicia. The day was wet and cold, the sky heavy and grey. Since the last cold snap at Christmas, the temperature had been unseasonably mild, but now a weather front was moving in from the west bringing with it the threat of heavy rain.

Mia pushed against the glass door and holding it open with her foot, shook off her sodden umbrella.

"Miss Ashton." The receptionist cried as she glanced up and rising to her feet, she moved noisily across the foyer on heels that would cripple her before the day was out. "Please, let me take that for you."

Grasping the dripping umbrella, she held it away from herself and retreated quickly back to her desk where she propped it up in the waste paper bin.

"I'm here to see Alicia," Mia told the girl who appeared young enough to qualify as a day release student from a local school or college.

"I will let her know that you have arrived." Her smile was genuine. "If you would care to take a seat." She indicated to a collection of easy chairs arranged around a tiny table by the window.

Mia settled herself and unbuttoned her coat. Heat rising from the under floor system did its best to dry her shoes, but she knew that if she sat there long enough she would be forced to remove her coat.

"Ms Wicks will see you now Miss Ashton," the receptionist appeared at her side. "You are to go right up, she is looking forward to your meeting."

"I'm sure she is," Mia smiled uncertainly.

The lift door opened the moment the button was pressed and she stepped in, Alicia must have sent it down for her. Mia knew that it went directly to her floor; the lifts on the other side of the reception area serviced the levels above.

"Mia," Alicia said as soon as she arrived. They hugged briefly then Alicia led the way to her office. "Sit," she demanded, then sliding behind her desk she said. "Make yourself comfortable."

The garishly upholstered chairs were typical of the brightly coloured office. Alicia adored colour and dressed accordingly, but Mia almost shuddered as she sat down. She decided to keep her coat on, as her outfit would clash terribly with the decor.

"I'm sorry that I was not available when you called yesterday," Mia began. "It's not that I have been ignoring you, in fact I have been helping the police with their inquiries."

"Poor you," Alicia pursed her lips, "how utterly beastly."

Mia couldn't help thinking that Alicia would relish the attention of a room full of detectives.

"It was not a pleasant experience I can assure you of that." She wanted to say that the police seemed convinced that she was somehow involved in the murders, but she kept her thoughts to herself.

"It's a terrible business but we must strive to rise above it."

Mia stared at her agent and wondered how she could remain so cool and detached from it all. Alicia must be up to something, she would find a way to turn this dreadful business to her advantage, she had said on more than one occasion that no publicity is bad publicity. It didn't seem to matter who was disadvantaged as long as her precious organisation came out on top.

"I'm thinking about pulling out of my next concert." There, she had said it and now all she had to do was to brace herself for the reaction.

"There's no need for that," Alicia replied, her eyes wide with alarm. "You have plenty of time to prepare, besides, it's all arranged."

"How can we possibly go ahead, don't you understand, people have been murdered?"

"Well that may be so, but the show has to go on, you know that. It would be grossly unprofessional to pull out now."

Alicia seemed to have had a change of heart. It was not so long ago that she had suggested postponing the remaining concerts.

"Unprofessional," Mia seethed. "Three people have been killed and I'm not prepared to risk the life of another."

"Look, you don't have to worry about a thing. I can assure you that procedures will be put in place, safeguards designed to protect you and your colleagues."

Leaning forward in her chair, Mia struggled to control her anger. "How can you possibly assure me? There were police officers all over the Barbican and still Suzie Chahal was murdered."

"You are overreacting."

Mia was speechless, she stared at her agent for several seconds before finding her voice.

"People have died Alicia..."

"You don't have to remind me of that," Alicia said cutting her off. "I am fully aware of the situation."

They glared at each other having reached an impasse and both women realised that to go further would prove to be disastrous. Mia had to remain calm, she could hardly say what she was really thinking. Alicia might be a complete and utter bitch, but she wielded great power and could quite easily destroy her career.

"Listen to me," Alicia hissed icily as her elegantly manicured fingertips played over the keys of her laptop. "The musician who will be accompanying you at your next concert is a Russian pianist by the name of Viktor Vasiliev." She positioned the laptop so Mia could see the screen. "Viktor is a pianist of some repute who has performed with some prestigious orchestras in Russia and across Europe. We are extremely fortunate that he has agreed to step in and work with you."

Mia studied the screen in silence. She had of course heard of Viktor Vasiliev but had never seen him perform.

"I have also managed to re-arrange your schedule." Alicia chose not to mention that the pianist originally booked to appear with Mia had cancelled, or the fact that she was now in the process of speaking with her lawyers for breach of contract.

"As you can see, he is something of a catch. Viktor is a proven talent and very much available."

Mia looked up just in time to see Alicia's eyes flash. The prospect of meeting Viktor obviously excited her very much.

"When did he agree to this?" she asked.

"He's already in the UK playing in Cardiff at the moment. He has concerts booked in Lancashire and Scotland and in a few weeks time will be in London. His agent was overjoyed at the prospect of working with us."

"Really?" Mia frowned suspiciously, hardly able to take in what Alicia was saying.

"He genuinely wants to perform with you. Apparently he has heard of you and admires your work." Alicia watched her closely, looking for a reaction before going on. "It's not as if the murderer is likely to strike here, it's young women he's after." She paused again. "This is an opportunity that you can hardly afford to miss, performing with Viktor Vasiliev will be very good for us."

"The date for this concert is only six weeks away so what is the theme and the musical arrangements?"

The title of the concert is 'Over the Rainbow'. The first half will be dedicated to theme tune variations and other selected music from the film Wizard of Oz." Alicia passed a file across the table.

"As you can see, the movement lasts for twenty six minutes and is an arrangement that Viktor knows well."

Mia studied the file in silence.

"The second half comprises of an exciting collection of Oriental influenced movements. As it says there in the file, these are arrangements for piano and cello and listed as beautifully mystical melodies from the Far East."

Mia looked up. "Has Viktor seen this?"

"Oh yes, his agent has a copy of that file. We discussed it at some length and he assures me that Viktor will be more than happy with the arrangements."

"I see," Mia replied and looking at the paperwork again, she thought about the practicalities of learning the pieces, taking into consideration the time frame. There would hardly be an opportunity to rehearse with Viktor himself, but it was essential to go through the music with a pianist. Someone would have to be available to play Viktor's part.

"Don't worry," Alicia could see what was going through her mind. "I have organised a pianist, in fact she is already learning her part. You will have enough time to rehearse using both instruments."

"You had better get me the sheet music then. I'm not entirely happy with this but I will of course take a look at it."

Alicia was convinced that Mia was hooked, she could hardly afford to turn down an offer like this.

"As I said before, this will be a great opportunity for you to work with one of the world's top pianists. I must admit though I was astonished when he agreed to step in."

"He is such a big name," Mia agreed. "I assume his team will be taking care of publicity and ticket sales."

"Well, that's where you're wrong," Alicia looked up and smiled triumphantly. "His agent made it quite clear that we are to arrange everything. It's your concert and Viktor sees himself as accompanying you."

Mia was shocked at that. "So, will we be performing at the little theatre in Barking as arranged?"

"No, did I not say," Alicia paused for effect. "The Royal Albert Hall has offered us a date."

Again, Mia was shocked. "No pressure then," she mumbled, her eyes glazing over at the prospect.

Belenos laid down his pen and massaged the sides of his head with his fingertips. His eyes felt gritty and he was in need of coffee. The first draft of his introduction into the lives of transgender people was complete and he was pleased with the results. Of course, now the editing process would have to begin but the hard work had been done. Taking a deep breath, he held onto it for a few seconds before letting it out then he began to read through what he had written. His red pen was already in his hand and occasionally he used it to make a correction or to re-arrange words so they read more easily. He took particular care when using the quotes that Chrissie Bird and Michael Faith had provided, to use anything out of context at this stage would be a disaster.

Belenos liked to work using a pen, he was a champion at writing his first draft by hand. Only when that was done and the first edit complete would he commit it to his laptop. He would have it no other way. When he had worked in an office his colleagues had ridiculed him mercilessly, but this system worked for him. He found that by using a pen, he could express his thoughts more effectively and he regarded copy typing as just another part of the editing process.

Glancing at his notes, he began to read a section that he originally wanted to include in his first piece, but decided that with a little more work it would do as the foundation for the second instalment. Flicking back through the pages, he found the notes he had taken when talking to Jenna O'Brien. She had told him about Lizzie Baines, one of Josie MacDonald's friends. Lizzie had been a transgender woman and unfortunately a victim of William Randolph, or Mr Mac as he had liked to be called. Belenos had intended to ask Robert Nixon about Lizzie when visiting TG International but the opportunity never presented itself. Reaching for his mobile phone, he looked up the number before pressing the dial button.

"Hello, Robert Nixon." He answered after the second ring.

"Mr Nixon, its Belenos Falzone here."

"Mr Falzone, good afternoon. How can I help you?"

Belenos told him that he had completed the first draft of the introduction piece and asked if he would care to see it before it was released it to his editor.

"As I told you before Mr Falzone, if you have been objective in your report and dealt with issues sensitively then I see no reason to appraise it before publication."

"That is very good of you. I can assure you that there is nothing derogatory in my account. I'm certain that both Chrissie and Michael will be happy with what I have written."

"Good," Nixon said before rising to his feet. He had been sitting down for too long.

"There is something that I meant to ask you the other day."

"Oh yes," Nixon replied as he shuffled away from his desk.

"I'm interested in a case of abduction and murder that took place last year. One of the victims was a transgender woman called Lizzie Baines."

"Ah yes, Lizzie Baines." He stopped at the window and stared down at the car park.

"Was she one of your clients?"

"Yes she was," Nixon frowned as he remembered Lizzie. "She used to attend some of the sessions here at the centre, but as you are aware I'm not obliged to give you any of her details."

"I quite understand, I just wondered if Lizzie was known to you and what kind of a person she was."

"I see," he said turning away from the window. "I got to know Lizzie quite well over the time that she attended the centre, I also became acquainted with her parents." His voice took on a lower tone. "She was a loving and caring person, devoted to her family. It's such a pity that she was taken from us and in such distressing circumstances."

He was silent for several seconds before Belenos realised that he would say no more.

"Thank you Mr Nixon. I'm not working on that particular case at the moment, but it does intrigue me. There are so many questions about the abductions and murders left unanswered and I'm determined to find out why that is."

"I would be very careful with that Mr Falzone. Perhaps these questions remain unanswered for a very good reason."

Chapter
FORTY ONE

DI Ashton was at the Westminster Mortuary.

"The only prints that we could find on that letter belong to your daughter."

Ashton grimaced, he was hoping for more.

"Sorry Terry," Pat's expression softened as she stepped towards him. "The author has been very careful, she must have been wearing gloves."

"She?" he said picking up instantly on what Pat had just said.

"Analysis experts agree that it was written by a woman using a ballpoint pen. The ink was cheap, so probably a plastic disposable pen and given the range of colours it was probably one of those multi colour retractable point types."

"Like we used to have at school?" Terry smiled.

"Exactly," she replied.

"Was the woman who wrote it right handed?"

"Yes." Pat chose not to go into the science used to determine this fact.

Terry thought for a moment, pinching the bridge of his nose between his thumb and forefinger.

"Is there anything you can tell me about the Suzie Chahal autopsy?"

Pat knew that he was not officially investigating the case but this did not stop her from giving him the details.

"The MO is the same as the others then?"

Pat nodded, she had seen the CCTV photographs from the King Edward Hotel and knew that the suspect was a woman. In her mind this made complete sense, she was convinced that a woman had killed Suzie

Chahal. She also thought the same in the case of Victoria Stevens, in fact, the report she had received from Dr Ralph Hughes in York regarding Alison Morley was almost identical to the ones she had written.

"Thank you Pat, I really appreciate this." He held up the evidence bag containing the letter.

"So," she smiled sweetly at him. "Where are you taking me then?"

"Where would you like to go?" he turned the question back onto her with a shrug of his shoulders.

"Anywhere expensive as long as it's not the Richmond. I understand that has become a regular watering hole for officers of the Met, besides isn't that where DI Mallinson is staying?"

"I'll have to think of somewhere else then."

"Do you like French cuisine?" she asked.

"Yes I don't mind."

"Then I know where we can go. There is a place called 'Raymond Duval's' or something like that. I've been meaning to try it out, it has some very good reviews."

"Okay," Terry nodded. "I'll check it out and see if they have a table available for later this week. Friday evening suit you?"

"Friday suits me very well indeed," she responded with a satisfied grin.

When Ashton returned to the Yard there were more officers working in the murder room, but still Mallinson and Keable were nowhere to be seen. DS Woods was sitting at a desk talking on the telephone and as he walked past, she looked up at him and raised her eyebrows. She was talking to someone at the Information Commissioners Office.

Going into his office, he unlocked the top drawer of his desk and pulled out the notes from the TG International interviews. An idea had just occurred to him and he wanted to check the dates of the attacks on Debbie Sotheby and Ruth Smith. Jotting the information down in his notebook, he looked to see that he still had the CCTV photographs in his pocket, then locking away Mia's letter he turned and left.

PC Bill Yearsley was known by his colleagues as a 'Super Recogniser'. He could identify more than eight hundred suspects from photographs, computer and CCTV screens. Ashton had used his predecessor before to help identify suspects but had yet to meet PC Yearsley.

"Bill, I wonder if you can help me."

PC Yearsley was twenty eight years old and had been in the force since joining as a cadet. His close cropped fair hair, angular features, and well formed shoulders reminded Ashton of a military type and when he got to his feet the young man towered over him.

"My name is DI Ashton," Terry said by way of introduction. "I'm currently working on a case of multiple assaults whilst assisting on a murder inquiry." He put that last bit in to lend credibility to his request.

"How can I help you sir?" PC Yearsley asked as they shook hands.

"Do you recognise this woman?"

Yearsley took the photographs and scrutinised them carefully before replying.

"The Matron has beaten you to it sir."

"Ah," Terry replied looking sheepish. "I haven't had chance to speak with DS Woods yet," was all he could think of saying.

"Are these the CCTV shots taken from the King Edward Hotel?"

Ashton nodded in agreement.

"I'm afraid to say that I don't recognise this woman."

"I'm not surprised." Terry said as he took the photographs from Yearsley. "The picture quality isn't that good."

"It's not just the features, I study the whole body." He explained.

"Do you have access to surveillance cameras around the city?"

"Yes sir."

"Could you check some of those cameras if I gave you times and dates?"

"I could try." Yearsley replied, eager to please.

Taking his place behind an oversized computer screen, he tapped a button on the keyboard and entered a password whilst Ashton pulled his notebook from his pocket. Opening it up on the page, he placed it on the desk beside the keyboard.

"These dates are more than a year old." Yearsley said turning to face Ashton.

"Is that a problem?"

"Yes, most hard drives connected to cameras where the footage is stored, will delete the older images once the memory is full to make way for the new stuff. Typically this will happen every thirty to ninety days depending on the storage capacity of the system being used."

"Ah," was Ashton's reply.

"We could try, see what I can find." He didn't sound hopeful.

Entering the location followed by the dates he stared at his screen, but it was no use. If anything had been stored in the first place, it had been deleted long ago.

"The building these cameras overlook may have its own surveillance equipment." Yearsley began. "It all depends of course on the business occupying it."

Ashton nodded in encouragement and Yearsley went on.

"If they were aware of an assault taking place on their premises and they managed to capture it on camera they might still have it saved on a computer, especially if it was reported at the time."

"Okay," Ashton nodded, "good work." Why had he not thought of that? "I have another location for you and yesterday's date."

Ashton read out the details including the time span then leaning closer to the screen he watched as Yearsley typed in the parameters.

"There appears to be several cameras in that area."

"Can we start with the closest one to that location then work out from there?"

"Yes sir."

Mia's flat was not overlooked by a camera, the nearest was situated further along the street. The picture that appeared on the screen was black and white, the image made worse by the glare from a nearby streetlamp. The system produced sixteen frames per minute so the film jerked from still to still. Anyone passing by quickly would either not show up at all or appear as a partial image.

"What are we looking for sir?"

"A female runner dressed in a tracksuit and a baseball cap."

"Okay," Yearsley muttered as he focussed his attention on the screen.

After several moments, he began to switch between cameras widening their search and on several occasions, they thought they saw something only to discover an arm or leg disappearing off screen. The monotone stills flashing rhythmically one after the other reminded Ashton of an old black and white film.

"What is that?" he said suddenly, poking his finger at the screen.

The image was partially hidden by the shadows but it seemed to reveal a figure dressed in dark clothing getting into a car.

"It's a Ford Focus," Yearsley said identifying the make of the car, "but it's impossible to read the licence plate."

The next still revealed an empty space.

"Let's check them all again but this time we are looking for a car." Extending the timeframe by five minutes, they still failed to spot anything useful.

"Perhaps we are going about this the wrong way."

Ashton glanced at the young officer and waited for him to continue.

"We have an image from this camera." He pointed at one of the squares on the screen, which had been split into a dozen frames each representing an individual location. "Why don't we concentrate on this one and try to find out when the car arrived."

"Good idea," Ashton nodded. "Let's do that."

Yearsley minimised all the other views and enlarged the one they were interested in, then running the film backwards, they waited for something to happen.

"Here we go," Yearsley said, his voice filled with excitement.

They watched as the car appeared.

"It's our Ford Focus but I can only get a partial index number."

Zooming in, the picture quality deteriorated but it was enough to see that the vehicle was empty. The time delay meant they had missed the occupant exiting the car.

"We can now check the cameras using this new timeframe."

After a few minutes, they picked up a figure wandering along the footpath.

"I know this person," Ashton said as he recognised the back of Benjamin Sykes. "He told me that a female runner passed him along one of these streets."

Tracking his progress along the footpath they watched as he stepped into the road, then they struck lucky.

"Freeze that one," Ashton whispered as he peered at the screen.

It was only a partial, a female runner with her head turned slightly towards the camera. Half of her body was missing, an arm and leg out of shot, but it was enough for Ashton, this was the woman he had seen outside Mia's flat.

"Can I see your photographs again sir?"

Studying the screen closely Yearsley fiddled with the resolution in a bid to sharpen the image then he compared the results with the photographs of the woman from the King Edward Hotel.

"It's the same person," he said confidently. "I'll print this off for you, maybe it will give you a clearer perspective sir."

With the print in his hand, Ashton could indeed see it better. Yearsley went on to explain the similarities between the women, the size and shape of her face, her posture and even her body language. The runner also had long hair, but Ashton couldn't see it clearly in this new image, it was a merely a blur rising over her left shoulder. Benjamin Sykes had told him that the woman he had seen had her hair pulled back into a ponytail. The peak of her cap was shading her face and even with further enhancing, it was impossible to improve the picture. Yearsley was confident however that she was the woman from the hotel.

"Thank you Bill," Ashton said. "It seems I owe you a drink."

"Anytime sir," he smiled. "Maybe I'll see you one day after a shift in the Richmond."

On his way to his car, Ashton telephoned Robert Nixon.

"Inspector, good afternoon. What can I do for you?"

Ashton asked if his organisation used a surveillance system.

"Yes we do have cameras set up around the perimeter of the property."

"Debbie Sutherby and Ruth Smith were both attacked in the car park. Do you have CCTV coverage of either event?"

"Yes Inspector, now you come to mention it I'm sure it was saved on one of the computers here."

"Could you find it for me?"

"Of course, I'll try my best."

"I'm on my way."

By the time Aston arrived, Robert Nixon had recovered the file.

"Inspector Ashton." Nixon met him at the door, and climbing the stairs to his office he said, "I have what you asked for."

A kaleidoscope of lines and colours swirled around the computer screen on his desk but with the touch of a key, the confusion disappeared. The computer would not reveal its secrets until Nixon typed in a password then he activated an icon on his home page and the first image appeared.

"This is Debbie," Nixon said.

A woman lying face down on the tarmac was clearly the victim of an assault, but her attacker was only partially visible.

"The next one is much clearer," Nixon promised.

He was right. This image revealed Ruth Smith frozen in an awkward manoeuvre having just received a blow to the back of her head. Her mouth was partially open in an expression of surprise and only one of her feet was in contact with the ground. If the camera had taken the next shot, she would have been completely airborne.

The attacker was in profile, poised in what looked like a golfers swing. She was wielding a stick-like weapon of some kind with her ponytail fanned out behind her head, frozen in an action shot as she twisted away from the camera. She was dressed in a brightly coloured tracksuit.

Nixon zoomed in.

"Sorry Inspector," he said as the picture blurred.

Pulling the pictures from his pocket, Ashton compared them to the image on the screen.

"The same person wouldn't you say?" glancing at Nixon he sought confirmation.

Chapter
FORTY TWO

Mia was in her music room tuning her cello to the key required to play the next set of arrangements. A portfolio of sheet music lay on top of the little cabinet beside the door and gradually she was working her way through it, acquainting herself with the unfamiliar tunes.

Her meeting with Alicia had taken an unexpected turn, the thought of performing with someone like Viktor Vasiliev at the Royal Albert Hall was completely insane. To have been noticed by a musician of his calibre was both exciting and terrifying. Her career seemed to be heading in the right direction after all despite the recent terrible events.

Mia had convinced herself that given the circumstances, her next concert at the very least should be cancelled then she would be excused the pressure of preparing, but suddenly everything was back on track. It was true that she had several weeks in which to prepare, but with everything else going on in her life, she was in for an intense time ahead.

Alicia had made it quite clear that there was no room for negotiation and if she insisted on not fulfilling her contractual obligations then dire consequences could follow. This unbending attitude only added to the growing pressure that surrounded Mia.

Embracing her cello, she took a deep breath and banished all other thoughts from her mind it was now time to concentrate on nothing else but the music. Drawing her bow across the strings, she arranged her fingers and began to play.

Belenos decided to spend some time working on what he called 'The

William Randolph Affair'. He had started a portfolio, which contained notes about the once wealthy landowner and his serial killer son, Mr Mac. What interested him most however was discovering more about Randolph's illegitimate daughter Phillipa Weston.

Going to his computer, he accessed an on-line people search site that he had used before. The service provided search results from various social networks including public records and search engines. Entering the name Phillipa into the information box, he added her surname and date of birth before hitting the search button he then waited for the results. The name of her mother appeared with a few random dates, information that he had seen before so refining his search he settled for a more detailed approach and this time was not disappointed. He explored people in the UK with the name Phillipa Weston and seventy hits appeared on the screen. Sitting back in his chair, he pursed his lips before deciding how to filter the results. First, he deleted all those from the wrong age category, this reduced his list to fifteen, then he began to look at regions. He was only interested in those born in London. He could have used her date of birth and reduced the list even further but he wanted to see who else could potentially be the woman he was looking for. He was left with three names, two had emigrated, one to New Zealand, the other to Spain but the remaining file proved interesting. It was an address in Blackheath, with an e-mail address and a social network profile attached to the dossier. This he tried first, but her profile had been abandoned two years previously. There was however, a photograph of Phillipa so he saved it to his file. Next, he tried the address in Blackheath, clicking the link that would take him to the postal address, he discovered that Phillipa no longer lived there. Now all he had was the e-mail address, so compiling a short message he sent it and waited for a response. It was as expected, the message came back as undeliverable, the e-mail address no longer existed. Before giving up, he checked out the women who had emigrated but they appeared to be genuine.

Next, he tried the Births, Marriages and Deaths website looking specifically at deaths, but Phillipa was not amongst the ranks of the deceased. It seemed that the person he was interested in had simply vanished. Going into his file, he studied the photograph. An almost boyish face stared back at him with piercing blue eyes, her fair hair was cropped short revealing ears that were not pierced. There was nothing appealing about her.

"Where have you gone?" he mumbled thoughtfully.

He wondered if she would appear on the police missing persons register, but he could not access that file so he decided to trawl the newspapers, see if there were any articles about missing persons in the London area from around two years ago. Thirty minutes later, he gave up, there were several reports from the period he was interested in, but none of them related to Phillipa.

Suddenly his telephone began to ring.

"Hello Belenos Falzone."

"Hi Belenos, it's Jenna, Jenna O'Brien."

Her bow travelled lightly over the strings as she played a bass note that signified the end of the movement then Mia hung her head and breathed deeply. She felt disorientated and struggled to make the transition back to reality, but the music was not ready to give her up yet.

The title of the Oriental piece that she had just played was not translated into English so she had no idea what it meant. The notes accompanying the music told her that it was a mix of ancient music set to a modern theme, its emotive powers both hypnotic and soothing. It was quite different from the first part of the performance and she was worried that the arrangements were not compatible. A theme on 'The Wizard of Oz', would hardly sit well beside ancient Oriental music she had thought, but she was wrong. The juxtaposition worked well, whoever had put these quite different pieces together was a genius as far as she was concerned.

Taking another deep breath, Mia opened her eyes and began to move her shoulders, her overworked muscles were tired and would soon stiffen if she did not go through her warm down routine. The music was still playing inside her head, echoes of the mysterious composition refusing to let her go, but rising slowly to her feet, she placed her cello on its stand then tiptoed around the sheets that lay on the floor. These she had flicked from the music stand with the tip of her bow as each movement ended revealing the one beneath. She would have to be more careful when at the Royal Albert Hall, it would not do to have the audience see her throwing sheet music all over the floor during her performance. She decided to leave them where they were, collect them up later, what she needed now was a mug of strong coffee.

Going into the kitchen, she filled the kettle before reaching for a cafétiére then waiting for the kettle to boil, she began to analyse her performance whilst rotating the stiffness from her shoulders. The first part, 'Over the Rainbow', was simple enough, having played it through twice with no obvious problems, she was happy with the arrangement. It was an engaging piece designed to connect with the audience and maybe even induce a little foot tapping. This part of the concert would be popular with every age group, she thought, but the second part was quite different.

The kettle began to rumble as it came to the boil and all thoughts of music were forgotten as Mia prepared her coffee. Pouring it into a mug, she added a splash of milk before carrying it into the living room where she settled carefully on the sofa. She was looking forward to relaxing for a few moments but thoughts of Alicia popped into her head and cursing under her breath, any prospect of tranquillity was lost. Going over the events of their meeting, she knew that her agent could be hard-nosed at times and in the past, this had often worked to her advantage, but being on the receiving end was not a pleasant experience. She was not used to Alicia's bullying tactics and was not happy about doing another concert, but she had no choice. Alicia had made it quite clear that she had contractual obligations, this was true, but given the circumstances, she had expected a postponement of her next concert. It would be a prudent interlude, allow the police time to put an end to the killings. She couldn't help thinking that if it were not for her, those poor young women would still be alive. She should have fought harder, made her agent appreciate the dangers, but it was pointless. Alicia would not listen.

Breathing in the vapours rising from her mug she turned her thoughts to Viktor Vasiliev. When Alicia first mentioned the Russian pianist, she was convinced that her agent had been joking, but then she produced an official document from Viktor's agent proving his intention to perform with her.

"Perhaps this will be an opportunity to break this chain of unfortunate events that accompany your concerts." Alicia had said.

Surely, the killer would not be interested in Viktor, it was young female musicians that were targeted, so he would be quite safe. Not once did it occur to Mia that this time she might be the victim.

Suddenly her thoughts were disturbed by a ring tone and reaching for her mobile phone, she checked the screen before answering. It was her father calling.

Chapter
FORTY THREE

When DI Ashton returned to his office, he found an envelope waiting for him on his desk. It was his daughter's telephone records. Laying the documents out in front of him, he reached for his notebook and found the dates that she had given him. These were the times of the anonymous telephone calls to both her home phone and mobile. He studied the documents, cross referencing the information but something did not add up, there was no record of incoming calls at the times she had suggested. Perhaps she had made a mistake, he thought, so highlighting the numbers closest to the dates in question, he wanted to know who had made these calls. He decided the best way would be to ask her himself. He also wanted her to look at the latest print of the attacker from the car park at TG International; it was the clearest image so far. There was not yet enough evidence to confirm that this was the murderer of Suzie Chahal, but there were a number of similarities emerging. He should take what he had to Mallinson, but Ashton decided to keep it to himself for the time being, besides he felt sure that DS Woods was not too far behind him with her own investigations.

Pushing the telephone records back into the envelope, he reached for his computer keyboard and accessing the system, ran a check on the car he had seen on the CCTV camera close to Mia's home. With only a partial licence plate number, he was not confident of a result.

There were over nine hundred Ford Focus' on file, so by entering additional information he managed to reduce that number down to one hundred and five. Fifty of these were silver or grey, twenty seven were red and the remaining cars were either blue, black or white. The partial licence plate did however confirm that he was looking for a red car. This surprised him given that the most popular colour was either silver or grey.

He sighed and looked away from the screen. It was all conjecture, without the full licence plate details there was no way of identifying the vehicle or its owner, besides it might not even be on their system. If he were to link this to the murder of Alison Morley then the traffic cameras in York would need to be checked. Perhaps the killer had used the vehicle to travel north. This was another job for PC Yearsley.

Yearsley was on the telephone when Ashton arrived at the surveillance centre. Not wanting to disturb his colleague, he remained out of sight in the corridor contemplating the purchase of coffee from the hot drinks dispenser, but he decided against this foolhardy notion. He'd already had the misfortune of sampling the dirty grey liquid that masqueraded as coffee and had vowed never to repeat the experience.

Yearsley ended his call and was about to scribble down a note when DI Ashton appeared.

"Sir," he called out amiably, inviting him into his domain.

"Bill, I'm sorry to be a nuisance, but something has come up that I would like you to take a look at."

His note forgotten, Yearsley swivelled his chair so he was facing Ashton.

"I have here a clearer picture of the person I showed you earlier." He said presenting his colleague with the print from TG International.

"You have been busy sir," Yearsley grinned, "but I still don't recognise the attacker I'm afraid."

"Can you access traffic cameras?"

Surprised by the sudden question he raised his eyebrows.

"Sure, we can access that information from NTOC."

"NTOC?"

"National Traffic Operations Centre."

"I see," Ashton said before asking. "Would they operate a recording system or are all their cameras live?"

"The Highways Authority operates a recording system but not all of the time. It rather depends on the location of the camera. Accident hot spots and city centres are more likely to be recorded."

"Okay," Ashton nodded thoughtfully. "I'm looking for a vehicle that may have been used in the city of York in December."

"There is a chance that some cameras would still have data from December. It's within the ninety day memory period."

Ashton gave him all the information he had.

"Not much to go on," Yearsley grumbled.

"We could narrow our search by concentrating on the cameras at the university campus. That is where the murder of a young woman took place and I'm hoping the killer drove there."

Turning to his computer, Yearsley typed in a command and carried out a search.

"The university is well outside the city centre so the cameras will not be so numerous." He waited for the information to appear, then reading from the screen he said. "There are six hundred and sixty CCTV cameras strategically placed across campus that are monitored and recorded twenty four hours a day." He was surprised, he had no idea there would be so many cameras.

"York Security Services operate all security measures on campus."

"Can we access those cameras?"

"I could, but given the amount of work I have and considering the fact that it could take days to search the city centre looking for your Ford Focus, I suggest that you contact the officials at the university." He tapped the screen with his fingertip before going on. "It says here that York security officials are trained professionals who are available twenty four hours a day. Why don't you get them to check their system?"

Ashton grunted before saying. "Good work. Can I leave the city centre search to you? I will contact the security people operating the system at the university."

"Yes sir, I'll let you know the moment I have anything."

Ashton returned to his office and telephoned the security operation in York, then he called his daughter.

Chapter
FORTY FOUR

Belenos was surprised at her invitation. She wanted him to accompany her to an art exhibition; the artist was Josie MacDonald so he agreed readily. He realised that that she must have a hidden agenda, Jenna O'Brien would not have asked him otherwise.

He picked her up at seven thirty.

"I'm so glad you agreed to drive," she said as he held the passenger door open for her.

Rain was beginning to fall heavily, the forecast shower turning into something more substantial.

"I couldn't bear the thought of traipsing across London in this weather." Jenna said glancing up at the sky.

"Tube and taxi would have done just as well," Belenos replied as he climbed in beside her, but she had begged him to drive and he could see no point in arguing.

Jenna was convinced that her father was having her followed. A man was trailing her wherever she went, he was always on foot, using the same public transport as her. She had never seen him behind the wheel of a car so by driving to the art exhibition she was hoping to shake him off.

Sitting quietly as Belenos steered his car through the puddles in the road, she clasped her hands together in her lap as thoughts raced through her head. Was she being paranoid? Did her father know about her meeting with a solicitor? Surely, he could not suspect her of applying for a marriage protection order.

"Are you okay?" Belenos asked. "You seem unusually quiet."

She looked at him and smiled, delighted by his concern.

"Oh, it's just this weather. I must be suffering from SAD Syndrome. What I need is a dose of sunshine."

"Don't we all," he laughed. He sensed there was more, but decided not to pry, she would probably tell him in her own time. Jenna was not a fan of keeping secrets.

Forty minutes later, they arrived at Timothy Granger's gallery, the venue for the exhibition. Belenos found a parking space close by and as the rain had eased, they decided to walk back without the aid of an umbrella.

"Jenna O'Brien and Belenos Falzone." She told the man at the door who simply smiled and took his time looking her over.

He checked the invitation that she held out towards him, then eventually he nodded and held the door open for them.

"Security at an art exhibition," Belenos whispered as they made their way towards the gallery.

"After what Josie has been through I guess she takes every precaution these days."

The gallery was filled with light, warmth and laughter. People were milling about enjoying the champagne and admiring the paintings. Everyone seemed to know each other and Belenos felt as if they had just crashed a private party. He did not see her at first, but Josie MacDonald was holding court surrounded by her friends. She was sitting at a small table piled with coloured brochures, Belenos had seen them dotted around the exhibition space, so picking one up he glanced at its contents. Easy to read paragraphs told him about the paintings and he discovered the inspiration behind each one. There was also a chart with price tags confirming that Josie's reputation as an artist was soaring, he should have invested in her work twelve months ago.

Tim Granger had done an impressive job showcasing her work, but Belenos realised that the publicity surrounding her terrible ordeal must have worked in her favour.

Glancing at the first exhibit, he was drawn towards it. Josie was a watercolourist and landscapes were her specialism. Some critics labelled her as a modern day Turner, although looking around the room Belenos thought her style more Constable than Turner.

"I simply adore this one," Jenna said and taking his arm, she guided him towards a pastoral scene.

A distant mountain range rose up in the background expertly captured by simple washes of purples and greys, but the eye was drawn to the foreground where a collection of pretty cottages was set around a village green.

"It looks as if it could have been painted a hundred years ago, don't you think?" She looked up at him, her expression full of admiration.

"Yes," he agreed and looking closer he realised that there were no cars in the composition. "I wonder if the lack of traffic was done by design?" he said in an effort to appear critically responsive.

"The only reference to modern day is the television aerial on the roof here and this satellite dish." Jenna had an eye for the finer details.

"I know this place," she told him. "It's a little village just outside Inverness. I can't remember the name of the place but I do recognise it."

Belenos doubted her certainty, to him it looked just like a thousand other village scenes.

Digging her elbow into his ribs, she looked hurt. "You don't believe me?"

"Yes, of course I do, your knowledge of Scotland is obviously far superior to mine."

"Check in your brochure, but note, I don't have one so I'm not cheating."

They laughed together. Belenos was glimpsing another side of Jenna. Usually she was loud, flirtatious and often half drunk, but tonight she was quite different.

"Come on, let's go and meet Josie."

"I didn't know she was a friend of yours."

"She isn't but she's greeting all her guests and as I'm a friend of a friend..."

They picked up a glass of champagne each and Jenna slipped her arm through his, holding onto him tightly as they made their way across the room.

Tim Granger was standing close behind Josie MacDonald with his hands resting protectively on her shoulders, but he did not remain there for long. He was a busy man, much in demand. It was his job to ensure that her work sold and at every opportunity, he was off to speak with another prospective buyer.

Belenos studied the group as they approached and it struck him that Josie was far more striking than he realised. Tabloid photographs did not do her justice. When she laughed her face lit up and he watched as she brushed stray hair from her face with the back of her hand. She was in the later stages of pregnancy and seemed to be carrying it well, but curiously, her ivory coloured dress was designed to hide her bump from the casual observer.

A petite dark haired woman stood close beside her, Belenos knew this was Tim's sister but he couldn't remember her name. He had read an article about her engineering design work in a magazine a few months ago and had found it fascinating. He would love the opportunity to talk to her.

Jenna introduced herself to Josie and they began talking animatedly. It seemed they had something in common but he failed to hear what passed between them. He smiled, content to stand back, the placid observer. He couldn't help thinking how similar they looked, they shared the same colouring and physical structure. Jenna was a very attractive woman but Belenos had never regarded her as a suitable partner, she was hardly his type. It seemed to him that she was far more vulnerable than she let on, perhaps this was the reason for her wild and irritating style.

"Can I introduce you to a dear friend of mine?" Jenna was saying then he realised that she was talking about him. Jenna had never referred to him as that before and stepping forward he took Josie's hand.

"Belenos," Josie smiled, "what an unusual name."

Resisting the urge to roll his eyes he looked at her and grinned. He had experienced this reaction a thousand times before, then, he launched into an explanation.

"My mother is Welsh, she adores Celtic mythology so named me after a Sun God."

"How fascinating, so where does Falzone come from, surely that's not a typical Welsh name."

"You are quite right," he paused as polite laughter rippled around the group. "My grandfather was an Italian immigrant who settled in Herefordshire during the 1930s."

Josie looked at him delighted by his story.

"How long did it take you to complete this fascinating collection?" Jenna asked drawing Josie's attention away from Belenos.

"About six months," came the reply.

Josie did not elaborate. The depression that followed her terrible ordeal had almost ended her career, but with the support of friends especially Tim she managed to return to her painting style.

"They are simply marvellous. I love Scotland and looking at your paintings I'm inspired to go for an extended visit."

"I would wait until summer if I were you, it can be rather chilly in Scotland at this time of year." Again, laughter followed Josie's comment.

Stepping away, Belenos moved closer to the dark haired woman.

"Hi," he said looking down at her.

She was barely five feet tall and he towered above her.

"Forgive me, I know you are Tim's sister but I can't remember your name."

"Oh," she replied. "Have we met before?"

"No, but I read an article about you recently in a magazine."

He was hoping that she would respond with a smile, but her expression remained neutral.

"I'm Belenos by the way."

"I know who you are," she snapped. "I heard your introduction speech." She paused as if trying to make up her mind then she told him. "My name is Kate Granger."

"Of course, how could I possibly forget?" This time she smiled but it was not as genuine as he would have liked.

"Your brother has done a fantastic job here," he tried again, hoping to find some common ground.

"He has worked very hard," she agreed, "they both have." Glancing around she searched for her brother, but he was on the other side of the room talking to another group of people.

"Will the exhibition continue after this evening?"

"Of course, it's due to run for the rest of the week, but it rather depends on what's left at the end of the evening."

"Quite," he nodded, "it does appear to be a successful evening so far."

Belenos watched as another little sold sticker was applied to a painting.

"Why are you here?" she asked suddenly.

"I'm here as a guest," he replied, surprised by her frosty attitude.

"I know you are a journalist."

"Ah," he smiled, now they were getting somewhere. "That may be my day job but at the moment I'm well and truly off duty." He wondered how she knew about him and his business.

"I know as much about you as you do about me," she told him.

"That makes us equal then," he laughed in an attempt to lighten the atmosphere, but there was something about her that unnerved him.

"You don't have to worry about me," she told him as if reading his thoughts. "Just be very careful when you open Pandora's Box."

Staring at her, he frowned.

"I know what you are doing," she hissed under her breath so no one else could hear.

"What is that exactly?" Taking her arm, he drew her away from the others.

"You have no right to go raking up the past, just stay away from Josie and my brother."

"How could you possibly know about my plans?" He had told no one about his research regarding William Randolph.

"Let's just call it women's intuition." She replied staring at him hatefully.

"Have you heard of a woman named Phillipa Weston?" Belenos couldn't help himself and as he watched, her expression changed. It told him all he wanted to know.

Hissing her annoyance, she moved away from him.

Emilia Sykes had received an invitation to attend the open evening at Timothy Granger's gallery. It had come via the Shopkeepers Association and she had intended to ask Mia and Ben to accompany her but unfortunately, Mia was busy. She was spending the evening with her father and wanted Ben to be there with her. She could have asked Mark, the guy she had shared St Valentine's Evening with, but regrettably, they had very little in common so there was little point in pursuing that relationship. The weather was foul anyway and did nothing to encourage her to hike half way across London on her own so she decided to stay in and relax.

Filling the bath with hot water, she opened a new pack of floating candles and set them adrift, delighted at the way light from their flames danced with the swirling steam. Shrugging off her robe, she eased herself into the rising scent, carefully avoiding the candles and with a contented sigh, stretched out. Closing her eyes, heat soaked into her body and she relaxed, but her mind would not stop working. Her first thoughts were of Jenna O'Brien. Had she been to see a lawyer yet or at least spoken to Belenos? She felt so sorry for Jenna and was at a loss as how she could support her through her crisis. All she could realistically do was to be there for her if she needed a friend to confide in. Jenna appeared to be a popular woman but Emilia suspected that she had no real friends. This was a disturbing thought, but sadly, it was true.

After a while, her thoughts inevitably turned to business. Since the beginning of the year, things had been going much better than she could have hoped. Nothing much was supposed to happen until Easter when spring weddings were popular, but February was proving to be a good month. This was probably due to the romance surrounding St Valentine's Day.

Introducing her brother to her business was a very sound move.

His knowledge of working with computers was invaluable. He had straightened out her accounts, redesigned her stock sheets and came up with a program that predicted her monthly sales based on past performance and current trends. He had already identified a number of items that were not doing very well and by replacing these with stock that was more popular, she had seen her sales figures improve. She would never have thought about scrutinising her business in such a way and decided that she should have a serious chat with him regarding his future. Now that he had found Mia, he seemed more settled and she felt that it was time to invite him to join her permanently. Emilia liked the idea and began making plans of her own. She would need to set up a meeting with her business manager at the bank and armed with Ben's predicted sales figures she felt sure that she could extend her business loan. This was the only way that she could raise the money to pay him a decent salary. Her accountant would probably tell her that she was being foolhardy in taking an unnecessary risk, but she believed that in the long run it would be worth it. She would talk to the bank before making her proposal to Ben.

Breathing deeply she was satisfied with her decision and savouring the sweet scent rising up from the water, wished that she had thought to bring a glass of wine into the bathroom. It would probably have helped to stop her mind from racing. Sinking lower into the water, she pushed away her thoughts, it was time to enjoy her bath and her candles.

Mia poured more wine into Ben's glass before topping up her own then she passed him a little bowl of peanuts. Her father settled in one of the armchairs leaving them to sit together on the sofa. He declined a glass of wine.

"I'm going out later to a French restaurant with a colleague." He confessed and Mia pressed him for more but without success.

It had always been her wish that he find someone to settle down with. After the death of her mother, he had been too busy juggling his career with bringing her up. There had been a couple of flings along the way but they had come to nothing. Her father refused to move on, he would always love her mother and the thought of replacing her with someone else had never crossed his mind. At one time Mia thought there was something special between him and Isobel Woods.

"She is far too young," he had said, "besides, Izzy is a colleague, it would never work."

Finally, he relented and gave her the name of his date.

"Pat Fleming is a pathologist and before you ask, she is single, a divorcee, but I can assure you that she is not looking for a husband."

Mia was surprised that he had told her this much, but she remained hopeful.

"What I want to show you is this," he said changing the subject and digging into his pocket he drew out a folded piece of paper. "Do you recognise this woman?"

Mia studied the image, it was an action shot of an assault. The face of the victim had been shaded out, but the details of the assailant were quite clear.

"This is the woman from the hotel photographs that you showed me the other day."

"Yes," he nodded.

"I don't recognise her, but as I said before, there is something about her that looks familiar. Perhaps she reminds me of someone else."

Terry wanted her to see the CCTV images from the camera outside in the street, but he realised there was little value in showing her another picture of the same woman. It would unsettle her to know that she had been so close to her home.

"I have here copies of your telephone records," he said waving them in the air. "The dates and times that you gave me don't seem to correspond with these," pausing mid sentence, he passed them to her. "I have highlighted the numbers that I would like you to identify."

Mia remained silent as she studied the list of dates and times and her hair fell over her face as she leaned forward. Ben peered at her father and frowned, the atmosphere in the room changed and he began to feel uncomfortable. Reaching for the bowl, he scooped up a handful of peanuts and popped them into his mouth. What was going on here he wondered. Terry was obviously being diplomatic by not demanding an explanation, but this was a murder case and like it or not Mia was caught up in the middle of it.

Reaching for her mobile phone, Mia went into her list of contacts and finding what she was looking for jotted down the names against the highlighted numbers.

"There must be some mistake," she said. "Why don't the anonymous calls show up?"

"I don't know the answer to that," her father replied.

He had contacted the telephone providers to ask them the same question and they had both came back with the same answer. The records were complete, even if the caller had blocked their number from appearing on Mia's phone they would have been on that list. If he was conducting a formal interview, Terry would have persisted with his questioning, but he could hardly accuse his daughter of making this up. Why would she do such a thing?

He knew how things could affect her. Throughout her childhood, there had been occasions especially during times of great stress when she would retreat into herself and begin to act strangely. Her teenage years had been particularly difficult but he was sure that she would grow out of it. Perhaps he was wrong.

"Look," he told her, "don't worry. My investigation is ongoing so we are bound to get to the bottom of this eventually. If you get another of these calls be sure to let me know immediately."

He made a point of looking at his watch.

"I had better be off." Climbing to his feet, he smiled then he said. "You have a good evening, try to put this behind you."

"You have a lovely evening too." Mia hugged him and followed him to the door.

She seemed subdued, not as carefree as she had been earlier and he was sorry for that, it saddened him to think that he was the cause of her distress.

Chapter
FORTY FIVE

The following morning DS Woods met Ashton in the corridor, he was on his way to his office.

"Good morning Terry," she said cheerfully. "Did you have a good evening?"

Ashton frowned, how could she possibly know about his date.

"Izzy, good morning," he decided to ignore her comment. "How is it going working with the Dynamic Duo?"

Shrugging her shoulders, she replied. "They pretty much leave me to my own devices. It's like being back at school, as long as I appear to be working..."

He nodded before asking. "Do they appear to be working?"

"We don't see them much," she admitted, "the murder room can be a lonely place, but they do surprise us from time to time."

"In what way?"

"Well, the blood sample found on Victoria Stevens' wheelchair for example. They have asked the pathologist to have another look at it."

Terry wondered why Pat had not mentioned this the previous evening, but then he realised that she probably didn't know. Mallinson may have asked one of her colleagues to do further tests.

"Do you know why they have done that?"

"I have no idea," she shrugged her shoulders again. "I've also been talking to PC Yearsley."

Terry was not surprised to hear her mention his name. Woods was a good detective and would realise that CCTV could play a big part in identifying the killer.

"You realise that we are treading the same path."

"Yes," Aston replied.

"Don't you think it's time that we shared information?"

She hardly needed to remind him that she had given him everything she had on the Suzie Chahal murder case.

"Okay Izzy, but only because it's you. The file you need to see is here." Holding up his briefcase, he went on. "I don't want to show it to you yet, it probably wouldn't be wise for us to be seen together in my office."

"I'm sure it's nothing personal." She smiled.

"Do you know Sammy's Sandwich Bar?"

"No, but I'm sure I could find it."

"Good, meet me there in half an hour and I'll buy you a late breakfast."

"It's a date," she said touching his arm, "but I think you'll find that at this time of the morning it's called brunch."

When he got to his office, he telephoned Pat Fleming only to be informed that she was busy in the cutting room. Thirty minutes later, he was sitting at a table in the sandwich bar. Sammy or Samuel West was the proprietor. He was a huge man with a personality to match, he always appeared happy but Terry realised that sometimes that was merely a shield hiding a sombre face. Originally, from the Caribbean Sammy had inherited his business from his cousin who had passed away suddenly. He seemed content to remain in London, which surprised Terry. Surely, the lure of the southern hemisphere and a more relaxed way of life would be almost too much to ignore.

"Will be with you in a short while." Was Sammy's mantra, his voice booming around the tiny space. He was currently selling freshly made rolls and sandwiches to a line of customers.

Five minutes later DS Woods arrived.

"Sorry to keep you waiting," she apologised and slipping into a chair opposite him, she went on. "Mallinson came in just as I was about to leave and he was asking some very awkward questions."

"What would you good people like?" Sammy asked as he cast a shadow over their table. He was eager to take their order before the next influx of customers.

Ashton ordered a full breakfast baguette and a mug of tea whilst Woods went for an egg and bacon Bap. She also ordered tea.

"What is Mallinson's problem then?" Ashton enquired the moment Sammy had moved away.

"You seem to have monopolised PC Yearsley. He refused our request for surveillance records saying that he is already overstretched. It seems that he is flat out working for you. Mallinson is furious, he's convinced that you are deliberately obstructing his investigation."

"Does he indeed," Ashton smiled. "That is a serious allegation."

"Be careful Terry. Mallinson won't think twice about bringing you down, he's already thinking about lodging a formal complaint."

"I can handle him," Ashton said becoming serious. "You don't have to worry."

They sat in silence as their tea arrived then he began telling her about the case he was working on.

"At first I thought it was just me trying to find a connection that wasn't there," he put his hand on the file sitting on the table between them, "but then I found this." He showed her the image of Ruth Smith's attacker.

"If you compare this with the CCTV images taken from the King Edward Hotel you will see that it's the same woman."

"Mallinson has no idea about this connection with the attacks on transgender women." Izzy whispered.

"He wouldn't would he. It's an old case, he wasn't around when these attacks took place, besides no one seems to remember them."

"Do you think our attacker was simply honing her skills by targeting random women?"

"Maybe," he glanced at her, knowing that she was about to make another comment.

"Do you think she targeted these women because they are transgender, some kind of personal hate campaign?"

"It's possible I suppose. She may even have something to do with TG International." Reaching for his mug, he took a swig of tea. It was strong and sweet, just how he liked it.

Woods followed suit but was much more cautious, blowing across the top of her mug first before taking a sip.

"Why the acceleration then? Attacking women in a car park is one thing, but murder is something quite different."

Their food arrived and DS Woods was amazed at the size of the bap on her plate.

"I think I might need a knife and fork," she said glancing over her shoulder.

"The other thing I don't understand," Ashton ignored her remark, "is why target young musicians."

"It could be a jealousy thing," Woods looked up at him. "Perhaps our murderer is a failed musician."

Ashton grunted before biting into his baguette then chewing slowly, he considered his next observation.

"I still don't get this mutilation thing. Why would our murderer feel the need to disfigure these women? Is it because she harbours a grudge of some kind?"

Woods stared at him thoughtfully. She knew plenty of women who would readily smash the face of another if she thought her a threat, especially where relationships were concerned. She decided to keep these thoughts to herself, DI Ashton being a man would probably not understand.

"Jealousy is a powerful emotion." She informed him before taking another bite of her bap. She had given up searching for cutlery and had resorted to using her fingers. "Have you managed to find out why Mallinson ordered another check on the blood sample?" She knew that he would have been straight on to the pathologists.

"No, Dr Fleming was not available when I telephoned earlier."

"How is Mia holding up?" She indicated that he had egg on his chin and he wiped it off with his serviette.

"She was rather upset after the Goons dragged her in for questioning."

"That's understandable. You do realise why Mallinson did that?" She glanced up at him again before going on. "It was to get back at you. There was no need to bring her into the station for a formal interview."

"I'm aware of that," he said, his eyes flashing with anger.

"That is why you need to be careful Terry. Don't cross Mallinson too often, we have no idea what he might do next."

Ashton stopped eating and let his half-eaten baguette fall onto his plate. It was true that Mallinson could make life very difficult for Mia especially if he found out about the alleged telephone calls.

"Is here anything else you should tell me Terry?"

He didn't want to let her in on the CCTV images from the camera close to Mia's home or the fact that he had seen the alleged murderer outside in the street. He was not going to tell her anything that might get back to Mallinson and encourage him to talk to his daughter again.

"No Izzy, there is nothing else." He glanced down at his food before going on. "I will let you know what PC Yearsley comes up with. I won't keep you in the dark, I promise."

"I appreciate that Terry." She accepted what he said but was not entirely convinced of his sincerity. Pushing her plate away, she said. "There's no way I can eat all of that."

"Tell Mallinson that we are sharing information, maybe it will keep him off PC Yearsley's back."

"Can I tell him about the connection between the murder case and your transgender investigation?"

"Not yet, let's keep that between ourselves for now. I'm thinking about taking it to the Chief myself, but let's just see what we can come up with over the next couple of days."

He was thinking about Yearsley and his own request for CCTV camera archive footage from the university at York. If he could track down the Ford Focus then they would have something solid to go on. It wouldn't do to let Mallinson in on all of his business, not just yet.

Chapter
FORTY SIX

Mia lay in her bed listening to the sounds of her home. The creaking of the structure and the tapping of pipes were part of the symphony of an old house that was seldom heard during the daytime, but as soon as darkness arrived, the mysterious noises would begin. When she was young, her father would tell her not to be afraid; it was only the house breathing. Thoughts of Ben were a pleasant interlude. She had reluctantly told him that they shouldn't spend the night together and although disappointed he had taken it well. They both needed to be up early in the morning, he had work to do and she was going to meet the pianist who would be playing Viktor's parts during rehearsal.

The house creaked louder this time and she began to regret sending Ben away. She should have told him about the noises she had heard at the bathroom window, get him to take a look, make sure everything was secure, but now she was not entirely certain that she had heard it at all.

Rolling over onto her side, she pulled the duvet up around her ears and reminded herself that she was quite safe. All the windows and doors were locked and the alarm was set. If an intruder did manage to breach her security measures, the alarm would go off and wake the whole neighbourhood. Taking comfort from this she closed her eyes and at last managed to drift off to sleep.

Several hours later, she woke suddenly. It was still dark, the bedside alarm clock yet to herald in the new day. Something was wrong, she could sense it and straining her ears she listened for sounds that should not be there. The boiler had fired up earlier and now hot water was expanding in the radiators, ticking and gurgling as it surged through the central heating pipes. Rolling onto her side, pain shot through her abdomen and Mia took a sharp intake of breath. Slowly the burning sensation eased and breathing out she felt under the duvet, she was naked her nightdress was gone. Carefully reaching for the bedside lamp, she closed her eyes against the sudden light and when she opened them again she discovered four angry lines extending across her body. Scratches punctured her skin leaving it swollen and angry. Traces of blood had left their mark on the cotton sheet then throwing back the duvet she sat up and stared at her wounds. How had she managed to do that? Studying her fingertips, she found no trace of blood or skin beneath her nails then searching for her nightdress, it was not under the cover. Glancing at the floor beside the bed it was not there either, but her slippers were in their place warming beside the radiator.

Reaching for her gown, she shrugged it around her shoulders and pulled the belt carefully around her waist before edging reluctantly towards the door. Putting her ear to the cold surface, she listened for sounds but the hallway beyond was silent then finding the courage, she pulled the door open slowly before creeping towards the kitchen. It was empty and tidy, just as she had left it the previous evening. A quick search of the bathroom confirmed that an intruder could not have come in that way either and glancing up at the window she could see that it remained firmly shut.

Going into the living room she threw open the curtains in an effort to let in what light there was, but the sky was still dark and overcast, the earth damp from last night's rain. The room was silent. Ben's flowers were in their vase on the coffee table, the hardiest having survived were still on display and scenting the room. There was no sign of her night-dress, she was certain that she had put one on before climbing into bed the previous evening, she was not in the habit of sleeping naked especially at this time of the year. Pushing open the door to her music room, she reached for the light switch before peering in. Her cello was in its case against the wall and sheet music was piled up neatly where she had left it, then draped over the stool she found her nightdress. It was in tatters, reduced to rags. Reaching for it, she ran her fingers through the ruined material searching for signs of blood or clues as to what could possibly have happened. She had no idea how it had ended up in shreds in her music room. Only her father and Ben had been there the previous evening and once they had gone, she went straight to bed. She had not entered her music room, so who could have done this and how had she got the scratches?

Returning to the living room, she sat down on the sofa and opened her gown. The wounds were ugly, scabbed over with dried blood. She would have to clean them carefully then apply some cream to aid the healing process, she didn't want to be left with scars.

How could this have happened? She asked herself again. The alarm system was still active so no one could have got in. A thought at the back of her mind kept nagging at her, taunting her mercilessly with bitter recriminations, but she pushed it away. It would never go completely, it was always there waiting patiently to emerge again, but soon she would have to face up to it and deal with the consequences.

Belenos telephoned Jenna soon after finishing his breakfast, he knew that it would be no good calling her before ten in the morning.

"Hey," he said as soon as she answered. "Thank you for such a lovely evening."

"I told you that you would enjoy attending an art exhibition." She replied sleepily.

"I wouldn't as a rule, but seeing as it was Josie MacDonald."

Belenos was a traditionalist where art was concerned, he preferred the old masters and Jenna was aware that portraits were his preference. She smiled and ran her fingers through her hair. She was sitting at her dressing table, about to go through her morning routine when her mobile phone had rung and now, checking her face in the mirror, she was relieved that Belenos could not see her.

"Do you know Tim Granger's sister?" He asked suddenly.

"Kate, why do you ask?"

"We didn't hit it off last night and I was wondering if it was me or is she always so intimidating." He was tempted to use another word to describe her but he decided to spare Jenna her blushes.

"I understand that she can be something of a cow," she told him bluntly, "her reputation precedes her."

"She is obviously a very clever woman but I can hardly recommend her bedside manner."

"Don't let that worry you," Jenna laughed, "I'm sure you're not the first man to suffer her rebuffs." Clearly, he was not happy with his lack of progress with Tim's sister.

"You know that I'm interested in researching William Randolph and his son Mr Mac, well, Miss Granger warned me off."

"Did she indeed, how interesting. You are aware that she was mixed up in this abduction and rape thing. Apparently she almost became a victim herself."

"I did read something about it, but I thought Kate and her brother were instrumental in rescuing Josie from '*the dungeon of hell*' as the tabloids of the time put it."

"Yes they did, but it almost cost them their lives."

"Of course, I remember now. That was probably why she was so reluctant to talk to me."

"So what did you actually say to her?"

"I asked if she had heard of a woman called Phillipa Weston."

Jenna thought for a moment before replying. "Never heard of her, what did she say to that?"

"Not a lot I'm afraid, but it was then that she became hostile."

He chose not to tell her about William Randolph's illegitimate daughter and was relieved when she did not ask.

"What are you doing today?" she asked feigning interest."

"Working," he told her. "I'm currently writing articles for a magazine and need to complete the second instalment." He doubted that she read the magazines that he worked for so he decided not to elaborate.

"I've got nothing planned so if you are interested we could meet up for lunch or something."

"I don't know Jenna," he replied trying his best not to sound too unenthusiastic. "Let's see how I get on, I could call you later."

He had enjoyed her company the previous evening but he did not want to make a habit of going out with her.

"Okay," she replied recognising a brush off.

Ending the call, Belenos stared thoughtfully at the notebook on his desk. It was obvious that Jenna hardly knew Kate Granger so had no useful gossip to impart. He had definitely upset the woman by mentioning Phillipa Weston and she was quite adamant that he leave Josie MacDonald and her affairs alone, but now he was even more convinced that there was a story waiting to be told. Opening his notebook, he turned to his research notes. He had to discover more about Randolph's daughter and he realised the only way to do that was to become more proactive, the place to begin his investigation was at her last known address.

Chapter

FORTY SEVEN

Mia was in her kitchen making a fresh pot of coffee when her mobile phone rang. It was Ben.

"I didn't sleep well," he confessed. "I was awake half the night worrying about you."

"Oh Ben, I shouldn't have sent you away. I'm sorry."

"Don't be," he said, "you have a lot to think about at the moment, besides you need your rest."

"But I didn't sleep well either." She decided not to tell him about her ruined nightdress or the scratches across her stomach.

She had cleaned the wounds and applied an Aloe Vera balm that cooled the heat and took away the sting that accompanied her every move. Now with her mobile tucked under her chin, she continued to make her coffee whilst listening to the sound of his voice.

"We should meet up this evening," he suggested. "I'm busy with Emilia all day so lunch is out of the question."

"Dinner this evening will be perfect." Mia told him. "Leave it to me, I'll reserve us a table somewhere."

She smiled as their conversation ended. It was sweet of him to be concerned but she didn't want him to worry. She liked him a lot and was pleased with the way their relationship was developing. She felt so fortunate at having met him. Adding a dash of milk to her coffee, she took it into the living room where she made herself comfortable on the sofa. She had already spent over an hour working in her music room and after this short break was determined to rehearse the oriental section again. This afternoon she was going to meet a woman called Margaret Marshall. Alicia had arranged it and told her that the pianist was already acquainted with Viktor Vasiliev and his work. Margaret was going to help Mia by playing Viktor's parts, she already had a recording of the piano accompaniment, but Mia preferred to work with a pianist. So much more could be achieved when working with live music, besides she enjoyed the company, her music room could be a very lonely place.

Turning her thoughts back to Ben, she wondered where they could go this evening. She would like to return to Raymond Duval's French restaurant but it was a place that should be kept for a special occasion. Ben liked spicy food. There was a little Thai restaurant close by so reaching for her mobile she looked up the telephone number and made a reservation. With that done, she sat back and sipped at her coffee, wondering how her father had got on the previous evening with his date. He had insisted that there was nothing in it and he was merely socialising with a work colleague, but it pleased her to think that he had some kind of social life outside of work.

The business with the telephone calls had shocked her and she couldn't understand why they had not appeared on the itemised record. She was hoping that once they had identified the caller her father could make them stop. Taking another sip of coffee, she grimaced at the memory of being presented with the evidence or lack of it in this case. It had been an awkward moment but what could she say, the calls were real enough so there must be a record, surely it was a mistake. She was certain that her father believed her, but it was his job to question everything, he was bound to solve the mystery eventually.

Her coffee cup was empty but she craved more so swinging her legs from beneath her she got to her feet and went into the kitchen. Glancing up at the clock, she was appalled to see how quickly time was slipping by. If she were going to keep her appointment with Margaret then she would have to get back to work.

DI Ashton was sitting at his desk talking on the telephone to the Security Services in York. The person he had spoken to before had been helpful enough but he doubted their ability to get the job done. He was anxious at not being in control, the only pressure he could exert was to remind them that he was conducting a murder investigation and the information they could provide might be crucial to his case. He could of course take an official line, formalise the request, but he believed that a friendly approach would work best.

The woman he was speaking to assured him that everything was being done to fulfil his request. They had already looked at the CCTV footage from the night of the concert but had found no trace of the vehicle that he was interested in. She sounded sincere, telling him that most of her shift would be dedicated to studying the files and she would call him the moment there was anything to report.

He jotted down her name and extension number and thanked her before ending the call then he turned his attention to Mia's telephone records. She had written the names of her friends against the numbers he had highlighted and under different circumstances he would have checked them out, confirm their validity, but he had no reason to doubt his daughter's word. He sighed and retuned them to the file before slipping it back into his desk drawer then suddenly the telephone at his elbow began to ring.

"DI Ashton," he spoke formally into the mouthpiece.

"Terry," came the reply, "no need to be quite so formal."

"Sorry Pat, I was miles away."

"Have I caught you at a busy moment?"

"No, not at all, it's good to hear from you."

"Thank you for such a lovely meal last night," she purred. "Raymond Duval is such a charmer."

"What do you expect from a Frenchman?"

She laughed. "We must do it again soon, my treat next time."

"Sounds great," he replied with as much enthusiasm as he could muster. It was not as if he found the prospect daunting, but he had never imagined himself flirting with someone as challenging as Dr Patricia Fleming.

"It won't be that bad," she teased sensing his unease. "You know that I don't bite and I promise to be on my best behaviour."

"Sorry," he said again then feeling foolish, he continued. "You are right, we should do it again soon."

With the pleasantries out of the way, Pat became serious.

"I understand you are interested in a request made by DI Mallinson."

"Yes that's right, but he doesn't know that I'm checking up on him so I would like to keep it that way."

"I see, well my team have been working on it during their night shift and have come up with some startling results." He could hear the sound of shuffling notes then she continued.

"The blood sample found on Victoria Stevens' wheelchair is a common blood group containing XX chromosomes, to you that means female blood, but we have discovered something else." She paused again. "Tests have revealed an unusual amount of male hormones present in the sample."

"Male hormones?" Ashton repeated. "Could the blood samples have become contaminated?"

"Not at our end," she told him, "and I can't see how anything like that could happen when our team collected the sample from the murder scene either."

"Perhaps there were two blood smears on the wheelchair. What if she ran into two people?"

Pat could understand his thinking but thought it unlikely.

"If that were the case then we would have had two quite different blood sample results. The blood we tested definitely came from one person. I would say that whoever it belongs to is taking a course of male hormones."

"What, do you mean like a sportswoman hoping to build up muscle structure or something?"

"No, I don't think so," Pat replied. "I would suggest that the hormone treatment is for something much more personal." She paused again as if inviting his comments but he remained silent. "These are the results I would expect to find in an individual undergoing a gender transition."

"What, a transgender man?"

"That's what I think, yes."

"Why wasn't this picked up in the initial blood test?"

"We were not looking for this then, we were only interested in establishing a blood type."

"I see," Ashton ran his hand over his face and frowned. "So our suspect is a transgender man."

"Assuming the blood is from the murderer." She reminded him.

He wanted to tell her what he had discovered so far, but stopped himself.

"Thank you Pat, this certainly shines a different light on the subject. It seems that I owe you another evening out."

"As I said before, next time it's my treat."

He stared at the telephone once their call was over. This was just another twist in and increasingly complicated case and he was yet to consider the implications fully. What would Mallinson make of it he wondered?

Chapter
FORTY EIGHT

Belenos decided to take the tube to New Cross Gate then a taxi to Blackheath. He didn't know the area well so used a navigation aid on his mobile phone to find his way. The address that he was looking for was in a rundown area of Victorian terraces built either side of a narrow street. It was not far from Blackheath train station and clearly, the residential area was used as free parking for commuters. Belenos would never leave his car in such a grim neighbourhood and he wondered how Phillipa Weston had ended up here.

Finding the house, he stepped up to the door and regarded it with interest. It had been once painted midnight blue but that was clearly a long time ago, now the paint was chipped and peeling and where a brass knocker had taken pride of place four small screw holes remained in the rotting wood. There was no doorbell so reaching for the letterbox flap it rattled ineffectually so he rapped loudly on the door.

"What?" A woman appeared and glared at him.

She was in need of a meal and a shower and Belenos stepped back. Between her fingers, she held a cigarette its smoke giving off a sweet herbal aroma.

"Good afternoon," he said amiably. I'm looking for someone called Phillipa." Fumbling in his pocket, he pulled out the photograph he had printed from the internet then he continued. "Phillpa Weston, I believe she used to live here."

The woman appeared much older than her years and beyond her mask of hardship and abuse, Belenos thought that she was no more than forty years old. She hardly glanced at his picture and slowly lifting her hand, she took a drag from her cigarette. Holding the smoke in, her eyes never left his face but eventually she came to a decision.

"Yeah, she used to live here but she doesn't anymore." Stepping back into the darkened room, she swung the door closed.

"Do you know where she has gone?" Belenos asked, prevented the door from closing fully.

"Why should I care?"

"It's important to me to know where my friend has gone." His act was perfect, the concerned friend desperate for information.

This outpouring of emotion roused her interest so she opened the door again and this time her eyes were no longer dull.

"What's in it for me?" she hissed.

Reaching for his wallet, he pulled out a twenty pound note.

"This is all I have."

Snatching it from his hand, she held it up to the light and grinned, her black uneven teeth looking as if they came from the same period as the house.

"Phillipa moved out months ago, she was a mad cow, used to dress up as a man and scare us half to death with talk about cutting someone's throat. Now we couldn't have that could we, so we threw her out."

"Where did she go, do you have a forwarding address?"

Her face turned red as laughter rattled at the back of her throat and she doubled over. Belenos thought that she would never regain her breath, the last thing he wanted to do was to administer CPR. When at last she recovered, she swiped tears from her cheeks with the back of her hand before saying.

"No forwarding address." This set her off again but she managed to continue. "Try the doorways around Victoria, plenty of begging going on there."

The door was slammed in his face, leaving Belenos standing in the street. He thought about what she had said, especially the part about Phillipa dressing up as a man and threatening murder. He had played his part well. Years of chasing stories as a journalist had taught him many things and quick to learn, he soon realised that it didn't always do to tell people the whole truth, not all of the time.

The moment Ashton was finished on the telephone, he went to see Robert Nixon at TG International. Pat's news about the blood sample was significant and may have startling consequences, but Ashton was ahead of the game. Mallinson would have no idea what to make of this new discovery and he just hoped that DS Woods would keep her word and not share what they had discussed earlier. Before leaving his office, he used the printer to enlarge the photographs of the suspect including those taken close to Mia's home.

"Thank you for seeing me at such short notice," Ashton said as he met Nixon in the car park.

They shook hands before Nixon replied amiably. "If you would like to follow me, we'll go to my office."

The centre was busy with a number of activities taking place and people were milling about in the corridor. Through the window of a closed door, Ashton could see a group engaged in some kind of exercise class and he nodded when he recognised one of the women from the group he had interviewed before.

When they were settled in the privacy of his office, Nixon asked.

"What's this all about Inspector?"

"Some new evidence has come to light recently which I think may be related to the attacks on the women from this centre."

"New evidence, what do you mean?"

Ashton could not reveal much about the ongoing murder investigation but he had to give Nixon something.

"I think the person responsible for the attacks on your people may be implicated in a murder inquiry," he paused as he opened his briefcase. "I have some photographs that I would like you to look at. Some of them you have seen before, but I want you to look at them again but in a different way this time."

"How do you mean?" Nixon replied leaning forward with interest.

"Tell me if you know the person in these photographs." Ashton held up the file but did not open it. "Has this person been here before, maybe they have a connection with someone associated with this centre?"

He stared at Nixon who nodded his understanding then opening his file he began to lay the photographs out randomly on the desk and when he was finished, Nixon said.

"I recognise this woman as the attacker from the file I sent you."

The photographs had been enlarged showing nothing but a close up of the woman's features.

"What about the others?"

"Well, they are not as clearly defined but I can see that they are the same woman."

Ashton nodded before asking. "Have you seen her before?"

Nixon remained silent and a deep frown appeared between his eyes. He thought carefully before answering.

"I'm sure that I haven't," he said at last. "I know most of the people who visit this centre. Of course there are a few who remain on the periphery." He paused and pursed his lips. "No, I'm certain, I have no idea who this woman is."

Ashton nodded again before saying.

"Now have another look but this time try to imagine her as a man."

Nixon looked up, his eyes wide with astonishment.

"How would her appearance change?"

"Facial hair, shorter hairstyle, glasses," Nixon replied, "all these things will change her image. Make-up would help too, it's not only women who use make-up."

"What about male hormones. How would that change a person's appearance?"

Nixon sat back in his chair and studied Ashton. He was curious at the way their conversation was going and it was a few seconds before he could answer.

"Testosterone taken in controlled doses would not change a person's appearance overnight Inspector. Depending on the treatment, it could take months to achieve the desired result."

"Okay," Ashton nodded, "but what changes would you expect to see?"

"Facial hair growth is the obvious one, followed by a deepening of the voice. Muscle growth, widening of shoulders and thickening of the arms would take a little longer. This would lead to an increase in strength and stamina."

"Would there be any behavioural changes?"

"Yes you can expect to see changes but nothing significant, it's impossible to change the personality that's already there. The person might begin to act instinctively like a man, have a larger appetite for example. There could also be an increase in aggression and sexual urges, but it really does depend on the personality to begin with."

"Would it be possible once the hormone therapy has begun to pass yourself off as a woman again?"

"A transgender man would never forget the person he was before, but surely the whole point of transitioning is to become more comfortable with yourself. Don't forget, these people were born into the wrong bodies so I can't imagine why anyone would want to switch regularly between genders."

"I understand what you are saying, but is it possible?"

"Yes, anything is possible, but it all depends on what has already been achieved. As I said before it may take months before changes begin to take effect so in the early stages of transition it would be very easy to present as both male and female."

"Androgynous, I think is the term."

"Very good Inspector, you are quite right. Some people choose to live as what we term 'gender fluid'. That means they are neither male nor female and can pass convincingly as both."

Ashton nodded, trying to understand the psychology behind the urge to live like that, but he failed dismally.

"So, can you imagine this person as a male?" Ashton tapped one of the photographs with his fingertip.

"I don't need to imagine Inspector," Nixon smiled. "We have a computer programme that we use to change facial images. By manipulating a photograph we can produce a pretty fair indication of how one may appear as the opposite gender."

"A bit like a photo fit."

"Exactly that. We use it to allow clients to see what might be achieved."

"Can we access it from here?" Ashton glanced at the computer screen sitting on the desk.

"Sure, all we have to do is scan one of your photographs, feed it into the computer then run the programme."

"Do you mind if we have a go?"

"Not at all," Nixon said reaching for his keyboard.

Ashton selected one of the photographs and slipped it into the printer as Nixon prepared his computer. They scanned the image and when it appeared on the screen, Nixon got to work. The various stages of transition emerged and as he worked, the face gradually changed from female to male, these he saved to a file. Choosing one, they worked until they had what was thought to be the most likely outcome.

"This of course would only be achieved after years of hormone treatment and possibly even surgery."

"It's very impressive," Ashton admitted as he studied the image on the screen.

The face staring back at him was the perfect male version of the female they had started with.

"It could almost be her twin brother," Nixon said. "There is a definite family likeness. I still don't recognise him by the way."

"So he's not one of your clients then?"

Nixon shook his head.

"The images of the woman in the early stages of transition are more likely to be as our suspect is presenting today." Ashton reminded him.

"Yes, given that she is able to switch between genders so convincingly."

Clicking on the file, Nixon brought up one of the earlier profiles and began to manipulate it, adding a five o'clock shadow and a male hairstyle to make the face in the picture look more realistic.

"Not bad," Ashton nodded. "To the casual observer this would be convincing enough."

"Yes, with the right body language and attitude." Nixon agreed.

"Can you print some of those off for me?"

"Of course, would you like me to e-mail the whole file to you?"

"Excellent idea, but still do me a copy or two."

The printer began to whirr.

Chapter
FORTY NINE

Mia stepped onto the platform at Epsom and the difference between central London and this little market town was shocking. It had taken just under forty minutes for her world to change completely.

Margaret Marshall had promised to meet her at the station and take her to the house where they would be rehearsing. Mia had never met Margaret before and her agent, Alicia had told her almost nothing about the woman whom she would be working with so closely, but Mia need not have worried.

"Miss Ashton," a voice sounded from along the platform.

Mia turned to see a woman dressed in a tweed two-piece suit coming towards her. She appeared to be from another era and reminded her of Miss Marple.

"Miss Ashton," she said again slightly breathless. "I'm Margaret Marshall."

The hand she held out was clad in a soft leather driving glove and in the other she clutched a crocodile skin handbag.

"Pleased to meet you," Mia smiled, "but you must call me Mia."

"Did you have a pleasant journey?"

"Yes, I'm surprised at how quickly it went."

"We are not far from the great Metropolis." Margaret told her. "Welcome to Epsom, our little gem of a town." She paused before going on. "The main street is not far away and we have some wonderful little shops. Now, let's find the car and I'll whisk you home for a nice cup of tea."

Leading the way, Margaret set a brisk pace that belied her age and dodging past the guard standing at the entrance, she steered Mia out towards the car park.

"Here we are," she said and taking a bunch of keys from her handbag, Margaret unlocked the passenger door and held it open for Mia.

The old Morris Minor Traveller was a fine example. It looked brand new, but Mia knew from the number plate that it was old. She was impressed, she had never been in a car like this before.

"Wow," she exclaimed as she climbed in.

The car was Snowberry White with a Cherokee Red interior, the cracked leather seats giving off an aroma that she associated with prestigious cars. The simple metal dashboard was the same colour as the car and in the centre was a single speedometer, there were no other fancy lights or gauges. Margaret appeared on the driver's side and fumbled with the door then throwing it open, she climbed in.

"What a splendid little car."

"She's called 'Woody'. Bit of a cliché I must admit but she's been in the family for years," Margaret explained as she inserted the key into the ignition, "belonged to my aunt. I remember when she bought it in 1965."

The ignition key was not turned like in a modern car, to start the engine a little black knob beside the huge steering wheel had to be pulled, then, the engine burst into life.

"This car is never fifty two years old," Mia gasped, her eyes huge with amazement.

"Oh yes," Margaret nodded. "I had her restored on her fiftieth birthday. Like me, cracks were beginning to appear, but I couldn't bear to part with her. Us old girls must stick together you know."

Margaret glanced at her, her face full of mischief, then pushing the gearstick forward they began to move.

"Have you been to Epsom before?" she asked once they were on their way.

"No, I'm afraid not," Mia replied ruefully.

"Then you are in for a treat." Margaret pulled up at the lights. "It was the Springs that made Epsom fashionable. In the latter part of the 17th century it gave its name to Epsom Salts."

"Oh, I didn't know that," Mia smiled as she thought about the way these things came about.

"We also have the Epsom Derby," Margaret continued and as the lights turned green, she eased 'Woody' forward. "Do you follow the horses?"

"No, but I've seen the Grand National on the television."

"Not the same as actually being there." Margaret glanced at her and shook her head. "You need to experience the atmosphere, the excitement of the horses, the noise of their hooves as they thunder across the turf and of course have a little flutter."

"That's another thing I have never done," Mia admitted, "is put a bet on a horse."

"You really should get to a Ladies' day. You don't have to go to Ascot for that you know, we have them here at Epsom, first Friday in June come rain or shine. It really is a splendid affair and if you like dressing up you should try to get into the Queen's or Duchess's stand because then you will be invited to enter the Style Awards. A young woman like you could win the title and go home with some splendid prizes."

"Sounds lovely," Mia smiled, not sure that it would be her thing.

"It was here that in 1913 the Suffragette Emily Davison threw herself in front of King George V's horse, Anmer, bringing him down."

"That was here?"

"Oh yes, at the Epsom Derby."

Margaret sounded the horn as they passed a row of little shops and waved her gloved hand at the window.

"Bertie Bromsgrove," she chuckled, "almost married him once."

"When was that?" Mia asked wanting to know more.

"Oh, it was in the 1960s, not long after my aunt bought this car. Eligible young things we were then, a bit like you now dear."

They glanced at each other and Mia laughed.

"Do you have a young man?"

"Yes I do." Mia told her all about Ben and when she was finished, Margaret said.

"He sounds like a very fine catch indeed. I wouldn't play him for too long before you reel him in."

Mia laughed again. It was as if she had known Margaret all of her life and sitting there next to her in the car, she felt that she could tell her anything.

"Are you married Margaret?"

"No, never had the time for marriage. I became a teacher you see, taught music in a girls school. Teaching was a vocation in those days, women were not given time off to have babies, maternity leave and job security had not been invented then. Anyway, I've always been an independent woman so couldn't see the point in marriage."

"My life is like that at the moment." Mia confessed. "My career is finally taking off and there never seems to be time for anything else. It will only get worse as overseas concerts become a reality."

"Is that what you really want?" Margaret asked as she steered 'Woody' around a series of bends.

"It's what I have always dreamed of, I've been working towards this moment for as long as I can remember."

"One creates the monster then it takes over." Margaret nodded thoughtfully, "but if it is what you desire then you must embrace it with both hands."

Fifteen minutes later they arrived outside a neat 1930s house complete with cottage garden and picket fence.

"What a lovely house," Mia said as she climbed out of the car.

"It also belonged to my aunt, it came with the car."

"How marvellous," Mia replied eager to know more.

"Like myself, my aunt never married so had no one to pass it on to. She was a Civil Servant you see, something in the city then during the war she was with SOE."

Mia frowned, not familiar with the term.

"Special Operations Executive," Margaret explained. "She was a spy."

Again, Mia was amazed and just had to know more.

"She didn't talk about it much, not one to blow her own trumpet so to speak, but then they were all like that. She was an independent old stick, probably why she never married. Always had a great enthusiasm for life, loved to travel. I suppose that was down to her experiences during the war. My father used to say that the war changed everything, his sister most of all, but to me she was the perfect role model."

Following Margaret into the house, they went into a beautifully proportioned sitting room.

"I'll pop the kettle on whilst you take off your coat and make yourself at home."

Mia did as she was told and taking a tour of the room studied the many framed photographs that were dotted about. She was drawn to one in particular, a black and white portrait of a striking young woman dressed in a fur-collared coat and stylish felt hat. Her smile radiant, she looked into the camera, her expression one of innocence and youth. It saddened Mia to think of the horrors that this woman must have encountered.

"That one is a favourite of mine." Margaret said as she appeared carrying a tray loaded with cups, saucers and a teapot.

"She was a very beautiful woman," Mia said wistfully and turning to face Margaret, she asked. "What was her name?"

240

"Alice. She was my father's only sister. She would have been about nineteen when that picture was taken."

Mia made herself comfortable in an old armchair and Margaret handed her a cup of tea.

"Earl Grey with a spot of bergamot, I hope you don't mind, but it's my favourite."

"No, not at all, I love Earl Grey tea."

They chatted for a little longer and as they got to know each other Margaret began to realise that there was more to Mia than she was prepared to reveal. Something from her past gave her no peace. She knew that her mother and brother had been killed tragically in a car crash when Mia was a young girl and that she had survived the ordeal, but Margaret was convinced that this was just the root of the problem. She was determined to find the underlying cause and discover what it was that plagued her, but now was not the right time.

Once they had finished their tea, Margaret took Mia into an extension at the back of the house.

"I had this built just before I retired." She explained. "It was so I could continue giving music lessons."

"Wow," Mia exclaimed.

A Baby Grand piano stood in the centre of the room and drawn towards it, she took a closer look.

"It's a Steinway, a Model B Classical Grand." Margaret told her proudly as she came to stand beside her. "The Model B is often referred to as the perfect piano, and I have to say that I agree."

Opening the lid, she ran her fingers expertly over the keys giving Mia a taste of its quality.

"It really is a wonderfully balanced and versatile instrument and it does me extremely well."

"It sounds terrific," Mia said, her eyes wide with envy.

"I understand that your cello is something rather special."

"Yes, it's a Guadagnini dating from 1777."

It was now Margaret's turn to be impressed.

"It must be very precious," she said.

"It is, and much more to me. It's a real privilege to play an instrument like that. I love the idea that many other musicians down through the ages have played and cherished it. I have most of its provenance, but it does have a few secrets." She laughed.

"And why not?" Margaret laughed too. "This is not that old I'm afraid and I have no idea where it has been." She ran her hand lovingly over the dark wood. "It was built in 1978 I think. I wonder if it will still be around in three hundred years time."

"I can't see why not, it is a quality instrument."

"Right," Margaret said becoming serious. "I had better introduce you to your cello, but I warn you, it's nothing like a Guadagnini I'm afraid."

She produced a La Chambre that looked hardly used. It was a standard size cello made from richly coloured woods that glowed warmly under the light.

"Wow that's very nice." Mia crooned and in her expert hands, it looked perfect.

"I have my own bow," she murmured, indicating to a slim case that she had brought with her.

"You settle in and as soon as you are ready we'll begin."

Mia drew her bow experimentally over the strings and each note reverberated through the air, warm rich lows, and brilliant highs. Not much tuning was required, the instrument was in perfect condition.

"Shall we start with 'Over the Rainbow'?"

Mia nodded her agreement and on a count of three, they began.

An hour later, they had gone through the first musical arrangement.

"You need to be ready for Viktor's little peculiarities." Margaret told her.

She had played the pieces the way Viktor would on the night of the concert and Mia had been caught out on more than one occasion.

"I have studied him for quite some time now, you won't find this on a recording, you need to see him live to appreciate his particular style."

Mia found the session extremely useful and they spent most of their time perfecting her technique. She was grateful to have this opportunity to discover just how difficult it could be to perform with the Russian pianist.

Chapter
FIFTY

DI Ashton was in his office studying the file that Robert Nixon had sent him. On his desk lay Mia's telephone records, he had decided to check the names she had given him against the numbers he had highlighted. He was hoping that maybe one of them would be linked in some way to the suspect but it turned out these numbers belonged to her friends and there was no connection. He struggled with his conscience, but in the end convinced himself that he was doing the right thing. It was not that he doubted her, but still, checking the numbers left him feeling awkward.

The anonymous letter that Mia had received interested him. He had not yet had it checked out by a handwriting analyst, he was hoping that it might reveal the profile of the author, but now he had CCTV images of the suspect it hardly seemed worth the effort. The handwriting certainly looked like it had been written by a female hand, if the author was going through a transition from female to male, then they had some work to do perfecting their penmanship.

Suddenly the door burst open and DI Mallinson appeared. Closing down the screen, Ashton discreetly covered the file on his desk before looking up.

"What the hell are you playing at?" Mallinson snarled, his face puce with anger.

"Sit down," Ashton told him indicating to a chair by the door. He didn't want everyone in the outer office to witness a stand up argument.

"Now tell me, what's this all about?"

"As if you don't know. You have been sniffing round the pathologists behind my back."

"Ah," Ashton said wondering how he had discovered that so soon. "You must also be aware of the contents of that report," he continued, searching for a convincing excuse. "I have reasons to believe that it might have a bearing on an old case I'm working on."

"What old case?"

Ashton explained about the attacks on women from TG International and how this new evidence might possibly tie in. He omitted to mention the CCTV images apart from those from the King Edward Hotel.

"PC Yearsley refuses to co-operate with me, why do you think that is?"

"I can only guess it's because he's a very busy man." Ashton found it difficult to keep a straight face.

"It's because he's snowed under working for you. I might be an outsider, but we are on the same side. I expect a little co-operation from my colleagues."

"I'll have a word with him, see if I can persuade him to be a little more accommodating."

"Don't worry yourself Ashton, if he continues to refuse my requests then he will find himself on the end of a disciplinary."

It was clear that Mallinson was no further ahead with his investigation and was not yet ready to accept the links between the attacks on the transgender women and the murdered musicians.

"Look Mallinson," Ashton said staring at him earnestly. "If I come across anything that I think may be useful to your investigation then naturally I will pass it on to you."

"Why don't I believe that?" he hissed through clenched teeth. "Listen Ashton, I'll be watching you very closely from now on."

Ashton nodded but remained silent, he did not want to say anything that might prolong the argument.

Suddenly the telephone on his desk began to ring and his hand went to the receiver but he did not lift it.

"Are we done?" he said not wanting Mallinson to listen in on his conversation.

The phone stopped ringing.

Slowly Mallinson got to his feet and turning his back on Ashton flung himself from the office.

"What was that all about?" DC James asked as he poked his head around the door.

Ashton remained tight-lipped, James was currently on Mallinson's team so he told him nothing. When eventually he was alone, he checked the incoming number, it was the Security Services from York. Returning the call, he let the phone ring for a couple of minutes but clearly, no one was in so he gave up.

Chapter
FIFTY ONE

Belenos asked Jenna to accompany him on his trip to Victoria station. It was not her idea of fun, traipsing around hostels talking to homeless people, but she readily agreed when he promised to take her somewhere nice for lunch.

They took the tube across the city and at first Belenos struggled to make conversation. Jenna seemed pre-occupied, she kept glancing over her shoulder.

"What is it?" he asked when he could stand it no more.

"I'm sure that we are being followed."

He stared at her, his face etched with doubt.

"I assure you that I'm not being paranoid," she snapped. "It's my father."

She went on to tell him about the arranged marriage that was being forced upon her. She also mentioned the steps she had taken to prevent this from happening.

"Is he aware that you are opposed to his plans?" Belenos asked, shocked at what she had just told him.

"He suspects that I'm not keen to go ahead." She gave him the full story including her father's plans to disinherit her if she refused to marry his business associate's son. She went on to tell him about the fabulous wealth and lifestyle that she could expect from the arrangement.

"But would you be happy committing yourself to a marriage devoid of love?"

"I suppose I could get used to it," she said uncertainly. "It wouldn't be the first time a woman was forced to marry against her will."

Belenos stared at her in disbelief. Although she was known to possess a hard and resourceful exterior, cracks were starting to appear and a vulnerable woman was emerging.

"So what do you intend to do?"

He suspected that Jenna would not survive for long without the support of her father and he could hardly see her holding down a job.

"At first I thought that I could go through with it, but to tell you the truth I don't think I can." She looked away so he could not see her tears. "I simply cannot become somebody's plaything."

Suddenly she pointed at a man in the crowd. "Look, there he is."

He was dressed in a dark grey suit and carried a raincoat over his arm. Belenos thought he looked like any other commuter and he didn't know what to think, she had told him so much, but he committed the man to memory.

"What does your father think he is going to achieve by having you followed?"

"I'm sure that he suspects me of seeing someone else. He is probably aware that I no longer want to go on playing his game. He hardly knows me at all and shows no interest in the life I lead. All he cares about is using me as a pawn to further his precious empire."

"So he engaged a Private Investigator to follow you."

"I guess he wants to know what I'm up to." She glanced at him nervously. "I dread to think what he might do when he discovers the steps I've taken to prevent this marriage from happening."

"Where is your father now?"

"Oh, he's overseas somewhere on another of his business trips."

"I suppose his absence does not prevent him from discovering your business."

"Believe me," she said turning to face him. "He is a man with unlimited resources, he has eyes and ears everywhere. I'm expecting something really unpleasant to happen any day now."

The change in her was palpable, no longer was she the carefree heiress. She was close to tears and it dismayed Belenos to see her like this. He considered approaching her pursuer, but what good would it do? It would hardly be difficult to lose him in the tunnels beneath the streets of London, but he realised that might make the situation worse so slipping his hand into hers he guided her towards the platform where the train was waiting. Glancing over his shoulder, he could see that the man was no longer there. Either they had lost him or he was very good.

"It seems that Phillipa Weston may be a much darker character than I first thought," he said once they were on the train. It was standing room only so they huddled close together by the door.

Jenna looked at him questioningly so he went on.

"The woman at the house in Blackheath told me that Phillipa likes to dress up as a man."

"What do you mean, play acting or for real?"

"I don't know, she didn't go into details, but she told me that Phillipa also displayed violent tendencies. She would often talk about killing someone."

Jenna's eyes widened. "Killing who?"

"No one in particular," he shrugged, "I guess it was merely a passing comment."

"Perhaps Phillipa has lesbian inclinations," Jenna said thoughtfully. "You know, the type who likes to dress up and play the role of a man."

"What do you know about lesbians?" Belenos asked with a smile.

He said this a little too loudly and now those standing around them were taking an interest. She flushed as they waited for her to reply her cheeks burning as she tried to move away, but there were too many people, there was no escape.

"No more than the next person," she said defensively, "and before you ask I'm not that type, I'm purely heterosexual. I'm no homophobe either." She stopped herself, sensing that she had probably said too much already.

"I'm glad to hear that," Belenos smiled and pulling her closer he wrapped his arms around her protectively. This was an unconscious act on his part rather than one of passion but Jenna did not seem to mind. Some of the faces around them grinned and Belenos winked at a woman who was staring at them.

"Do you really think she could be a lesbian?" Jenna whispered.

"You came up with the idea it was not me, besides does it really matter?"

"No of course not, but it's strange to think that she likes to dress up as a man." She thought for a moment before going on. "What about the threat of murder? It's not usually the kind of thing that women think about."

"What about Mary Wilson, Ruth Ellis, Fiona Donnison, Myra Hindley?" he replied reeling off names.

She continued to look at him, her face blank. She had never heard of these people before apart from Myra Hindley then after a moment, she admitted.

"Okay, some women think about murder."

"I have no idea what to make of it. The woman I spoke to told me that they were spooked by Phillipa's strange behaviour so they all agreed that she had to go."

Jenna had recovered some of her colour but now looked pale by comparison.

When they arrived at Victoria Station Belenos was amazed to find their pursuer standing by the exit of the underground waiting for them to emerge. Leading Jenna towards him, he wanted to get a better look. She didn't seem to notice, she simply held onto his hand and allowed herself to be led from the station.

The first homeless shelter they came to was called 'Centrepoint'. It provided a host of services designed to help people living on the streets. A Polish man named Ozzy made time to speak to them.

"I'm trying to trace a friend who went missing some months ago," Belenos began.

"When did you last see your friend?" Ozzy asked, his eastern European accent pleasant to listen too.

Belenos pretended to be uncertain about dates and avoided the question but at the same time gave the impression that he was very concerned. It was obvious that Ozzy was not willing to give anything away without being certain that Belenos was genuine.

"I have a picture," Belenos said pushing his hand into his coat pocket. He produced the print that he had taken from the internet. "This is Phillipa."

Ozzy studied it impassively then he said.

"I have never seen this woman before."

"How can you be sure?" Belenos pressed.

"Many people pass through here every day," Ozzy explained. "Most of these are regular visitors, they are like old friends. You do not see many outsiders." He paused to write something on the back of the print.

"You should try this place."

Handing the paper back to Belenos he continued.

"Ask for Athena."

They thanked him before heading out onto the street. The air was shockingly cold after the heat of Centrepoint and as Belenos pulled his coat tighter around himself, he noticed a man across the road peering into a shop window. It was the man from the station although he was now wearing his overcoat. Belenos made a show of taking Jenna's hand but said nothing.

Athena Gladstone was an ageing hippy whose colourful clothes billowed loosely around her thin frame. Brightly coloured ribbons decorated her hair and there were bangles at her wrists and when she spoke, her voice was almost as cultured as Jenna's.

"We are looking for our friend," Jenna began surprising Belenos with her boldness. "We think she may be living rough or maybe in a hostel nearby."

"Why did she want to disappear?" Athena asked clearly suspicious of Jenna.

"Who said she wanted to disappear?"

"Well, you said that you are friends, only careless friends would lose track of each other."

"Phillipa took it upon herself to shun her friends, but we are very concerned. We only want to know if she is okay."

Belenos was impressed by her performance, there was genuine emotion in her voice.

"Look, we had a falling out if you must know. It was nothing serious but Phillipa took it very badly. We were foolish to allow the situation to go as far as it has."

"Show Athena Phillipa's picture." She said turning towards Belenos.

"This is our friend."

"What's her surname?"

"Weston, Phillipa Weston." Belenos noticed her frown as she studied the print.

"She was here last summer, but she didn't remain for long."

"Was she okay?" Jenna said feigning concern.

"Phillipa is a troubled soul, she did not stay with us because we didn't know how to help her."

"What do you mean?"

"Phillipa is very strange," Athena said, doing her best not to shudder.

"In what way?" Jenna persisted.

Athena looked at her and scowled.

"Surely as a friend you must know what she is like."

Jenna realised that they were in danger of losing her confidence so she asked.

"Is she still dressing up and acting like a man?"

"It's worse than that." Athena replied, her eyes blazing. "She often became violent, in fact she assaulted some of the people here at the hostel then one day she went too far."

Athena wrung her hands nervously and the bangles at her wrists danced.

"One night she took a knife from the kitchen and stabbed one of our volunteer staff."

"Oh my god!" Jenna exclaimed, the colour draining from her face. "What happened?"

"Phillipa had become involved in some kind of argument and the situation escalated out of control. The stabbing was not life threatening, but we've not seen her since."

"Do you know where she went?"

Athena handed Jenna a leaflet, it was printed with the names of dozens of street kitchens.

"If she's still on the street she probably uses some of those."

Belenos thanked her and before they left made a donation to the collection box.

"I had no idea there would be so many," Jenna exclaimed miserably as she studied the leaflet. It dismayed her to see the names of so many church halls and community centres across the region.

Starting at the top, they began to work their way down the list by visiting those closest to Victoria Station. For Jenna this was something of a shock, the lives that these people lived was in total contrast to her own and after a while, the reality of extreme poverty began to leave its mark. Jenna became subdued and Belenos, aware of her changing mood began to question the wisdom of asking her to accompany him. Given her current situation, it could soon be her begging on the streets.

"Are you okay?" he asked as they left the third street kitchen. It was a shockingly grim place, run on a shoestring, relying on handouts from local restaurants and shops.

By mid afternoon, the light was fading fast and heavy clouds were beginning to gather overhead bringing the promise of more rain.

"Let's try just one more then we'll stop for a hot drink and a bite to eat." Belenos suggested.

The next kitchen was housed in a disused church. The space inside was magnificent and the calm that she had come to expect from a place of worship remained. Improvements were ongoing, but the idea of turning the building into a community centre dismayed her.

"It's such a shame that churches are being turned into places like this."

"Sign of the times," Belenos said pragmatically. "At least it will remain as a community centre, it could easily have been developed into a house."

Jenna shuddered at the idea.

"Yes we know Phillipa." A slightly built man wearing thick round lenses said once they had gone through their routine.

"She's more like Phillip these days though," he told them with a crooked smile.

"What do you mean?" Jenna eyed him warily.

"Well, I think she's convinced that she is a man, acts and dresses like one too. We advised her to seek counselling at one of those centres."

"You mean a transgender clinic." Belenos said.

"Yes that's right."

"Do you know where?"

"I can find out for you," he replied helpfully.

He offered them both a cup of coffee before going off to search for the information and they made themselves comfortable at a table. There was hardly anyone at the centre, the midday rush was over so the volunteer cooks were taking a break before preparing the evening meal. Their coffees arrived in chipped mugs and Jenna hid her disgust. The grey liquid looked unappetising and contained more chicory than coffee. Pushing it aside, she whispered.

"I couldn't possibly drink that."

"What are you going to do Jenna?"

The question took her completely by surprise and it made her feel incredibly sad. She looked up at him and their eyes locked.

"I really have no idea," she told him.

The man returned sooner than expected and turning her face away Jenna swallowed down the lump that had formed at the back of her throat. Belenos, giving her a little time to recover focussed on what he had to say.

"I have the address of the transgender clinic and also I managed to find this."

He handed Belenos a piece of paper containing Phillipa's last known address.

Jenna turned to face them, then getting to their feet they thanked him before heading towards the door. Belenos left another generous donation in the collection box.

Chapter
FIFTY TWO

"Emilia has asked me to join her on a full time basis at her shop," Ben told her once they had settled at their table.

The aroma of delicious Thai cuisine filled the air around them, a welcome relief after the damp chill of the night.

"She is willing to pay me a salary," he continued.

"That's marvellous news," Mia beamed at him from across the table.

"I must admit though, I'm a little worried that she may be overstretching herself."

"She must have thought it through very carefully because I can't imagine Emilia putting her business at risk."

"I'm sure you are right, but still I'm concerned."

"You must have some idea about the state of her business. The work you have done for her recently has paid dividends, she told me herself."

"True," he nodded in agreement. "She wants me to help organise the weddings, develop that side of the business. You know that she is determined to offer the complete package."

"I'm sure your sister is more than capable of making that happen and with your help and support it's bound to be a success."

She knew that Ben was practically minded and like an accountant would do nothing to upset the balance sheet, Emilia on the other hand tended to follow her heart, there were some things in life worth taking a risk for.

"Have a little faith in your sister."

A waitress arrived with menus and she took their drinks order.

"I guess you are right, Emilia must know what she's doing." Ben said once she had gone.

"You should feel privileged that she has so much faith in you."

"That's part of the problem I suppose. Working in her shadow and rising to her exacting standards will certainly be a challenge."

"Don't belittle yourself, you will hardly be working in her shadow, you'll be perfect together."

Their drinks arrived and lifting her glass, she proposed a toast.

"To success and harmony."

Ben smiled and touched the rim of her glass with his own.

"So, how was your day? Was it so very stressful meeting your pianist?"

"No, not at all," Mia replied her eyes lighting up with joy. "Margaret is simply amazing. She is very 'old school', we got on famously."

She went on to describe Margaret then she told him about 'Woody'.

"You do realise that all Morris Minor Travellers are called 'Woody'."

Mia looked at him and smiled. "She did say that it was a bit of a cliché, but I didn't understand why at the time and didn't like to ask."

"It's because of the wooden frame that surrounds the bodywork of the car."

"Oh," she replied, still none the wiser.

She went on to tell him about Margaret's aunt Alice.

"SOE," he said raising his eyebrows. "Blimey, that was a very risky business during the war." He knew a lot more about it than she did.

"When are you seeing her again?"

"Day after tomorrow," she told him. "I need to go over what we did today then rehearse the second part of the concert a little more before we meet up again."

"You are so fortunate to be performing with someone like Viktor Vasiliev," Ben said. "It will be such a boost to your career."

"I'm so thrilled," Mia smiled, "especially at the prospect of performing at the Royal Albert Hall. I never imagined that, not for a while at least."

"I bet your agent is rubbing her hands together."

"I suppose she is," Mia agreed.

They had not yet discussed the financial arrangements.

They made their choices form the menu and when the waitress had taken their order a figure appeared from behind Mia.

"Miss Ashton," he said surprised to see her.

"Hello Jim," Mia turned towards him. "Fancy seeing you here."

"I like Thai food so occasionally eat here," he explained.

"Ben, you remember Jim, he's a sound engineer. I'm sure that you must have met before at one of my concerts."

Ben inclined his head. He remembered Jim Peters all too well, he did not like him then, and his opinion remained the same. Neither man extended the hand of friendship, Jim simply stared at Ben sensing his hostility.

"I do like this restaurant," Mia continued oblivious to the tension between them.

"I've just finished eating so I'll leave you in peace," Jim said with a smile. "Enjoy your evening."

Ben watched as Jim made his way towards the door and as he glanced back at Mia, Ben was certain that he saw malice in his glare.

"Don't you think him strange?" Ben asked the moment he was gone.

"In what way?" she asked reaching for her drink.

"I don't know," he frowned, "but there is something about him that I don't like." He paused for a moment as if finding his words. "He's so effeminate."

Mia raised her eyebrows, shocked at his unworthy comment.

"There's no crime in that," she said. "He's always pleasant and helpful and he's very good at his job."

Ben got the impression that it was all an act with Jim Peters, but Mia would have none of it.

"What do you know about him?"

"Nothing really, why should I? He's simply a sound engineer who I bump into from time to time behind the scenes at my concerts."

"Was he with you in York?"

"No, the university have their own stage crew. Why do you ask?"

Ben remained silent, his expression betraying his opinion. A thought nagged at him from the recesses of his mind, but it remained elusive.

Their food arrived and the delicate fragrance of spicy food rising up from their plates drove away any unpleasant thoughts of Jim Peters.

After their meal, Ben sat back in his chair and groaned, he was as exhausted as a marathon runner at the end of a long race. The mountain of food had floored him and now he could hardly move.

"Wow, that was amazing, but I didn't expect there to be so much."

"You didn't have to eat it all," Mia told him looking smug.

She had avoided the heavier foods, selecting the dishes that overflowed with flavour.

"I don't think I have room left for coffee," he admitted.

"We could take a slow walk back to my place if the rain has stopped. Perhaps by then you will have room for coffee."

Checking his watch Ben nodded in agreement.

"Sounds perfect, but I can't stay for too long. I have an early meeting with Emilia in the morning. We are talking to a representative from Wellington House. She is hoping to persuade him to let us organise some of the civil ceremonies that are held there."

"That sounds interesting." Mia said rising to her feet.

"They are a huge outfit and in my opinion may prove to be a little too ambitious."

"Look Ben," Mia said turning to face him. "Don't be so negative. Emilia obviously has her sights set high so just humour her. Try not to say anything that may undermine her ambitions, especially not in front of this representative."

"I wouldn't do that to her," he replied looking hurt that she should think him capable of such a thing.

The rain had eased leaving puddle filled hollows along the pathway. Light from overhead lamps and shop fronts danced on the surface of the road creating colourful patches and leaning into him, Mia kissed his cheek before they set off. Their evening had been perfect, but she wished that Ben would stop worrying about his sister. Perhaps it was not such a good idea after all, him agreeing to join her. They may be brother and sister but were quite different in many ways. Emilia possessed an enthusiasm for life that showed in everything that she did. She was obviously a very capable woman and clearly not afraid of taking a risk. Mia sometimes wished that Ben could be more like his sister.

Suddenly a runner brushed past them forcing Mia against Ben as water splashed up from a puddle.

"That was a bit close," Ben said loudly. "You should watch where you are going."

The runner did not break her stride and Mia watched as the distance between them lengthened, her ponytail swinging between her shoulder blades as she went.

Chapter
FIFTY THREE

The following morning Mia woke from a dreamless sleep. Her bedroom was in semi-darkness as the weak wintery light battled to penetrate the curtains at the window. The temperature had fallen during the night turning the rain to sleet, which now rattled against the windows like grit. Mia was glad that she was not going out today.

Exploring with her fingers under the duvet she pulled up her night-dress and ran her hand across her stomach. The scratches were fading quickly and the swelling had gone. Constant moisturising had seen to that and now she was confident there would be no scars. Luckily, she did not have to explain her injuries to Ben, they had not spent the night together recently, their busy schedules confounding any thoughts of an intimate relationship. She decided to make it up to him. As soon as they were able, they should get away for a few days. The idea pleased her and she imagined a winter break somewhere relaxing, a country retreat perhaps or a spa where they could be pampered and enjoy each other's company. She smiled, the idea was appealing, but the reality was not quite that simple. It would be impossible for her to get away before the next concert and by then winter would be over. Maybe they should plan a spring break, she thought not wanting to be outdone.

Throwing back the duvet, she swung her legs over the side of the bed then reaching for her gown pulled it around her. Her slippers were warming beside the radiator as usual so slipping them on she moved towards the door. The house was still and silent apart from the occasional squall against the windowpanes and making her way towards the kitchen, coffee was her first priority, it would help kick start her day. She couldn't face breakfast, she was still full from the meal they had enjoyed the previous evening. Reaching for the coffee pot she automatically went for the strong French mix from the collection of blends on the shelf. She favoured this one the most first thing in the morning.

Placing the steaming pot on a tray, she added her mug and a jug of milk, then stepping into the hallway she headed for the living room. Something caught her eye and turning towards the front door saw a card lying on the mat. Stooping to pick it up she carried it into the other room where she placed the tray down on the coffee table and switched on a lamp.

The front of the card was decorated with scenes from a country town and across the centre was printed *'Welcome to Epsom'.* Turning it over, she discovered a simple message.

'Wish you were here'.

Mia frowned as she studied the hand written message then the muscles in her stomach tightened. It was the same as the anonymous note that she had received before. There was no address this time, no stamp or postmark. She shuddered again, realising that it must have been hand delivered during the night. It had not been there when she and Ben returned from the restaurant or when he left an hour later. Her coffee remained forgotten on the table beside the flowers that had now lost their scent and reaching for the telephone, her hands trembled as she dialled the number.

Terry was about to leave for work when his phone began to ring. He wanted to get an early start so he muttered an oath under his breath as he snatched up the receiver.

"Hello dad, it's Mia."

He knew immediately that something was wrong, the tone of her voice told him all he needed to know.

"I'll be there right away."

By the time her father arrived, she was dressed and had recovered some of her composed.

"So, tell me what happened." Terry settled himself in an armchair.

Mia explained how she had found the card on the mat earlier, insisting that it had not been there when she had gone to bed the previous evening.

"Is that it?" he asked inclining his head towards the innocent looking postcard.

Mia nodded but remained silent.

Fumbling in his jacket pocket, he pulled out an evidence bag.

"I want you to pop it into this. I don't want to touch it, my fingerprints will only add to the confusion."

Mia did as she was told and once the evidence bag was sealed, Terry studied the card through the polythene.

"Epsom," he frowned, "why Epsom?"

"I was there yesterday," she said, "it's where the pianist who is helping me to rehearse for my next concert lives."

Terry produced a notebook and pen from his pocket.

"I'll need to take down some details."

Mia told him about Margaret, where they went and how they spent their day.

"Mostly we worked in her music room." She smiled weakly.

"How old is Margaret?"

His question caught her off guard.

"I really don't know," she murmured. "Margaret is a retired music teacher," she paused thinking for a moment before going on. "She told me that she could remember her aunt buying a car in 1965 and I got the impression that Margaret must have been a teenager or in her early twenties then."

"So early seventies perhaps."

Mia nodded in agreement.

"Assuming this card was sent by the killer," Terry said thoughtfully, "she must have followed you to Epsom."

"I suppose so," Mia agreed.

"You didn't see or notice anything out of the ordinary when you were travelling yesterday?"

"Of course not, there were crowds of people about all the time. I didn't expect to be followed so took no notice."

Terry scribbled something in his notebook.

"Margaret needs to be informed about this," he said.

He didn't want to alarm Mia, but from the way the blood had drained from her face he was convinced that she was aware of the implications. He asked a few more questions mostly about her immediate plans and movements. The killer could still be nearby.

"I'm going to work with Margaret again tomorrow." She told him.

"At her home in Epsom?"

"Yes," she nodded, "the same arrangement. She will collect me from the station."

Writing down the time of the train that she intended to catch, he made up his mind, he should also be on it, stage a covert operation in the hope of spotting the killer.

Suddenly his mobile phone began to ring.

"Sorry," he said peering at the little neon screen. "I have to take this."

"I'll make us some tea," Mia said as she got to her feet.

"DI Ashton," he spoke into the phone.

"Inspector Ashton, it's the Security Services in York."

"Hello," he greeted the female voice warmly. He couldn't remember her name and she did not remind him.

"I have some information for you regarding the Ford Focus that you are looking for."

"That's great news," he said unable to hide his excitement.

"I wouldn't get your hopes up," she laughed. "We only managed to get a partial number plate I'm afraid." She read it out to him but unfortunately, it was nothing new. The letters were the same as those he already had.

Biting down on his bottom lip, he muttered an oath.

"I can confirm that it's a red car. The camera in the city spotted it on the evening of the concert at the university," she paused as if consulting her notes. "It was being driven by a male."

"Are you sure?"

"I'm certain, but I can't give you a description of the driver." She paused again. "On the same evening about an hour later the car was seen on the university campus, but this time it was being driven by a female. Again a clear description is impossible."

"Thank you for this," Terry said. "Can you send copies of both images to me by e-mail?"

She agreed to do as he asked then he ended the call. He now had clear evidence that the suspect was at the murder scene in York. His frown deepened as he thought about the male driver. If it was his transgender murderer then this could be the first real image of him as a man. He would need to compare it with the photo fit images that Robert Nixon had produced. At least now, he felt that he was getting somewhere, he could even be on the verge of identifying both personalities of his suspect.

"You are looking thoughtful," Mia told him as she placed a mug of tea on the table in front of him.

Terry grunted, he was tempted to tell her about what was on his mind, but he couldn't. This was a murder investigation and like it or not his daughter was caught up in it.

"I'll get this to the lab," he said nodding towards the evidence bag. "We may discover some prints or DNA." He didn't think it likely though, the killer would be far too devious for that.

Terry returned to his office, but he had to wait a couple of hours for PC Yearsley to come on shift.

"Good morning Bill," he said at last, "how are you today?"

PC Yearsley turned to face him. "Inspector Ashton," he said without enthusiasm. Clearly, he was not pleased to see him.

"Sorry about the hassle you are getting from DI Mallinson. He's a thorn in my side too." Ashton laughed and Yearsley relaxed a little.

"He did get a bit hot under the collar I must admit."

"Don't you worry about him. Now, could you have a quick look at these for me?"

Terry produced two A4 prints from his file and placed them on the desk in front of him.

"What am I looking for?"

"Is it possible to clean these images up, make them a little clearer?"

"We could run them through the computer programme and see what happens."

"Good, I was hoping you would say that. I've already e-mailed them to you. It's the faces of both drivers that I want you to concentrate on."

Yearsley nodded then got down to work. Accessing his e-mails, he downloaded the images to a file before highlighting the areas that he was interested in then he initiated the computer programme.

"It will take a couple of minutes," he said glancing up at Ashton. "Is this the same woman we were looking at the other day?"

"I hope so Bill," Ashton replied.

His mobile phone began to ring, so stepping aside he answered it.

"DI Ashton."

"Terry, it's Isobel Woods."

"DS Woods, thank you for returning my call, we need to meet up. I want to share some information with you regarding the murder case that DI Mallinson is working on."

From the tone of his voice, she guessed that he was not alone and he obviously wanted whoever was listening to know his business.

"A formal meeting or is this a lunch invitation?" she asked.

"Let's meet in the bar at the Richmond Hotel. Shall we say 13:00 hours?"

He finished his call then glanced towards PC Yearsley. He was looking at an image on his computer screen, it was the face of a young man

261

behind the wheel of a car. The features were still unclear, the face in shadow revealed nothing but it was good enough to make a comparison with the profile that Nixon had put together.

"Let's have a look at the other one." Ashton whispered as he moved closer.

With the click of the mouse, the image changed. This one was much clearer, the interior of the car brighter than the first. Pulling a print from his file, Ashton compared it to the face on the screen.

"It's the same woman," Yearsley confirmed.

"That's the result I was hoping for." Ashton patted him on the shoulder. "Can you e-mail those to me?"

Chapter
FIFTY FOUR

On his way to the Richmond Hotel Terry stopped off at the Public Mortuary where the Forensic Suite was situated. The main doors led directly onto a reception area that reminded him of a well appointed hotel and there was always someone perched behind the desk ready to help with any enquiry. On this occasion, he was here to speak with Dr Patricia Fleming so the receptionist asked him politely to wait while she made a call to the pathologist.

"Dr Fleming will be with you shortly," the woman informed him, her smile artificially bright, she forgot all about him the moment she got back to work.

In less than five minutes Pat appeared.

"Terry, what a pleasant surprise." Unable to hide her affection she threw her arms around his neck and hugged him tightly. "Have you come here to ask me out on another date?"

Terry was conscious that the receptionist had a front seat view of their performance, but diplomatically she kept her head down and looked busy.

"That is partly the reason for my visit," he lied. "I have another exhibit that needs processing. Same as before but this time there's no need to keep it from Mallinson."

"Have you boys made up?" Pat smiled and drawing him towards the comfortable chairs arranged in an alcove she sat down and crossed her legs.

"I will soon be back on the case officially," he told her. "It turns out that what I'm currently working on is linked to the murders of the young musicians and although Mia is involved, they won't be able to stop me from investigating both cases. In fact, I'm hoping to have a satisfactory result very soon."

Pat looked at him and her face lit up with pleasure.

"You have been busy."

"It's partly down to you," he told her. "The blood sample found on Victoria Stevens' wheelchair ties both cases together, I've also got CCTV images that proves it."

He didn't want to tell her too much but felt obliged to reveal some of the details.

"So, you want to have this postcard checked for prints and DNA?" she asked holding the evidence bag between her fingertips.

"Yes. You will of course find Mia's prints on it, but this time it was hand delivered so hopefully not much else in the way of contamination."

"So what about your other business, where do you intend to take me this time?"

"I seem to remember you saying something about the next time being your treat so more to the point, where are you going to take me?"

Throwing her head back, Pat roared with laughter.

"Quite right," she said wiping a tear from the corner of her eye. "Let me think about it and I'll get back to you."

Terry checked his watch and got to his feet.

"I really must go, I have a one o'clock meeting."

"I'll ring you," Pat said as she watched him walk towards the door.

The receptionist lifted her head and smiled as he passed.

The Richmond Hotel was busy with lunchtime revellers, but there was a room permanently set aside for members of the Metropolitan police force. DS Woods was already there occupying one of the huge leather armchairs.

"Izzy," he smiled as he lowered himself in the chair opposite her. A low circular table separated them and in front of her was an empty cup and saucer.

"Would you like another one of those or something stronger perhaps?"

She gave him a withering look, leaving him in no doubt that he had asked the wrong question.

"Should I ask for a couple of menus?"

"Don't bother, I know exactly what I'm having."

She told him to get her a cheddar cheese ploughman's and a half pint of dry cider and moving towards the bar, Terry realised that he should have known what she would order. They had spent enough time together over the years.

He returned carrying their drinks and placing hers down carefully on the table, he asked.

"Are you okay sitting here or would you prefer a table?"

"I'm fine thanks."

He grunted before sitting down.

A copy of his file lay unopened on the table but before reaching for it, he took a mouthful of his drink.

"You are aware that I'm working on an old case," he began, "assaults on transgender people from TG International in the Docklands area."

She inclined her head but made no comment.

"I now have reasons to believe that it is linked to the murders of the musicians including Alison Morley in York."

Her eyebrows shot up and she leaned forward.

"I have CCTV evidence that places the car used by my suspect in the area at the time of the murder."

He went on to tell her about the images he had in addition to those from the King Edward Hotel.

"It was Mallinson's request for another look at the blood sample that drew it all together." He admitted

"I've also been looking for CCTV evidence."

"I know, but what progress have you made?"

She looked at him sourly. "Well as you already know, PC Yearsley has been a little monopolised of late so I have not been able to get very far."

"You can blame Mallinson for that, he must have mishandled Yearsley. I don't suppose his bedside manner is as well developed as mine."

This made her smile.

"True, but Mallinson is a good detective. Apart from the business with the blood sample there are other aspects of the case that you may not be aware of."

They traded secrets and as he went through the notes in his file, many of her suspicions were confirmed. He then told her about the anonymous notes that Mia had received.

"We know nothing about this," she said glancing up at him. "Have you been withholding vital information?"

"Given the fact that Mallinson regards my daughter as a murder suspect there was no way I was going to bring this to his attention. He would have brought her in for further interrogations."

He chose to say nothing about the alleged telephone calls; they remained a mystery. There was nothing to show that they had actually happened and until he had evidence, he would keep them to himself. He then told her about Margaret Marshall.

"I think I should be on that train in the morning when Mia goes to Epsom."

"I think you should too," Izzy nodded in agreement. "We must take this to Mallinson first, he should know what's going on. The Chief should also be informed, he needs to give you the nod to work on the case officially."

"His support is irrelevant nothing will stop me from looking out for my daughter. She may be in grave danger and I am not prepared to rely on others to save her from a maniac."

"I think that I should also be on that train in the morning."

"Okay," he murmured.

Belenos stared at the computer screen. The second article exploring the lives of transgender people was open in front of him but he could not find the enthusiasm to work on it. It required some very careful editing but all he could think about was Phillipa Weston. He found the prospect of researching the half sister of a serial killer appealing, but suddenly she had become inexorably connected with his current work. He could never have imagined a link between them and was now going to have to re-think his strategy. Everyone he had spoken to had told him the same thing; she liked to dress as a man and was obsessed with death. This could be a reaction to her half brother being a serial killer, but it could also be something much deeper.

Reaching for his notebook, he pulled it closer and began to write down his thoughts before they got away. This was just another angle that would need some consideration once he began to write about Mr Mac the serial killer.

The notes he had made the previous day were there in his book along with the scrap of paper containing her address. Turning to his computer, he saved the changes he had made to his article before accessing a search engine then typing in the postal code, he sat back and waited for the information to appear. He knew that the address was in Hackney but was unfamiliar with the area.

The house where Phillipa Weston lived appeared to be in another row of Victorian terraces, further information told him that it had been converted into flats some years before. Clicking on the map icon, he discovered that it was situated just off the Amhurst road and the nearest train station was Hackney Downs. Checking the train network and timetables, he decided to travel to Hackney Central, it would be more convenient as the house was just a short distance away from the station. He decided to telephone Jenna, she had performed surprisingly well the previous day, amazing him with her role-play and improvisation. It seemed fitting that she should be involved in the next stage of his investigation.

Reaching for his mobile phone, he searched for her number then pressing the call button, he listened to the sound of the ringtone. She did not pick up, her answer phone service kicked in, inviting him to leave a message, but he declined and rang off. Shutting down his computer, he reached for his scarf and coat. He would telephone her again from the train station.

The air was charged with vitality as people rushed about their business and the noise of a major train station was deafening. Belenos considered his options. The journey to Hackney Central was not straight-forward, he would have to change trains at Highbury and Islington. Before purchasing his ticket, he called Jenna again but still she did not answer so he composed a text message asking her to contact him as soon as possible. He wondered what she could be doing, it was unusual for her not to answer her phone.

Hackney seemed just as busy as central London, but on a much reduced scale. Stepping from the station, he was transported into a multi-cultural main street filled with colour and fragrance and pulling up his collar against a passing shower, he put his head down and set off.

The road he was searching for was further from the station than he thought, but eventually he arrived at his destination and staring up at the house from the pavement, he noticed few similarities with the property in Blackheath. Here the front door was painted bright red, the paintwork in good condition and there were two buzzers. One was marked 'Flat A' and the other 'Flat B'. Phillipa lived on the upper floor so pushing buzzer A, he stepped back and looked up. No discernable shadows passed the windows and the curtains remained still so he rang the buzzer again.

Suddenly the door opened revealing an Afro-Caribbean woman.

"There's nobody in." She informed him.

"Good afternoon," Belenos smiled amiably. "I'm looking for my friend, I think she lives here."

The woman's eyes narrowed then she asked. "What's your friend called?"

"Phillipa, Phillipa Weston."

"Ain't nobody by that name lives here." She folded her arms and leaned against the doorframe.

"I was given this address," he said, making a hopeless gesture.

"Is a man who lives here." She nodded her head towards the stairs.

"A man?" Belenos said surprised at her response.

"Don't know his name, keeps hisself to hisself."

"I see, I must have been given the wrong address."

He was tempted to show her the print of Phillipa, but something held him back.

"I suppose you could ask at the corner shop," she told him, her expression softening. "They know everyone from around here."

He thanked her before moving away.

The shop had been carved out of a corner house sometime in the previous century and when Belenos opened the door, an overhead bell tinkled and a middle aged man standing behind the counter looked up.

"Good afternoon," Belenos said pleasantly before going through his routine. He then showed the man Phillipa's picture.

He shrugged his shoulders before stepping out from behind the counter. Going to the back of the shop he nudged open a door and barked something harshly before a woman appeared looking fearful. He showed her the picture and she said something in a language that Belenos did not recognise then the man returned to his place behind the counter.

It seemed to be another dead end, Phillipa had disappeared completely, but it could of course be the result of her choosing to present as a man. He left the shop and retracing his steps, passed the house where he thought she lived. He was tempted to ring the bell, speak to the woman again, ask her some questions about the man who lived in the flat above but he decided to leave it for now. Pulling his mobile phone from his pocket, he checked his messages, but still there was no word from Jenna.

Chapter

FIFTY FIVE

Mia walked quickly along the platform at London Victoria. She had just gone through the automated gates and was now heading towards the waiting train. She glanced nervously over her shoulder, her father's words ringing loudly in her ears. He had told her to be vigilant, the killer had obviously followed her to Epsom earlier in the week and could be doing the same today, but it was an impossible task. How could she spot a murderer when everyone appeared so normal?

What had shocked her most was discovering that the murder suspect was a woman, now everyone she looked at was a potential killer. A smartly dressed woman stopped in front of her suddenly causing Mia to step sideways to avoid a collision. They made eye contact as Mia passed, but she simply smiled and crouched down to adjust her shoe. The killer could be anyone, she thought, a student or sightseer, or maybe one of the thousands of shoppers that were milling about the station.

Mia stopped and took a deep breath, she was in danger of becoming overwhelmed at the prospect of becoming caught up in something sinister and if she was not careful, a panic attack was a distinct possibility. She had to focus on her day ahead, it was going to be intense, but she was prepared for that, she had worked hard learning the music for the concert. Viktor Vasiliev was an extraordinary pianist who did not always play to the rules. Margaret had already introduced her to some of his peculiarities, but she was certain there would be more to come.

Going towards the nearest carriage, the doors were already open so climbing aboard she discovered that the first few seats were taken.

Moving along the walkway, she spotted a few empty seats close to where a group of women were sitting. Ordinarily she would have sat with them, begin a friendly conversation with whoever was close by but today she decided against that idea. On her left, an elderly man was sitting alone at a little table so moving towards him she smiled before swinging her bag onto the seat.

"Good morning," he said cheerfully as Mia made herself comfortable then he continued to read his newspaper.

Unbuttoning her coat, she kept it on but unwound the scarf from her neck. She kept her bag containing her sheet music, bow and blocks of rosin close beside her. She realised that it would be no use studying her music, she was far too tense so had to be content with resting her head back against the seat and staring out of the window. The train began to move and in just under forty minutes, she would arrive at her destination.

DI Ashton and DS Woods began their surveillance from the cover of a coffee and bagel kiosk. They watched as Mia walked through the station and onto the platform and as soon as she had boarded the train, they made their move. Dodging quickly amongst the crowd, they glanced at all the women, searching for anyone who might resemble the suspect. Ashton hoped that Mia had chosen a seat on the far side of the train or at least not be looking out of the window as they passed. If she spotted them, their cover would be blown. She had gone into the first carriage so they targeted the second and climbing aboard, stayed close to the inter-connecting door. There was only one seat available here so were forced to split up, Ashton moving further along the carriage. DS Woods peered through the window into the adjoining carriage but could see nothing of Mia. No one was standing in the aisle, it was unlikely that this train would become overcrowded. Turning to check her fellow passengers there was only one woman sitting close by and she was busy entertaining a child. Ashton was doing the same, casually glancing at those around him taking particular interest in the female passengers. He was unlikely to spot the killer, but as it was his daughter travelling alone, he wanted to do everything possible to ensure her safety.

The train began its journey and as it stopped at stations along the way, the number of passengers decreased only to rise again as it neared Epsom. DS Woods had been to the town before and was familiar with the station layout so when the train finally stopped, she held back waiting for Mia to alight before stepping out onto the platform herself. Ashton had emerged from further along the carriage and watched as Mia made her way towards the exit with Woods just a short distance behind. He noticed an older woman talking to one of the guards and when she spotted Mia, she waved cheerily. This must be Margaret, he thought. He knew that she would have a car parked close by so they would need to find some transport of their own.

DS Woods slowed her pace and watched as the women hugged affectionately, then they disappeared out onto the street. DI Ashton appeared beside her.

"We could call the local nick and request a car." She suggested but Ashton shook his head.

"No, let's grab a taxi. It would raise the alarm if we turned up outside Margaret's house in a squad car."

She knew that he was right and glancing towards the taxi rank she watched as the last car pulled away.

"I had a visit from the police last night," Margaret told her once they were on their way.

"I'm so sorry to have brought all this to your door." Mia glanced at Margaret apologetically. "She must have followed me from London."

"She?" Margaret said her eyes wide with amazement.

"Yes, didn't the police tell you? The murder suspect is a woman."

"No they did not, they just referred to the person as the suspect."

"Ah," Mia swallowed noisily. "I don't think it's widely known yet, but the police are looking for a woman."

"Well whoever it is I'm sure they won't be interested in an old wreck like me."

She didn't need to remind Mia that all the victims were young and attractive, it was an established pattern that Margaret thought she did not fit into.

"We should still be careful," Mia said.

She went on to explain that her father was one of the detectives involved in the case and had been explicit in his advice. He insisted that she remain vigilant and take every precaution to protect herself.

"So," Margaret said brightly. "Are you ready for the day ahead? We need to focus on the Oriental music today. How did you get on with it?"

"Very well," Mia smiled. The music was technically challenging but by adding Viktor Vasiliev it could become even more testing.

"Don't look so worried," Margaret laughed as if reading her thoughts. "Viktor might have his own way of interpreting the music, but I assure you there are no surprises, in fact I think that what he's done with the arrangement is a stroke of pure genius."

271

"I can't wait," Mia groaned.

It took a few minutes to track down a taxi, but now Ashton and Woods were mobile. The Morris Minor Traveller was out of sight and there was no longer any danger of them being spotted.

"What do you expect to find?" Woods asked once they were settled.

"Hopefully nothing out of the ordinary. I just want to see for myself where Margaret lives. If Mia is going to be visiting the house regularly it might be useful to be familiar with it and its surroundings."

He didn't need to say more, Woods knew that if the killer had been drawn here then Margaret's house could potentially become a killing ground. Knowledge was power and the more information they had the better equipped they would be in having to deal with whatever came their way.

The taxi dropped them off at the end of the road and Ashton made a note of the telephone number displayed on the side of the car. The driver gave him his name and said.

"Ask for me and I'll come out and collect you."

The road was quiet and was home to a mixture of 1930s and 1940s dwellings, each surrounded by neat little gardens. Some of the gardens had been converted into driveways, but most retained their picket fences and wooden gates. The house they were looking for was partially obscured by trees and shrubs, the pathway leading to the front door widened to accommodate the Morris, which now sat on a hard standing in front of a window.

"It must look very pretty during the summer," Woods smiled.

Ashton simply grunted all he could see was a collection of barriers that could conceal a crime. Going past the house they made their way along the street doing their best to blend in, but in reality they stood out like a couple of unwanted door-to-door canvassers.

Circling behind the houses Ashton wanted to see if alleyways ran between the properties, but the gardens backed onto each other, the boundaries established by hedge or fence.

"The psychological profilers would tell us that our suspect is likely to kill again before Mia's next concert." Woods told him. This was a particular interest of hers, but Ashton was not a great fan of criminal profiling.

"We know there is a pattern forming," she continued. "There were two killings in December then one in February, so we can expect another one soon."

"Don't you think that the killer simply struck on the dates of Mia's concerts?" Ashton glanced at her. "I think it's more likely to be opportunity rather than planning."

"That could be true." She nodded reluctantly, but was not convinced. The killer was working to some kind of pattern.

"The last crime took place on 14th February, the one before that on Christmas Eve, about six weeks separating them. The murder in York was at the beginning of December, so I'm convinced that she will strike again before Mia's next concert."

"Her next concert is just over five weeks away."

"Exactly, our killer won't wait that long, besides Mia will be performing with a man."

Ashton thought about what she was saying. It was true that once a serial killer began to operate regularly it would develop into an addiction and as the desire to kill became stronger mistakes would be made. Even the most disciplined serial killer would eventually become careless.

"Margaret hardly fits our victim profile," he acknowledge.

"That may be so," Woods stopped walking and turned to face him. "She is however a female musician with a connection to Mia. She might not be performing with her on the night of the concert, but she could be the next best thing."

Ashton rubbed his finger against the side of his nose and sighed deeply.

"Either that or this time Mia is the target."

"No, I don't think so. Why would the killer follow her out here if she was going to be next?" They began walking again before she continued. "I'm sure that Margaret is the target here. The killer may have been closing in on Mia, but with Margaret coming onto the scene I'm convinced that things have changed."

Chapter

FIFTY SIX

There was still no word from Jenna. Belenos had left numerous text messages, he had even used voicemail, which is something that he seldom did. It was so unlike Jenna, she always returned her messages and now he was beginning to think the worst. She had told him about her father and the arranged marriage and he had seen for himself the Private Detective hired to keep watch over her. The more he thought about it the more he believed that foul play was at the root of her disappearance.

He could not have imagined the effect she would have on him. Over the last few weeks, she had become more transparent and as he got to know her better, the more he liked what he saw, now he was finding it impossible to stop thinking about her.

He had already decided to drive to Hackney, do a bit of sleuthing, watch the place where Phillipa Weston lived. He needed to know more about her before his notes were complete, but first he would go to Pimlico. Jenna lived there and he wanted to know if she was at home.

The area was in total contrast to Hackney. Huge mansions and villas lined grand avenues where luxury cars were parked in a display of power and wealth. Only the privileged could afford to live in this desirable postcode.

Finding a space to leave his car was almost impossible. Driving restrictions and one-way streets confounded the likes of Belenos, only the locals would know how to circumnavigate the road system. Eventually he found a space some distance away from where Jenna lived, this was an area mainly reserved for residential permit holders, but with a few spaces available for visitors, which of course came at a premium. Armed with his mobile phone and a credit card he rented a space for an hour and baulked at the expense. It left him feeling cheated, but at least his car would be safe. He could hardly imagine street crime happening here, the place was bristling with CCTV and security cameras.

Jenna lived in an apartment in one of the Georgian mansions just off the main road and as Belenos approached the building, he couldn't help being impressed. He had never been to her home before and although he expected opulence, he was not prepared for anything as imposing as this. If her apartment occupied just one floor, his humble home would fit into it many times over.

Climbing the steps leading an ornate front door, he was confronted by several bells each with names of the occupants printed clearly below. Finding the bell for Jenna's apartment he pushed it then standing back, waited for an announcement from the intercom, but suddenly the door opened.

"Good evening," he said, startled when a well-dressed middle-aged woman appeared. "I'm here to see Jenna."

She studied him as if he was a scientific specimen then she said.

"I'm afraid that Miss O'Brien is not currently at home," she paused before going on. "If you would care to leave your card I will see that she is informed of your visit." Speaking slowly and impeccably there was no trace of a local accent.

Belenos raised his eyebrows and opened his mouth to speak but nothing came out, he was at a loss for words. He must be addressing a member of the household staff he thought. This was something else that Jenna had failed to mention and it amused him to think that she would take staff for granted.

"Would you be so kind as to tell her that Belenos Falzone called?" he said at last. "I have been trying to contact her but with no success."

From the way she stared at him he got the impression that he had probably said too much.

"I will be glad to pass on your message."

"Do you know when she will be back?" He decided to ask.

"Miss O'Brien is not expected back for several days." Her reply was blunt, her expression stern and guarded.

He realised that nothing more would be forthcoming so thanking her he backed away down the steps to the pavement below. Returning to his car, he thought about what he had just learnt. It was strange that

Jenna had said nothing to him about going away in fact, she was keen to help with his search for Phillipa Weston. It did not explain why she was not answering her phone or returning his messages, so pulling his mobile phone from his pocket, he tried her number again.

Ashton was on his way to see his daughter but first he intended to walk the streets where she lived. He had seen the suspect loitering there before and it only seemed logical that she would return to spy on her quarry again, besides someone had hand delivered the anonymous note to her door. He wanted to be ready this time. He had circulated her image amongst his colleagues and squad cars had been alerted, but that would not be enough. There were precious little resources available to cover every angle all of the time.

Parking his car a few streets away he began to walk towards Mia's flat. The hour was late and the night air heavy with moisture. The temperature was dropping rapidly and soon the damp patches on the pavements would turn to ice. Walking silently on the balls of his feet he kept to the shadows listening for the footfalls of a runner. He also took note of every passing car. A dog walker hurried past, intent on returning home as quickly as possible. His dog sniffed at the shadows where Ashton was standing but that was the extent of its interest, like its master, it too craved the comfort and warmth of a fireplace. Ashton smiled and hunching his shoulders against the chill, he pushed his hands deeper into his pockets. He should have thought to bring gloves and a scarf.

The houses on each side of the road were silent, lights showed at some of the windows and he imagined the occupants snuggled up in front of the television or enjoying their supper. He wondered what Margaret Marshall was doing and he pictured her house in his mind. He had requested that a squad car sweep past at regular intervals and hoped that it would actually happen. He had very little influence over his colleagues in Epsom, all he could hope for was their co operation.

Looking up at a CCTV camera, he was tempted to wave, but he could not be sure that an operative would be looking down at him so he decided to ignore it, not draw attention to himself or the position of the camera.

Further along the street, a puddle had formed on a bend. Water from a previous shower had failed to drain away and now tiny ice crystals were beginning to form on its surface. Ashton thought that soon it would freeze entirely turning that section of road into an accident spot. Suddenly a car appeared, its headlights slicing into the darkness. Turning his face away in an attempt to preserve his night vision Ashton recognised the shape of the car, but it was impossible to make out the driver. The vehicle careered around the bend, so he moved to the edge of the pathway in order to get a better view of the number plate. Tyres hissed throwing up a wall of freezing water and Ashton gasped as it soaked through his trousers and seeped into his shoes. Holding his position, he managed to see what he wanted and reaching for his mobile phone, he called in the number plate and asked his colleague to run a check. It took several minutes to get a response, but eventually he was rewarded with an answer. The car was registered to a woman by the name of Phillipa Weston and her address was in Blackheath. Jotting this down in his notebook, he smiled.

He decided not to call in on Mia, he was soaked and wanted to get off home. He would telephone her instead, make sure that she was okay and her windows and doors were secure.

Belenos was engaged in some surveillance of his own. Sitting in his car opposite a house in Hackney, he stayed low in his seat in an effort to remain out of sight. The lights in both flats were out and there had been no movement in the last two hours. The temperature had dropped until the interior of the car resembled a freezer, his breath curling from his mouth. He did not run the engine and turn the heater up for fear of being exposed, the area hardly boasted an inviting atmosphere. He decided to remain for another half hour then call it a night.

Twenty nine minutes later he'd had enough and pulling away, the only car that he passed on his way to the Amhurst road was a red Ford Focus.

The following morning began dry but cold. Lorries loaded with salt had been out during the night servicing the main roads, which were now clogged with commuters. Ashton glanced at Woods who was sitting beside him. He had considered calling her out during the night to investigate the address in Blackheath, but he had been wet and cold and what difference would a few hours make.

"We could use the siren," she eyed him mischievously.

"No, the noise would drive me mad and on these roads I don't think it would make any difference."

Cars were everywhere, some inching their way slowly along the road whilst others were parked beside the pavement adding to the congestion. Buses were forced to dodge in and out of the traffic frustrating the motorists even more, but Ashton remained calm and focussed on the job ahead. He could hardly believe that in just a few hours they may have apprehended the killer, Mallinson and Keable would be on their way home and his daughter would be safe.

"The place we want is near here," Ashton said breaking his thought pattern. "We had better look out for somewhere to leave the car."

Parking close to the house was impossible. The streets between the terraced rows were narrow and not designed to accommodate so many cars. He could see no sign of a red Ford Focus but this did not concern him, like them, the driver had probably been forced to leave it some distance away.

They found a spot that appeared to be too small but Ashton manoeuvred the car skilfully and Woods wondered if he would ever manage to get it out again. She remained silent as they made their way along the pathway. She was appalled at how rundown this area was and shuddered to think about the kind of characters who might be lurking within the slums that surrounded them. Ashton eyed her sympathetically he could sense her apprehension. Perhaps they should have told someone where they were going.

Bracing her shoulders Woods settled a serious expression on her face and when she was ready, Ashton rapped loudly on the door. A man appeared a few moments later and eyed them scornfully.

"Gawd blimey, I can smell bacon." Laughing at his own joke, he exposed his blackened teeth. "It must be time for breakfast."

Woods could only wish that it was bacon she could smell.

"I don't need to produce my Warrant Card then." Ashton remarked as he inched closer to the door.

"We are looking for Phillipa Weston," Woods said incurring the man's full attention.

He leered at her lecherously then suddenly snapped out of his trance.

"That mad bitch moved out months ago."

"This is the address that we have for her," Woods informed him.

"That may be so but she doesn't live here anymore."

"How long ago did she move out?"

"I told you, months ago."

"How many months?"

"I don't know, four or five I expect."

"Where did she go?"

"I ain't her keeper," he shrugged his shoulders violently sending up another cloud of unpleasant aromas.

"She is a very bad person," he continued, "that's why we threw her out."

There was hardly any point in prolonging their questioning, it was unlikely that they would learn more and Woods was relieved when Ashton did not insist on entering the property.

"So," he moaned as they walked back to their car, "another dead end."

"At least we have the registration details of the car," Woods reminded him. "Uniform can keep an eye out for it, I'm sure it won't take long to track it down."

"Providing Phillipa Weston doesn't realise that we are closing in on her. She could easily dump the car."

Woods looked at him, he was obviously disappointed, but that was often the way things went. Clues could often be misleading but she knew from experience that something else always came along, another lead that might prove useful. They had to remain positive.

Chapter
FIFTY SEVEN

It rained all weekend and as the month slipped from February to March, there was no immediate prospect of improvement. DI Ashton was in his office, he had been there for much of the time searching through official websites and registers looking for anything that might lead him to Phillipa Weston. He discovered a page on a social media site but it was inactive. There was however, a passport size photograph of the woman, which he saved to his file before printing off a copy. It matched the images that he already had and was further proof that he had identified the killer, all he needed to do now was to work out how to track her down before she struck again. Preventative policing methods were in place, Margaret Marshall's home was under constant surveillance, and he had taken it upon himself to patrol the streets where his daughter lived. The whole force was on the lookout for the red Ford Focus and a detailed description of the suspect had been circulated.

DS Woods appeared at his door.

"Morning Terry," she said as she slipped into his office. She was carrying a plastic cup filled with tea but showed no interest in drinking it.

"Mallinson is on his way," she warned him, "and he's not happy."

"What have I done this time?" Ashton sighed.

"Nothing, it's not you, it's Phillipa Weston."

Mallinson burst into his office almost knocking Woods off her feet, she just about managed to avoid spilling her tea.

"What else are you holding back regarding this case?" he snarled, his face flushed with anger, he was clearly upset.

"I've given you everything that I have," Ashton began defensively. "I shared her name and address the moment I knew it myself along with details of her vehicle."

"Do you know what she has been up to this weekend?"

"No," Ashton admitted, "she has disappeared off my radar."

"That's because she has been active elsewhere. Whilst you have been keeping watch over your daughter, Phillipa bloody Weston has struck again."

"That's hardly fair..." DS Woods began but Mallinson cut her off.

"Obviously you will take his side," he stared at her. "I thought you were a team player but the only team I can see here is made up exclusively of you two."

"There's no need to vent your anger on DS Woods," Ashton said rising to his feet. "What have you been doing all weekend?" Moving around his desk, he squared up to Mallinson.

DS Woods, not wanting to witness a contest of male bravado, pushed between them. Her heart was racing but she held onto her plastic cup as if it was some kind of shield.

"We had all better calm down," she told them. "This kind of behaviour will do no good at all."

There was a tense moment as the men stared at each other and holding her breath, Woods braced herself, but it was Ashton who backed away.

"You had better give me the details," he said calmly.

"A victim has been found in Kensington, a female music teacher from a private school." Mallinson's voice trembled with stress. "It happened some time over the weekend, but wasn't discovered until earlier this morning."

"Do we know if there is a connection between the victim and Mia Ashton?" Woods asked.

"Nothing is certain yet."

"So there has been a change in her pattern." Woods was expecting something like this to happen. The psychological profile of the killer suggested that things were likely to change and she would strike again.

"Don't you dare say I told you so," Ashton said glancing at her. He knew the way her mind worked.

"We didn't expect anything like this, not so soon anyway. There was no indication that the killer was seeking another target," Woods said mainly for Mallinson's benefit. "Based on the information we have we were convinced that the likely victim was Margaret Marshall."

"We were wrong to assume that," Mallinson whispered, running his hand over his face.

He sounded tired and Woods felt sorry for him. He could be incredibly annoying at times, but he was basically a good man who took his job very seriously. She guessed that he had already seen the Chief who would almost certainly have given him a rough time. She was relieved not to have been up in front of him herself, she knew how fearsome he could be. It was however clear whom he considered to be running the case.

"Was the MO the same?" Ashton asked.

"Yes," Mallinson nodded, "blow to the back of the head then mutilation of the torso."

"It's strange this mutilation business." Woods said, wondering what the psychologists would make of that.

"SOCO are at the scene now," Mallinson continued. "I'm heading over there shortly."

Ashton sat down and sighed.

"Do you want us to accompany you?"

"No, I don't think there is any point, both Keable and James are there. You will have a full report just as soon as we have it." Mallinson frowned before adding. "I'll telephone you with the victim's name, perhaps you can make a start by finding out what you can about her."

"Do you think the killer knows that we are closing in on her and is using this to distract our attention away from the intended victims?" Ashton said thinking out loud.

"We can't rule that out." Mallinson agreed. "We may have been duped into thinking that Margaret Marshall would be next."

"It was just a matter of time before Weston killed again and looking at the pattern..." Woods said hardly needing to spell it out.

"You are right," Mallinson nodded. "We should have been ready for something like this. The psychologists report warned us well in advance."

Ashton snorted, he did not share their confidence in such reports.

"The facts are that Weston was seen in areas where both Margaret Marshall and my daughter live and given the emerging pattern one of them was believed to be the next victim."

"Did you actually see Phillipa Weston for yourself? Can you be sure that it was in fact her behind the wheel of that car?"

Ashton stared at him, he had a point, but he decided to say nothing. Mallinson was convinced that Weston had a male accomplice although there was no clear evidence to substantiate that. He refused to believe that she could be a transgender man and was reluctant to consider the evidence that Ashton had put before him. Suddenly the telephone at his elbow began to ring.

"Hello Pat," he said. "Look, I'm in the middle of something. Can I call you back?"

"It's about the postcard that you gave me to examine," she said ignoring his plea.

"Okay, go on."

"We have picked up traces of DNA that are not a match for your daughter, but of course the only prints we could find belong to her."

"Do you have a match for the DNA?"

"We do indeed," she told him, excitement creeping into her voice. "It matches the blood sample found on Victoria Stevens' wheelchair."

"So it was the killer who sent her that card."

"We can be certain that at some point it came into contact with your suspect."

Years of working with the police had taught her to be non committal. She rarely gave her opinion, she merely pointed out the facts. "Thank you Pat."

She realised that their conversation was at an end so would have to wait for another opportunity to talk to him socially.

Mia was at home working in her music room. She would not see Margaret again for a few days, but had plenty to work on. Margaret was a great support and her teaching methods revolutionary, consequently Mia found it much easier to modify her style to accommodate the way Viktor Vasiliev played.

Ben would soon be joining her for lunch and she suspected that he was planning to stay all afternoon. They had seen very little of each other over the weekend and she was looking forward to spending some time with him, but first she was determined to make the most of her morning rehearsal session.

At one o'clock sharp, he arrived damp and cold and shrugging off his coat, he held her in his arms and kissed her enthusiastically. His face was like ice but his passion burned with desire.

"Wow," Mia gasped. "Are you really that pleased to see me or are you simply full of lust and testosterone?"

"Feed me first then I'll let you know."

She giggled then taking his hand, led him into the kitchen. Eager to prove that she could cook, she had spent the previous evening preparing soup from fresh vegetables and earlier that morning had made a loaf with the help of her new bread making machine. The results were pleasing.

"This smells wonderful," Ben said. He guessed that she was looking for praise and in this instance it was truly justified.

Mia stirred the soup as it simmered gently on the stove.

"Em's shop was busy on Saturday," he told her as he looked round searching for something to do.

"That's good. I guess it's the spring wedding season that's responsible for that."

He decided to help by slicing the bread so selecting a knife from the rack on the wall he got to work. The loaf was soft and smelled amazing and as he cut into the rich brown interior, it was full of seeds that he would never be able to identify.

"This is great," he told her.

"I hope it's okay, I'm going to try other recipes if you like that one."

He loved it when she included him in her future. Mia was by far the best thing that had happened to him and he was determined to make their relationship last forever. It was true they had only known each other for a short time, but he was certain that she was the woman for him. He had already bought a ring, but was nervous about presenting it to her. Perhaps he should wait a little longer, take time to engineer a special occasion. His sister suggested that he take Mia away somewhere romantic, if he lavished enough attention on her then she could hardly refuse. He realised that she was right, Emilia knew about such things.

"Belenos came into the shop earlier," he said once they had sat down to eat. "He wanted to know if Em had seen or heard from Jenna O'Brien. It seems that she has disappeared."

"Disappeared?" Mia frowned, her spoon half way to her mouth.

"Apparently she is not answering her phone, he even went round to her house, but she's not there."

"Somebody must know where she is."

"Well that's the thing, Belenos told us that her housekeeper seemed evasive and not very helpful at all. Em agrees with him, it does seem unlikely, Jenna is not the type of person to suddenly disappear."

Mia hardly knew Jenna, but she was great friends with Belenos. If he was concerned then there must be something going on. She decided to call him later, see if he was okay.

"How are your rehearsals going?" he asked, eager to get the latest news.

"Very well," she nodded enthusiastically. She had already told him about Margaret. "I'm now fully aware of what to expect from Viktor."

She told him about his unusual playing style and the changes he had made to the musical arrangements.

"I thought you were the main attraction at this concert," he said eyeing her with concern. "It seems to me that Viktor Vasiliev is having it all his own way."

"He is an internationally renowned pianist," she reminded him. "He's bound to have some eccentricities, besides I'm sure Alicia only said that to get me to agree to the performance." She popped a piece of bread into her mouth and when she had finished chewing, she went on. "I'm under no illusions; Viktor Vasiliev will be the star of the show."

Ashton was at his desk studying a file that Mallinson had given him. It contained details of the latest victim along with photographs taken at the murder scene and sliding a sheet of typed notes from the file, he began to read.

Evelyn Constance Pearson was thirty four years old, a musician working for a private music school in Kensington. She had been employed there for just over two years and her clients were the children of wealthy parents, the type who could afford the exorbitant fees charged by the school. Evelyn was a multi-instrumentalist who taught Jazz, modern and contemporary music. Reading the notes carefully, he was looking for anything that might link her to his daughter, but so far, the only obvious similarity was her profession and like Margaret Marshall, she was a music teacher.

The photographs told a grim story and he was satisfied that this was the work of Phillipa Weston. They had deliberately not released specific details of the previous murders, by keeping the killer's modus operandi from the press it was unlikely that this could be the work of a copycat murderer.

There was a recent photograph of the victim, which he studied closely. Evelyn was an attractive young woman whose colouring was similar to Mia. Her hairstyle was almost identical and her clothing suggested that they shared similar tastes in fashion. This could be a possible link. The murderer could have selected Evelyn because she resembled Mia. Perhaps they were wrong and Margaret was not the next victim, maybe this was another trial run and Mia would be next. Thoughts rushed into his mind and his head began to throb, so pushing them aside he concentrated on the SOCO report.

Evelyn's parents had been informed and would have to make a formal identification. Ashton could find no details of a boyfriend or partner, it seemed that she lived alone. He made a note on a clean sheet of paper before reading on.

Mallinson and Keable were at the victims address searching through her personal effects. This was a formality that had to be undertaken even though they were certain of the killer's identity. Ashton paused and stared at the wall, seeing the faces of other young woman whose lives had been cut tragically short. He sighed and held his head in his hands. He had to do something, work out how to prevent the killer from reaching his daughter.

DS Woods appeared at his door and knocking gently she pushed it open.

"Terry," she whispered. "I think I might have found something."

Chapter
FIFTY EIGHT

There was still no news of Jenna. Nobody had seen or heard from her for several days now and despite his best efforts, Belenos had drawn a blank. He had continued to send messages and had contacted everyone that he could think of who knew her, he could no longer stand the silence. He was on the verge of contacting the police but first he decided to pay a visit to her parent's home in Windsor.

The property was easy enough to find, he simply followed the river until he came to a rambling Tudor mansion set low in the landscape. An ancient brick wall surrounded the estate and he was astonished to find the heavy wrought iron gates open allowing him access from the narrow country road. Swinging his car onto the long gravel drive, he steered slowly between ornamental trees and formal gardens. Eventually the property came into view and entering the carriage sweep, he stopped his car in front of the house. He was amazed as he stared up at the building. Jenna had once told him that her childhood home was an ancient Royal hunting lodge, but he never expected anything like this. The opulence of his surroundings was stunning and he could easily imagine this to be the meeting place of kings.

The house appeared to contain many of its original features and there was nothing to suggest that it had undergone alterations in recent years. Pushing open the car door, he stepped out onto the immaculately swept gravel before reaching back in for his coat. Shrugging it on, he turned the collar up against the breeze and continued to study the house. The walls were elegantly decorated with patterned brickwork typical of the Tudor period. Huge oak beams, blackened by time formed the framework of the building and there were more leaded windows and gabled dormers than he could count. He wondered how many rooms were contained within these walls.

Stepping up to the richly decorated front door, he passed beneath a magnificent Tudor arch. He had never seen an entrance like this before and suddenly he felt intimidated. Clearly, he did not belong here he was out of place, an intruder surrounded by gems that he could never afford to own. Jenna was definitely out of his league, he thought miserably.

He rang the bell then took a step back. From beyond the door, he could hear the muffled sound of a chime, a fanfare to herald his arrival, but nothing happened. An arrogant silence settled around him, but the door remained firmly closed. Reaching for the bell once more, he stopped himself. There was little point in ringing again he might as well try around the back.

A stone archway drew him along the front of the house where formal gardens dropped away to his left. Box hedging clipped to perfection lined the flagstone pathway where borders of winter colour pleased the eye and parkland spilled into the valley ahead. He expected to see deer or sheep grazing amongst the trees, but the place was deserted.

Reaching the corner of the house, he turned and was astonished to discover that it was almost as deep as it was long. Buildings some distance away told a story of their own. An orangery appeared like an overgrown greenhouse, it was in use that much was clear, even from this distance he could see benches loaded with trays of young plants waiting to be transferred to the borders. There was also a stable block and coach house. These buildings were in good condition but there was no evidence of horses so Belenos guessed they were used for general storage or garages.

Half way along the side of the house, he found a door so rapping loudly on the panel he pushed his face up against the glass and peered in. Nothing moved, the house seemed as deserted as the gardens so turning away, he continued along the path. The atmosphere of calm that he associated with grand country residences was present here, even the quality of the air seemed better than in the city. This was truly an impressive estate and he found it hard to believe that it was Jenna's family home. She had described her father as a ruthless businessman and Belenos wondered just how many others had been destroyed so he could own a place as grand as this.

Jenna seemed dissatisfied with her lot, it was true that she doted on the trappings of wealth and did not seem to appreciate what she had, but he supposed this was natural. Hers had been a privileged upbringing so she would know nothing of working class living.

Retracing his steps along the pathway, he had not gone far before he heard a noise. Turning his head, he searched for its source but could see nothing, then holding his breath he listened but all he could hear were the doves in the eaves and the breeze in the treetops, so he continued on his way.

This time there was no mistaking the muffled scream that stopped him in his tracks. Swinging round he scanned the wall of the house until he spotted a window low to the ground then he began to move towards it. This must be part of an old cellar or storeroom complex. The noise seemed to be coming from there so dropping to his knees, he reached between the bars that protected the window and wiped grime from the glass with his hand. He could make out movement, someone was inside so cleaning the glass more thoroughly he pushed his face up against the bars and peered in.

"What the hell!" he exclaimed as he recognised Jenna.

She was screaming wildly now, waving her arms in an effort to attract his attention. She was not yet aware that he had spotted her and was inconsolable but with a series of frantic hand gestures, he was able to make her understand. He could almost feel her relief and once she had calmed down, she peered up at him helplessly. Belenos could hardly believe that she was a prisoner and testing the bars against the window, he gauged their strength. Clearly, they had been there a long time and formed an integral part of the window. One end was fixed firmly into the brickwork with the other disappearing into the flagstone pathway at his feet. Heaving his weight against them one at a time he soon realised that they would not budge so with the use of more hand signals, he reassured Jenna before dashing back along the pathway. He checked the door on the way but it was locked. The main door at the front of the house was also impenetrable, so stepping back he looked up at the windows, they were all closed. He considered breaking one and thought about the consequences of gaining access to the house. He would first have to locate the cellar then find a key or try to force the door to her cell, it was sure to be locked. He could not imagine doing that so turning towards his car he wrenched open the door and threw himself in. Starting the engine, he swept around in an arc shooting gravel up from beneath the tyres. There was a gap in the hedge allowing him access to the lawn, lining his car up with the bank, he felt the wheels spin as they searched for grip. The car lurched sideways so easing back on the accelerator he steered away from a hedge, but the rear of the car clipped it, ripping a section from the ground. Straightening up, he narrowly missed an ornamental tree before ploughing across a flowerbed full of young plants. Bringing the car to a stop, he flung himself from the seat and went to the window. Kneeling down he gesticulated wildly and when he was satisfied that Jenna understood he went back to his car. Securing the seatbelt and selecting reverse the wheels spun as he shot backwards. Lining the bonnet up with the window, he stood on the brake pedal then pushing the gearstick forward, the engine howled as the car picked up speed. Belenos braced himself for the impact. The shock and the noise was far greater than he expected and dazed, he shook his head before reaching for the gearstick. Selecting reverse again, he worked the accelerator with his foot but nothing happened, the car remained impaled in the brickwork. Seconds later, he realised that the engine had stalled so turning the ignition key he was relieved when it burst into life. Easing backwards, the damage to the wall became apparent. One of the window bars had been wrenched from the wall and the other was bent at an impossible angle. Nothing was left of the glass or the brickwork surrounding the wooden frame and dust was rising from the gaping hole like smoke from a fire. Leaping from his car, Belenos raced to the scene of devastation.

"Jenna, are you okay?"

Slowly she emerged from beneath a narrow bed where she had taken cover. She was a mess and her face ghostly pale. Dust and chippings plastered her hair and covered the clothes that she had been forced to wear for several days.

The cellar was well below the level of the pavement and Belenos could not reach her.

"Use a chair to stand on."

Doing as she was told, Jenna reached up towards him and taking hold of her wrists Belenos pulled her up through the gap.

"What the hell is going on here?" he asked, holding her upright.

Her eyes wide with shock Jenna stared at the devastation, her gaze veering from the hole in the wall to his damaged car and tears rolled over her cheeks then she collapsed against him.

"Come on," he said wrapping his arms around her. "Let's get you out of here."

Chapter
FIFTY NINE

"James William Peterson," she said bringing the name to life.

An online chat forum had led her to a social media site where she had discovered the name.

"Unfortunately I've not been able to uncover anything more." Woods looked up at him from her chair.

"You've done well to get this," Ashton told her indicating with his chin towards the computer screen.

"The forum was set up as a discussion point for transgender people," she explained. "I've been exploring the site hoping to find out more about Phillipa Weston."

Woods had taken part in several conversations in the hope of gaining the users confidence and had cleverly avoided asking questions that would make her sound like a police officer. James Peterson was one of the people in on the conversations. It had taken a while before she realised that there was something different about this character. He had used a number of key words that had alerted her to him and it was at times like this that she realised just how important her studies into psychology and human behaviour really was.

James Peterson did not admit that he was transgender, but by simply being there in the forum was a good indication that he probably was. She was certain that he was Phillipa Weston, too many coincidences had emerged during their conversation, but what she needed now was solid evidence.

"There is nothing about Peterson in the official records," she told Ashton.

"I don't suppose there is," he replied. He thought for a moment before going on. "If Weston is using an alias, then perhaps she has used this name to rent a property or secure a job. I suppose it depends on how convincing she is at presenting as a man."

Woods nodded in agreement and realised that effectively they were looking for two suspects. No wonder Mallinson was convinced that Phillipa Weston was operating with a male accomplice.

"I'll check the electoral role and associated agencies, see what other surprises I can find."

Ashton nodded and putting his hand on her shoulder said.

"Good work Izzy."

At least now, they had a name to go with the computerised photo fit profile that he and Nixon had put together. Ashton was pleased about that, they had taken another step closer in apprehending the murderer. He decided to run the name past Nixon, see if it stirred any emotions. Taking his time, he studied the computerised image of James William Peterson and wondered if it was a good likeness. Mallinson would have to be informed, but Ashton was not convinced that it would make any difference. At least now he would be forced to accept the transgender element of the case, the evidence was beginning to stack up.

During her continued investigation, Woods decided to look further back and delving into historical records discovered a link between Weston and the serial killer William Randolph, known as Mr Mac. It turned out that Phillipa Weston was the illegitimate daughter of Mr Mac's father also named William Randolph. Woods remembered the case vividly because Josie MacDonald was a local person. She and a number of her friends had become victims of the serial killer, but miraculously Josie and her friend Sarah had survived their ordeal.

Sitting back in her chair, she toyed with the end of her pen before scribbling in her notebook. She wondered what the psychologists would make of Phillipa Weston being the half sister of a serial killer. Would they suggest that her lust for murder was the result of a rogue gene? There was no evidence in the archives to suggest that others from the Randolph bloodline were linked to historic murder cases.

Woods was also interested in what drove Weston to become a man. Could it be that she was obsessed with her half brother and would stop at nothing to become more like him or was it simply that she had been born into the wrong body? Pushing her thoughts away, she printed off the relevant information before highlighting the items of interest with a coloured pen. Ashton and Mallinson would need to see this even if they did not share her confidence in the psychological aspect of their job.

Jenna was sitting at the kitchen table in his flat wearing a dressing gown that Belenos had given her. She had bathed and washed her hair and now her clothes were spinning in the washing machine.

"We can call by your place in the morning and pick up a few things," Belenos suggested.

"No," Jenna shook her head. "I simply can't return home. I'm sure that my housekeeper is in league with my father."

Belenos had already told her that he had met the woman when calling at her house previously.

"Poor you," Jenna cringed. "Was she really so beastly?"

She was heartened by the fact that he had tried so hard to find her and if it wasn't for him she would still be locked up in the cellar or worse.

"I can't see why you chose to employ such a disagreeable woman."

"I had no choice," Jenna explained. "She came with the house. My father organised it all."

Belenos raised his eyebrows amazed at the extent of her reliance on her father.

"We should go into town and buy you some clothes. I'm afraid that I don't possess an extensive collection of women's clothing that you could borrow."

"I'm glad to hear it." Jenna laughed. "I doubt very much that your style would suit me anyway." Becoming serious, she said. "I need to go to the bank and arrange for new cards. I have no way of accessing my accounts because my bag containing my purse, phone and passport was taken from me when I was thrown into that wretched dungeon."

"Money is no problem," Belenos told her. "I can let you have some until you are sorted."

Jenna smiled again and Belenos couldn't help thinking that he might have made an error. He was certain that her shopping habits would be way beyond his own spending power. Jenna would not be content to patronise budget boutiques, he just hoped that it would not take long to sort out her finances.

"I've made a bed up for you in the spare room and have left a tee shirt for you to sleep in. It's the best I can do I'm afraid."

"Thank you," she replied. "I'm so grateful to you for everything. I hate to think about what might have happened if you had not come along."

"We'll discuss it further in the morning, work out what we should do next."

Jenna was exhausted. The strain of the past few days and the treatment that she had received left her drained and demoralised and he couldn't help thinking how vulnerable she looked. He had never expected to see her like this, her hair wrapped up in a towel and her face devoid of make-up. He didn't even possess a hair dryer that she could use.

The following morning he rose early. There was hardly any food in the house so he would have to visit the corner shop before Jenna got up. Closing the front door quietly behind him, Belenos hurried to the end of the road then glancing over his shoulder he spotted a car that he did not recognise. It was parked close to his flat and the driver was watching him carefully. The hairs on the back of his neck bristled as he recognised the man.

Pretending not to have noticed, Belenos walked calmly across the road and turning the corner, he stopped. Questions filled his head. How did this man know where he lived? Did he know that Jenna was there and no longer a prisoner in her father's house?

Abandoning all thoughts of visiting the corner shop, he hurried unseen back to his flat and letting himself in by the rear door went straight to the spare room. Gently knocking on the door, he called out her name.

Jenna stirred and pulling the duvet up to her chin as she sat up in bed.

"Come in," she said expecting a tray of tea and toast.

Belenos stood in the doorway looking anxious.

"The guy who was following you the other day is outside," he told her.

She gasped and clutched the duvet tighter around her naked body. The tee shirt was still on the chair.

"Don't worry," he said as panic gripped her.

He wanted to go to her, wrap her up in his arms and keep her safe, but he resisted the urge.

"I'll get your clothes from the airing cupboard. Get dressed quickly then we'll slip out the back door."

Going to the front window, he kept his head down so as not to alert the man in the car. He was talking on his mobile phone and Belenos wondered how long it would be before he made his move. If he thought that Jenna was there alone he may attempt to gain access to the building. It could be that he was waiting for others to arrive before making an assault. Belenos had an overwhelming urge to flee, his fight or flight instincts telling him to run.

Jenna appeared beside him, she was dressed and attempting to tidy her hair with a comb that she had found in her room. She smelled of toothpaste, there was no spare toothbrush in the bathroom so he guessed that she must have improvised and used her finger.

"Here," he said thrusting a coat at her.

It was a military style trench coat and it swamped her. Doing her best to make it more comfortable she pulled the belt tight around her waist.

They left the house and moving swiftly, Belenos dragged her along the alleyway that ran along the back of the buildings but she stumbled on a sack of abandoned rubbish. He managed to catch her before she fell.

"Sorry," she mumbled, "I'm not used to this."

"Let's go a bit slower, I'm sure your man doesn't suspect anything yet."

At the end of the alley, they turned left avoiding the front of the house and two streets further on, Belenos suddenly pulled her down beside a parked car. She squealed as her heart filled with terror.

"There's a car coming our way," he explained. "It doesn't look like the kind of vehicle my neighbours could afford."

A large SUV with blacked out windows cruised past. Belenos was unable to see the driver but he realised that the occupants were not planning a social visit. This must be the backup team. Obviously, Jenna's escape had been discovered and they knew exactly where to find her. The situation was far worse than he could have imagined.

Chapter
SIXTY

Ben had not only stayed for the afternoon, he was still there the following morning. Their lovemaking had been frantic at first but once they reached the bedroom, they settled down and satisfied each other with care and consideration. He said nothing about her wounds but now as she scrutinised herself in front of the bathroom mirror she could see why. The ugly scars had all but disappeared, a single ghostly white line was all that remained. A little more moisturiser and few sessions on the tanning machine would take care of that.

Wrapping herself in her robe, she patted her hair gently with a towel before reaching for her hair dryer. Ben was still in bed and she didn't expect to see him until he smelt the aroma of freshly brewed coffee. She had a busy day ahead and wanted to be dressed before he got up.

She dried her hair in the living room so as not to disturb him but to her surprise, by the time she had finished Ben was up and in the shower. Taking the opportunity of an empty bedroom, she went in to find her clothes and get dressed.

"Good morning," he said when he joined her in the kitchen.

Standing behind her, he wrapped his arms around her waist and nuzzled the back of her neck.

"You smell wonderful," he said as she leaned back against him.

After a moment, she turned to face him and planted a kiss on his cheek.

"I've been thinking," he began. "We should plan a little break, an extended weekend away perhaps."

"I have been having the same thoughts," she said, her eyes gleaming as she looked up at him. "I was daydreaming just the other day."

"You like the idea then?"

"Yes please, but you do realise I couldn't possibly get away until after the concert."

"I'm aware of that," he reassured her before going on. "How about Venice, I understand its lovely at this time of the year."

"Venice?" she said, surprised at his choice.

"Yes," he nodded, "why not?"

"It's just that I was expecting somewhere a little less exotic, Hampshire or Dorset perhaps or a little country cottage in the Home Counties."

"You need to get out more," he laughed, "broaden your horizons."

Mia laughed too and leaning forward she hugged him.

"Seriously," he continued. "We could travel to Venice on the Orient Express."

Stepping away, she leaned back against the counter and scrutinised his face. He appeared to be serious.

"How long would it take?" She asked, warming to the idea.

"A short round trip will take five days," he replied. "We can leave from Victoria, travel through the Swiss Alps, spend a couple of days in Venice before returning home on a scheduled train." Before she could respond, he added. "We could always stay longer in Venice."

"No, five days sounds perfect and on the Orient Express." She danced with excitement.

Emilia was right, Ben thought. This would be an ideal opportunity for him to present Mia with his ring.

"We could go in five or six week's time. It will be half way through April by then so the weather should be a little milder."

"Will your sister be able to do without you?" she asked. "You will probably be busy with Easter weddings."

"I'm sure it will be fine, besides, it will only be for a few days."

She hugged him again and whispered in his ear. "I'm looking forward to it already."

Later that morning Mia met Alicia at her office in the city and this time their meeting was less formal than before.

"So," Alicia said once Mia had settled on the garishly upholstered chair. "How are you getting on with Margaret Marshall?"

"Very well," Mia replied enthusiastically. "Margaret is lovely and a fantastic teacher. She really seems to know Viktor Vasiliev well."

"She should do," Alicia responded. "They spent several months travelling and performing together in Europe some years ago."

"Did they really?" Mia was surprised to hear that. "She never mentioned that to me, no wonder she knows all about him."

They discussed Viktor and Margaret for a while longer before Alicia steered their conversation onto business matters.

"We need to discuss your fee in reference to your upcoming concert. As it's the Royal Albert Hall and you are performing with an internationally renowned pianist your reward will be much greater," she paused and slipped a report across her desk. "This is a projection of what you might expect."

Mia studied the account, it was a simple arrangement of columns detailing income and expenditure and there were some very large numbers appearing.

"Of course you don't need to concern yourself with the details, my accounts people will take care of that. The figure that you need to be aware of is at the bottom of the second column."

"Wow," she murmured, it was much larger than she had expected.

"As you can see we have done our best for you."

It was true, her fee for performing with Viktor Vasiliev was substantial, much more than she had ever earned from a single concert.

"How do you feel about performing abroad?" Alicia asked, eyeing her keenly.

"Abroad?" Mia looked up at her agent.

"Paris, Rome, Venice."

Mia blinked, it was the second time that Venice had come up in conversation that morning.

"If this concert is as big a success as we are expecting then there may be an opportunity to work with Viktor in Europe."

Mia was stunned and took a few moments to take it all in.

"No pressure then," she laughed nervously.

"You don't have to agree now, the idea is purely in the early stages."

"Obviously we can't go back to my place," Belenos said, "and yours is out of the question, so it seems to me that we only have a couple of options left to us."

Jenna looked much more like her old self. She had discarded her trench coat in favour of a stylish, bright yellow high-collar wrap and she had spent some time in the make-up department of a large high street store. She was now ready to face her bank manager.

"We could go to the police," he said voicing their first option.

"I hardly think that would do any good," Jenna told him. "We would have to prove that I was imprisoned against my will. Without evidence a crime cannot have been committed."

"Okay, so not one of my better ideas." He knew that it wouldn't work but he wanted her opinion. "We could remain in London, move around a bit, never stay in the same place for long, live like fugitives."

"For how long do you think we'd get away with that? It might work in the short term, but as I told you before, my father has unlimited resources so it won't take him long to track us down."

"Well, we can't ask friends for help, it wouldn't do to implicate anyone."

Jenna agreed and waited for his next idea.

"The only option that we have left is to disappear completely," he shot her a look before continuing. "If staying in London is too risky then we need to get as far away from here as possible."

"Where do you have in mind? I can't go abroad as they have my passport."

"We don't need to go abroad," he explained. "My mother lives in the Black Mountains in Wales. Her smallholding is in a remote area near the Marches, that's the border between England and Wales."

Jenna thought about what he had said before asking.

"Won't your mother mind if we just turn up unannounced?"

"I will of course telephone ahead. She may live in a remote area, but some technological advances have managed to reach that far, but I warn you now, it's basic." He eyed her new coat. "You should have kept that old trench coat I lent you."

"Oh, I gave that to some poor soul sleeping rough in a doorway."

Belenos laughed before saying.

"We should at least buy you some wellington boots."

"I'm used to living in the country," she huffed. "You seem to forget that I was brought up on a Royal hunting estate."

He almost laughed again but managed to stop himself. There was hardly much in common between a country estate in Windsor and a Welsh mountainside.

"My mother will be pleased to see us, but I think that you should know, she will have us married within a week. My turning up with a woman in tow without so much as a ring on her finger would be scandalous."

It was Jenna's turn to laugh.

"Do you honestly think that she would consider me suitable daughter-in-law material?"

Belenos simply looked at her and raised his eyebrows.

"Well, in that case I can't wait to meet her."

By the time Jenna returned from her meeting at the bank, Belenos had bought them a suitcase and some essentials for himself. He had also reserved their train tickets.

"Well at least he hasn't frozen my bank accounts," she told him with a sigh of relief.

"Your father wouldn't do that," Belenos said. "He can trace you by checking your cash point withdrawals and card purchases."

"That's why I withdrew this." Reaching into her new shoulder bag, she produced a brown envelope. Inside was five thousand pounds in cash.

"Five grand!" Belenos exclaimed. "What did the bank manager think of that?"

"Nothing I imagine, he is used to my spending habits."

"But withdrawing such a large sum of cash, surely there were questions asked."

"Large sum?" she replied making a face. "It's merely our expenses."

"Well, it should keep us going for a while."

"I also transferred five hundred to your account." That was to cover what she had spent already.

"Right," she said eyeing the suitcase suspiciously. "Let's go shopping."

By the time they had finished, their luggage had expanded to two suitcases and a vanity case for her make-up. She told him that she had been very restrained; just over half their cash remained.

Chapter
SIXTY ONE

Mia left her flat early the following morning. The weather had improved slightly, the temperature rising, but the sky refused to relinquish its hold on the rain clouds. At the end of the road, she stood at the curb and waited for a break in the traffic. It was always busy here especially early in the day, the residents had campaigned for a pedestrian crossing of some kind, but the local authority resisted.

Suddenly a runner joined her and standing shoulder to shoulder, they greeted each other. From the corner of her eye, Mia studied the woman. She was dressed in a pink sweatshirt with grey leggings and on her head, she wore a baseball cap with the peak pulled low over her eyes. There was something familiar about her but before Mia could talk to her she was gone. She watched as the runner weaved her way amongst the cars her ponytail swinging pendulum-like between her shoulder blades.

London Victoria was as busy as usual but Mia knew exactly where to go. She had timed her arrival to perfection and the Epsom train was waiting for her at the platform. Going through the gate, she made her way quickly towards the nearest carriage when suddenly she felt a hand on her shoulder. Swinging round, she came face to face with someone she knew.

"Jim," she said, "fancy meeting you here."

"Miss Ashton, where are you charging off too so early in the day?"

Jim Peters was dressed for work. It wasn't the long overcoat pulled down over his jeans that gave him away, it was the sturdy boots on his feet.

"I'm working in Epsom today," she told him.

"What a coincidence, I'm going that way too."

"Oh," Mia said and an unspoken agreement passed between them as they moved towards the train.

"What are you doing in Epsom?" she asked.

"I'm helping a friend with some electrical work." He replied and avoiding a group of students, he stepped aside as they piled out from one of the carriages.

"You do that kind of work too?" Mia asked as he rejoined her.

"Oh yes," he nodded. "I'm a qualified electrician I do it between jobs at the theatre."

Mia knew Jim as a sound engineer whom she had worked with on several occasions before, but it never crossed her mind that he possessed other skills.

"So you are not working at a theatre at the moment then?"

They climbed aboard the train and settled in the first available seats.

"No, your concert at the Barbican was the last theatre job I did."

"Oh," Mia said again. "It's lucky that you can turn your hand to other things."

"Yes," he nodded as he stared out of the window. "I'm helping to re-wire a house."

They chatted about work for a while longer then their conversation drifted naturally to other topics. Mia knew very little about Jim and this was an opportunity to discover more about him. She liked him, he was very good at his job, attentive to detail and he was always pleasant. She knew that there was something different about him, Ben was convinced that he was gay, but this made little difference to her. Jim had an easy way about him and always went out of his way to help others, but sometimes he could appear distant and moody.

The train pulled into Epsom station and Mia was amazed at how the time had flown by. Jim got to his feet and allowed her to step onto the platform ahead of him then he said.

"It was lovely to bump into you."

He accompanied her along the platform for a little way before stopping at a bench.

"I should wait here for my mate to arrive."

"You have a good day Jim." Mia said then she was gone.

He watched as Mia walked towards the exit where she was met by an older woman. They hugged each other affectionately and when they had disappeared from view, he got to his feet and left the station.

Mallinson had called a meeting and as Ashton waited for the team to arrive, he studied the evidence board in the murder room. Photographs of the victims had been arranged chronologically with notes about the ongoing investigation, it was a linear record of the progress that was being made. There were gaps between some of the events where someone had written vague prompts and memos that were relevant to the case. Today it was hoped that more information could be added to this board. A photograph of Evelyn Pearson was the latest addition and although Ashton had seen it before he was startled by the physical similarities between this young woman and his daughter.

Once everyone was assembled, Mallinson began with an opening address and bringing them up to speed he went through the progress that had been made.

"We need to understand what links Evelyn Pearson to the other victims. We know that she did not work with the cellist Mia Ashton, so what made her a target?" he paused and glanced around the room.

"Evelyn was once a pupil of Margaret Marshall," Ashton was the first to respond. "Marshall is a retired music teacher who lives in Epsom. She is currently working with my daughter."

"So, tenuous though it may sound, this could be the link," Mallinson added.

"Evelyn Pearson resembled Mia Ashton," DS Woods told them and drawing their attention to the photographs on the board, she continued. "As you can see, the similarity is uncanny."

"They could be twin sisters," DC James pointed out needlessly as he moved closer for a better look.

Ignoring his comment Mallinson took up the commentary.

"Do we think that the killer is trying to tell us something?" he paused, taking a moment he chose the right words. "A young woman who resembled Mia Ashton has become the latest victim, a woman with only the vaguest connection to the other victims. We were convinced that Margaret Marshall would be the next target given the pattern that our suspect was following."

"It's true that given a logical pattern Margaret should have been the next target," Woods said getting to her feet. "We all agree that Mia is the ultimate prize, the killer seems to be closing in on her slowly, but now the rules have changed. The killing of Evelyn Pearson opens up a new field of possibilities; anyone vaguely connected to Mia could now be a potential target."

"It's still not clear just how far the killer will go," Keable added. "We know so little about our suspect."

Woods looked at him and frowned.

"DNA results taken from the blood sample collected from Victoria Stevens wheelchair suggests that we might be looking for a transgender man or at least a woman taking large doses of male hormones," she paused and was about to go on but Aston took the stand.

"We know that the suspect is a woman, we have photographic evidence linking her to the murder scenes. Let's just assume for a moment that we are searching for a woman who also presents as a man, it could in effect make our job easier. The transgender world is a relatively close knit community so perhaps we should concentrate our investigations in that quarter."

He glanced at Mallinson expecting him to contradict, but was allowed to continue so he told them about his own investigation and where it had taken him.

"The name of our suspect is Phillipa Weston, but she seems to have disappeared completely, we have however come up with another name that we think she may be using."

Stepping up to the board, he wrote the name James William Peterson in a space before fixing the photo fit image beneath it. DS Woods got to her feet again and began by giving them details of Phillipa Weston's history telling them that she was related to a serial killer from Scotland. She did not labour the point as many of the officers in the room were unfamiliar with the Josie MacDonald case but she thought it relevant information.

"So," Mallinson said when she had finished. "We now have names to focus on and we also have details of a vehicle that our suspect has been using." He stabbed his finger against the licence plate number on the board.

"We need to know where this red Ford Focus car is right now, where our suspect lives and or works and where she spends her spare time."

He began to delegate jobs to the members of his team before winding up the meeting.

"At least he didn't dismiss the transgender angle," Woods said as she and Ashton made their way along the corridor. "I believe that he may be coming round to our way of thinking."

"Thanks to you Izzy, I think you may be right."

Chapter
SIXTY TWO

His mother met them at the train station at Abergavenny as the grey sky darkened overhead. She was overjoyed to see her son and they hugged fiercely before Belenos introduced her to Jenna.

"I'm Bethan," his mother said and taking Jenna's hand, noticed how soft and elegant her fingers were.

Jenna was not keen to load their new luggage into the back of an old Land Rover, but Belenos didn't seem to mind.

"It's about a forty minute drive into the hills," he explained as she settled into the back seat.

Her surroundings were less than opulent and the interior smelt of something unpleasant, so burying her nose into the fresh lining of her coat she did her best to ignore it. Belenos joined his mother in the front leaving Jenna to listen to their conversation from the rear seat. Bethan asked him about London and they chatted nonstop about ordinary things. Belenos was careful however not to say anything about their current circumstances, he told her that they intended to stay for only for a few days. Bethan grunted but said nothing. She realised from the amount of luggage they had between them that their stay was likely to be extended.

It was completely dark when they pulled into the yard. The temperature had fallen to below freezing and as they climbed out of the Land Rover a raw breeze ruffled Jenna's hair. She shivered and glanced towards the house. It was a squat stone cottage, the slate roof white with frost, but warmth spilled from the windows and it looked inviting.

"Best you get yourself in beside the fire," Bethan said leading the way. "Belenos will bring your bags."

Once inside Jenna was amazed at how cosy it was. Traditional furniture filled the room and where an open fire had once been, a huge log burning stove glowed warmly.

"This was all there was once," Bethan explained as they shrugged off their coats. "The old crofters that lived here before cooked and slept in this room, they even brought their animals in when the weather became harsh outside."

Over the years, the house had undergone many changes and now boasted a basic country kitchen and three small bedrooms.

"It's not what you are used to in London," Bethan said glancing at Jenna, "but it's homely." She smiled then rubbing her hands together said. "How about a nice cup of tea."

"That would be lovely."

Belenos appeared at the door laden down with luggage so rushing towards him, Jenna took hold of her vanity case before he collapsed.

"Put your stuff in your rooms," his mother told them. "I've put you in here Jenna."

She opened the door onto a small room. A narrow single bed took up much of the space leaving just enough room for a single wardrobe and a chest of drawers. Jenna wondered where she was supposed to store her cases.

"My brother's old room," Belenos said, peering over her shoulder.

Jenna was shocked but could hardly complain. Her dressing room in Pimlico was larger than this, but at least it was clean and smelled of fresh mountain air.

Belenos left her to settle in and went to find his mother.

"She doesn't say much." Bethan remarked as she poured boiling water into the teapot.

"Give her time," Belenos smiled. "It's all a bit strange for her and we've had a long day." He didn't add that Jenna was recovering from a traumatic experience having been locked up in a cellar for days, before fleeing London for their lives. It would not do to worry her, but he was sure that his mother would get the truth before long.

"It really is lovely to see you." Wrapping him up in her arms, Bethan squeezed him tightly.

Belenos felt guilty, he had not seen his mother for several months.

"She is a very striking girl." She told him.

"Jenna is a good friend," he replied dispelling any thoughts of romance.

"We have known each other for a long time."

His mother looked at him and smiled. She knew there was more to it than that; she had seen the way her son looked at the girl.

"What does she do for a living?"

He could hardly tell her that Jenna was a socialite and wealthy enough not to work.

"She's between jobs at the moment," he said casually, "taking a career break, enjoying a few months off."

"I see," she studied him carefully and he could tell that she was not impressed. His mother hated the thought of idle hands.

"Jenna is quite well off," he felt the need to defend her. "She can quite easily afford time away from work."

"None of my business," Bethan said holding up her hands.

Suddenly the bedroom door opened and Jenna appeared. She had changed into jeans and a white jumper and looked fresh and bright. Belenos was relieved to see her, he was rapidly talking himself into an awkward situation.

"Make yourself comfortable my lovely, sit by the fire."

Carrying the tray of tea into the living room, she set it down on the little table before lowering herself down onto the sofa beside Jenna.

"Sugar?" she asked.

"No thank you, just a dash of milk please."

"So Jenna, what brings you to Wales?"

"I've never been before, well apart from Anglesey. I was on my way to Ireland once and stayed in Holyhead for a few days."

"Is that so, Anglesey was it? Land of the Druids."

"To be honest, I can't remember much about it. I was a young child then."

"It's a little different here I can assure you of that," Bethan told her, taking a sip of tea before going on. "You see, outsiders might think that living here is idyllic, but in reality it can be a little harsh."

"I imagine it can be," Jenna agreed, "but it's so peaceful here compared to London."

"That is why I love it so much."

Jenna asked questions about the area delighting Bethan with her enquiring mind.

"Culturally this is a lively area, known for its busy market towns, galleries, food scene and festivals."

Belenos almost choked on his tea.

"Not at this time of the year mother."

"No, you are right, but in the summer the place fills up with holiday makers and hill walkers. It's the sheep that outnumber the residents during the winter months."

Jenna could feel Bethan's passion for the mountains and it was clear that she was immensely proud of her heritage.

"There was much unrest hereabouts during the medieval period," she continued. "Norman Marcher Lords inhabited many of the castles along the border where they fought bloody battles against the Welsh princes. Luckily it was these very hills that helped keep the raiders out."

Belenos didn't like to remind her that it was a war that the Welsh did not win.

"I love history," Jenna confessed. "I read historical novels all of the time."

They chatted long into the night establishing bonds as they discovered more about each other. Belenos was right, it didn't take his mother long to discover that Jenna came from a very privileged background and from her impressed glances, he was left in no doubt that she approved of their friendship.

In London DS Woods was still at work. Although it had been a long day, she was still no further in discovering where James Peterson lived. There was very little to find, the name had not been entered onto the electoral role, or the local authorities register. There was nothing to show that Phillpa Weston had changed her name.

Ashton appeared in the murder room surprised to see her still at her desk.

"Izzy, what are you doing here at this hour?"

She looked up, startled to see him.

"I could ask the same of you."

"I have just spent the last hour with Robert Nixon from TG International." He approached her desk and pulling a chair from a neighbouring workstation, sat down wearily.

"I just stopped off here to pick up a file."

"Has Nixon heard of Peterson?"

"No, but he has heard of Phillipa Weston. He gave me a couple of leads, other centres in the area where she might be known. It seems that psychological counsellors have to be involved when a person decides to undergo the gender realignment process, so someone must have a record."

Woods nodded, but remained thoughtful as they studied each other.

"Have you eaten yet?" she asked, breaking the silence.

"No, not had time."

She checked the clock on her computer screen before saying.

"If we hurry we might just be in time to grab a bite to eat at the Richmond."

Ashton glanced at his watch.

"Do you know what Izzy, let's get out of here."

Chapter
SIXTY THREE

Mia was sitting at the kitchen table with Margaret enjoying a cup of tea and a chat. They had just completed another gruelling session of rehearsal and both were feeling the need to unwind.

"My agent told me the other day that you have travelled and performed with Viktor Vasiliev."

"Did she indeed?" Margaret replied dryly.

Mia thought that she might have spoken out of turn, but once Margaret had finished drinking her tea, she confessed.

"That was a very long time ago, well before I became a teacher. I was a struggling musician once you know and Viktor was not much better himself. He was quite unknown outside of Russia. That was before the time of free travel in Europe and Russians were seldom allowed to set foot out of their own country."

Sitting back in her chair, she glanced at Mia and smiled.

"He was such a dashing young man and a brilliant musician even then."

"Did you fall in love with him?"

"Oh yes, of course," Margaret's eyes flashed like jewels and the years fell away. "It was the same with every young woman that he met."

Reaching for the pot, she refilled their cups before continuing.

"That was almost forty years ago, a lifetime in fact."

"Wow," Mia's eyes widened, "as long ago as that?"

"It may seem a long time to you as it was before you were born, but to me it seems like only yesterday."

Memories clouded her vision and as she sipped at her tea, she smiled at images from the past.

"I have never forgotten that summer I shared with Viktor," she said after a while. "We performed duets together in some of the greatest cities in Europe. I thought it was never going to end."

"What happened?"

"My contract came to an end and it was time to move on. I might have been young and impetuous but I was no fool. I realised there could be no future for us. Viktor was not the type to settle down, besides, it would never have been allowed, his career had to come first. In Russia, he was a national icon and a rapidly rising star in Europe so there was no room for me. It would never have worked."

"Oh Margaret," Mia reached out, her voice soft and full of compassion. "Is that why you never married?"

"Partly I suppose," Margaret whispered, she sighed and pushing her regrets aside, she continued. "No one could measure up to Viktor, he was my first love you see. It was not for want of trying, there were men from time to time, but I had set the bar too high." She sniffed before placing her cup on the table. "What about you dear and your young man?"

Mia told her all about their plans to travel to Venice on the Orient Express.

"Have you known him for very long?" Margaret asked, noting how animated Mia became when talking about Ben.

"Just a few months, but he has transformed my life. He is a very special man."

"Do you love him?" Margaret hardly needed to ask, but she wanted Mia to hear herself admitting it.

"Oh yes I do, very much." She replied without hesitation.

"Then never let him go." Margaret said fiercely and reaching out she took hold of Mia's hand. "Don't make the same mistakes I did, the love of a good man is a rare thing. If you let him slip away you will regret it for the rest of your life."

They sat in companionable silence for a while before Margaret asked. "Who is Ethan?"

Mia was startled, it was as if she had been struck and she frowned.

"Ethan. Why do you ask?"

"It's a name that surrounds you. I have been meaning to ask for some time now."

Mia took a deep breath and her nostrils flared.

"You don't have to say anything if it upsets you."

"No, it's okay, you just caught me unawares that's all."

Margaret was concerned, Mia's problems obviously went far deeper than she thought, but she felt that whatever was troubling her, needed to come out.

"Ethan was my brother."

She told her how Ethan and their mother had died in a car crash when she was a child. Margaret was aware of the tragedy but knew nothing of the details, she could only imagine how deeply it had affected Mia.

"You do realise that Ethan is still with you."

Mia's frown grew deeper and she began to feel uneasy.

"I have always been aware of his presence, especially as a child, but as I've grown older he seems to have faded into the background." She did not mention the psychological problems that she had experienced as a child, or the guilt she felt at having survived.

"Forgive me for asking but how does he make you feel now?"

"How can he make me feel anything, surely it's all in my head. Ethan died a long time ago."

"You know that's not true. Some spirits seem prone to unrest and I feel sure this is true with Ethan. It's because of the way he died, not that he is evil or unable to cross over to the other side, it's just that he has unfinished business here."

"Ethan was a child when he died so how could he possibly have unfinished business?"

"People who are killed suddenly or accidently sometimes do not realise or understand what has taken place because it happened so fast and without warning."

"How do you know about all this stuff?" Mia asked, shifting in her seat.

"It's an interest of mine. I have read extensively about the subject over the years and find it fascinating. Occasionally I come across someone who may be in need of my help." She paused to study Mia's reaction. "Do you mind talking about it?"

"Yes I do, but strangely I don't feel so bad discussing it with you."

Margaret inclined her head, she did not feel entirely comfortable talking about it herself.

"You say that you were there beside him when he died."

"Yes, we were clinging onto each other."

"Clearly he was not ready to go so finds it very difficult to have peace. I can feel his frustration and I know that he sometimes takes it out on you. Am I right?"

Mia said nothing but simply nodded.

"He is very unhappy about sharing your body."

"I was told when I was young that I had a multiple personality disorder."

"Was that when you were a teenager?"

"Yes," Mia replied miserably.

"You must understand that the changes you were experiencing as you developed into a young woman would have frustrated him further. He was a typical little boy who should have grown into a man, but once he died he found himself trapped inside your body."

Mia blinked rapidly and her eyes filled with tears.

"Imagine the frustration and turmoil that he must be feeling."

Margaret passed her a tissue and Mia wiped away her tears.

"You must seek help for this because if you don't, the abuse that you have been experiencing will continue, it could even become a lot worse."

Everything fell into place as Mia thought about the times she had woken up naked in bed with her clothes strewn around the floor torn to shreds. The bruises and scratches she had suffered as a teenager continued even now and then there were times when she had found herself in a strange place with no memory of having got there.

"Your brother's spirit needs to find peace if he is to move on to a better place."

Belenos received a telephone call from the editor of the magazine he was writing for.

"I'm going to have to return to London," he told Jenna as they walked through the ruins of Abergavenny castle.

She had just learnt that Welsh noblemen had been slaughtered there in the great hall in medieval times when meeting with an English nobleman and the story had touched her deeply, now her joy at being with him was about to suffer a similar fate.

"I need to check my flat anyway, see what damage your father's thugs have caused. I should only be away for a couple of days."

"Okay," she replied sadly and linking her arm through his asked. "When do you intend on leaving?"

"Tomorrow will be soon enough. Once I have my laptop and notes I can work from here. Internet connection might be a problem up in the mountains though."

"We'll just have to come down here, find a cafe or library with Wi-Fi connection."

Once she had recovered from the shock of the size and lack of amenities at his mother's croft, Jenna relaxed and became more settled. She no longer worried about the constant threat of surveillance or being snatched by her father and imprisoned against her will. Here in Wales, she found peace and her wretched life in London seemed so insignificant.

In the short time they had been in Wales, Belenos' accent had broadened until he sounded more like his mother and Jenna found it appealing. She loved the way they talked, some of the phrases and words they used were quite different to her own. Unlike her own mother, Bethan was warm and understanding, she had welcomed her into her home and Jenna was grateful for that.

"We had best get ourselves some lunch then head back," Belenos said glancing up at the sky.

The morning had begun brilliantly with a cold clear sky, but more rain was forecast and the weather could change quite rapidly in the mountains.

Chapter
SIXTY FOUR

By mid afternoon the following day, Mia and Margaret had completed another rehearsal session. They did not mention Viktor Vasiliev or Mia's brother Ethan again. Enough had been said about both subjects and the bond between them had strengthened.

"Perhaps we should go on tour together." Mia laughed.

"Nice idea, but I fear that I'm too old for all that." She glanced at Mia and knew what she was thinking. Viktor was a similar age and he was more active than ever.

"Time I got you back to the station." Margaret said and heaving herself to her feet, went into the hallway to get their coats.

"You should come to London soon," Mia said. "We could take in a show or have a meal, both perhaps. You could stay overnight at my place."

"That would be nice. I could see your cello, it's been ages since I saw a Guadagnini. We'll have to make a date."

'Woody' accelerated at a stately pace along the main road leading into Epsom. There was hardly any traffic, which was unusual for this time of day, but Margaret was not complaining. Leaving the houses behind, they drove out into open countryside and soon entered a section of woodland. Up ahead on the side of the road they spotted a car with its hazard lights flashing. Standing beside the open bonnet was a young woman who appeared to be alone. Bringing 'Woody' to a standstill, Margaret got out.

"My car has broken down," the woman explained miserably, "and stupidly I forgot to charge my mobile phone."

"Oh dear," Margaret eyed her sympathetically. "Is there anything we can do to help?" She glanced at the engine but the collection of wires and hoses meant nothing to her.

Mia remained in the car, she was uneasy, something felt wrong. Reaching into her pocket her fingers folded around her mobile phone then she opened the door and got out. Glancing along the road, she could see no other vehicles, so edging round the stranded car she moved towards the front.

Margaret was lying on the ground, she was on her side and not moving. Mia gasped and called out her name before throwing herself down beside her.

"Margaret," she exclaimed and putting her hand on her shoulder squeezed gently, but it was no good she did not move.

Glancing over her shoulder, Mia could see nothing of the woman they had stopped to help, so concentrating on her mobile phone she began to dial the emergency services. Suddenly something smashed into the side of her head knocking sideways and losing grip of her mobile phone it sailed out of her hand.

It was easy to lift Mia into the car, since taking the male hormones Phillipa found that she had more strength and her level of aggression was heightened. The old woman was no bother either, she was taller than Mia, but seemed to weigh less. Dragging her towards her own car, Phillipa lifted her into the passenger seat before jumping in behind the wheel. Starting the engine, she reversed before running the Morris into the trees. Next, she pulled Margaret over into the driver's seat, any passing motorist would think that she had run off the road and hit her head against the windscreen. Returning to her car, she tied Mia's arms behind her back with tape then applied some across her mouth. She did not want any trouble when driving.

Belenos was on the train heading towards London. He was intending to return to Wales the following morning, but it rather depended on what he might find when he returned home. He would have to be cautious, the men trailing Jenna might still be there waiting for him to return.

There was something that he wanted to do first, he should have done it days ago when in Hackney. He was going to return to the house where Phillipa Weston lived and speak to the neighbour about the man in the flat above.

Changing trains along the way, it was just a short hop to Hackney Downs. He knew from experience that this station was closer to the

Amhurst road than Hackney Central. Making his way quickly towards the terraced houses, the road he wanted was full of cars, when he was there previously the street had seemed less crowded. Crossing the road, he watched as a red car pulled up, the driver finding a gap close to the house reversed into the space. A woman got out and went to the passenger door then reaching in she pulled another woman up from the seat. She seemed to be having difficulties holding onto her companion, so increasing his pace he was about to offer his help when he saw the tape covering the woman's mouth, he then realised that it was Mia. He was shocked, he should have gone forward, find out what was going on, but he didn't. Something warned him of the danger so ducking behind a car he watched. The woman supporting Mia snarled before getting the door of the house open, then shoving her inside it slammed behind them. Belenos hesitated, he was tempted to knock on the door and demand an explanation, but still he held back. Reaching for his mobile phone, he found Terry Ashton's number before hitting the dial button.

Mia drifted in and out of consciousness as she lay on her back. She had made numerous attempts to move, but her limbs were heavy and the constant throb from inside her head was making her feel nauseas. A breeze drifted across the room and her skin puckered against the chill, she groaned again. There was someone in the room with her she could sense it, but it was too much effort to open her eyes.

Phillipa Weston stood beside the bed looking down at Mia and was irritated by what she saw. Her flawless skin, well formed breasts, and flat stomach annoyed her and she hated Mia even more, but these soft feminine attributes would soon be turned to mush and her spirit prised from its shell. Her pulse quickened at the prospect and she spared a thought for those she had already destroyed. Slaying such gentle creatures helped to ease her pain, but nothing could make up for the suffering that she had endured already. Her whole life had been a long cruel episode of torment and disaster but she had taken steps to correct the defects assigned to her at birth. She realised however that she could never be whole, she would always remain a half person, neither male nor female, she would be left in limbo and this made her angry.

Mia groaned and tried again to roll away. All she wanted to do was to curl up somewhere safe and warm until all the misery and hatred that surrounded her had gone away. She could see her brother standing in the shadows, he was still a child, but there was something different about him. She tried to call out to him, she desperately needed his help,

317

but she didn't have the strength. He looked so sad, Margaret was right, she would have to do something to help him find his way.

Climbing onto the bed Weston straddled Mia and was delighted by the reaction, the frown between Mia's eyes deepened and she groaned. She was obviously aware so could feel pain. This time it would be different, she would use her knife while Mia was still alive. Her first cut was deliberate and controlled, the blade slicing through flesh caused maximum discomfort, but was not deep enough to be fatal. Lights flashed behind Mia's eyes as pain seared up into her brain. She wanted to scream but nothing louder than a pathetic mewl came out.

Weston raised her knife again and light flared from its razor edge. It felt good in her hand, and as she drew it across Mia's ribs, she felt empowered. She could end it all now, plunge the knife into her heart, snuff her out in an instant, but what good would that do? Mia Ashton would have to suffer just as she had suffered all of her life.

Ashton, Mallinson and some of their team formed up in the street outside. Belenos was there to identify the house and immediately the area was cordoned off. Soon after that, the Armed Response Team arrived.

"The ground floor flat is occupied by a woman," Belenos told them. "The flat above is where Mia has been taken."

Ashton wanted to move in right away, but there was a short delay whilst armed officers secured the back of the building. Suddenly a radio transmitter stuttered into life, the team were in position and standing by.

He was already wearing a stab proof jacket and was determined to be in on the action. Glancing at his watch, he sighed, Mia had been inside the house with the killer for just under half an hour and with every passing minute the chances of him seeing her alive again were fading away.

Suddenly the order was given, the ordinary front door leading to an innocuous looking house was splintered and armed men stormed in. Ashton, swept up in the advance, entered the building. A scream sounded from somewhere followed the all clear then they thundered up the stairs. The men in front wasted no time, doors were flung open and shouts confirmed their progress until one door remained. They paused and exchanged glances then the door was kicked open. The lead man dropped to his knees with the man behind standing over him in support.

"Armed Police, drop your weapon or I will fire." A clear order rang out.

Phillipa Weston was kneeling on the bed with Mia splayed out beneath her. The knife in her hand was covered in blood and as if in slow

318

motion, she turned her head towards Ashton and their eyes locked. The anger and rage etched across her face horrified him, her eyes glowed like coals and he shuddered.

Another warning sounded then suddenly her head snapped back as two rounds slammed into her chest. The force of the impact knocked her sideways and the wig that she was wearing fell to the floor.

Ashton moved quickly. Mia's face was deathly pale and her eyes were closed, her naked torso was a mass of wounds and he was surprised at the amount of blood. Calling out her name, his throat tightened and he began to tremble.

Mallinson was not far behind and entering the room, he took in the scene. Reaching out he felt the side of Mia's neck and his fingers tingled as he found a pulse.

"Get an ambulance," he yelled.

She was still alive but time was not on her side. One of the armed officers appeared with a large medical bag, part of his training included advanced first aid and putting his weapon aside, it was now his job to help save her life.

DS Woods entered the room, her face as pale as Mia's, her expression pinched with stress. She knew that it would not be long before the room filled up, but she was there for Ashton. He should never have to see his daughter like this and reaching out she put her arm around his shoulders and gently prised him away.

"Come on Terry," she whispered, "let the man do his job."

Ashton was numb, emotions bottled up for years began to surface. Mia was all that remained of his once perfect family he simply couldn't lose her too. She was his life, the reason he got out of bed each morning and glancing up at Woods, he saw tears streaming over her face. From somewhere in the distance came the urgent sound of an ambulance.

EPILOGUE

The noise inside the Royal Albert Hall rose to a crescendo as the audience got to their feet. Viktor Vasiliev stood beside his grand piano his expression easy, he was satisfied with their performance. Taking a step forward he bowed stiffly before turning to Mia then taking her hand, he helped her up from her chair and the roar grew even louder. This time there were cheers and whistles. Tears of relief dampened her face, it had been a particularly harrowing few weeks, but she was determined to honour her contract and make the performance of her life.

Her father was there in the front row and beside him beaming with joy was Isobel Woods. Emilia and Ben were there too, both as emotional as Mia. They had been there throughout, supporting her through the darkest time of her life and now they looked on proudly.

Brushing away her tears Mia bowed carefully in salute to her family and friends then turning she looked up at a box overlooking the stage. She raised her hand and blew a kiss, and the audience cheered again as Mia acknowledged the help and support that she had received from Margaret, her mentor and friend.

DS Woods had continued doggedly with her investigation discovering the transgender clinic that Phillipa Weston had attended during the early stages of her transition. She had taken possession of Weston's notes including a psychological assessment; it made for interesting reading. Months earlier concerns had been raised regarding the state of Weston's mind and it was considered unwise to support her bid for hormone therapy. It was then that Weston turned her back on professional help and sought direction from the internet. Unprescribed and unregulated doses of male hormones proved to be a catastrophic cocktail, the changes in her personality leading to the deaths of many innocent young women. Even with these professional conclusions, Woods couldn't help thinking that Phillipa Weston must have shared a murderous gene with her half brother William Randolph.

Ashton had not been back to work since that fateful afternoon in Hackney. He was taking a well earned rest, but was seriously considering early retirement from the Force. If Mia was going to be spending prolonged periods abroad then he was thinking about accompanying her. They had discussed this at length and Mia was overjoyed at the prospect of travelling with her father. She was also looking forward to spending more time with Ben, they were about to join the Orient Express as it made its way to Venice.

It was Belenos who experienced the greatest changes. The Metropolitan Police Service had put a stop to the intimidation caused by the thugs that Jenna's father had employed and now the Fraud Squad were looking into a number of his business deals.

His articles for the magazine were a great success and now there was a book offer. A literary agent was keen to see a draft based on serial killers but what they were interested in most was an in depth study into the life of William Randolph; AKA Mr Mac.

When eventually he returned to Wales Jenna had changed beyond recognition. Gone were her designer clothes, make-up and beautifully painted nails. She met him at the station in Abergavenny behind the wheel of his mother's Land Rover. She was dressed in dungarees, wellington boots and an old duffel coat and she looked fantastic.

"Wow," he said wide eyed with shock. "What happened to Jenna O'Brien, she was supposed to be meeting me."

Jenna smiled and slapped his arm playfully, then throwing her arms around his neck she held onto him tightly.

"I'm here you fool and I'm never going away. From now on things are going to be quite different."

Jenna had fallen in love with Wales and she adored living in the mountains. The croft was proving to be too much for Bethan so the women had come up with a plan. The simple life was indeed much harder than she had thought, but it was honest work and it helped to fill the huge void in her life so Jenna decided to turn her back on her alcohol fuelled existence in London, there were more things to life than material wealth. She was determined to make a go of it in Wales and longed for Belenos to be there at her side.

He wondered if she was being sincere or was this just another ill-conceived idea. He hoped that it would work because he was about to make a serious commitment to Jenna.

Their trip through the Alps had been stunning; the Orient Express was all they imagined and much more besides. This was their last night aboard the train before it reached its destination in Venice.

Easing himself back in the richly upholstered chair Ben toyed with the stem of his glass. Their meal had been superb and now the hypnotic motion of the train was making him feel sleepy. Mia was in a chair beside him and as he glanced at her, she took his breath away, she looked simply marvellous. Gone were the shadows that haunted her face and her physical scars were on the mend. Aware that he was staring at her, she looked up at him and smiled.

"I have something for you," he said and putting down his glass, he slipped his hand into his pocket.

Rising slowly from his chair he knelt at her feet and opening his hand, declared his love for her with the ultimate promise.

Mia was overjoyed and her face beamed with love.

"I would be honoured," she whispered and slipping his ring onto her heart finger, she leaned forward and kissed him passionately.

Author's note

The Cellist began life as a modern day/historical novel. I completed a few chapters several years ago before setting it aside to write The Gordian Knot, the second book in The Torc Trilogy. It was always my intention to return to this novel and complete it so, with that in mind, I wrote notes on how the plot was to develop and made up comprehensive character profiles.

When I eventually picked up the file and began to familiarise myself with the story I discovered that other ideas were beginning to develop. It is true that certain characters appear as real people in the mind of their creator and often drive the plot, sometimes with alarming consequences. I have had characters in previous books end up in some strange and rather unexpected situations leaving me to come up with a solution to get them out of it. Anyway, out went the historical element along with some of the principal characters from that part of the story. Most of the modern day characters remained. Mia underwent a surname change don't ask me why, it was probably something to with the plot lurching in a completely different direction. Who am I to question the Principal character?

The Cellist was always going to be linked with The Witness, I see it as book two in a series of stories that share characters and places. Although not a sequel, The Cellist does seem to answer some of the questions left open at the end of The Witness. It would be an advantage to have read The Witness before tackling this book as you will have a greater understanding of where previous characters and events fit.

Many interesting subjects have been explored in The Cellist and I had fun researching certain aspects of the plot before weaving a story around my findings. It was never my intention to alienate specific groups of society so hopefully I have dealt with issues sympathetically.

I am planning to write further thrillers that link these books together so some of my characters will appear again.

October 2017

Acknowledgements

I would like to thank Mark Webb at Paragon Publishing for all his help and guidance in getting this novel into print. Also with the initial proof reading, Annick Martin and Maria who did a fantastic job ironing out the wrinkles, any remaining are purely down to me.

Finally a big thank you to Maria who continues to be a 'writing widow', as most of my time is spent working on the next book in my study.

Other books by Kevin Marsh

The Torc Trilogy:

The Belgae Torc

The Gordian Knot

Cutting the Gordian Knot

Psychological Thriller:

The Witness

Website:

www.kevinmarshnovels.co.uk

Blog:

mynovelsandotherthings.blogspot.co.uk

Lightning Source UK Ltd.
Milton Keynes UK
UKHW021320300320
361075UK00007B/2126

9 781782 225293